Challenge The Wind

by

Christine Echeverria Bender

Published by
Caxton Press
312 Main St.
Caldwell, ID 83605

I.S.B.N. 0-87004-422-2

Caxton Press is a division of
The Caxton Printers Ltd.

Printed in the United States of America.
167598

THIS BOOK IS DEDICATED WITH GRATITUDE
TO MY PARENTS;
MY MOTHER, PHYLLIS ECHEVERRIA, FOR HER UNWAVERING
AND BOUNDLESS FAITH IN MY ENDEAVORS,
AND MY FATHER, ISAAC ECHEVERRIA, FOR TEACHING ME
TO CHALLENGE THE WIND.

Acknowledgements

Of the many to whom I am grateful for their help on this novel, I would first like to express my deep indebtedness to a special collection of men and women in Corpus Christi, Texas. These are the officers and crewmembers of the Niña, a replica of the original ship. When I discovered the existence of not only the Niña but also recreations of the Pinta and the Santa Maria, I knew that there would be no better way of understanding life at sea in 1492 than to sail on one. I contacted their captain in the spring of 1999 with that request. Captain Barrera explained that the Santa Maria and the Pinta were not sailable but that I was welcome aboard the Niña.

From the moment I arrived, these fine people embraced me as one of their own crewmembers. They educated me about the countless details of the ship and her workings, and even let me haul on the sail lines along with the rest of them. They answered my endless questions with grace and kindness. Some of them continued to assist me in my research long after I had left their city.

By allowing me to sail with them, the Niña crew enabled me to experience first-hand what Domingo saw and smelled, what he heard, touched, and felt during his voyage. These devoted volunteers also instilled in me a love for those magnificent ships that I will not outlive. Sadly, the future of this historic fleet is uncertain. Funding is in serious question and the ships are no longer sailing. I sincerely hope that a way can be found to bring them back to their full glory, and to keep them carefully maintained and in full service.

Special recognition must be given Captain Jose Antonio Barrera for sharing his ship, his crew, and his knowledge. Captain Barrera served as the historical navigator aboard the Santa Maria when the Columbus fleet sailed from Spain to America in 1992, reenacting the first westward voyage of Christopher Columbus. May his career be as generous and kind to him as he is to those who seek to learn from his vast experience. I also offer my gratitude to crewmember Rafael Resendiz, a noble seaman who became a friend during my work on this story, for his continual flow of invaluable information and insights.

In addition to experiencing life aboard the Niña, I was fortunate enough to sail aboard a replica of the Santa Maria, named the Marigallante, in Puerto Vallarta, Mexico. Although the Marigallante has been somewhat converted for commercial use, providing entertainment and dining rather than a historical sailing experience, she still sails proudly. I happily applaud those who keep her silhouette gracing the waters of the Pacific.

Another who gave so willingly of her time and resources was Patty Miller, curator of the Basque Museum and Cultural Center in Boise, Idaho. Her gracious assistance during my visits, and through emails and phone calls is greatly appreciated. Though too young to bear such a title, Patty's dedication and tireless work to promote a deeper understanding of the Basque culture, as well as her boundless generosity of spirit, has already made her a legend in Boise.

Dr. Errol Jones, who is a professor of history at Boise State University, assisted me in obtaining reference materials and source documents that I could not have easily found without his help. Because of his support of my project, I was able to add greater depth and accuracy to my research, for which I am deeply grateful.

For her help with editing and her enthusiastic encouragement, I heartily thank Sue Oakes, one of the truest and most generous hearts I have ever met.

Finally, I want to acknowledge my family members who helped me so much throughout this journey. My parents, Isaac and Phyllis Echeverria, and my sisters, Teresa Townsend, Felisa Wood and Diana Echeverria provided many positive but perceptive criticisms and suggestions. I thank my sister, Debra Geraghty, for accompanying me in my adventures in Corpus Christi and for her consultations and advice every step along the way.

I extend warmest appreciation to my dear children;

Anna, Nicholas, Adam, and Gideon Bender, always my inspirations and joy, for their enthusiastic faith and support. It was for them and their children that I started this book. It was with their love that I finished it. To my husband, Douglas Bender, I offer my thankfulness for accepting the fact that Domingo and the other characters of this book lived so vividly and with such prominence in my mind while they came to life on these pages. Thank you, Doug, for understanding my need to complete their story, and for sharing me with them.

Author's Notes

There are few people who do not, at least to some degree, recognize the name of Christopher Columbus. Some have learned the names of his ships, the dates of his voyages, and even who financed his trips. Some have learned much more.

Although this work is one of historical fiction, it is intended to tell a story that is more broad, more real, than was generally known to exist before these pages were opened. It is told from the perspective of the era, and from the standpoints of the most powerful to the most humble of its participants. If the reader is surpised by some of the events that unfold, I assure him or her that the episodes described during the ocean voyage closely follow those recorded by Columbus himself. They were taken, wherever possible, from his own logbook. His journal was diligently used to describe the manner and the order in which things occurred. Accounts of other witnesses from this time period were also utilized to support many historical aspects of the book.

The depictions of the sailors aboard the now famous three ships, by name, role, and nature, were delineated from the notes left by Columbus, as well as historians who have spent much of their lives studying this adventure.

There is no known record of the original names of the Tainos who encountered the men of Columbus',s fleet. Therefore, names were chosen for them from the Taino language with the intent to match the individual with a name that reflected his or her nature. Again, Columbus provided descriptive information for this purpose.

The main character of the book, Domingo, his friends in Lequetio, and his family were created to tell a story of the events that actually took place. How and why events evolved as they did were carefully considered before the characters were allowed to disclose either their methods or motives within the book. Interepretations of relationships, as well as descriptive details, were added to enable the reader to envision this incomparable experience in man's history to the fullest.

Christine Echeverria Bender

Table of Contents

Illustrations

The Cave

1

A breeze from the sea swept over Domingo's body as he scrambled up the steep slope. An occasional gust ruffled his dark hair into bushy disarray and tugged at his clothes, but he barely noticed the wind. Staring straight ahead, he climbed the grassy incline with determined steps.

He advanced steadily, feeling the sweat trickle down his back and dampen his woven shirt. His breathing grew more and more ragged but he did not slow his pace. At the age of seventeen, he was young and strong, and he welcomed the pressure in his lungs and the burning in his tired legs. He needed this physical straining of muscles and organs to quiet his clouded mind.

He pressed on without stopping, laboring until his head filled with the pounding of blood. And still he forced himself upward. Finally, near a quartz-seamed boulder just below the mountain's peak, he slowed his pace. Panting heavily, he shielded his eyes with his hand and searched the ground ahead until he spotted a nearly hidden path. He immediately took to the tiny trail and followed its sweeping arch along a wide stone mantle. No more than a half mile from where it started the mountain track ended abruptly. Domingo stopped at the edge of a high cliff. The valley floor was over fifteen hundred feet below.

He turned back to face the way he had come and stood scanning the horizon, slowly and carefully. If someone had been watching him, he would force himself to retrace his many steps. And if others were watching him now, it would appear to them that he had no other choice. But Domingo Laca knew this place. He knew its secrets.

When he was satisfied that he had not been seen he lowered himself to the ground. Facedown, with his head still pointed toward the trail he had just traveled, Domingo scooted backward until his legs dangled over the lip of the cliff. With great care he lowered himself over the edge, stretching his body, reaching with his feet until his toes touched the thin overhang below. He tried not to think about the fall that awaited him if he lost his footing on the narrow ridge.

He clung to the rock and waited, needing to steady his balance and his hammering pulse. After a few moments, he began inching his way to the right. He hugged the wall so closely that his face scratched against one of the sharp outcroppings, but he didn't dare pull away. For what seemed like an hour, he took one tiny sidestep after another until, at last, the ledge curved, broadened, then opened wide.

He stepped onto safer ground, turned slowly away from the ridge, and stared at the scene before him. Without closing his eyes, he wiped his forehead with his sleeve. He inhaled deeply, and let out a long, low breath.

Directly in front of him, two giant stones, twice the height of a man, loomed gray and brooding. In massive shape and ashen color, these ancient sentinels were nearly identical. Domingo, as he had done many times before, stood before them wondering who had placed them here, and for what purpose. The shadows cast by the great rocks leaned toward him as if to reach out and gather him in.

Taking a few steps forward, Domingo let his gaze follow the stone pathway that led between the two pillars. The line of flat stones dissected the center of a large, nearly perfect circle of gray boulders, each roughly the size of a table. Beyond the circle, dark and beckoning, yawned the mouth of a cavern. As quietly as possible, out of a sense of reverence, he moved toward the cave.

Domingo had noticed long before that even the birds seemed to know that this was a holy place. The birds were here, but they sang very little and in hushed tones, or not at all. The silence seemed especially heavy today and he welcomed this. More than ever before he wanted the stillness and solemnity that was here. He hoped it would help him gather the courage to accept what he must face tonight.

Domingo had told no one about this site. Not once in the five years since he had found it. He came here to be alone, and to be with the spirits of the old ones.

Although he was a Christian, Domingo knew that his people, the Euskaldunak, had long ago worshipped other gods. He believed that this place had once been, and perhaps still was, the home of their ancient deity. His grandmother had told him how the Euskaldunak of old had prayed to a female deity called Mari. Sometimes appearing to mortals as a breathtakingly beautiful woman, Mari had lived in caves that reached into the depths of the earth. The goddess had used the moon to influence the fertility and childbirth of mortals. Mari had streaked from mountaintop to mountaintop in the form of a ball of fire, protected from all dangers by a huge red bull called Beigorri. On nights of a full moon, their village priestesses once paid homage to this goddess. These chosen women had danced and sang, and had offered the life of a ram as a sacrifice. All of this Domingo had heard since he was a small child.

The oldest people in his village, including his grandmother, remembered many of the stories of the ancient ways. These memories were treasured greatly, especially because the language of the Euskaldunak was not written. Few who lived in his town of Lequetio could read and write. Those who had been taught these skills used the language of the Spanish for such things. Since Domingo's people had existed, their own language had been retained through the spoken word. Exceptions were extremely rare, and Basque inscriptions held deep meanings. This practice had kept them safer from outsiders and had held them closer to one another.

Some of Domingo's earliest memories were of sitting on his grandmother's lap, listening to her tales and legends. If his grandmother, his amuma, had not grown too old to climb the steep trail, Domingo might have told her about the cave long ago. He sensed that she would understand it, and knew that she would tell no one else of its existence. But to tell her now, when she could not see it for herself, would be like inflicting a wound on the old woman. She would want to see it so badly, to touch it, and to feel the presence of the ghosts around her.

Although this concern was enough to justify his silence, there was another reason that Domingo did not tell her, that he did not tell anyone. He held his tongue because of a deep-rooted fear. Powerful rulers had taken people from his countryside and burned them to death, burned them for things much less serious than the knowledge of a cave that housed ancient spirits. Domingo did not view his visits to the cave as the commissions of a sacrilege, but others might. He was afraid for his family, influential as they were, if his discovery of the cave were ever disclosed to the inquisitors.

He pushed these thoughts aside and advanced to the mouth of the cave. Hesitating briefly before the low opening, he stooped slightly and entered. He squatted low and braced his feet against the sunken floor that sloped down and away from the entrance. Pressing his hands against both walls, he inched ahead until he met the downward slope and pushed himself forward. With the rustle of sand and small rocks, he slid down a short tunnel and landed with a soft thump on the dirt floor below.

Picking himself up in the gloom, Domingo waited for the dust to settle. He breathed in the scent of the cave, the scent of minerals and mustiness, and something not quite explainable. There was something in the smell that spoke of ages long past. With a renewed awareness of the antiquity and mystery of the place he had just entered, Domingo glanced from side to side. After another pause, he moved deeper into the cave.

He entered the an oval-shaped chamber that ran ninety feet into the mountain and spread some twenty feet in width. The space grew to a height well above his head, then dropped sharply to the floor. He walked to the deepest region of the cave and lay down on the hard packed earth. He waited, letting his eyes adjust to the dim light. With his feet pointing toward the cave's opening, he watched the smooth expanse of stone above the entrance. Gradually the ceiling came to life above his body.

The first image to meet his gaze was that of a giant red bull guarding the entrance. Its power leaped from the vivid painting. The massive shoulders and neck, the horned head thrown back as if in anger, conveyed undefeatable, immortal strength. The picture and its meaning held Domingo. But Mari's bull was only one of many creatures to compete for Domingo's attention, and soon his eyes were drawn away from the cave's guardian. Racing over and around him, strange images of wild men and animals revealed themselves.

Hundreds of figures in vivid oranges, golds, and browns, stampeded across the light gray ceiling and walls. These animals were proud and powerful, massive and mysterious. There were giant bison, thick-necked horses, deer with huge antlers, and animals totally foreign to Domingo. Some of the men in the mural pursued the beasts holding heavy spears over their heads. The images were clean and clear. The hunters and their prey.

Yet, the pictures showed much more than a hunting scene to Domingo as he gazed up at them. Here was a story, an explanation, of an entire culture long since erased from his land. He stared at the drawings, and questioned anew. Who had these people been? Were they *his* people as they had lived ages ago? Was it possible that his ancestors had lived for so many ages in the same region? Had they looked at all like he did, with his high cheekbones and dark, thick hair? Were their eyes the shape of almonds and their skin the color of honey?

As he watched, Domingo decided that the drawings were not only created with the talent of an artist, but also with the imagination of a holy man, and the intent of a historian. The people on the walls and ceiling looked so free and wild. Free to test their strength as well as their courage, as men ought to do. Today, he envied them for that. His own freedom was to be given up for the sake of his family and his village. He must leave his childhood longings behind and take on the duties of a man.

His gaze traced the edge of the ceiling until he saw the figure of a man tumbling, bleeding before a huge tusked animal. He saw the shapes of other men running to the aid of this fallen hunter, spears held ready to strike their monstrous adversary. Closing his eyes, Domingo considered that even these ancient men had made sacrifices for the good of their people, as he must. Their lives must have been filled with tragedies and hardships. Their existence was undoubtedly harder to endure than was his own. This realization, however, gave him little comfort.

Sitting up, then rising, Domingo walked to the edge of one of the rock walls. He followed the wall, touching the rough face with his left hand as he searched the ground with his eyes. The light was so limited this far into the cave that it wasn't until his foot touched something pointed that he knew he had found what he sought. Bending down he peered at the dim pile of objects before him.

These were his treasures. Over the years, Domingo had gathered pieces of bones and shaped rocks that he had found half or fully buried around the floor of the cave. He picked up a bowl-shaped stone and fingered its once smooth edges. He wondered how long it had been since someone else had touched this bowl. What had he, or she, been like? Had it been a holy man making a magic brew or a young mother preparing a meal for her mate and child?

Growing restless, Domingo set down the bowl and picked up the digging stick that he kept in the cave. He began poking and digging around the edges of the back wall. It was here that he had found one or two of his relics in the past. As he worked, careful not to dig with too much strength and break any new discovery, the people painted above his head kept him company.

Unable to further postpone the thoughts that were haunting him, Domingo let his mind drift back several hours. He thought back to the look on his mother's face when she had come into the room where he and his tutor had sat bent over his books. At first, she had only watched him, as if she were dreading what her words must be. Then she had uttered, "Your father wishes to speak with you after we eat." That was all she had said, but there had been a heaviness in her voice that had spoken much more than her words.

They thought alike, he and his mother, and he read a great deal in her expression and her tone of voice. Domingo had always felt that she knew what was in his heart. She might fear for his safety a little too much, but she understood his dream of sailing on the big ships.

Yet even if his mother understood, Domingo's father, Aitor Laca, had made it clear that he had other plans for his youngest son. Aitor occasionally pointed out that he was getting older. One day it would be Domingo's duty to keep track of the family business.

Aitor had seen to it that Domingo learned how to read and write Spanish, as well as how to keep records and accounts. His father had even hired a military expert to teach him how to use a sword. Much time and money had been spent to insure that Domingo had the best education available.

"You will have nothing to be ashamed of when you trade with the Spanish, Domingo," Aitor had told him. "You have learned quickly and well. Your whole family is proud of you, Son."

Domingo worked hard and tried not to be ungrateful for his father's generosity. It was just that he could not accept the idea of staying behind for the rest of his life, sitting at a desk or wandering around a warehouse. Not when his brothers were free to hunt the mighty creatures of the sea.

How many nights had Domingo sat listening to the tales his brothers would weave of their shipboard adventures? And if they ever tired of retelling the details of their own experiences, they would describe those of their ancestors. The men of the Laca family had been whalers for nearly two hundred years, and there were stories enough for many nights.

He had heard numerous tales of how one of his father's ships had managed to survive a terrible storm at sea. Domingo was convinced that no one built better long-distance ships than his people did. Their vessels were strong and dependable, made from the wood of ancient forests by skillful craftsmen.

His mother and grandmother had made sure Domingo understood that keeping their whalers well fed was just as important as building the ships in the first place. The Euskaldunak, the Basques as the Spanish called them, had learned long before how to catch, salt, and dry codfish. They could process the fish in such a way that it would stay edible and nutritious for months. This secret knowledge, which allowed them to stay at sea for great periods of time, was well guarded. After all, if they could survive longer at sea than others, they could also sail farther, sometimes much farther.

But, as Aitor often reminded Domingo, "More than strong men and ships are needed to keep our trade alive. Markets for the whale oil must be found and supplied. Provisions must be paid for and records must be kept. These duties you will see to little by little as you get older."

Domingo continued to dig in the hard dirt, feeling the heavy weight of these responsibilities. Reluctantly, he admitted that there was more than just the well-being of the Laca family at stake. Many people in their village relied on them to hire their men.

The people of Lequetio were known far and wide for their expertise in three areas; the building of sturdy ships, the forging of the world's best iron and the hunting of whales. Whale oil was so valuable it was sometimes used as currency. The crewmembers aboard the Laca ships were paid handsomely, every seaman receiving a share in the precious whale oil. The lucrative whaling trade, along with the manufacture of their superior iron and strong ships, both greatly sought by the English, kept the region prosperous.

Domingo knew and accepted all of this but his yearning to sail would not lessen. He had prayed that he might be allowed to go once, just once, on a whale hunt. That would be enough for him to let go of his own aspirations. He had asked his father several weeks ago if he might be granted this opportunity but his father had only looked at him as if he were not thinking clearly. Then he had walked away.

Two whaling ships were leaving in the morning and Domingo felt that this was his last chance. If his father refused to allow him to go on this trip, there would be no other opportunity. Again, he thought of his mother's expression. It had been so sad. Did she know that his father was intending to refuse his request? It must be so. But then, perhaps, she was merely concerned about something else altogether. Domingo frowned deeply at his unwillingness to face his disappointment. Jabbing the dirt forcefully with his stick, Domingo told himself to stop his foolish wishing. Wishing was useless. He had been wishing for too long. After a moment, more gently now, he started to dig again.

Nearly an hour had passed without success when his stick hit the edge of something solid. Squatting down quickly, he could just make out the end of a small, elongated object. With difficulty, he forced himself to keep his breathing even and his hands steady. Carefully digging around it, Domingo watched as its shape began to reveal itself. Ever so gently he eased the object free of the soil and cleaned some of the dirt from its interior with his fingers. He raised it toward the mouth of the cave to see it more clearly, and his brown eyes widened. His mouth opened slightly as he stared at the item he held.

In his hands, eight inches in length, was the carved and hollowed out body of a boat. "It *is* a boat," he whispered in amazement, for the shape was unmistakable. Everything he had previously found had implied that these people had used only the simplest of tools, but here was something totally unexpected. There were detailed designs meticulously engraved along the sides of the small craft. The color and texture of the wood from which the boat had been carved were different from any he had seen in the cave.

"A boat," he breathed again, and this time his words seemed to circle the cave and return to him. His spine quivered at the eerie sound of his own voice within these walls. He glanced almost nervously at the onlookers above his head.

Peering at the wild men Domingo was struck by a question. Could these people have sailed? No, surely not. They must have used boats with oars or poles, for fishing perhaps. His mind raced with possible explanations for his find. Was this carved artifact simply something out of place? Was it left here by someone from a later race who had stumbled onto the discovery of the cave as he had? This idea did not agree with him and he quickly discarded it. He did not want to imagine that someone else had found the cave before he had.

Domingo looked harder at the men above him, trying to find an answer. Then a thought came to him that turned his eyes back to the small wooden object he held. Was it possible that this was a sign for him? Was he *meant* to find this boat? Could it mean that he was going to sail after all? Oh please, God, let it be so.

Excitement surged up his chest so violently that he sucked in a deep breath of air. Yes, this was a sign. Something would happen to let him have his dreams. Looking up once more, Domingo smiled at the primitive men above. He could not guess what would occur to help him but something, surely, would happen.

Quickly yet gently Domingo tucked his treasure behind his pile of collectibles. He turned, scrambled up the crawlway, and hurried out of the cave. Once outside he paused and turned back, looking again into the darkness. "Thank you for the boat," he said, not knowing exactly whom he was thanking. It might have been the ancient men, their gods, or his own God.

Then he spun around and leaped forward. He bounded through the circle of rocks like a young deer, his feet barely touching the ground. He would face whatever his father was to tell him. And he would find a way to have his dream.

He looked at the sky and realized that he must hurry. The sun was low and he had far to run. His mother would be displeased if he appeared at their door dirty as well as late. But she could never stay angry with him. He grinned at this thought as he raced to the ridge.

He slowed his pace only long enough to slide around the

rock wall and lift himself up to the top of the ledge. Then
Domingo careened down the path with his arms flying wide.
A great cry of joy and hope rolled down the mountain ahead
of him.

A Visitor

2

Domingo drew near the road leading to his town, slowed his pace, and glanced around. He wanted to avoid being seen until he had a chance to wash himself off. Sweaty and filthy, he strode toward the river that fed into the bay edging the north side of the hamlet. Nearing the water he was greeted by a loud, "Hey, my friend, have you been playing in the mud again?" Domingo looked upriver to see three naked young men swimming in the water beneath a stone bridge. "Just trying out these new clothes," he yelled back to them.

Domingo kicked off his shoes, took a running start, and leaped far out into the cold water. The current caught at his body, swirling around him, chilling his skin almost painfully. He held his breath and stayed under the surface for as long as his lungs would allow, reveling in the cold, moving sensation. At last he pushed up, burst through the clear plane of the water, and took in a huge breath of clean air. Barely had he reached the surface when his friends called to him again. They beckoned him to join them with teasing curses and gestures. Weighted down by his clothes he swam back to the edge of the river and waded towards his friends.

"New clothes? They don't look so new anymore," laughed Iban, a tall, skinny youth with wet hair curling in front of his eyes.

Domingo shed his clothes and spread them on nearby bushes to dry. He was of average height, well proportioned, and agile in his movements. His large eyes and strong eyebrows heightened his expressions of wonder, mischief, and anger. The men of his village tended to mature early, sometimes growing beards and hair on their chests by the age of fifteen. Strangers would have guessed that Domingo and Josu were several years older than they actually were.

Iban, in spite of his height, and Andoni because of his lack of it, still retained boyish appearances. All of the boys stood shivering from the frigid water and cool wind, but they were not ready to leave before one more swim. Andoni, Iban and Josu each had put in a hard day working with their respective families and the water felt too good to abandon any sooner than necessary.

"The last one to reach the other side has to marry my sister," shouted Josu with a dimpled grin. This challenge was all that was needed to jolt the mob into sudden motion. They pounded toward the water bellowing and pushing each other. Tired from his mountain trek, Domingo was last to reach the other side of the river. Laughing and panting, they collapsed on the sandy bank.

"I'll have to tell my sister that you're to be her future husband when I get home. But she probably won't have you when I *also* tell her you swim like an old woman," Josu announced, not even trying to hide his smile.

"Don't you think she's a little young for Domingo?" Andoni asked. Andoni was a jokester, always reminding his companions how the young ladies in town admired his good looks. By far the least handsome of the four, Andoni's good nature was his most attractive feature.

"Besides, our friend is too much the wanderer these days," Andoni added. "He's always walking off and sulking by himself. He has no time for a woman. And his real betrothed just might object to someone else eyeing him."

"You may be right about Carmen, Andoni," Josu chimed in as if he had given the matter some serious thought. "She might have a word or two to say about matching Domingo up with my sister. What she sees in him is a mystery, but anyone can tell by the way she looks at him that she thinks he is some kind of prize." Josu proceeded to make such ridiculous expressions of longing that they all burst out laughing.

Everyone in the town knew that Domingo and Carmen were betrothed, of course. Each of the other three boys had also been betrothed before the age of ten. But at the boy's current ages of sixteen and seventeen, marriage was still a

13

few years away. They were all grateful that there was still time for a little foolishness at the end of the day.

Carmen, two years younger than Domingo, was the second daughter of Imanol Barrutia, the village silversmith. Imanol's pride in his pretty daughter was as obvious as his distrust of Domingo's worthiness of her. Domingo was convinced that Imanol had only agreed to the match because of the respectability and wealth of the Laca family. Even so, Imanol had demanded assurance that Domingo would never become a common whaler.

"It's not that I have anything against whaling in general, you understand," Imanol had explained to Aitor and Domingo years before. "I simply do not want my daughter left a widow by a storm or some other tragedy at sea." Although Domingo had been only nine years old at the time, he remembered Imanol's words.

Over the last year, whenever Domingo left the village to wander in the hills Imanol had watched him closely as he had passed by the silversmith's shop on his way back home. Imanol's expression grew more disapproving with each of Domingo's wanderings. Lately Carmen's father scowled at him whenever they met as if Domingo had already committed some sort of crime. Domingo's polite greetings were answered by indistinct grunts, if at all.

At least Imanol had not spotted him today and Domingo was relieved. It raised his optimism even higher and confirmed that this was indeed a special day.

"Ah, that sun feels good," Domingo leaned back and smiled at his cohorts. "Now that the weather is getting warmer we should meet here every day."

Josu looked at him. "Every day? Will your father let you leave your studies to swim with us every day?"

Before Domingo could answer Andoni asked, "Even if your father will let you, would you want to swim with us more than go off wandering?"

Domingo returned his friends' gazes and grinned. "Yes, I'll want to swim more, Andoni. Who knows what trouble you three will get into if I'm not here to keep an eye on you."

Everyone smiled with satisfaction at his answer.

14

Domingo felt guilty for seeing so little of his friends recently. Even when he had been with them, he had been preoccupied and unusually quiet. They had been raised together since birth, and had been constant companions since they were old enough to walk. It was difficult for the others to understand why Domingo studied so hard and needed his long stretches of solitude. Although it didn't seem natural to them, they had tried to accept his peculiar behavior. They had teased him good-naturedly and said he was the thinker of their group, and that his oddities were simply burdens that went along with his "unusual" intelligence. Today Domingo realized how much he had missed their company.

They sat in the sand rubbing their arms and stamping their feet in an effort to stay warm. Andoni, the shortest of the group, noticed Iban's gangly knees poking up between the arms that were wrapped around them. Iban looked like a grasshopper trying to fold itself in half. "Iban are you ever going to stop growing?" Andoni demanded.

Iban glanced down at his long frame. "I wonder that myself. My feet already hang over the end of my bed. If I don't stop growing soon, I'll have to sleep on the floor."

"Oh, quit complaining. You know you love being the first one who's noticed when we meet a pretty girl," Domingo teased him. Iban's cheeks reddened at the truth of Domingo's words and all of them laughed out loud. They sat in contented silence until their bodies began to shiver and their teeth to chatter.

"Come on, let's get back across the river before we freeze to death," Josu suggested. With yells and a great deal of splashing the young men plunged into the water and swam through the chilling wetness, each fighting to reach the other bank first.

The family finished their evening meal, and Domingo's older brother, Eneko, left to visit some friends. Domingo sensed that his father was about to speak to him. But before Aitor had the chance to say a word, Domingo stood up and

15

announced that he wanted to look in on their horse that was about to foal. It was an excuse to buy time, to consider his words to his father once more. He left the room and headed toward the stall to make sure that the mare was fine, knowing full well that it would be hours or even days before the foal arrived.

As evening deepened, Domingo walked slowly around his home lost in thought. When he found himself at the far corner of the yard he turned and looked back at the familiar outline of his father's house.

Like all Basque houses, it faced the east to better meet the rising of the morning sun. Its large square outline was peaked with a high pyramid shaped roof. A broad, open entrance, wide enough for an ox cart to pass through, evenly divided the front of the first floor. Their animals as well as fodder and farming tools occupied the stalls in the half of the house to the south. The door that led to the rooms used by Domingo's family was built into the north wall of the entrance hall. Domingo traced the shape of the house with his gaze and wondered if he would be leaving it soon.

After several minutes had passed, Domingo admitted to himself that he had delayed his talk with Aitor longer than he should have, and he resolutely headed back. He paused a few yards in front of the house and let his eyes scan the words that were engraved into the long stone slab above the entryway. Such inscriptions were rare examples of the Basque language in written form. His grandfather had repeated this inscription to him until he had memorized it. He was only five years old at the time, and could not yet read them. He read them aloud now. "May our friends, the poor, and our enemies find peace within our house. With little, and peace, we have enough."

Staring at these words, Domingo hoped that he would not cause the peace of his house to be disturbed tonight. Still, he had to speak from his heart. He entered the darkening passage and opened the door leading to the kitchen.

The light from the whale oil lamp and the fire in the hearth shed warm glows around the light walls and dark beams. The hearth was built up off of the floor and located in the center of the room. From it, a thin line of smoke trailed upward, dancing through a smoke-hole and into the storage attic on the second floor. Chunks of salted fish and meat, as well as strings of sausages hung from the beams overhead. Pots and crockery sat on shelves built into the south wall by the door.

Forming a triangle around the hearth, three benches, txitxilus, had been pushed close enough to catch the fire's warmth. Each bench had a middle section that was pulled forward and down to form a small table for the two people at either end during meals. Domingo went to the bench next to the one occupied by Aitor and raised the table section. He could not bring himself to meet his father's questioning glance.

His amuma, dressed in black with her gray hair tied up at the nape of her neck, bent over the coals of the fire and stirred them to new life. His mother, Enara, who was of middle age, slightly plump, with a long braid hanging down her back, seemed busy drying newly washed wooden bowls with a white cloth. Domingo could tell that Enara was purposely avoiding eye contact with him or Aitor. His amuma also seemed unusually occupied with anything that drew her away from the males. Yet, neither woman left the room. They merely busied themselves with cleaning up and pretending they weren't waiting for Aitor to speak.

"It was a good supper, Enara and Mother," Aitor complimented.

The women glanced at each other. "I'm glad you enjoyed it, Aitor," said his wife, returning her attention to the bowl she held.

When no one else said anything, Aitor sat back and watched his hands resting in his lap. He did not succeed in his attempt to hide his own uneasiness. He remained silent, deep in his own reflections again.

Domingo had been born on a Sunday, and it was the village priest who had suggested that the baby be called by the Spanish name for that holy day rather than by a Basque name. The old padre had seen something in the tiny boy that had made him think Domingo would have a life that touched many people, even people outside of Lequetio. Aitor's plans for his newest son would involve dealings with the Spanish, so he had accepted the priest's suggestion. At home, however, Domingo had always been called by his Basque nickname, Txomin. With strict inflexibility, Domingo's tutor had demanded that he spell even his nickname in the Spanish fashion, as "Chomin."

Eneko, because he was the oldest of their children, would inherit their ships, their land, and the family dwelling place. Even if their first-born had been a girl, she would have inherited their property. This custom was unique to the Basque country where it was upheld as one of their strictest laws. If the oldest child was a male, he would not marry until he was older. Not until he had helped raise enough money to see that each of his brothers and sisters could begin a family of their own. If the first-born was a girl, it was her responsibility to find a mate wealthy and generous enough to insure the stability and continuation of her house.

The "house" was much more than the building in which they lived. The house was the family, its traditions, customs, and values. There was no cause for jealousy among the younger siblings because they were supported and guided by the head of the house, always. The household head was viewed as the main trunk of a branched tree, giving whatever was needed for the entire tree to flourish. One of the greatest compliments a parent could give an offspring was to proclaim that the child was "good for the house."

Eneko, who was now twenty-five, would marry later, after Domingo was closer to being settled. Eneko had worked with Kepa, the brother two years his junior, on Aitor's whaling ships until they had saved enough to build a ship with their father. The ship had been for Kepa, so he could marry and begin his own family. Eneko and Kepa would sail the new ship out of their harbor in the morning for its second voyage into the far reaches of the sea.

Aitor and Enara had made it no secret that having Eneko and Kepa exposed to the dangers and hardships at sea was more than enough for them to bear. Right now

18

Kepa was sharing the last night he would have with his young wife in many, many months. He had been married only eight months and his wife, Catalin, was expecting a baby. The child would almost certainly be born before Kepa returned to port. Fortunately, the young woman had her own mother and Enara, as well as two grown sisters, to help her when her time came.

Domingo knew that his amuma loved him no less than his parents did, but she disagreed with their keeping him in Lequetio. Just a few weeks earlier she had quietly told Aitor that Domingo would never be happy tied to a small village, not unless he got his chance to see something more of the world. Some things were worth risking one's life for, and for Domingo it was to sail. The old woman had stated her opinion only once, and had left the decision and the outcome to her son.

Still staring at his rough hands, Aitor let his thoughts dwell on all of the good reasons why he was making the right choice where Domingo was concerned. Carmen's father, Domingo's future father-in-law, had made it clear that he would cause trouble if Domingo became a whaler. Carmen would need the boy to be with her in a few short years. The family business needed him here. Domingo's mother and Amuma would never forgive Aitor if he sent the boy out on the next ship. And, what was more important to Aitor than all of the other reasons, he wanted his son to live.

Aitor had hunted the whales himself when he was young, and he had almost died from a sickness on his last voyage. Fifteen years earlier his own cousin, Iker Landaluze, and his entire crew were lost when their ship, badly damaged by a storm, sank near the Portuguese islands of Madeira off the coast of Africa. Iker had barely managed to reach shore, and had died within days. The perils of the sea were too strong, too undeniable to needlessly expose Domingo to them.

Aitor had noticed when Domingo had entered the room. His son was now sitting on the bench next to him, waiting. But Aitor had not yet said a word, and his thoughts were still unsettled when someone yelled a greeting from outside the house. A moment later the door was unbolted and swung open. One of their neighbors, Mikel Berria, entered with the evening chill.

"Mikel, welcome," said Aitor, relieved by the interruption.

"Forgive my disturbing you all so late."

"Not at all, my friend. Come in. Sit down."

Mikel smiled but shook his head. "I came only as a messenger tonight, Aitor. I was asked to tell you that Diego De Arana has just arrived from Madrid. He is staying with my brother, Jon, and he told me he has news for you that can not wait. He asks that you go and meet with them now.

"I haven't seen Diego for many years," said Aitor pleased to hear that his old friend had returned. "The news must be important if he wants to speak with me before he has even rested from his journey." Aitor looked inquiringly at his visitor.

"I have been told nothing of his news, Aitor," said Mikel. "I only know that Diego seems excited one moment and deeply concerned the next. Neither Diego nor Jon invited me to this meeting of yours. They just asked me to send you to them since I was passing by your house on my way home."

Aitor was already rising and heading toward the door. He paused and turned back, gazing first at his wife and mother who stood together near the fire, then at his son. "I must speak with you when I return, Txomin," he said in such a serious tone that Domingo merely nodded. The boy, crestfallen at the implied message in his father's voice, watched the two men depart. The door closed behind them with a loud "clunk" as the bolt was driven shut.

It was not long before the women went to their respective rooms and their own sleeping cots. Domingo remained in the kitchen staring at the fire for awhile, then he moved toward the door and quietly slipped outside.

As he stood silently in the shadows of Jon Berria's home, Domingo could hear voices drifting through the slightly open shutter of a window. He carefully raised himself and peered inside the window at the corner of the house.

The men inside the Berria home were seated on txitxilus, bent toward one another deep in conversation. Other than his father, Domingo could see only Jon and Diego De Arana. Jon's kind and lovely wife, who was Diego's sister, must have gone to bed.

Beside Aitor, who was stout and strongly built, Diego looked almost like a Spanish nobleman. It was not only his clothes that gave this impression, although they were finer than any Domingo had ever seen, it was also his tall thinness and the way he held himself. Diego's face, however, was markedly Basque. Jon, handsome and quick to smile, was also thin, but he had a ruddy outdoor color to his skin, and a brow that showed less strain than that of the visitor. Though Jon was a wealthy man, owning many hundreds of sheep, he dressed as a simple shepherd.

Domingo could easily make out their words as he huddled beneath the window.

"You surprise me, Diego," said Aitor. "Your cousin is a beautiful young woman. Why would she take a man from Genoa as her lover? Your father has been her guardian for many years. Did either he or you approve of this?"

"In spite of how it sounds, Aitor, Beatriz has chosen a man of honor," came the voice Domingo had not heard since he was small. "Soon after I met him he told me how his wife had died in Portugal years before. He seemed to have had no time for women since he arrived in Madrid. Then one night I brought him home to dine with my family, and when he met our Beatriz he was immediately taken with her. A few weeks later Beatriz came to me and said she loved him. She said she would *not* marry him *because* she loved him. She believed her lack of nobility could limit his ambitions. What was I to do? She was an orphan under my father's care, but she was old enough to make up her own mind. And the two of them are more than casual lovers, Aitor. Columbus seems truly dedicated to her and he is a good father to their son, Fernando. He has given the boy his name."

Diego glanced at Jon then continued, "To tell you the

21

truth, I was not totally against the match. He is an extraordinary navigator, Aitor. He has much influence, evidently even with the queen. I'd like you to meet this man, my friend. You will see why I feel he was not a bad choice for my cousin. Besides, he wants very much to know you."

Puzzled by this, Aitor could only ask, "Why would this Columbus want to meet me so badly? What would a man who has the ear of the queen, as you say, want with a humble trader like me?"

Diego looked intently at Aitor before replying, "Because, Aitor, he wants you to sail with him."

A look of suspicion appeared and began to spread across Aitor's face. "You know very well, Diego, that it has been years since I left port." Aitor looked from Diego to Jon and saw that they were hesitating to tell him the rest. "Why would a navigator from Genoa want me to sail with him?" he asked, his brows furrowing and his voice growing lower.

"Aitor, listen to me," Diego began speaking each word slowly, clearly. "Columbus intends to sail west, to the Indies. He wants to develop a trade agreement with the Great Khan for spices and silks. He is determined to sail west with or without our help. Of this, there is no doubt. But if we..."

Aitor interrupted him in disbelief and rising anger. "Are you suggesting, Diego, that I lead this *stranger* to our whaling grounds?"

"No, Aitor, not exactly, but..." Diego tried again.

"You and I have known one another since before we took our first steps," Aitor interrupted once more, color rising to his face and his breath coming faster. "Do you think that I would betray the secrets of my people, secrets we have kept for *hundreds of years*, to some, some, *Italian*? Someone who would surely sell the knowledge to the Spanish and whoever else would pay his price? How could you have even considered that I would play a part in this?" Aitor, glaring now at Diego, began to rise from his bench.

Diego, standing quickly, grabbed Aitor's arm and stared him in the eyes, anger now flashing between the two men. "I am no traitor, Aitor. No more than you. If you will sit down and let me explain, you will see that it is for the good of our people that I have come." They stood scowling at one another for a moment, then both slowly sat down again.

Before Aitor had a chance to start, Diego stopped him cold with one statement. "He already has a copy of our charts."

Stunned for a moment, Aitor finally growled, "That's impossible. He could not have our charts."

"Yes, Aitor, he does." As angry as Diego was at Aitor's accusations, he hesitated before telling Aitor what he knew he must. "They were given to him by your cousin, Iker."

Aitor sat with his eyes wide and his mouth slightly open, as if he had just been shot. "Iker would not have done that," he managed to say in a weak voice.

"He was dying, Aitor. You were told years ago of the shipwreck and the circumstances of Iker's death. One of his final actions was to give the maps to Columbus."

Aitor leaned his elbows on his knees and buried his face in his hands. Diego gave him a moment.

Gently now, Diego went on, "Iker had the charts on him, wrapped tightly in oilskins, when he reached Madeira. All but two of his crewmen were dead, and the last two were so sick that the townspeople told Iker there was no hope for them. Columbus brought Iker to his home and tried to save your cousin. The two men talked, shared their tales of the sea. Iker eventually told him where he had been sailing and some stories of the lands he had reached far to the west. He may have been delirious from his illness, I don't know, but before he died Iker did hand the maps to Columbus."

Aitor raised red eyes to Diego, searching his face.

Barely above a whisper, Diego said, "Columbus showed me the charts. They are Iker's, Aitor."

Aitor just managed to say, "I have believed all these years that the charts went to the bottom of the sea with my cousin."

Somewhat steadier after another pause, Aitor asked, "If this man has the charts, what does he want with me?"

"He wants your experience, your feel for the currents. I've told him of your sons and of the other men you have trained, but he wants you. I have told him that you are the best. Because you are."

"And why, Diego, would I ever agree to go with this foreigner? This man who has stolen one of the most valuable secrets of our people from my own kinsman as he lay dying?" asked Aitor in a voice growing stronger again with emotion.

"Because," Diego stated flatly, "it may be the only way to safeguard our fishing rights."

When he could see that Aitor had understood the implication of his words, Diego continued. "The queen is offering Columbus *and* those who sail with him great rewards if they succeed. Many people think he's completely mad but Columbus is persuasive, Aitor. I think he will succeed in gathering his crews. And if he reaches the Indies, the wealth he could bring back is nearly unimaginable. I have agreed to act as master-at-arms for his fleet, but I am no pilot. You are, and more. You know those waters better than anyone alive. If the two of us help him, and we live to see our own homes again, Columbus has promised to do everything he can to convince the queen to grant us permanent fishing privileges to all of the western seas. That is my great hope. That is why I've come."

Jon sat watching the other two men. He had silently watched the play of outrage, anguish, and resignation on their faces.

"But we have seen no signs of the wealth you describe on any of our voyages," Aitor protested.

"Aitor, the maps that Iker gave Columbus show a route to the south of our normal whaling grounds. He told Columbus that a tornado forced his ship in that direction. It is this southern route that Columbus intends to take," Diego explained.

"And just why has it taken so many years for Columbus to gather his crew and make his plans?"

"He has just received permission from the queen, Aitor," said Diego. "Columbus has had little money of his own and needed royal assistance as well as permission. Before he would set out, he wanted guarantees of a noble title and other explicit compensations for discovering and claiming the new lands." Aitor gave him a disgusted look but Diego continued. "He sought support from Portugal for several years before he finally accepted that King John would not help him, and he came to Spain. Queen Isabella gave him only brief attention at first, committed as she was to finalizing the war against the Moors. Finally, after the queen's victory in Granada a few months ago, she agreed to see Columbus again. Even so, she evidently put him off once more by telling him that there was no money available to fund his voyage because of the war."

"Now, Columbus has not admitted this to me, Aitor, but I believe, out of desperation perhaps, he showed the queen Iker's maps. Why else, after seven years of pleading, and only after a private meeting, did she finally give her consent for his voyage? Suddenly she is very optimistic about his chances for success. She's even determined to bring the church to the people of the Indies. More souls to God. I tell you, I think he showed Iker's maps to the queen to prove he could reach the Indies."

"When? When does he plan to sail?" asked Aitor.

"He wants us to find a ship and crew from our own land if possible. Then we are to return as soon as we can to Palos, from where he intends to set sail."

"He plans to sail with only one ship?"

"No, the people of Palos are providing two other ships," explained Diego. "It seems that some of their townspeople went tuna fishing a little too far south last year, interfering with the treaty with the Portuguese. The king penalized the town by commanding that they provide two ships, and full crews, for whatever service he would require in the future. The queen has decided to give the use of the ships to Columbus."

Aitor, listening to every word, looked as though the weight that had descended on his chest was growing heavier with each passing moment.

"Columbus plans to gather a crew from a town of men being *ordered* to go? To a place they have never sailed, never even dreamed of sailing?" Aitor asked incredulously. "And how will these Spaniards feel when they are told that they will be sailing under an Genoese captain-general, a Basque captain and a Basque pilot? Diego, surely you see the problems that would arise. Such a voyage would be all but cursed from the beginning."

"Columbus wants as many of our sailors as we can gather," said Diego. "He knows that our men are the most skilled sailors to be found anywhere. He knows that our people have sailed to the west before. These are two good reasons for him to want Basque sailors with him on this voyage."

"But our men leave with the morning tide to hunt whales. Everything is ready for their departure and I refuse to try to keep them here. And I doubt they will return soon enough to please your Columbus."

"Then we will have to look elsewhere for good men, other villages," Diego said with resolution. "Aitor, I know that there are a hundred reasons why we may fail in this undertaking, but we must try. Those fishing grounds are too important to our people for us to turn away. Columbus will try to help us secure them."

Aitor stared at his friend. "I don't know. I doubt I could ever trust this man you speak so highly of, Diego."

"I realize that we have no real guarantees, only Columbus' word to try to help us if we help him. But we can contribute our own hard work, and our prayers. The ultimate outcome of our efforts we must entrust to God," Diego said.

The three men sat for awhile letting the quiet surround them, each deep in his own thoughts. At last Aitor rose again, slowly this time, as if he were suddenly very old, and said, "We need to meet with our townspeople, of course. This decision must be made by all of us."

"Of course," the other two said softly together.

"Will you forgive the angry words I spoke earlier, Diego?" Aitor asked with sincere regret.

Diego looked at his lifelong friend with deep understanding and nodded. "I know this has been terrible news for you, late at night and with no warning. Remember,

26

Aitor, that we both want the same thing. We both want what is best for our people."

"Yes." Aitor said meeting his eyes.

Inhaling deeply, Aitor continued. "I must see my sons off in the morning, then we can meet with the others. I don't want my men to know that this may be their last hunt without the Spanish watching their every move."

"Yes, Aitor, of course," Diego repeated.

Domingo hardly dared to breathe as he watched and listened in the darkness. He pushed himself away from the wall and was running toward home before his father had reached Jon's doorway.

Preparations

3

The Lacas walked along the seaside road that led from the village square to their home. Each one of them quietly reflected on the town meeting that had just concluded. As they neared the shop of the silversmith, they saw a young girl sweeping the already clean stones of the stoop in front of the shop. She glanced at them furtively as they approached.

She was neither tall nor stout, but she gave the impression of strength in spite of her small size. Her thick, mahogany colored hair was held back from her face by a scarf. Her hair swayed back and forth about her waist as she swept in sure, swift strokes. Her lips were full and dark pink in color, and her nose was small and shapely. She had inherited a fine jaw and defined cheekbones. Even with her eyes cast downward, Domingo noticed how delicately her long lashes framed the shape of her eyes. She raised her face to them as they came up to her.

"Hello, Carmen," greeted Enara.

"Good morning," Carmen returned softly.

They stopped in front of the girl and Enara and Amuma exchanged small talk with her.

Aitor glanced at Domingo impatiently but waited for the women as politely as he could manage. When Aitor seemed unable to wait any longer he said to Domingo, "You may stay and speak with Carmen for a little while, Txomin, but don't stay long. There is much to discuss."

"I'll be along in a minute, Aitor," said Enara with a wave. "You go on ahead if you like." Her husband looked at her with slight surprise, then shrugged and started down the road.

Enara reached out and took Carmen's hand and studied the girl's face intently. She had always been greatly fond of Carmen's mother and she already considered Carmen one of her own. What Enara thought of Carmen's irascible father she tried not to voice. It was Enara who had first chosen Carmen to be Domingo's wife.

Amuma and Domingo watched the other two, waiting for Enara to say something. But the woman and the girl just looked at one another, Enara searchingly, Carmen with openness. Then, as if some question had been answered, Enara sighed and patted Carmen's tiny hand firmly.

"Yes, you are a strong girl," was all she said before she released Carmen's hand and turned to Domingo.

"We will leave you two alone now," Enara said. She and Amuma headed after Aitor, his figure already disappearing in the distance.

Domingo watched the rest of his family leave, wanting badly to speak to his father, to plead for the chance to go with him and Diego when they sailed.

"Your father is doing a brave thing for us, Txomin," the girl said to him when the others were out of hearing. "My father told me that this voyage, with strange men and strange ships, will be difficult for him."

"What else did your father say?" Domingo asked, wondering just how angry her father would be if he left with the older men.

"He said that I shouldn't worry about you going. He is certain that you will not be allowed to go because you will be put in charge of the warehouses while your father is away."

Domingo stared out at the waves beyond the wooden wharf, watching the sun's reflection dance on the moving surface. Perhaps Carmen's father was right and he would be ordered to stay behind. But even if he were told to stay, he would find some way to be aboard one of the ships when they sailed. He was sure, at least he hoped, that his father wouldn't have him thrown overboard once they were far out to sea.

"You look as though you are already a thousand miles away," Carmen said to him.

Domingo looked at her and could see that she read his thoughts. It was a mystery to him how she could do this so often. Sometimes she seemed to know his mind and feelings better than he did himself. She looked so concerned now, and so pleasing in the morning sunshine, that he wanted to take her hand and pull her close to him.

"Will you go with them?" she asked.

"I don't know. My father has said nothing to me yet."

"But you want to go." It was not a question. Carmen knew her betrothed well.

Domingo did not hesitate. "Yes, Carmen, I want to go. It's not that I want to leave anything that is here," he said smiling his meaning to her. "Everything I love is here. But I feel this need to see strange places and people, to face the dangers of a long journey. I feel it so strongly sometimes that it is almost painful." Carmen looked away from him.

"I will make you a better husband after I have had my adventure, because then I will be content to stay by your side for my whole life."

Carmen, although younger in years, shook her head at his childish words.

"You will be no husband at all if you do not return, if you end up starving or drowning. You may have no power over these things." After a pause she asked, "And what if you *choose* not to come home?" Although Carmen did not believe that Domingo would want a life away from his village and his people, she needed to hear him say as much.

Domingo glanced up and down the lane and into the shop, seeing not a soul. Then he slipped his arms around her. "I am not a fool, Carmen. I would come home to you." She leaned against him as he gently pressed his lips to her forehead. Lifting her face to him she watched as Domingo slowly lowered his lips, and closed her eyes when she felt his warmth meet hers. The kiss was brief. It was broad daylight and her father might see them. Domingo pulled away first, but held her hand a moment longer.

"I will tell you what my father decides," he said softly.

30

"I think they will let you go, Txomin," Carmen said as if she knew. Tightening her grip on his hand, she amazed him by saying, "I wish we could marry before you leave." She mistook his look of surprise for disbelief. "I do, Txomin," she confirmed.

Risking outraging her father Domingo again pulled her to him and held her tightly, trying to comfort her with his arms, not knowing the right words to say. Finally, she pushed him away.

"You must go speak to your parents...and I must finish sweeping," she said in a strained voice, looking away from him so that he could not see her eyes. Taking up her broom again she attacked the spotless stones as if he were no longer there. Domingo ran his finger slowly along her cheek, but she missed only one stroke with her broom before its motion started again, and she did not look at him.

"I will see you after my father and I have talked," he said, but she did not acknowledge him. He turned from her and walked up the road with his face showing a mixture of hope and worry. After walking a short way, Domingo glanced back to see if Carmen would wave to him but she stubbornly continued to brutalize the ground with her broom.

The older Lacas had barely entered their home when Enara faced her husband and said, "Aitor, I have been thinking, and Amuma and I have been talking." Something in her tone made Aitor hesitate as he hung his coat on its peg.

"Yes?"

"I think we have been wrong in believing we could stop Txomin from leaving here." Before Aitor could raise his voice, she hurried on. "We were right to want to protect him, but he is growing up, Aitor, and soon he will make his own choices. I'm now sure that he will choose the sea. I think it would be best for him if he goes with you and Diego."

Aitor stared at her for a moment as if she were a stranger. Amuma went to the hearth and busied herself with the pot that hung suspended over the coals.

31

"*Best* for him?" Aitor took a breath and began shaking his head back and forth. "How can you say that everything we ever planned for the boy was wrong, that now it would be *best* for Domingo to come along on this godforsaken voyage? We have not even discussed whether *I* would go, Enara, and now you say that Domingo should go too."

"The village voted that you should go," she reminded him. "Are you actually considering not going?"

Aitor went to his bench and sat down heavily. He did not answer her right away.

"No," he said at last. "I cannot let our whaling be handed over to the Spanish without doing what I can to stop it. But I don't want Domingo to be in the middle of all the trouble that could be stirred up on this trip. I imagine this Columbus to be a thief. I seriously question his honesty. I know him only through Diego's words. Diego trusts him, but it will take a great deal for me to believe the man is capable of keeping all of the pieces of this plan together. Italian, Spanish and Euskari sailors? He'll probably ask some Irish and English to come along too," he said with a snort. Enara knew that much of Aitor's resentment of Columbus was due to the loss of the charts, and the shame he felt because it had been his own cousin who had given them away.

"Aitor, husband," Enara began as she sat beside him. "I want our boy in danger no more than you do. But if we do not let him go on this trip, I'm afraid he will leave Lequetio, find some other ship to sail with. He might sail anywhere, with just about anyone. Wouldn't you rather have him go with you and Diego than with an entire crew of strangers?"

"You think the boy would be so disobedient that he would run off just because we denied him this?" Aitor demanded.

Enara smiled kindly at him. "How old were you, husband, when you first sailed?"

They both knew that Aitor had been just thirteen years old when his father took him on his first hunt. And they knew that Aitor had been every bit as excited to go as Domingo was now. "I was the oldest son," he said as if that made the difference perfectly plain.

"It is not Domingo's fault that he is the youngest," said Enara. "You know, this is not easy for me, trying to convince you to let him go when I don't want him to leave either." They looked at one another for a moment.

Aitor shifted in his chair, wishing Enara would be reasonable. She was usually such a reasonable woman. But, after all, Enara knew almost nothing of what this kind of a trip would really be like. Then he remembered an argument that she couldn't deny. "And what of Carmen, and her father? You know how Imanol feels," Aitor said almost triumphantly.

"I think Carmen has already guessed that Domingo will go. She will manage, as much as she loves him. As for her father, well...well, Domingo *wouldn't* be going on a whale hunt. He would be going on an expedition for the queen."

In spite of his best efforts not too, Aitor grinned. "An expedition for the queen. Ah, and you think that description of this adventure will make any difference to Imanol?"

Changing tactics, Enara continued, "And just why would he have to know Domingo was going, until he was gone?" she asked not quite meeting her husband's eyes.

Aitor's smile broadened at this. "Oh, my wife, I never knew you to be such a deceptive woman." He glanced up at his mother and caught a glimpse of her grin before she turned her back to him. Then, his expression sobering, he ran his rough hand through his thinning hair and continued. "I must have a chance to think about all of this. I will tell Domingo only that our talk will have to wait. Of course, that alone will be enough to send his hopes soaring. So don't you two say anything to encourage him." He looked sternly at Enara.

"Oh no, Aitor. I won't," Enara said very seriously.

Aitor got up and walked over to his tiny mother and looked down into her timeworn face. She smiled up at him, patted his face, and said, "Of course not, my son," almost as if she meant it.

As the days of preparation passed, Diego and Aitor tried

to hire a ship and men from the surrounding villages. Both were proving to be hard to find. Domingo became like a shadow to his father. He raced to do the smallest errand and never complained at the end of a long hard day. As he tried in every way to please the two men, Domingo could see that he was beginning to earn Diego's approval. Soon Diego, Domingo's mother, and his grandmother were all trying in small ways to persuade Aitor to take him on the excursion.

Aitor found it harder and harder to send Domingo off on some other task as they poured over the charts or discussed details of the trip. They took great pains in planning the food, supplies, and arms they would need. Usually Domingo said very little, afraid that any interference would result in him being told to leave them. But when he did speak, Domingo often surprised his father with his knowledge of celestial navigation and how easily he understood the maps as well as the quadrant, their main tool of navigation other than the stars.

After much convincing, Juan De La Cosa, owner of a square rigged cargo vessel called La Gallega, agreed to charter his ship and most of his men to Diego as an agent of Columbus. Neither Diego nor Aitor knew De La Cosa well, but he was said to be an honorable man and a just captain. He had previously sailed as far as the Canary Islands and, being a bold man, was willing to take the much greater risks associated with this voyage. True to his word, De La Cosa sailed his ship into the Lequetio harbor promptly on the prearranged date.

As Diego, Aitor, and Domingo stood on the beach gazing out at the incoming ship, Aitor commented, "Well, she isn't exactly beautiful. She will be slow and clumsy in the water compared to our whaling boats. But she's the best we could find and still meet Columbus' time frame."

"She will do well," said Diego. "Our biggest needs are for stability in the water and plenty of storage room. The queen will be happier with us if the holds of all the ships are full of valuables when we return. Besides, your whaling ships are all out doing what they were designed to do. You are right, we can't wait for them."

34

"Diego, you said that Columbus intends to sail to the south of our usual whaling grounds. What does he expect to find there? What *exactly* has Columbus promised Her Majesty?"

"Like everyone else, Columbus has heard the stories of Marco Polo, of the gold and spices and riches in the Indies. Iker told him a little about some islands he had landed on, but his descriptions were not exactly the ones Columbus hoped for. I don't believe Iker mentioned any treasures. Still, Columbus intends to meet the Great Khan somehow. He plans to convince him to accept a trading treaty with Spain."

"But remember, Aitor, it is not just the wealth of the Indies that the queen is after. She is fiercely religious, as you know. She has made it clear to Columbus that she plans to spread the Catholic faith to the people of the East. She has even stated publicly that she means to use any gold they bring back to help pay for a holy war. She means to regain Jerusalem for Christianity."

"I see," said Aitor with a raised eyebrow. "You describe a man and a woman who have more than a small amount of ambition."

"Sometimes it is hard to tell who is more ambitious, Columbus or the queen," Diego admitted.

"I hope he has some idea where to find this Great Khan," said Aitor.

"If he does, Aitor, he is keeping it to himself so far."

Aitor shook his head. "Ai, Ai, Ai."

Diego slapped him on the back. "Come, don't judge him too harshly. Wait until you meet the man, Aitor."

They continued to watch La Gallega and saw a small rowboat leave the ship. Its hands began to pull at the oars. As it neared, the captain hailed them with a wave of his hat.

Returning the salute, Aitor asked his companion, "How do you suppose Columbus is faring in Palos?"

"You said yourself that it would not be easy gathering men from a town when there is little expectation of payment. We can only hope that he has more luck finding ships than we have had. But Columbus is a resourceful man."

35

Diego grinned at Domingo and added, "And he's almost as tenacious as we Euskaldunak are." They all laughed at this, knowing the truth of Diego's accusation toward his own people. All three of them headed down to the water to greet De La Cosa and his men when they landed.

Days passed as they busied themselves with the buying, packing, and stowing of goods. They planned the duties of the crewmen already available to them, and those that they would need to hire in Palos. Although Aitor had still not told Domingo whether he would be permitted to accompany them, his silence on the subject allowed him to believe it.

Domingo was so busy that he saw little of Carmen. When they did meet, Domingo told her that he did not know whether he would be leaving; yet, she could tell what he presumed. She said nothing of this to her father.

Respect for Juan De La Cosa grew quickly as his capabilities and knowledge became obvious to the men of Lequetio. They correctly judged him to be a man that would accept no insubordination but, although he was firm, he dealt with his men so justly that it was doubtful the crew would give him trouble.

Domingo was greatly impressed by this man, and never more so than when he joined his family for dinner one night. Generally serious yet polite, after a good supper and tall mug of wine, De La Cosa sat back on his bench and began to hum, then to sing in a rich deep voice. It was a very old Basque song that they all knew. The words told of the women of a village going down to the sea with their nets to fish. Soon Domingo's own tenor voice, which was nothing to be ashamed of, merged with De La Cosa's. Then one by one the rest of the Lacas joined in until the small room was filled with the resonating melody. When it ended there was only a short hesitation before they burst into another tune. This one was somewhat faster than the first.

Everyone was tapping their toes to the lively music. De La Cosa stood up, walked to the end of his bench, pulled Amuma up from her stool, stood her in front of him on the floor, and started to dance. Amuma was so surprised that she just stood there with her mouth open for a moment. She couldn't help laughing and objecting to such antics. In spite of her protests, however, in no time at all her hands went up in the air and her feet started moving, and there they were, dancing like two dervishes as the song grew louder and faster. The hands of those still seated clapped or beat out the rhythm on their small tables. The singers were doing a valiant job of keeping the song going in spite of their laughter. When they finally ran out of words to sing, Amuma, with a final swirl of her long black skirt, collapsed onto her stool. Her cheeks were red, her breath was short, and her eyes were shining as they hadn't for a long, long time. De La Cosa stood over the old woman trying to catch his breath and smiling broadly. Domingo, seeing the expression on his grandmother's face, was grateful to De La Cosa.

As Domingo sat at the bench watching his grandmother's profile, he was abruptly struck with the thought, "What if Amuma is not here when I return from the sea? What if she dies while I'm away."

Amuma's husband had died two years earlier while Domingo's brothers were on a whale hunt. The young men had mourned their grandfather deeply when they learned what had happened in their absence. His amuma was so dear to Domingo that the thought of losing her made him realize for the first time just how deeply he would feel the emptiness in his heart at her death. Still watching her he thought, "This is how I will remember her while I'm at sea, like she is right now."

After things had quieted down a little, Enara nudged her husband's elbow and glanced at Domingo. Aitor frowned at her, looked at the ceiling, frowned at her again, took a deep breath and said, "Txomin." It was his official sounding voice and it snapped Domingo's head around to face his father. "Txomin, I have decided," he cleared his throat, "that you may come with us to Palos." Domingo was on his feet with a shout of joy before he realized that his father had mentioned a destination that he had not expected. The realization cut his excitement like a knife blade, and he froze. "*Palos,* father?" It was as far as Aitor had decided to allow, in spite of his mother, his wife, Diego, or anyone else.

"Yes, Palos. We will see how you handle yourself over a short voyage before I send you across any ocean. And I must meet this Columbus and learn of his plans, his other ships and crew."

Very slowly, Domingo lowered himself onto his bench.

Seeing the sinking expression on his son's face, Aitor started to talk faster. "It's just so dangerous, son, and you are still young." Domingo looked so crushed that Aitor couldn't stop himself from adding, "But, if all looks well, I may let you sail with us from Palos." Aitor looked even more surprised by what had just come out of his mouth than Enara.

Domingo sprang from his seat again and danced around the room, whooping and twirling with reckless joy. He was going to cross the ocean with his father, Diego, and De La Cosa. Their adventures would be something to tell his grandchildren about. He was going to sail to the western seas!

Aitor sat watching his son's wild dancing for a moment, and his look of surprise grew glum with resignation. Enara and De La Cosa smiled at each other while Amuma tried to smother her laughter behind her hand.

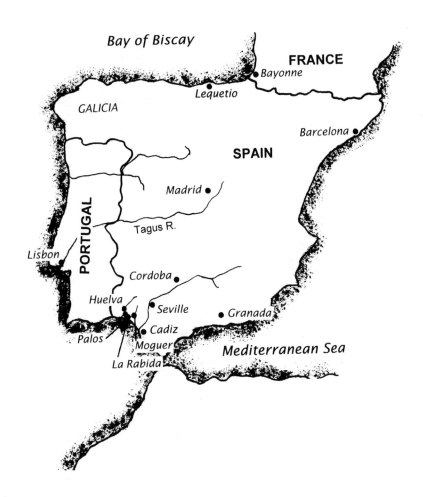

SPAIN

A Decision

4

"Come walk with me, Txomin," Amuma beckoned to Domingo as he threw one more fork full of hay to the young bull standing just inside the half open door of its stall.

The last few days had been so strange to him. As his departure date drew nearer, Domingo kept thinking how this would be the last time, for such a long time, that he would see, or hear, or taste, or feel all the familiar things around him. He had just been thinking that he would even miss the ill-tempered young bull he was feeding, which he told himself was ridiculous. He had never even liked this bull. What was the matter with him? At the sound of his grandmother's voice he leaned the hay rake against the wall and turned to her, brushing the stray pieces of hay from his hair. She made a sign to follow her and he fell in with her plodding steps as she led them to a quiet, grassy place up the road. From here they could sit and watch the sea.

She did not speak at once. She just stared ahead at the waves and let the breeze play with the strands of gray hair that had escaped her scarf. Domingo did not mind the silence; the two of them were comfortable with or without words. Finally Amuma took his young strong hand in her old worn one, something she had not done since he was small, and looked at him.

"How many times have we sat together like this and talked?" Domingo knew she did not want an answer from him, but her question made him think back on the thousands of times over the years of his life that she had told him her stories. Her tales had made up many of his first memories as a tiny child. She watched his handsome face as he remembered.

Her tone of voice grew serious as she continued. "You may encounter many hardships while you are away, Txomin, some that neither of us can imagine as we sit here. I pray that this never happens, but if a time should come when you do not know whether you have the strength to bear the challenges before you, I want you to remember what I tell you now." The old woman studied him to be sure that he was listening closely.

"You come from a remarkable race, Txomin. We Euskaldunak have been on this land for many ages. We have been strong enough and brave enough to hold it. I have heard strangers refer to us as ruthless. Perhaps, at times, we have been, but only because we have had to be in order to survive. We do not fight needlessly. Our people have not always made wise choices but we have never given up out of weakness or fear. When there is a storm brewing, no matter how fierce the lightening or how loud the thunder, we turn our eyes toward the wind. We face what is to come rather than hide from it. That is what you must do, my grandson. If you ever find yourself in danger, a danger that feels more powerful than you are, face it with your eyes wide open, and with the pride of your people behind you. It is the best way to fight."

Domingo covered her hand with both of his. "I will, Amuma. I won't forget where I come from." His expression bore the full confidence of youth and tender acknowledgment for all she had ever given him. He told himself that he would never forget this dear old woman who had taught him so much.

Gazing at him and knowing what she may lose with his going, her chin began to quiver. She stood up quickly, sniffed once, and said, "You must get back to your packing unless you want to sail tomorrow with only half of your things ready."

Domingo had been packed for three days but he rose and they headed back toward town. He must say goodbye to Carmen. She had told him not to come to her home or her

41

father may suspect that he was leaving. He was to meet her at a shady spot they both knew upriver from the bridge. He dreaded the tears he feared she would shed, and planned to make his farewell as brief as possible.

Carmen was waiting for him under a large pine tree. She sat with her head down, her long skirt flared around her. She was pulling pine needles one by one off a small branch. She did not look up at him as he approached her. He sat down so close to her that their shoulders touched, and still she did not look at him.

"I hoped you would not be angry with me," he said.

She kept her attention on the twig, pulling off its needles ever so slowly.

"Carmen, please look at me. Carmen."

In one sudden motion she threw her arms around him and buried her face in his shoulder. Domingo thought that she would cry, but she did not. He could feel each of her deep, warm breaths on his neck. He tried to pull her away so he could see her face but she would not let him. She merely clung to him more tightly. So he wrapped her in his arms and began to gently stroke her beautiful hair, telling her softly that everything would be fine, that he would come home to her, how much he loved her.

At last, Carmen raised her head but only high enough to kiss him, deeply. Domingo groaned inwardly, trying to hold onto his resolve to say good-bye quickly so it would be easier on them both.

"Carmen, we must..." he started, but she cut him off by kissing him with such passion that he lost his breath. Surrendering his feeble attempts to shorten their parting, he returned her kisses again and again. All he could do when she finally paused was to murmur her name and kiss her once more. Carmen was telling him how she would miss him with her lips but not with words. Any further declarations that Domingo had planned to make remained unspoken.

Two weeks later, Domingo stood on the deck of La Gallega beside his father and De La Cosa. Aitor watched the Palos harbor draw closer and closer through the spyglass he held to his eye. Their trip along the northern and western coasts of the Iberian Peninsula had gone smoothly. Although he was inexperienced, Domingo had learned his duties quickly and proved to be quite capable aboard ship. He was noticeably older than the other cabin boys but would be allowed no higher responsibilities until he had proven himself. As the days passed, his tasks became heavier. Aitor, much to his own wonder, found himself greatly enjoying this chance to be at sea once again. He had piloted the ship expertly and had often seen Domingo's looks of admiration directed his way.

De La Cosa's ship carried some of the goods they would need on the voyage, as well as those brought to barter in Palos. As they neared the harbor, the men were ordered to prepare to unload the trade merchandise. In the heat of the July sun Domingo joined the sweating men who were hauling up the wares from below deck.

La Gallega was still being secured when a shout came from a rowboat just beside them. Someone was asking permission to come aboard. De La Cosa peered over the side of the ship but did not recognize the nicely dressed white haired man asking to board. Diego approached the captain's side and followed his gaze. "Christopher!" he shouted with excitement. "How did you know we would be docking today?"

The tall, thin man of about forty years of age waved up at him. "I didn't know, Diego. Your letter that told me the name of the ship you were sailing on reached me just yesterday. I was already here on business when I spotted La Gallega." While Columbus was talking, De La Cosa had the ship's rope ladder lowered and Diego motioned for him to join them.

Domingo, standing in a line of hot, grimy men, each passing barrel after barrel of cargo along to the next man, tried to watch over his shoulder as Diego introduced Columbus to De La Cosa and Aitor. All of them bowed cordially enough,

43

but Aitor's bow was somewhat stiffer than those of the others. Columbus wanted to see the ship right away and was being taken without delay on an inspection tour by Diego and De La Cosa. The man next to him tossed Domingo one of the heavy kegs. Nearly dropping it, he decided that he had better keep his mind on his task.

That evening the four older men and Domingo sat at a long table in the sweltering darkness of an ancient inn's dining room. Empty platters and mugs in front of them drew the attention of buzzing flies that dove precariously close to the flame of the single candle on the table. Diego had been telling Columbus about the capabilities of the men who had agreed to sail with him. When Diego informed Columbus of Domingo's aptitude, Columbus looked Domingo over, smiled, and exclaimed, "This young man will be indispensable once we set sail!"

Domingo's study of the captain-general began at that moment. Though he was tired from the long day, he gave his full attention to the charismatic man's words and mannerisms.

Weeks earlier Diego had explained to the others what Columbus had been promised as reward for a fortuitous trip. Queen Isabela had agreed that Columbus would bear the title of Admiral of the ocean seas, and Governor of any new lands he claimed for the crown. He and his heirs would also be given the title of Don. Remembering this, Domingo continued watching the captain-general as he listened to Diego, wondering what riches he would bring back to the queen.

Domingo found himself grateful to his strict old tutor for his current ability to understand and reply to all of the Spanish being spoken. As the discussion flowed, Aitor discretely asked his son for clarification on one point or another, his own ability with that language being somewhat rusty. Aitor said very little and seemed to be weighing every word that Columbus spoke. He evidently intended to measure the foreigner's character, before revealing his own. De

44

La Cosa and Diego spoke this second tongue without difficulty.

"I am pleased that you have brought me a suitable ship and a more than suitable crew, Diego," Columbus said in a voice both sincere and pleasing. "I didn't want to write to you about my efforts here until I had had some success. Now I hope I am close to obtaining the two other ships we need."

Columbus bent over the table and said, "As I'm sure Diego told you, I was given a royal ordinance which authorized me to obtain two fully manned ships from Palos. I was to have these men and ships for a full two months. Well, when I read this ordinance at St. George's Church, let's just say that the reaction was not what I had hoped for. That was over seven weeks ago. At first I was ignored, then threatened. At last, I met the Pinzón brothers. These gentlemen have convinced their friends to supply two caravels that will be adequate for our needs. Cristobal Quintero owns the Pinta, and he has said he will come with us if Martín Alonso Pinzón will be her captain. I just hope Martín can hold Quintero to his commitment. I have heard nothing but grumbling from Quintero lately and he is slow in getting his ship seaworthy. We have all been calling Juan Niño's caravel the 'Niña', after him, although her christened name is the Santa Clara. Vicente Yañez Pinzón, Martín's younger brother, has agreed to act as the Niña's captain."

"Señor De La Cosa," Columbus continued, "I would like to make your vessel our flagship and I would like to call her the Santa Maria. Would that be acceptable to you?"

"If she is to be the flag ship for such a promising journey, I can think of no better name to give her," De La Cosa replied politely.

"Fine!" declared Columbus slapping his hands down onto the table. "Now let's go over a few details, that is, if you are not too tired." The hot, exhausted travelers all consented to stay. Though the evening was growing late, they were eager to solidify their new relationships, and the talk quickly resumed.

They began discussing which crewmembers were to be assigned to which ship. Most of the other Basques would stay with De La Cosa's ship, over which he would retain the title of master. Based on the composition of the Spanish crews Columbus had gathered, they decided to place three of their countrymen aboard the Pinta and two on the Niña.

Since some of the hands of La Gallega, now the Santa Maria, had planned to sail no further than Palos, they would need more men to bring her crew up to the proper number to fully man her. This would be their main task in the days to come. The discussion moved to how difficult it would be to hire the needed sailors when Columbus interrupted. "I must tell you that four convicted criminals were granted amnesty in exchange for agreeing to sail with me." In the stunned silence that followed, the other men looked at one another.

"What was the nature of their crimes?" asked Diego.

Columbus looked only slightly uncomfortable before saying, "One of them was convicted of murder. The other three helped him escape from prison. When all four of them were caught, they were convicted of the murder jointly."

"Murder?" exclaimed Aitor. De La Cosa asked in a low voice, "You would sail with a murderer on board my ship, sir?"

Columbus raised his hands to them. "Let me explain. I've interviewed the man at length. He said that there was a fight in a tavern and he admits that a man was killed. But he swears it was a matter of self-defense rather than murder. This accused man, Bartolome de Torres is his name, has never had any trouble with the authorities before. I firmly believe his story and I believe that he will be an asset to us, as will his three friends. You must meet them, and if you do not agree with my opinion after you have spoken with them, we can send them back to prison."

"Fair enough," said Diego. Aitor and De La Cosa looked far less at ease than Diego. They exchanged another concerned glance and let Diego take up the conversation.

It wasn't long, however, before they were all debating over what provisions to add to their stores, and what repairs to make to the ships before they could depart.

As he listened to the long discussions of the men,

Domingo leaned back against the wall behind him. Before long, his breathing began to deepen and the voices sounded little different than the droning of the flies. His eyelids became heavier and heavier, and his head began to droop. His thoughts returned to Columbus, and he pictured the captain-general placing great treasures before the queen.

When Domingo started to snore softly, Aitor looked over at him with mild surprise. A fond smile lightened Aitor's weary face and lingered a moment before he gave his attention back to the men and their talk.

"Aitor, I'd like you to come to my home tomorrow at mid-day so that we may discuss a few details," Columbus said.

Aitor, expecting it, had prepared himself for this request. "My son will come also." It was not a request

"Does Domingo know anything about...sailing, about the currents and the winds?" Columbus asked.

Aitor knew what this man from Genoa was really asking. He was inquiring whether the boy had been told that the route Columbus was proposing had previously been sailed by his own countrymen.

Diego had been adamant from the very first that they were to hire no one who had sailed to the western lands before, or who had any definite knowledge of it. Not even De La Cosa had been told that this voyage was one based on the maps of someone who had already been there. De La Cosa's experience, though substantial, had been gained in north-ern and southern waters alone. The only ones who knew that Columbus would be using Iker's maps, and that these western seas had been crossed long ago, were Diego, Aitor, and Domingo.

"He knows everything," Aitor answered Columbus direct-ly.

Columbus did not reveal a hint of his disappointment. "Well then, by all means, bring him along," he concluded. "I am a father of sons myself. I can see that you have reason to be proud of yours, as I am of mine. I will send a servant in the morning to bring you to my home."

"I will see you tomorrow then." Aitor rose stiffly and nod-

47

ded to Diego and De La Cosa. He roused his dozing son and led him down the hall to their room.

"If I hear one more complaint from Gomez Rascon, I'll have him thrown into prison instead of De Torres!" Aitor bellowed in Basque to Domingo who was standing in a warehouse trying to help with the purchase of wine and olive oil.

"You'd think he was the owner of the Pinta the way he keeps saying that she is not ready for such a journey. We've all been over her a hundred times and I've never seen a ship in better condition. It's plain enough that he is afraid to go with us. I wish he'd stay quiet or stay behind."

Domingo watched as his father sat down heavily on a bale of canvas. He noticed the redness in Aitor's cheeks and the sweat on his forehead. The heat did not usually bother Aitor as much as it did other men, and his son walked over to look at him more carefully.

"Father, you haven't had nearly enough rest lately. Are you feeling alright?"

"Perhaps I do need a little more rest but we have only four more days to tie everything down. If we aren't ready to sail by Friday who knows what Columbus will do."

"Your face is flushed. Is it more than the heat?"

"No, no, it's just that damned Rascon making my job harder. I'm fine."

Domingo sat down next to Aitor and they both looked on as the wine seller inspected his barrels for any damage they might have suffered along the road.

"So what do you think of Captain Columbus now, Father?"

Aitor raised his eyebrows and shrugged his shoulders. "I'll give him this much, he knows how to get what he wants. He also knows how to pick men with the experience he needs for this trip. It certainly didn't take him long to recognize De La Cosa's value. And the Pinzóns seem to be worthy captains. But it still amazes me that Columbus, the man in charge of this whole expedition, has never captained a ship. I can't help but wonder how this Italian is going to hold such strong men under his control."

"I agree that Captain Columbus knows a good man when one stands before him, Father. He obviously values and trusts your knowledge greatly," said Domingo, still keeping his eyes on the man inspecting the wine.

Aitor smiled, "I think he sees my coming as reassurance that there is *really* land where I've said it is. The fact that you and I and the other Basques will be with him seems to make him feel more comfortable." He wiped the sweat from his forehead with his sleeve and added, "You had better go on now and finish up with that merchant, my son."

"Are you sure you are feeling well? Will you stay here and relax for a while?"

"You're beginning to sound like your mother, worrying over me. Alright, alright. I'll just sit for a few minutes and cool off. You go on and get back to your work, Txomin." He said this with affection, patting his boy's shoulder as Domingo rose. Reluctantly, Domingo left his father's side to continue the negotiations over the price of the wine. When he glanced over his shoulder a moment or two later, Aitor had already gone back to the ships.

The next morning Domingo awoke before his father, which was highly unusual. Normally, Aitor had to just about haul his son off of his cot to get him up and going at an early hour. Sitting up, still rubbing the sleep from his eyes with the palms of his hands, Domingo snapped to attention as he heard his father groan painfully. Aitor's face was bathed in sweat and he was clinging to his cover and shivering.

Domingo knelt beside the cot and touched Aitor's burning brow. "Father," he said gently. When there was no response, he repeated the word more loudly. Aitor could barely squint at him, and the effort seemed to cause him extreme pain. When he tried to speak nothing came out but a hoarse raspy sound.

Domingo ran to get some fresh water. He lifted Aitor's head to help him drink, but only managed to get a few drops down before Aitor turned his head away. Even that little effort appeared to be too much for him.

"I'm going to find one of the ship's physicians, Father. I'll tell the innkeeper to send someone to stay with you. I'll be back very soon." Domingo talked as he threw his legs into his pants and jammed his boots on, not knowing if Aitor could understand what he was telling him. With one last look at Aitor, Domingo raced out the door and down the hall, grabbed the innkeeper's wife by the hand, and demanded that someone be sent to stay with his father. He told her that he was going for a physician and that someone had better be with his father when he returned. Receiving a confused nod from the surprised woman, Domingo sped out of the inn and down the road.

When he and the doctor returned, a young maid sat on a stool next to Aitor's cot laying a cool cloth on his face. She had covered him with another blanket to try to break his fever. The physician, Juan Sánchez, moved to the cot and examined Aitor's eyes and mouth. When he pulled the covers back, they could both see that the girl had made a hot poultice of some kind and laid it on his chest. Dr. Sánchez seemed to recognize the concoction that the girl had put into the poultice by its smell, and looked in wonder at the maid.

"You have been well trained for one so young." The girl's expression revealed fear as well as pride at the doctor's words. "Don't be afraid, my dear. I am not one of those who believes that women should be burned alive for their knowledge of herbs," he reassured her.

"Thank you for your kindness to my father," said Domingo as he reached into his pouch for some coins.

"No," she said, stilling his hand with a motion, "My gift of healing comes from God and I do not wish to be paid." She turned and would have gone out but Domingo reached out and took her arm. "Wait, tell me your name at least."

"It is Margarita, señor," she told him in a soft voice, then quickly left the room.

The doctor examined Aitor thoroughly then turned to Domingo and asked him several questions about Aitor's past and his health in general. Finally he said, "Your father obviously has a fever, but the most I can tell you is that it does not seem to be the plague or the scarlet fever. Beyond that, it is too soon to tell. I have seen your father many times at the shipyards, Domingo. He is there from dawn to dusk day after day. He has most likely exhausted himself and weakened his strength. If he is to fight this disease, he must have complete rest."

The doctor let the effects of his words settle on the youth. Dr. Sánchez knew well who Aitor and his son were since he had met each of the crewmembers over the last weeks. He knew also that their absence from the ship's roster could hinder Columbus' plans. It was easy enough to guess what remaining behind would mean to Domingo, however the doctor had no choice but to tell him the truth.

"Yes, doctor, I understand," said Domingo after a pause. And he did grasp all that the doctor had said. Aitor and he would not be sailing with the others. His understanding showed plainly on his face.

"When will my father begin to get better, doctor?" Domingo asked.

"Ah, youth," the doctor thought solemnly, "They think only of getting well, not of the alternative." But he was wrong, Domingo had indeed thought of the alternative. He simply chose not to voice this. Aloud Dr. Sánchez answered, "This evening I will come back to check on him but, Domingo, it may take days before we know how this fever will run its course. I will send my apprentice to you with a potion that should help your father rest. Now I must go and look over the other men to see if anyone else shows signs of this fever. If I learn anything from them I will tell you tonight."

"Captain Columbus," Domingo began, "Someone must tell him."

"I will take care of that, son," the doctor said kindly. "You stay with your father."

"Yes, Dr. Sánchez. I will. Thank you."

After the doctor left, Domingo sat by his father's bed staring into his face. It was bright with the fever. An enormous emptiness settled upon him. What would he do if he lost his father, if he were to die? Domingo thought of his mother, his amuma, his brothers, and so many others who relied on Aitor for strength, compassion, and direction. What would they all do without him? "Father," he whispered, knowing Aitor could not hear him. "Father." Then the young man bowed his head and began to pray as he had never before prayed, begging God to spare Aitor's life.

Things grew worse as the day wore on. Aitor began to cry out and thrash back and forth on his cot, at one point upsetting the cot altogether and falling to the floor before his son could stop him. Domingo's fear for his father's life became so great that he asked Margarita to stay with him. The girl's quiet manner, gentle care, and acceptance of whatever outcome God chose to grant, all helped to calm Domingo's thoughts.

When Dr. Sánchez returned that evening, he could give little in the way of reassurance. "I can only tell you that none of the other men show any signs of this illness," he told Domingo. "It is too soon to know how long it will take for the sickness to complete its cycle." He patted Domingo's shoulder as he left them. "I will see him tomorrow, unless you send for me sooner. Keep watch over him. There is little else you can do right now."

Margarita remained with Domingo through the long night, each of them tending to Aitor the best they could. Aitor lay quietly at times, but sometimes he groaned and shouted unintelligibly in his sleep. Domingo and Margarita sat at the stool by Aitor's side or on the cot, praying and waiting. Toward dawn, in spite of themselves, they began to doze. When Dr. Sánchez quietly opened the door the next morning, he found both of them sitting on Domingo's cot with their backs against the wall, sound asleep. Margarita's head had slid down and come to rest on Domingo's shoulder. Their young faces looked exhausted even in sleep.

Moving to Aitor's side, the physician checked his patient's face and chest. With great relief, he nodded. The fever had peaked, and mercifully fallen. The cloth that Margarita had laid on Aitor's forehead was merely warm now and would not need to be replaced. Aitor's breathing was deep and even.

"Aitor," the doctor said softly.

Domingo jumped up asking "What?" so quickly that the startled Margarita had to catch herself from falling off the cot. Half awake and unsteady on his feet, Domingo stared at the doctor.

"Calm yourself, son. Calm yourself," Dr. Sánchez said. "Are you awake enough to understand me, Domingo?" After receiving a quick nod, Dr. Sánchez went on, "Your father is better..." he began, but before he could say anything more, Domingo stepped quickly to his father's side.

He bent down and held his hand against his father's cheek, leaving it there long enough to be sure. Turning to Margarita with wide eyes he whispered, "Yes, his fever is down." A broad smile broke across his face. He sprang up, upsetting the nearby stool with a loud clatter, and ran back to Margarita. He squeezed her hands tightly, speaking his gratitude only with his eyes. A moment later he spun back around toward the physician. "His fever is down, Dr. Sánchez!" he shouted joyfully into the good doctor's face.

Dr. Sánchez couldn't keep from smiling himself. "Yes, Domingo, it is."

With all the commotion, Aitor began to stir. All three of the others turned their attentions to his cot.

"Aitor," Dr. Sánchez called to him again. Aitor's eyes fluttered open enough to squint at the three people leaning over him. There was the physician from the Santa Maria looking pleased, a young girl he did not know, and Domingo. Domingo's eyes were brimming with tears as he smiled down at him.

Aitor tried to speak but only managed a croak. Margarita was next to him in an instant with a cup of water.

He tried again and managed to squeak out, " I feel like I've been dragged over rough roads."

The three gathered around him and smiled as if he had just announced the birth of a grandchild.

"Ohhhh," he moaned softly and closed his eyes again.

More soberly now the doctor bent over his patient.

"You've been very ill, Aitor" the doctor told him, "but your fever has broken and the worst has passed. Still, this disease has weakened you and you are not yet out of danger. It is imperative that you have total rest for at least two weeks before venturing any further than the inn's dining room."

Aitor was too weak to argue. He meekly accepted the medicine the doctor gave him and rolled over, away from them all.

Dr. Sánchez gave Domingo and Margarita instructions for Aitor's care, then eyed them authoritatively.

"And both of you had better get some food and rest. I don't want to end up back here looking after the two of you as well as Aitor." They both nodded obediently and watched quietly as he left them.

That afternoon, after sleeping restfully and eating some hearty broth that Domingo had brought to him, Aitor wanted to talk.

"Txomin, please sit down over here for a moment and listen to me." Domingo left the small window he had been gazing out of and came to his father's side.

"I would be blind if I did not see how much it means to you to sail with this fleet," Aitor began.

"It is not as important now as it seemed only a few days ago, Father." Domingo said.

Aitor scanned his son's face.

"Perhaps not, my son. My illness must have been...a difficult thing. But if you miss this chance to go and come to regret it later, I would blame myself. If not for my being sick we would go together. That's no longer possible, not with them sailing the day after tomorrow. But, I have been thinking."

After a pause Aitor continued, "You can go under Diego's care and De La Cosa's guardianship, if they agree to stand in my place and watch over you."

Domingo realized that he had been holding his breath. Yesterday morning he had given up all hope of going and now it was being held up to him again. For the briefest of

54

moments he hesitated, then he said, "No, Father, I want to stay here now."

"Um. I see." Aitor said.

After a moment he asked, "Well, then, will you please see if you can go and find my good doctor so that I may speak with him? Surely he must have a potion that sits better with my bowels than that poison he's been forcing me to take."

Domingo nodded and hurried to comply with his father's request.

"How do you feel now, Father?" Domingo asked the following day after they had both had their morning meal. Aitor, much to the relief and pleasure of his son, had been able to sit up on his cot and feed himself.

"I feel almost like my old self," Aitor lied in a voice that he hoped sounded robust. He was still so weakened that every movement required a great effort.

A knock at the door interrupted Aitor's performance and De La Cosa entered, his tall frame dominating their small room.

"Well, my friend, you look much better than that gloomy doctor said you did," he said to Aitor.

"Yes, yes, I am much better today. It is good to see you, Juan."

De La Cosa turned to Domingo and said, "And you, young man, sorry as we are to lose the aid of your good father, we are all glad that you will be with us at dawn."

Domingo, who had been picking up Aitor's mug from the floor, froze in place. He looked up at De La Cosa, then at his father. "But, I am not going, sir."

"Yes, Txomin, you are," Aitor announced.

Aitor had made the arrangements through the doctor after sending his son on a string of unnecessary errands. He had not been sure that Columbus would allow the boy to go without him, knowing what he did. But Columbus had agreed.

For the next hour, Aitor attempted to convince his son that he was nearly well, and that it would be best if

Domingo went with the others. But even after Aitor's exhausting attempt at persuasion, Domingo was still torn with wanting desperately to go and hating to leave his father.

Seeing this, Aitor proclaimed to Diego, "With Margarita here to cluck over me like a mother hen, I couldn't be in better hands. With Domingo gone I'll get far more of the rest I need. There now, all is settled."

Looking at the tall dark man who dwarfed the small stool he was balancing on, Aitor said, "And, Juan, you will not forget your promise to me. You give your word that you will bring my son safely back to me?"

Very solemnly, De La Cosa once again promised, "If it is in my power, Aitor, your son will return to you sound and whole."

"There now," Aitor said again, and looked at his son with much more confidence than he felt. This son of his heart and soul, his Domingo, would be leaving him before first light.

Farewell to Palos

5

Domingo stood on the shore with the crowd that had begun to gather an hour earlier. It was the third of August and the day was as calm as a prayer. He waited with the others, watching in the false light of predawn. He could just make out the silhouettes of the three ships anchored in the river. The outlines of the red crosses painted on the sails were barely perceptible. The men on board were busy making final preparations for departure, their voices reaching Domingo across the short span of water in shouts and whispers.

He was late. Even with Aitor making a convincing show of being nearly recovered Domingo had wavered. He had not agreed to leave until his father had threatened to personally carry him to the ship. Yet here he stood, lingering on land, shifting his drawstring leather bag of personal things from one shoulder to the other. He felt a terrible apprehension that many things would not be the same if he left. At the same time, there was a gnawing in his gut that could only be stilled by stepping onto the deck of the flagship.

His eyes followed the launch from the Santa Maria, little more than a large rowboat with its sail tightly furled, as it landed on the beach to pick up its last load of provisions. The launches of the Niña and the Pinta had already been raised to the main decks of their respective ships, and were now being secured. Domingo continued to watch, moving neither forward or back, as if his feet were frozen to his place in the sand.

A sailor, still drunk from the night before, brushed by him, bumping his shoulder and pushing him forward a step. Slowly, Domingo followed it with another heavy step, then another and another, until his momentum propelled him steadily down the beach toward the water. Before he allowed himself to realize that he had made his ultimate decision, he was climbing like a sleepwalker into the launch. He didn't say a word.

The rowers, crewmembers of the Santa Maria, exchanged curious glances at Domingo's mute boarding. They had seen Domingo and his father with De La Cosa and Columbus many times and recognized him as a fellow ship-mate. Shrugging his shoulders, one of them nodded to the others. The kegs were quickly loaded and the launch pushed off. Muscular arms pulled at the oars, easily reducing the stretch of water between them and their ship.

Still silent and staring straight ahead, Domingo saw only the ship before him. "His" ship as he had come to think of her. Within two days of his arrival in Palos, the youth had studied and memorized the dimensions and features of the Niña and Pinta. He compared them to those of the newly renamed Santa Maria, which he already knew by heart. His flagship, a type of vessel known as a nao, was ninety-seven feet long and twenty-six feet wide, and from her first christening had sailed under De La Cosa's command with a crew of about thirty-three men. Along with the sailors, cabin boys, a physician and the officers, Domingo knew that today the Santa Maria bore several representatives of the queen. These included an interpreter, a scribe, and a royal over-seer. Together with Columbus, the total was brought to a slightly crowded thirty-nine. The Santa Maria's three decks made her stand high and majestic above the other two ships. The two caravels were smaller in dimension and had just two levels of decks. The mother ship was the only one of the three that bore a crow's nest high atop her main mast, adding even more height to her impressive stature.

During their short trip from Lequetio, Domingo had seen that De La Cosa loved his vessel like a lovely mistress. Now Domingo understood and shared that feeling. Even before he had learned that he would be sailing aboard her again, he had thought of the Santa Maria as proud and beautiful.

The Pinta was significantly smaller than the flagship at

seventy-five feet long and twenty-two feet wide, with a total crew of twenty-seven men. Her fore deck, at the front of the ship, was higher than that of the Niña and provided a work-space for the craftsmen on board as well as shelter during poor weather. The Niña, so small she almost seemed deli-cate to Domingo, was sailed by twenty-three men. She had a length of seventy feet and a width of twenty-one feet.

But it wasn't the size, capacity, or even the different per-sonalities of the ships that held Domingo's concentration this morning. He was trying hard to think of nothing at all, not his father bravely pretending that he felt fine, not his mother who didn't even know that Aitor was sick and alone at the inn, not Carmen whose own father must be furious that Domingo had left her for some crazy adventure. He focused solely on the Santa Maria as it loomed larger with each pull of the oarsmen.

The rowboat had no more than touched the side of the larger ship before Domingo leaped to the rope ladder. He scrambled up the lines and threw himself over the rail, his feet landing solidly on the main deck. Facing the bustling actions of the crew, Domingo saw Columbus just a few feet in front of him. The captain-general was dressed in clothing fit for a prince and was kneeling before a severe looking friar. The priest was bestowing a final blessing.

This was the only scene he was able to take in before the men he had left below in the rowboat began yelling up at him to send down the cargo tackle so that the barrels could be hauled up. Domingo quickly ran and grabbed the line tied next to the hatch and lowered the block. This done, he once again turned to face Columbus and the monk. Although the other men and boys did not slow their pace while performing their duties, they worked around these two with quiet respect. The pair in the center of the deck was praying in the eye of a storm of hushed activity. At another shout from the rowboat, a couple of deck hands came to help Domingo raise the barrels from the launch. They swung the main yardarm around, carefully avoiding Columbus and the friar, then lowered the kegs gently into the hold.

59

A moment later Domingo heard the two praying men say "amen," and Columbus stood up, inhaled deeply and smiled with satisfaction. Now that the benediction had concluded, the oarsmen were ordered to take the holy representative of the Church back to shore in the launch. Every seaman knew that it was unlucky to have a priest onboard a ship. This voyage was risky enough without tempting fate further. A blessing was one thing, bringing a priest along with them was quite another.

Scanning the ship, Domingo caught sight of De La Cosa standing on the half-deck. The ship's master faced the rear of the ship and critically eyed the men unfurling the mizzen-sail. As he watched, De La Cosa listened to one of his men report on some last minute details.

Still trying not to think too much, Domingo grabbed his bag, scrambled down the steps into the hold, and tied his gear securely to the hull. Avoiding the other men hard at work in the stale lamplight, Domingo hurried back up the steps and into the fresh air.

Chachu, one of their petty officers, a boatswain, spotted Domingo and called out to him over the increasing noise, "Domingo. Go help the cook make his final tie-down below."

Groaning inwardly but nodding obediently, Domingo slowly descended again into the hold and was soon swept up in the business at hand. As calmly as possible, Domingo tried to follow the barked instructions of the frantic cook, Francisco De Henao.

"Look at this mess! Nothing is where it should be! Get those bags of grain tied up higher. Move these damned ropes away from the fruit. What the hell are these barrels doing in the middle of everything?"

As Francisco grew more anxious, his cursing grew so vast and varied that Domingo had to admire the man's verbal creativity, if nothing else. From what Aitor had told him, Francisco's cooking style was nothing that would earn the gratitude of the men. Hopefully his cooking wouldn't be as bad as his temper appeared to be.

A tiny cabin boy named Pedro was attempting to secure a keg that was three times his weight while curses from

Francisco flowed over him like a waterfall. Domingo hurried to help him, and they exchanged a look. Rolling their eyes toward heaven at Francisco's seemingly endless vocal tirade, they began moving and tying the various containers into place.

It wasn't long before the voice of Columbus rang out loudly over the tumult of the men, "Cast away, in the name of Jesus our Lord!"

The ship moved gently with the raising of the anchor. Despite a new burst of obscene barking from Francisco demanding that Domingo stay until they had finished, he mounted the stairs three at a time, raced to the railing, and stared back at the shore. With the rising of the sun, it was lighter now. As the three ships eased away from land, Domingo could see the throng of people on the beach cheering wildly. Some of the women waved brightly colored cloths over their heads. A number of the younger children and women were crying, sobbing as if the voyagers were all sailing to certain ruin.

Domingo blinked twice and, finally, allowed himself to believe where he was, and what it meant. He was on the Santa Maria with Columbus and De La Cosa. He was really setting sail toward the Indies. Domingo closed his eyes and took a huge breath. Exhaling, he opened his eyes again and beamed at everything around him.

Glancing at the faces of the men standing on the deck near him, Domingo noticed many that looked less than eager to leave. Some revealed uncertainty, even fear, at their departure. The thought occurred to him for the first time that these men, everyone but Columbus and Diego De Arana, had more reason to be afraid than he did. Domingo was one of only three men on board who *knew* that there was a way to sail to the land that they sought. His ancestors had been there, or near there, long before. Although he wished he were free to share his secret, he was suddenly intensely grateful for his knowledge.

His smile grew larger and broader until the white gleam of his teeth shone from his face and his eyes glistened with moisture. Freedom to prove himself against the greatest of challenges lay before him. Domingo grew light-headed with the feeling that his life was beginning at this moment. Even though he knew not a single one of the people on the beach, he waved his arms over his head and bellowed farewells to them like a departing son. He cheered as if his entire family was watching his glorious departure. He shouted and waved until his face was red.

As Domingo's arms at last grew heavy and his voice became strained, the movement of a man standing to his right drew his attention. Luis de Torres, who had the misfortune to come from the same town as the convicted murderer on board, was the queen's appointed interpreter for their journey. He and Domingo had met several times and Luis, a valued member of the royal court, had shown an unusual cordiality toward the youth. Domingo had quickly taken to the gentleman's tolerant and generous nature. Of medium height and slight build, with a noble, expressive face, he stood not far from Domingo. Instead of looking at the still boisterous well-wishers on the beach, his gaze was drawn to a ship preparing to depart just down the shore.

First because of the darkness, then all of the commotion, Domingo hadn't even noticed the other ship earlier. He studied it now and was stunned by what he saw. Men, women, and children were being shoved and prodded up the rope ladders against the side of the ship. Then they were pushed or thrown into their places on the open decks. Some of the men had their hands tied in front of them and could barely manage to scale the drooping lines. They dropped like heavy dolls onto the deck. From where he stood, Domingo could occasionally hear the stifled wail of a passenger and the shouted demands and curses of the crewmembers over the din around him. He could do nothing but stare as one of the deckhands, ignored by the rest of the crew, viciously beat a prostrate man with a cat. The whip that had nine tails, each with a piece of metal hook tied to the end, was now crimson. A bent old woman sobbed and pleaded as the blows continued to fall. Repelled, Domingo turned to De Torres to ask for an explanation. He was silenced by the expression of terrible anguish on the older man's face. De Torres bowed his head into his hands as if he were deeply ashamed.

Domingo moved a step closer to Luis, hesitated, then asked softly, "Sir?"

"My people," he said with sadness so heavy that his head sunk even lower and he squeezed his eyes tightly closed. After a moment, rallying himself enough to look at the young man beside him, he added with difficulty. "They are the last, Domingo."

Confused, Domingo waited a moment. "I don't understand, sir. The last what?"

Glancing once again at the ship, which was adding more and more to its human cargo, Luis continued in little more than a whisper. "The last of the Jews to be expelled from Spain. The last few that refused to convert to Catholicism, and still managed to survive the inquisitors, go with that ship. How they will survive now, God alone knows."

Domingo watched once more and, even at that distance, he could make out the faces and the expressions of some of the people. Most of them looked down, avoiding the eyes of their loved ones as well as the strangers. Mothers clung to and tried to hush their children. The slightest glance of defiance brought quick blows from the guards.

"These are your people, sir?" he asked with sympathy and uncertainty in his young voice.

In another time or place, Luis would not have dreamed of telling Domingo what he was about to. But here and now, seeing the dreadful fate of his people before him, Luis bared his soul to another human being. "I have worked with the queen for many years," Luis said, his words sounding like a confession. "It was...necessary for me to convert to the Christian faith long ago." Although De Torres did not fear the character of the youth beside him, it would have been foolish to say more. He did not say that his conversion from Judaism had not been sincere or that he was ashamed beyond words of it now. But Domingo could guess all of this from the interpreter's careful speech.

"I am very sorry for your people, sir," Domingo said, mortified by what he saw before him, not caring at that moment that such words were gravely dangerous. The king and queen had fought for years to rid Spain of non-Christians, and had defeated the Moors just months before. The deportation of the Jews was merely the queen's last step in a victorious crusade for the glory of God. Domingo had known all of this, but now he asked himself how God could intend, could demand that such actions be carried out. Was this how Christ, God's own son, taught us to treat each other? No, it was not. This was a thing designed by men and women of power rather than by God. They must have wanted something from or feared something in these people, these Jews. Of this, the young man had no doubt.

"What is happening here is...disgraceful, sir. This does not honor God."

Domingo felt himself being watched and glanced down the ship's rail. His eyes met the eyes of Bartolome De Torres, the murderer. Bartolome merely nodded casually at him and slowly looked away. This was enough to make the hair on the back of Domingo's neck tingle. Drawing his own gaze away from the killer's profile, Domingo could feel what little remained of the exhilaration of his departure evaporate.

He turned his back to the rail and let his gaze climb the fore mast until he beheld the newly hoisted banner of the sovereigns of Spain. There was little wind but, as slack as the banner was, Domingo could still see that it bore a dark green cross on a white background. The initials of Ferdinand and Isabella stood out boldly on either side of the cross. There was a golden crown above each letter. Domingo stared at the flag. This same king and queen who were financing their voyage were also responsible for the treatment of the people on the ship not far from them. Gratitude, anger, and confusion fought for dominance in his mind. The fact that the same two leaders could manifest such hope and yet such misery was a hard reality for him to accept. He tried to tell himself that perhaps he would understand things better when he was an old man, when he had seen much more of how destiny played with the lives of men.

Today, all he could do was wonder at the twists and clashes in the paths of the powerful.

The air was so still that some of the hands were ordered to the oars, and the ships proceeded lazily down the Rio Tinto. As they passed beneath the silhouette of the monastery of Santa Maria de la Rábida, Columbus sank to his knees in homage, removed his hat, and bowed his head. Everyone knew that the good friars of the monastery had befriended Columbus and his young son, Diego, when they had first come to Spain. He had evidently not forgotten their kindness. Domingo joined the other men who followed the captain-general's example and kneeled on the deck. Luis hesitated then slowly sank to his knees also. The crews aboard the Niña and the Pinta observed the men of the flagship and knelt down as well.

Domingo humbly prayed, "Please Lord, help my father to get well, and keep him well while I am gone. Keep them all safe until I return, Heavenly Father." Deep in his prayer, Domingo was unexpectedly moved by a perception that the Lord was near him. He was illuminated by a strange sense of wellbeing. He interpreted what he was feeling as a sign that everything would turn out as he hoped. They would return unharmed, and with riches and knowledge that would gain them fame. He told himself that surely the queen, who now seemed to him both generous and brutal, would grant his people their fishing rights. Yes, this and much more. Carmen and his family would be so proud of how he, Domingo Laca of Lequetio, had conducted himself during his journey. He felt certain that he was doing what he was destined to do.

Rising from their knees, the older hands were quick to continue with their duties. Domingo glanced back toward Palos and watched the crowds gradually diminish as their ships drew farther down the river toward open sea. He could no longer see what was happening aboard the ship carrying the Jews.

Squaring his shoulders, he turned to face downstream. "No more looking back," he told himself. "Only ahead until we reach the Indies."

Domingo turned to Luis, who still bore a pained and haunted expression. "Will you excuse me, sir?" he asked, then headed back down into the hold to help Francisco with the stores.

Ship Diagram of the The Santa Maria

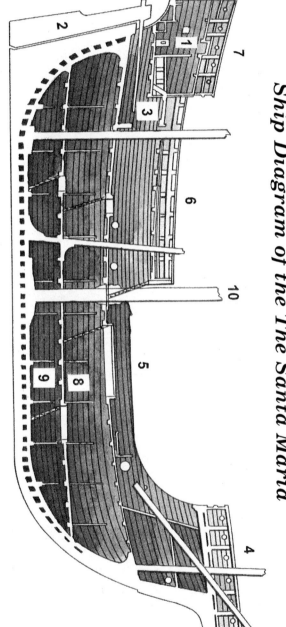

1 - Captain's Cabin
2 - Rudder
3 - Tiller
4 - Foredeck
5 - Main Deck

6 - Half deck
7 - Stern deck/stern castle
8 - Hold
9 - Lower hold for ballast storage
10 - Main Mast

Life at Sea

6

Once they reached open seas, the winds picked up masterfully and the fleet headed south. Domingo knew well that their first goal was to reach the Canary Islands off the coast of Africa, which were under Spanish rule. Though he was familiar with these waters only from the hours he had spent pouring over charts and talking with his father, this part of the route had been experienced first hand by many of the seasoned sailors. The fleet wouldn't head west until they reached the Canaries, and Domingo was confident that they wouldn't tempt fate until then. Even so, as much as he tried to look like an old hand, there were times he couldn't hide his own wonder and thrill at feeling the vastness of this stretch of the ocean for the first time.

There were only two things that dampened his excitement. He often worried about how Aitor was recovering, and prayed that he was better. In addition to his concern for his father, Domingo had to deal with mild seasickness the first day out of Palos. He succeeded in keeping this shameful reality carefully hidden, however, and was deeply thankful when his stomach once again became accustomed to the sea.

With the favorable weather and a well-known tract of the ocean, the crews fell good-naturedly into a regular work routine. From the outset, the men and boys were divided into two groups, each of which worked and rested in shifts lasting four hours.

Although Domingo had hoped to be assigned to the group of men and boys working under De La Cosa and his Basque sailors, Columbus had him placed with his own band of men. It wasn't that Domingo had anything against

Columbus or the Spaniards, he simply felt more at home with his countrymen.

As Domingo went about his duties, he couldn't help noticing the difference in the personalities of his two commanders. From the hour that land had disappeared from view, the captain-general had begun pacing the decks like a rooster just given a new flock of hens; excitement and optimism lightening his steps. His fine clothes, along with having his own servant and cabin boy, placed him clearly apart from the common men. Yet, he was cordial, even jovial with the crew as he roamed about the ship, and his friendly manner raised the spirits of those around him.

De La Cosa, on the other hand, wore simpler clothing, not much finer than Domingo's own. Like Domingo and the rest of the Basques, the ship's master wore a large red beret knitted from wool that could be pulled down over his ears on windy days. He seemed to take things calmly in stride from one day to the next. De La Cosa spoke seldom, but he had a way of giving a wayward crewmember a certain kind of look that got his meaning across without the need for words. The Basque crewmen referred to this particular stare of the ship's master as the "captain's betondu." Not even the roughest among them were immune from its restraining effects. Domingo did his best not to earn one of De La Cosa's betondus, and was appreciative for his occasional glances of encouragement or approval.

De La Cosa and Columbus took command of separate shifts, although both men were present on the decks much of the time. Often during his own shifts, Columbus was content to leave the command to De La Cosa while he went to the captain's cabin to study his charts and make notes in his log. It was understood that Columbus had the final word on every decision related to the fleet. But Domingo found it easy to see that the captain-general did not have the experience captaining a ship, especially this ship, that De La Cosa had.

Homesickness took posession of Domingo the night after they left Palos. His many tasks kept him so busy that this malady did not bother him much during the days. But the nights brought back all of the mental pictures of his home and a terrible longing.

As the afternoon sun beat down on Domingo, he swayed back and forth on his knees, mindlessly scrubbing the deck of the stern castle. He was singing an old Basque song softly to himself when a small shadow fell over him. With an effort, he stopped his motions and his voice, and lifted his head. Pedro was standing over him with a bucket in his hand and strands of hair hanging in his face. Domingo straightened but he didn't even try to let go of the rag in his hands yet. An hour earlier his arms had been so sore that he could barely keep them moving. Now his limbs were numb, and they seemed to have been moving round and round in endless circles all on their own.

Brushing the hair back from his eyes Pedro squatted down near Domingo. "Look at your hands," he said.

Slowly lifting them up in front of his face, Domingo said with acceptance, "Yes. They look like they're a hundred years old."

Pedro glanced around to make sure none of the men were within hearing range. With more pride than complaint he said in a low voice, "Us boys, we have the hardest jobs on the ship, you know, with all this scraping, and sanding, and swabbing, and rinsing. Just think what the Santa Maria would look like without us. Because of us, she is a thing of beauty."

To this, Domingo smiled and nodded.

Pedro and Domingo had been shipmates since they had left Lequetio. In a quiet moment during their trip to Palos, the pint-size boy had confided that his family was very poor. In the saddest of voices, Pedro had told Domingo that his mother had brought seven children into the world, but that only he and two sisters had survived. Diseases and lack of proper food had taken the others.

"My parents told me that the life of a seaman is hard," Pedro had explained to Domingo, "But they also said that a good sailor is always able to find work. They told me if I became a sailor, I would not starve. And they said they would be proud to have a son that was a sailor."

Not long after this talk with his parents, which had taken place about a year ago, De La Cosa's ship was preparing to weigh anchor at the bay near their village. Pedro's father had left their modest hut, and gone down to the beach to meet the captain. In less than half an hour, he had come home again, taken Pedro by the hand, and told his son to say goodbye to his mother.

De La Cosa had taken one look at the eight-year-old boy and said, "I'm sorry, sir, but your son is too small to be a cabin boy. He looks to be no more than six years old."

Pedro's father's great disappointment had been replaced by incredulity when Pedro strode from his side and up to the tall captain. Visibly shaking but with a brave, almost defiant expression, the small boy had announced, "I will work hard, Captain, sir, harder than the boys who are twice as big as me. I will not shame you or my parents."

When De La Cosa had not immediately replied, Pedro's father had moved forward and reached out to take his son. He had been stopped by a gesture from the shipmaster.

"And do you understand that you will be away from your mother for many months, boy?" De La Cosa had asked not unkindly.

"She will be alright, sir. She has my sisters to help her, and she has told me many times that she wants me to be a sailor."

De La Cosa had looked with approval at Pedro's father. "He thinks of his mother rather than himself when I speak of their separation. You must have a good wife." Then, speaking directly to the boy he had added, "I look for men who will sail with me for many years."

Pedro had replied with simple logic. "I have more years to give you than any of your other men, sir."

This statement had brought a slow smile. "Well, Pedro, can you be ready to sail with me within the hour?"

"I am ready now, sir."

And with that, Pedro had given his father a long embrace and had become an official member of De La Cosa's crew.

When Domingo had met the boy in Lequetio, and had explained that this was to be Domingo's first voyage, Pedro had taken him under his tiny wing. He had instructed Domingo in everything that a worthy cabin boy needed to know. Even now, Pedro tried to be helpful to Domingo and show him just how an experienced hand would best deal with things. Sometimes his recommendations, coming from one so young, amused Domingo immensely. But Domingo always kept his smiles to himself when Pedro was at his most serious. Pedro's eagerness to please and his willingness to perform his tasks had impressed Domingo greatly. The boy made up for his small stature every day.

And now here was Pedro, seriously giving full credit for the loveliness of the Santa Maria to the grueling efforts of the cabin boys. Although an exaggeration, Domingo was aware that much of what Pedro said was true.

"Oh, I don't mind the cleaning so much as long as I can stay out in the fresh air, even if my hands *do* look ancient," Domingo said still surveying his outstretched hands. "But there are times I'd like to see someone nail the hatchways closed. I would be happy if I never had to go below again." Pedro nodded in full agreement, grimacing at the mere mention of the hold.

Insufferably stifling and dank in the August heat, the hold was a place that Domingo had come to dread. The ship was constantly taking on water, and the cabin boys frequently had to wade through it. They also had to pump out and swab up the mess in the stinking murkiness that swirled through the belly of the ship.

Also among the cabin boys' duties was the job of fetching food and supplies from the hold. Domingo would have endured these excursions more willingly if rats, cockroaches and other crawling things had not made their homes in the darkness below. And the rats, in particular, seemed to be quite used to getting their way. The creatures were occasionally fearless enough to defend their territory, and their bites were something to avoid at all costs.

Domingo had soon developed the habit of keeping a billet, one of the long, rounded pieces of wood used to secure the ropes to the ship, at the base of the steps. Whenever he was sent to search for something below he took this club with him. He noticed with satisfaction that it didn't take long for the rats to learn to respect his billet.

Still, Domingo hated to be sent on missions to find something for Francisco's cook pot, or to fetch an item needed to repair the ropes or a piece of sail. Some days there seemed to be no end to the number of errands that forced him to leave the light and the fresh air, and descend the steps to what he considered the dungeon beneath the decks.

Because he was the oldest and most conscientious of the cabin boys, Domingo was often assigned the job of timekeeper. The half-hour glass was kept near the tiller under the roof of the half-deck. It was to be turned precisely as the last grain of sand fell from the top half of the glass to the bottom. At the turning of the glass, the time was called out in a loud clear voice. Eight turns were made during each shift. Any boy who kept the men of one shift working longer than they should have been due to a late accounting of the final half-hour would be dealt with in a way that would discourage a repetition of such carelessness. Domingo had carefully managed to avoid making such a mistake.

At sunset of the second day at sea, the men gathered on the open decks facing the western horizon. In their loudest and most reverent voices, they sang out the lonely tune of Salve Regina. The Niña and the Pinta sailed close enough for the voices of their crews to blend in the sky overhead with those of the men aboard the flagship. Through this religious song, almost a chant, the men praised the Almighty and gave Him thanks for seeing them through another day at sea.

Tonight, something in the song pulled at Domingo's emotions and his voice suddenly cracked and faltered. He could do no more than mouth the final words.

His last shift had ended hours earlier and Domingo knew that he should find an empty space on deck and try to get some sleep. His 11:00 p.m. shift was fast approaching and he had caught himself struggling to stay alert the night before. Instead of bedding down, however, he stood and watched the final rays of the sun disappear. He was held by the wondrous display of colors as they reflected their glory, first on the many shapes and textures of the clouds, then again on the vastness of the ocean. As darkness gradually swallowed the sun's performance, Domingo realized that Pedro was standing at his side.

The two of them remained at the rail in silence for awhile, then Pedro asked, "Domingo, do you think we will see any houses made of gold when we reach the Indies?"

Before Domingo had a chance to answer, a respected sailor by the name of Rodrigo De Jeres, who had a mass of curly black hair and the eyes of a poet, joined them. Rodrigo asked Pedro with a gentle smile, "Is it important to you that you see such houses, Pedro?"

"Oh yes, sir. I have heard stories about them. I long to see them very much," the young voice answered with yearning.

Rodrigo and his friend, Gonzalo Fernández, were two of the Spanish men that had hired on in Palos. Rodrigo seemed always to see the beauty in things that surrounded him. His handsome smile was peaceful, his expression quietly perceptive. He had told Domingo about his wife and two grown daughters, whom he missed while he was away. But this voyage was one that his heart had longed to join since it was first announced in St. George's church. His good wife, seeing his desire and knowing him well, had insisted that he go.

Rodrigo looked from Pedro to Domingo and asked. "And you, my young Basque friend, do you also long to see such wonders as golden houses?"

Domingo thought for a moment. He was a little surprised when he realized that he had never actually wished to see one thing in particular during this voyage.

"Not really, sir. What I want..." he searched for the right words, then continued. "What I want is to see *everything*, to *feel* everything that happens on our journey."

Rodrigo nodded thoughtfully at this. "I have watched you, Domingo. I see that you put your whole soul into your work, and I guess that it is this way with your dreams as well." He raised a questioning brow and could see by Domingo's self-conscious expression that he was right.

"My grandfather would have said that you are wise for one of so few years." A wistful look came into the seaman's dark eyes. "As I was growing up, my grandfather often told me that I should treat each day as something precious. He said to make love to life itself. He told me that I should put every bit of myself into what I did, no matter how humble the deed. In that way I could learn from everything I ever encountered, and enjoy some part of it." Then, clearly picturing the man he had held so dear, Rodrigo added, "That is how he lived, making love to life, and he died with no regrets. What more can a man hope for?"

"That is how I will live my life!" announced Pedro with such serious conviction that Rodrigo and Domingo couldn't help smiling at each other over the small boy's head.

"Good!" Rodrigo proclaimed. "And who knows? You just may get to see those golden houses, Pedro. They would indeed be wonders to tell your grandchildren about, eh? Now," Rodrigo added, giving each a pat on the shoulder, "You two had better get some sleep or one of you will undoubtedly fall overboard during your watch tonight."

The two followed this order without delay and were soon curled into their own meager spaces on the wooden planks of the deck. Domingo thought about the captain-general and De La Cosa, who were the only two aboard who did not have to find their sleeping places on the open decks.

"I will no doubt wish I could trade places with one of them if the weather turns bad," he mused sleepily to himself, "But I'd rather sleep where I am tonight. The breeze is cool and these ropes serve as a fine bed."

As they lay under the glow of the evening stars, the rolling and sighing of the ship rocked Domingo and Pedro to sleep with its own serene song. During the night, Domingo woke briefly when he heard Pedro mumble something about "houses of gold" in his sleep.

By the third day at sea, Domingo and the rest of the hands were painfully familiar with Francisco's lack of cooking talent. They didn't starve, but occasionally the braver hands grumbled that starvation might be preferable to eating what Francisco called "hearty meals". The morning diet was generally considered safe because it consisted of sea biscuits, nuts and cheese, as well as fruit for as long as it lasted. Once a day, however, they were served Francisco's hot meal, which was concocted with greatly varying quality and ingredients. Sometimes only half-cooked and often with foreign objects floating among the hard beans and less than clean vegetables, this mysterious mixture appeared with the changing of shifts at 11:00 a.m.

Watching Francisco face down the different men who approached his cooking fire became a daily amusement for Domingo and Pedro. Particularly entertaining to the cabin boys was Columbus' servant who would approach Francisco holding his master's bowl. He would all but hold his nose as the meal was scooped up. The fastidious servant would then proceed to pick out anything questionable and toss it back into the pot, all the while making faces and grunts of displeasure. Just as Francisco looked like he was about to bash the man with his iron ladle, the servant would conclude his sorting activities and declare loudly, "Thank heaven captain-general Columbus has a strong stomach and a generous nature." This proclamation never failed to produce a string of oaths from Francisco so impressive that the Domingo and Pedro had to turn their faces and busy themselves elsewhere in an effort to hide their silent laughter.

De La Cosa and his men ate next, just before the start of their shift work. At the calling of the hour, which marked the changing of the shift, the men just leaving their duties were fed. As was custom, the only ones on board who expected to eat from their own bowls or platters were the captain and the master. These luxuries were unnecessary for the crew. Each of the hands wore a spoon and a knife on his belt, both of which served them adequately at mealtime. In the evenings, the men who were courageous enough ate any leftovers from the same pot, which, by then, were even less appetizing. The rest of the crew made a meal much like they had gathered together for breakfast. Accompanying all of their meals was a mixture of water and wine, which the men grumbled was far too much water and too little wine.

Domingo had never considered himself overly picky about what he ate but on their fourth day at sea he was faced with the choice of going hungry or holding his breath and closing his eyes while he ate. For the last half-hour he had been down in the hold with two other hands moving barrels and shifting piles of canvas to higher places in an attempt to keep them dry. He had sweated through his clothes and was panting to catch his breath when he heard the blessed sound of a voice singing out the hour of 11:00 from above. Heavily climbing the stairs into the fresh breeze above, Domingo breathed in huge gulps of the clean air. Somewhat refreshed, he headed for the group of men who were waiting to eat.

One of the sailors who was about to start his shift passed Domingo and growled, "No sense in hurrying. That swill isn't fit to feed to the sharks."

When Domingo reached the pot he had to agree. Floating in the grayish-brown fluid were so many different pieces of fish anatomy that it appeared that Francisco had thrown the fish in whole. After being added to the soup and boiled for quite some time, the fish had fallen apart. Chunks of unpeeled potatoes bobbed between fish heads and tails. From the smell that drifted up from the mixture, some of the potatoes had been rotten when they were tossed in. Domingo shook his head and turned away. With his stomach growling like a wild thing, he took a few plums and a handful of sea biscuits rather than the soup. Most of the men and boys complained about the meal but sat down around the pot just the same. They pulled their spoons from their belts and began spooning mouthfuls of the stew directly from the kettle. Domingo saw Pedro squeezed between the larger boys and men, scooping his spoon into the pot's contents whenever opportunity allowed.

The next day when Francisco suggested that he might try his hand at fishing again, Domingo not only heartily encouraged him, he volunteered to start the meal for the crew. After having to listen to all of the whining from the men the day before, Francisco decided to let the lad prepare a meal. When Domingo failed miserably, the men would be begging him to return to his cooking duties. With this thought, Francisco gathered his fishing bait and headed to the rail of the ship.

Domingo reasoned that he could surely manage one decent meal. He was the youngest child of his family, and had spent many hours helping his mother and grandmother cook. Could he possibly do worse than Francisco?

Only slightly nervous, Domingo dropped the ingredients he had prepared into the huge kettle and hung it to cook over the coals of the fire. Domingo had heaped these coals inside of the ship's one fogon, a giant three-sided iron box. The fogon rested on two thick pieces of wood to insulate the ship's deck from the heat of the box. Sand had been spread on the bottom of the fogon on top of which Domingo had built his fire.

The weather had been so calm during the first few days of their journey that the fogon was used out on the open decks rather than under the cover of the half-deck. The portion of the main deck beneath the half-deck was crowded with the tiller men, the pilot and others laboring to navigate the ship. The heat of nature was bothersome enough without adding the warmth of a man-made fire.

Francisco returned from fishing just in time to see Domingo ladling out Columbus' portion of food. Francisco couldn't help grinning to himself as he waited for the servant to start fussing. Instead, the man merely sniffed the contents of the bowl, eyed it thoroughly, and said in a loud voice, "Well done, young man." Then Columbus' servant left without so much as a glance in Francisco's direction.

The soup Domingo had made was nothing extravagant. But the vegetables were washed and unspoiled, the salted meat was tasty and cut into manageable pieces, and Francisco's mystery ingredients were noticeably missing. Domingo had tended the pot with care so that the food was neither burnt nor half raw. De La Cosa took one taste and gave Domingo an approving lift of his eyebrows. The rest of the crew reacted to the meal by slapping Domingo on the back and bombarding him with bawdy, teasing praise. Pedro finished eating, patted his full belly, and said with great sincerity, "You cook almost as good as my mother." Everyone roared with laughter as Domingo's face grew bright red. All Francisco could do was stand back and frown.

From that day on, the entire crew began to encourage Francisco to fish for longer periods. And his cooking duties were more and more often relinquished to Domingo.

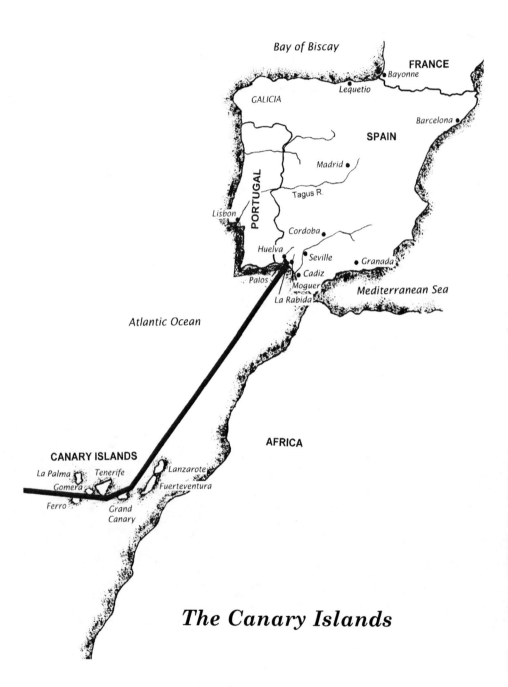

The Canary Islands

The Alboka

7

Domingo sat in the shade of the forecastle with Rodrigo and Gonzalo enjoying the last few minutes of relaxation before their stint of duty began. The Canary Islands were barely visible to the south and they had been speculating about their chances of going ashore as soon as they anchored. They knew that Columbus didn't intend to stay on the islands any longer than necessary before heading west. Still, they hoped for at least a short visit with the island inhabitants.

Gonzalo was not tall, but he was built with such strength in his chest and arms that he looked like he could gut a whale with his bare hands. Gonzalo's wife had died soon after the birth of his second son. He had told Domingo that he hoped to earn enough from this trip to raise his young sons in some comfort. Whenever he spoke of his boys, his chest swelled and his eyes shone with emotion.

"With this strong wind," Gonzalo said as his hands greased and twisted a section of rope, "We should be in port by tomorrow. That would make it just five days since we left Palos. I have never made this trip in less than eight days before, and usually it takes ten. Fortune is smiling on us, my friend. May she continue to do so once we head west."

"One lucky day at a time is all we can ask for," replied Rodrigo standing up and flexing his arms to loosen the muscles, anticipating the cabin boy's call to work. As he stretched, Rodrigo glanced in the direction of the Pinta, which was a little behind them on their starboard side. Gonzalo saw his friend's expression change to one of grave concern.

"What is it?" he asked as he and Domingo sprang up next to him and followed Rodrigo's gaze.

Rodrigo did not have to answer. Domingo and Gonzalo could see as clearly as their companion that a high plume of dark gray smoke was trailing the Pinta. An iron basin attached to her stern was used for building signal fires to communicate between the ships. The smoke now billowing from the Pinta's signal fire was a call for immediate help. Even without the smoke beacon they could easily see that the Pinta was in trouble. The ship was veering off course and the men on her decks were frantically hauling on the ropes in an attempt to maintain the Pinta's position.

Rodrigo turned in the direction of the half-deck and yelled against his cupped hand. "Captain De La Cosa! The Pinta! Look to the Pinta!"

De La Cosa raised his head at the shout and hurried to the rail. He was joined a moment later by Columbus. Both men stared at the Pinta's strange maneuverings. They could hear calls from her captain, Martín Alonso Pinzón, but were unable to make out his words.

"Something's happened to her rudder," said Columbus under his breath. He ordered the men to pull the Santa Maria as close to the Pinta as was safely possible.

The sea was too rough, however, for the Santa Maria to come alongside the Pinta and be of any direct help. Not without endangering the flagship. As soon as the two ships were closer, Columbus was rowed to the veering Pinta. He managed to board her and was met by a furious Martín Pinzón.

Storming and cursing, Pinzón led Columbus to the rear of the ship as his men scattered to stay out of their paths. Sure enough, the rudder had been torn from the tiller and now dangled loosely in the water. The ship was left to the mercy of the wind and ocean currents. Hands were straining to shift the sails in an effort to hold the ship steady. Pinzón glared back toward mid-ship where Gomez Rascon stood not far from Cristóbal Quintero, the Pinta's owner.

Columbus, his expression showing a mixture of disgust and worry, asked, "How did this happen?"

Pinzón did not remove his angry gaze from Rascon, who had grabbed onto a sail line and was keeping his eyes averted from the direction of his captain. In his rage, Pinzón barely managed to lower his voice and spit out, "I do not believe this was an accident."

Columbus, stunned, now paid closer attention to the direction in which Pinzón was still staring and spotted Rascon.

"You think Rascon has done this *intentionally?*" he demanded.

"I do. The bastard! I should hang him right now."

"Did anyone see him tampering with the rudder?"

"No, at least no one who will admit it. But he has not been subtle about saying that this voyage was a mistake from the beginning. I believe he and Quintero never intended that this ship be allowed to sail any farther than the Canaries."

Columbus considered for a moment, looking from one man to another. "There could be another explanation, Martín. We will not hang him without some sort of proof. Can you do anything to repair the rudder, so it'll hold long enough to reach the nearest island?"

Finally pulling his glower away from Rascon, Pinzón replied simply, "I will try."

Columbus walked to the main mast and told the crew that he had full faith that they, and their fine captain, would repair the rudder and bring the Pinta into port safely. He promised each of them some time ashore while the rudder was being fully reconstructed, which raised the spirits of the men considerably.

During the next few hours and after several exhausting attempts, Pinzón and some trusted men succeeded in rigging the rudder and tiller in place with a web of ropes. The Pinta was now handling more smoothly although far from perfectly in the water. The men aboard the Niña and the Santa Maria were ordered to reduce their ships' sails to slow their pace. This way they could better stay even with the Pinta, like a friend shortening his stride for an injured comrade. In this condition, the fleet slowly limped in the direction of the island of Grand Canary. Each man hoped to reach land by the next day.

By the next morning, however, Domingo and Pedro went to the ship's railing and saw that the Pinta's rudder had loosened again. When Columbus shouted to Pinzón to ask about the ship's condition, Pinzón yelled back that she had started taking on water during the night.

Pedro looked up at Domingo, shook his head, and said, "This is not a good omen."

Pinzón and his crew worked and reworked the ropes that held the rudder in place but the progress of the fleet was little better than a crawl. Grand Canary, ever closer, was still well out of reach when darkness fell again.

With the first rays of the following sunrise, Domingo joined his voice with those of the crews of all three ships as they cheered lustily at the proximity of the island. When Domingo turned to look at the Pinta he could see that, though she was limping along, her slow pace was still making some progress. Columbus ordered one of his men to signal Pinzón that the Santa Maria and the Niña would proceed to the island so they could learn what ships might be available to replace the Pinta. Pinzón answered the signal with agreement and the two undamaged ships pulled ahead, leaving the Pinta to catch up with them as quickly as she could.

As the Santa Maria neared the coast, Pedro and Domingo gaped in wonder at the lushness of the shoreline, their feet almost itching to set foot on the sand. They joined in to help as men hurried to secure the lines. Every man and boy anxiously waited to hear their next orders, each of them silently praying that they would be given time to enjoy themselves on the island. De La Cosa remained onboard ship and in command of the fleet while Columbus and Vicente Yañez Pinzón, captain of the Niña and Martín's brother, were rowed to shore.

While the men left onboard waited impatiently for news from their captains, De La Cosa decided to grant permission for his men to swim near the ship. He hoped this would give them some amusement, as well as relief from the beating rays of the equatorial sun. Before carrying out this decision, however, De La Cosa made certain that the Niña and the Santa Maria were far enough from shore to discourage anyone from attempting to swim to land. He knew and trusted the part of his crew that had been with him for years, but the new men aboard the Santa Maria, and those on the Niña, were unfamiliar to him. He would take no foolish chances. It was quite possible that some of them had thought twice about sailing west into unknown waters, and would be more than happy to hide in the Canaries until the others had left. Any man that jumped ship would not have to wait long before another vessel heading for Spain came into port looking for additional hands.

De La Cosa gave a nod to Chachu, his boatswain of many voyages. With a deep breath, Chachu bellowed out the order giving permission for the men to swim. This announcement started a stampede. Yipping men and boys, laughing and racing each other for the best positions, hurled themselves over the side of the ship. As De La Cosa had guessed, the men left in charge of the Niña saw what was happening and also granted their men authorization to swim. The crewmembers from that ship were instantly diving and jumping in to join the watery commotion.

Domingo, who had been climbing the stairs from the hold, yelled to Pedro to hurry and glanced over his shoulder just long enough to be sure that the boy was behind him. Seeing Pedro's grinning face following him closely, Domingo climbed up the rail, stood wobbling on top for a moment, then sprang into the air. He hit the water with a full splash and pushed himself deeper and deeper under the surface. His first thought as he savored the feel of the water surrounding him was that nothing in his life had ever felt so good. The ocean around the ships was teeming with splashing, paddling, playing, men and boys. Not a single one of them had bothered to take off his clothes. But then, from the smell and appearance of their clothes, they were in as great a need of rinsing as their bodies were.

Domingo surfaced, looked for Pedro, and saw him climbing down the ship's rope ladder to reach a safer distance from the water before jumping in. Swimming around the boisterous men, Domingo reached Pedro just as he let go of the ropes and landed in the water. When he resurfaced, all Pedro could manage to say to express his delight was, "Oh! Oh!" And the two of them laughed with pure joy. The small boy was a good swimmer, if less than an excellent diver. Just the same, Domingo was relieved when Pedro seemed satisfied to swim close to the ship. After a thorough rinsing off, Domingo and Pedro joined the others who began taking off their wet shirts and hanging them over the lower ropes of the ladder.

Pedro was paddling around in small circles when he noticed Gonzalo climbing back up the side of the ship. He pointed the sailor out to Domingo with a curious expression and asked, "Why is Gonzalo leaving the water so soon?"

Rodrigo swam closer to them with a grin on his face. He had evidently heard Pedro's question because he said, "Just watch and you will see."

They both watched as Gonzalo paused on deck to remove his sodden shirt then headed toward the prow. Once he had reached the highest point on the front of the ship, Gonzalo climbed up on top of the railing and stood there balancing. By now most of the men in the water were pointing and staring at him, wondering what he was up to. Gonzalo didn't seem to notice any of them. He held himself steady on his high perch for a moment, then bent his knees and threw himself far out into the air, falling into a beautifully executed dive. He entered the water like a sword thrust.

Amazed and delighted, Domingo and Pedro added their lusty cheers to those of the other swimmers when Gonzalo came up for air. Everyone loudly demanded another dive, and Gonzalo happily accepted their request. Without the slightest sign of uneasiness, he dove again and again from the dizzying height of the prow. Much to the admiration and encouragement of the onlookers, each dive was as graceful and precise as the first one had been. At last, tired but smiling, Gonzalo swam over to Rodrigo, Domingo, and Pedro. When several of the men gathered around and asked how Gonzalo had learned to dive like that, he only winked and said, "A man must not reveal all of his secrets at once." No amount of pleading from Pedro or anyone else could convince Gonzalo to dive again that day, and the four of them contented themselves with quietly enjoying the feel of the ocean.

Columbus and Vicente Pinzón returned to the ships less than an hour later with sweaty, disappointed faces. They spoke briefly with De La Cosa, who nodded his head in agreement. Then the officers gathered their men around them and Columbus gave them what news they had. No ships were available. The closest of the other Canary Islands was Tenerife to the west, but there would be no help for them there.

The governor of the islands, a young widow named Doña Beatriz De Peraza y Bobadilla, had a ship much like the Santa Maria. "Doña Bobadilla is an acquaintance of mine," Columbus told them. "She, like the previous governors, resides in a castle on Gomera, just west of Tenerife. I am hopeful that she will aid us if she can. We will, therefore, head directly to Gomera and offer to hire her ship."

"The Pinta will remain here on Grand Canary and her men will work to repair her, in case no other ship is available to us when we reach Gomera. If we are able to hire a ship, we will return here and pick up the crew of the Pinta to sail her. If not, we will return hoping that the repairs to the rudder have been completed so that the Pinta can rejoin the fleet. Either way, we should be back to join the Pinta's crew in just a few days. We have left word for them of our plans with some of the residents here. Captain Pinzón will be informed as soon as he lands."

The hands of the Santa Maria and the Niña were not happy to hear the order to weigh their anchors immediately. As the two ships moved away from Grand Canary, Domingo and Gonzalo watched the Pinta inch closer to shore. Gonzalo joined them at the rail.

"She should reach the harbor within a couple of hours," he said. Gonzalo turned to face the shoreline and could see some of the island natives walking along the sand. "The Pinta's hands are lucky devils. Most of them will have a week or so on land while that rudder is being repaired." Then with a sigh and a grin he added, "Ah well, no doubt there are some pretty women on Gomera just waiting to meet us."

Even with such optimism, the crew could only watch with longing as the shores of Grand Canary diminished behind them. Under the watchful eyes of the captain-general and De La Cosa, the men turned the two healthy ships to the west.

The flagship and the Niña had barely cleared the waters around Grand Canary when their crews were forced to contend with winds that blew from a conflicting direction, or not at all. They made frustratingly slow progress past Tenerife, and it took three days to reach Gomera.

Although very much relieved at finally anchoring near the island, and anxious to acquire a replacement for the Pinta, Columbus was cautious about contacting Doña Beatriz. She had only become governor after the natives of the island had killed the previous governor, her own husband. To be safe, only a small group of men was sent ashore in the launch to make inquiries. The landing party returned with the news that Doña Beatriz and her ship were not even on the island, but were expected to return any time.

So, they waited. They lingered and hoped as they watched the days pass one by one through an entire week. Longer than it had taken them to reach the islands all the way from Spain. For the most part, the men were kept on board to prevent desertion. As the days crawled by with no word of the ship, tempers and tolerance grew shorter and shorter.

Domingo found that he was one of the few hands whose duties had not lessened while the ships lay at anchor. In fact, every time Francisco cooked a meal, the jeering from the crew got worse. When the taunts became threats, the man gave up cooking altogether. That meant Domingo had to prepare all of the meals. This would have been quite bearable if it hadn't been for the bickering and petty arguments that sprung up among the men while he sweated over the hot coals of his cooking fire.

One blistering day, just before the mid-day shift was about to change, Domingo crouched down, stirred his kettle of stew one last time, then pushed himself away from the heat of the fogon. He plodded to the other side of the ship and sat down heavily, pulling his knees up and leaning his back against the ship's rail. He bent his head down to keep the sun's rays out of his eyes and watched as sweat began to drip from his nose and chin onto the deck. He was too hot and tired to bother searching for an unoccupied sliver of shade somewhere.

The idea of swimming in a cool mountain spring came into his mind and began to torment him. He wondered if there was such a spring somewhere on the island. Oh, if he could only go ashore long enough to swim in a cold, fresh pool of water. De La Cosa had been left in charge of the ship and was sweating along with the rest of them. Domingo thought of Columbus on shore with De Arana. The two of them were meeting with some of the Spanish noblemen who lived on the island. Were they swimming in his imaginary pool right now?

The men who were assigned to the next watch were gathered around the kettle eating. In a few minutes, Domingo and the rest of his shift would have their turn. But Domingo wasn't hungry, and he couldn't fathom how the other men could be. It was just too sweltering. He didn't want to move with the weight of the sun bearing down on him.

Mealtimes had been growing less and less enjoyable as the griping among the men escalated. Lately, Domingo had overheard Bartolome De Torres, the killer, and his three friends, Juan De Mogur, Pedro Yzquierdo, and Alonso Clavijo, complaining about having to sail with the Basques. They were careful not to let themselves be overheard by any of the Basque men, or the Spanish sailors who had sailed with De La Cosa and their Basque crewmates for years. But the four ex-criminals didn't seem to care much if Domingo heard them. Only yesterday, Bartolome had been watching a group of Basque sailors, then he had turned and commented to his friends, "Columbus should have hired only Spaniards for this voyage. These Basques, these northerners, are little more than barbarians. Just listen to that damned devil tongue they call a language." Domingo had silently fumed at this. If he had been able to arrange for Bartolome to spoon it up, he would have added a cockroach to his soup.

Chachu, the boatswain, finished his meal and wiped his spoon on his shirt as he stood up. Noticing Domingo seated dejectedly by himself, Chachu considered for a moment, then disappeared into the hold. When he came back on deck he headed for Domingo and hunkered down beside his young cook.

Domingo had learned quickly that when Chachu was on duty he was utterly professional. He was demanding of the men, but never asked more of them than he was willing to do. The hands who had sailed with Chachu for years, some growing to manhood during that time, had shared the terrors and wonderment of the sea with him, and this had forged a bond between them that was almost tangible. The men could trust Chachu and they could rely on him to be among the first to come to their defense against an outside threat. They could also rely on him to carry out all orders of discipline issued by De La Cosa without hesitation. Discipline at sea was crucial if they were to survive, and Chachu whole-heartedly agreed with De La Cosa's sense of justice.

Aitor had told Domingo long ago that maritime equity allowed the captain of a ship full discretion to brutally beat, chain, or hang a man for insubordination. Domingo's brothers had told him of terrible punishments carried out against wayward crewmembers. But a ship and its entire crew could go down because of the actions of one seaman. If a man were to threaten the safety of the Santa Maria, Domingo guessed that De La Cosa was more likely to chain him and keep him below than hang him. But if the captain ordered a man hanged, Domingo didn't doubt that Chachu would comply with the order. It would be Chachu's duty, and he wouldn't question the fairness of such a judgement if De La Cosa issued it.

When he was off duty, however, Chachu was much like one of the hands, approachable and easy to talk to. The boatswain had been born in a village not far from Domingo's own. They knew many people and places in common. Today, Domingo barely lifted his head when Chachu sat next to him. He wearily managed a short nod to be polite, then let his head fall again.

Chachu knew that all of the men were hot, bored, and pent-up at not being allowed to go ashore. Much worse, he knew that their fears of the trip were building with this long wait. Patience had worn threadbare. Tempers among many of them were barely being held in check. He had gone to the hold and retrieved something with which he hoped to lighten the tension aboard their ship.

Chachu watched Domingo for a minute, waiting for him to look up again, but the lad's head stayed down. At last, Chachu said in Basque, "I have something to show you."

Domingo swiped at the sweat on his face and raised his gaze. His eyes widened and a smile, a rare thing these days, spread across his face. "An alboka," he breathed.

"Yes, an alboka," replied Chachu, satisfied with himself for producing such a response.

"Can you play it?" asked Domingo hopefully.

"And why would I carry it around the world with me if I could *not* play it?" Chachu laughed.

The boatswain held in his hands a musical instrument of a design so ancient that no one there could have guessed its origin. A small piece of oxen horn had been fitted with a double reed and attached to a wooden base. This base was intricately carved with Basque symbols. A larger section of horn was mounted to the other end of the base, and acted as a resonator. Two rows of holes had been drilled into the top of the wood to allow the player to create a wide range of different tones.

"But you have not played it before now," Domingo pointed out, his eyes still fixed on the alboka.

"With this band of pirates?" Chachu demanded loud

91

enough for all of his men to hear. "I have to choose my timing just right or one of these uncivilized brutes might mistake it for a drinking horn and fill it with wine."

His men grinned at each other as if they had just been given the highest of compliments. In spite of Chachu's words, the hands knew that their boatswain cared about them as if they were his own younger brothers. His shipmates of many years also knew what was to come, and they looked almost as eager as Domingo to hear the alboka sing.

Chachu lifted the instrument and placed his fingers so that each hand could manipulate the nearest row of holes. Putting the mouthpiece to his lips, he couldn't help pausing just a moment when he saw the look of anticipation on Domingo's face. Then Chachu closed his eyes. At the sound of the first note, the crewmen onboard the Santa Maria became absolutely still. The sound of the alboka was new only to Gonzalo, Rodrigo, the four criminals, and a handful of others. These men exchanged curious glances. De La Cosa quietly came to the rail of the half-deck and listened along with the rest.

The unearthly music, which sounded similar to that of the bagpipe, flowed with haunting beauty from the simple looking instrument. The rich tones were long and smooth, and the sound pulled at the souls of the crew. Like a master who waits until he has entirely captured his audience, Chachu played in this beckoning manner until the men on his ship, as well as those on the Niña, could feel the music touch something deep and old within them. Only then did Chachu begin, gradually, to shorten the notes and increase the range and complexity of the melodies.

To Domingo, the songs of the alboka brought back, vividly and deeply, the sensations of being home. For as long as Domingo could remember his cousin, Paxti, had played the alboka at family gatherings. Sometimes when he and Domingo would sit by themselves gazing out at the ocean as the sun set, Paxti would play lovingly to the sea. At village festivals, drummers and flute players, the txistularis, joined Paxti to produce the ancient folk music of his people. Remembering, Domingo's heart tightened.

In his mind, he could see Carmen dancing with other young women at the last harvest celebration. Her long hair had been braided and tied up behind her head. The luster in her eyes and the glow in her cheeks had been accentuated by her full, teasing smile. Domingo had been unable to take his eyes from her. She had looked so exquisite, so vibrant, swirling and leaping, catching his glance each time she faced him, that he had ached to hold her. The memory made him ache for her now. The image was so clear and painful that Domingo, with a great effort of will, forced himself to turn his mind from it.

He allowed himself to picture his parents as they had looked at the same festival, standing with their shoulders touching, joyously clapping to the rhythm of the music. They had entered his mind countless times during the last two weeks, and he had eventually come to see them slightly differently, more fully as individuals, whole and separate from himself. Domingo had gained a deeper realization of just what fine, honorable people they were. He knew he was fortunate to have been born their son. The comfort they had always surrounded him with, in the form of support rather than indulgence, was something he missed greatly. He saw their love for him with a clarity that he had not possessed before. He had been valued and reassured by his mother and father on a daily basis, and he had taken this totally for granted. Now, in a world of great dangers and few assurances, Domingo prayed that he would be allowed to see them again, to show them in ways other than words all these things he had learned. He prayed that Aitor was alive and well. That his father would be there when he got home.

Domingo's thoughts drifted to his amuma, and he remembered the night that he had watched her dance with De La Cosa. It was strange to be sitting here on the ship and remembering the mental picture that he had tucked away with the intention of drawing it out at just such a time. Yes, he could see his dear amuma laughing and dancing with Captain De La Cosa. She had been so happy. He could almost sense what she had been like when she was young and carefree. How could it seem as if that night had happened so very long ago?

Glancing in the master's direction, Domingo caught sight of him on the half-deck. De La Cosa was watching the expressions of his men. His scanning gaze met Domingo's, and paused. An understanding, an acknowledgement of what the music meant passed between them. "Perhaps," Domingo thought, "he remembers that night of music and laughter as well as I do."

Chachu continued to increase the speed of the music until he was playing a lively, familiar Basque tune. The feet of some of the men could no longer remain still. One of them came to his feet, yanking a friend with him, and the two began to dance. A handful of others joined them, their feet tapping out the quick rhythm on the wooden deck, their hands held high in the air. Someone grabbed a small keg, turned it on its side, and began pounding on it with a couple of spoons, emphasizing the tempo of the alboka and heightening the emotion of the dancers and listeners alike. This was a dance that the Basque men had learned when they were young boys, and they danced now with as much precision as the hog-backed decks would allow. Chachu, not missing a note, nudged Domingo and with a jerk of his head indicated that he should join the dance.

Nearly forgetting the heat, Domingo got up and seized Pedro by the hand, yelling over the music and dancing, "Come on. I'll teach you."

Self-conscious for only a moment, the little boy quickly joined in, admirably imitating the quick-stepping, twirling Basques. Gonzalo looked at Rodrigo and grinned. "What the hell," he shrugged, and both of them bounded into the middle of the carousal. Their movements were clumsy and untrained, but their laughter and enthusiasm made up for any lack of experience. Domingo loudly encouraged their efforts.

One of the dancers, Pedro De Bilbao, took a step in preparation before making a spectacular leap into the air. With the balance of an expert, he landed softly on the balls of his feet. Loudly encouraged to repeat the move, De Bilbao graciously complied. This time, however, his landing was slightly uneven. He tumbled backward several steps, bumped Juan De Mogur hard in the chest, and they both fell down. De Bilbao quickly righted himself and extended a hand to his fallen shipmate. But instead of receiving the clasp of the man's hand, he was met with a fist smashing against the side of his jaw. The blow knocked him to one knee. The music stopped in mid-note. Before anyone could stop it, De Bilbao was back on his feet and the two men were swinging at each other. The sounds of fists meeting bone and muscle immediately replaced the strains of the melody. Chachu came to his feet and bellowed at both men to stop just as one of De Mogur's friends pushed De Bilbao roughly to one side. Instantly there were six more men, three Basques and three Spaniards, punching and kicking each other. Chachu and several of the other men tried to separate the brawlers without being pulled into the battle themselves. Amid the sudden clamor, one of the younger men was bumped backward and went tumbling over the ship's railing, hitting the water with a loud clap.

Pedro appeared from nowhere and stood beside Domingo, gaping at the milling men. Domingo pushed the boy behind him and stood wavering between helping his countrymen and staying out of the mess. He could see Chachu, Rodrigo, and Gonzalo in the middle of the chaos, attempting to separate the fighters while dodging wild swings.

Chachu pulled himself from the circle of men and grabbed a billet from the ship's rail near Domingo. As he yanked the makeshift club out of its hole, Chachu caught the look of uncertainty in Domingo's eyes and barked at him in a way that left no questions, "Stay here and watch Pedro!"

It was then that Domingo looked up on the half-deck and saw De La Cosa. The ship's master yelled out, "Enough you men!" But he was heeded no more than Chachu had been. His expression was terrible. His hands were clasping the half-deck's railing so tightly that Domingo wondered if it might crack. But De La Cosa did not move from his spot. At first, Domingo did not understand. Why didn't he come down and stop the fighting? Then he realized that De La Cosa, furious, barely containing himself, was forcing himself to stay out of the fight for Chachu's sake. If De La Cosa climbed down the steps and got involved, Chachu would forever lose a share of his authority among the men, and much of his own pride in performing his duties well. The master would enter the conflict only if absolutely necessary. Domingo could see how hard it was for De La Cosa to restrain himself when his men were at each other's throats. Domingo was watching a separate battle, a battle between one's inclination and ones will, being fought and won by a powerful man over himself.

Chachu approached Bartolome, whose back faced the outside of the circle of the fighters, and loudly called out his name. Bartolome didn't even turn toward him. Chachu held his club over the man's head, poised for a split second, then brought the billet down with the utmost precision. The blow landed with a "knock" against the man's skull and dropped him like a sack of grain. De Bilbao staggered back panting, his fists still held high. One eye was so bloody he could hardly see out of it. It seemed to take him a moment to see that his opponent had fallen. He looked up from De Mogur's inert body and was met by Chachu's glaring face. He lowered his arms wearily and looked down.

The two men fighting closest to De Bilbao had caught sight of Chachu's clubbing out of the corners of their eyes. They allowed Gonzalo to push them away from each other. One of the remaining fighters also refused to yield to Chachu's vocal warning. He too felt the sudden impact of the boatswain's weapon before everything went black and he crumpled to the deck. With that, the last of the opponents were pulled apart. All of those still on their feet swayed unsteadily. Cut, bruised, and bloody, they scowled at each other while they struggled to catch their breath.

Chachu turned to De La Cosa, who appeared slightly more relaxed than a moment earlier, if no less angry.

"With your permission, Captain," he said, "These men will be taken to the hold. If they so much as raise a hand toward each other, I'll lock them in chains."

96

"Very well," was all that De La Cosa said. He turned from the rail, climbed to the stern castle and stood staring out at the water.

The eight men were led or carried in the direction of the hatchway. As they passed Domingo, he could see the damaged faces of the men clearly. De Bilbao's bloody nose was attached to his face crookedly, and the bleeding skin around his left eye was split wide apart. As Bartolome was carried by, still unconscious, Domingo saw that the skin and tissues of his left cheek, as well as both of his lips, had burst open from the impact of heavy blows. Bartolome's mouth hung open, exposing one missing and one broken tooth. His blood flowed freely down his face, into his hair and onto the deck, leaving a red trail after him.

The faces of the other fighters were also swelling and bleeding in various places. Chins, lips, noses, eyes, and ears were torn, or bruised, or both. Blood ran from the knuckles of most of the men's hands.

The crewmen who accompanied their friends down the stairs soon returned alone wearing grave expressions. They all feared that their shipmates would die within a short period if they were left in the suffocating heat below decks.

Once the injured men were out of sight, Chachu ordered the men back to their duties even though there were too few to be done as the ship lay idle. The boatswain then went with Dr. Sánchez to tend to the wounds of his battered men. As Chachu passed by, Domingo heard him quietly cursing himself for letting his music cause so much trouble. Chachu glanced up at De La Cosa's back before his head disappeared from view.

There was no singing or laughter among the men as they resumed their duties. Occasional glances of animosity and low threats could be seen and heard between the friends of the injured men. De La Cosa remained on the stern castle, his eyes turned toward the sea, silently praying for an end to this intolerable waiting.

Diego De Arana, the official constable of the fleet, had

been ashore with Columbus when the fight broke out, and De La Cosa did not look forward to their return. De La Cosa had no doubt that the whole incident was more a result of inactivity, and the men being forced to remain at anchor for so long, than the desire to make trouble. He was determined to convince De Arana that it was unnecessary to punish the men.

De Arana and Columbus boarded the Santa Maria hours later, caught a glimpse of the beaten faces, and demanded a full explanation. De La Cosa asked them to join him on the stern castle. Speaking in low tones, he explained what had happened.

"Captain-general, the fight started by accident. One man simply fell into another. It was over quickly, and no one was seriously injured."

Columbus and De Arana scanned the swollen faces of the guilty crewmembers below them, all of whom avoided eye contact with their superiors.

"Were any knives drawn?" De Arana asked solemnly.

De La Cosa had been greatly relieved that the fighting had not risen to such a level. The punishment for pulling a knife in anger aboard a ship was to be tied to the mainmast and left there. If a guilty man was able to free himself, he survived and the matter was dropped. If not, he was left where he was unassisted. The penalty for murder at sea was enough to make a man think before acting out any anger or act of vengeance. A man who murdered another was securely tied to the dead body of his victim, and thrown into the sea. If a seaman killed a seaman, he died with the object of his hostility pulling him to his own watery grave. Many of the men and most of the boys had nightmares about such a fate.

"No knives were drawn," De La Cosa answered.

"And what of the punishments dealt to those involved in this? I know I don't have to tell you that fighting aboard a ship is a serious crime, and I'm sure you've dealt with this kind of thing before. Has the judgment already been executed in our absence?" asked De Arana.

The combatants had been kept in the hold only long

enough to bandage them up. They were now trying to carry out their work in spite of their injuries. De La Cosa answered, "The judgement has already been carried out, yes. These men have been judged with appropriate *severity*," He emphasized the word in a way that made De Arana guess that the cat had been liberally applied.

Chachu had been standing nearby in case he was needed, and Columbus now looked in his direction. The boatswain met his eyes and nodded once without so much as a blink of his eye. Forcing his countenance to appear especially harsh, Chachu's expression corroborated the implication made by De La Cosa. The punishment inflicted on the men had been more than adequate.

"This must not be allowed to happen again," Columbus stated firmly to De La Cosa.

"This *will not* happen again, sir," said De La Cosa loud enough for his men to hear him. His tone told them clearly that he was pledging his reputation on their future conduct.

The fight, in addition to the pain from the resulting bruises, sore muscles and torn up hands, further worsened the moods aboard the Santa Maria. Chachu was forced to watch over the men with less tolerance than usual in order to insure stability.

Even before the conflict between the men, Columbus was finding it harder to keep from showing his own frustration with their situation. Doña Bobadilla had not returned to her home with the ship that they hoped to borrow. In addition, the Pinta's crew had been on Grand Canary long enough to repair their ship and sail to meet them. But the Pinta had failed to arrive and her captain had sent no word of his progress. Everyone in Gomera's harbor, especially Martín Pinzón's brother, Vicente, worried that some bad luck had befallen the men of the Pinta.

Finally, Columbus called all of his hands together.

"Men, if we have heard nothing of Doña Bobadilla's ship and nothing of the Pinta within three days, we will sail back to Grand Canary. By now, the Pinta should be more than ready to sail again and we'll be able to proceed west."

This announcement did little to brighten spirits. Afterwards, Pedro turned to Domingo and said, "At least we won't have to sit in this bay forever."

"Yes," Domingo agreed, "But I hate to think of all the time we've wasted here. We should have been far out to sea by now."

The next three days dragged by with no word of the ships they waited for. Each day's passing further darkened the captain-general's countenance. On the fourth day after Columbus' declaration, with the fleet having made no progress in over ten days, sails were raised and the two ships headed east again. Even though they were moving in the direction opposite to their goal, and some feared that the Pinta's crew must be caught up in some kind of trouble, Domingo and the rest of the men were happier to be at sea than confined to the ships in a harbor.

From the moment they left Gomera, Columbus began to remind Domingo of a newly caged animal. The captain-general snapped orders with little patience, and men tried to stay out of his way.

Pedro was watching Columbus furtively as he helped Domingo peel potatoes one morning. He leaned toward Domingo and asked, "What do you think he's thinking about when he paces back and forth like that?"

Domingo looked up briefly then resumed his peeling. "I just hope he's not thinking of turning back toward Spain."

Pedro was startled by these words. "Do you think he would go back to Spain, Domingo?"

"As I said, I hope not. But every one of these delays makes it harder for us to turn west. It's hot now, but how cold will it be after we spend time in the Indies and then try to return to Spain? And, from what I've heard, the winds will be less favorable as the year wears on. If the Pinta can't be used, and there is no ship to replace her, I don't know what he'll decide to do."

"But we could go on with just two ships," Pedro offered.

"The voyage would be much more dangerous with only two ships, Pedro. And that would mean the Pinta's crew, or at least most of them, would have to stay behind."

"Well, I'm sure the Pinta has been repaired by now," said Pedro with conviction. But his expression grew worried when he added, "We just *have* to keep going. We *have* to see the Indies."

Domingo nodded reassuringly, and told himself to do a better job of hiding his concerns from Pedro in the future.

They reached Grand Canary on the morning of the third day after leaving Gomera. It wasn't until then that Domingo saw his captain-general in a full rage.

As he helped lower the sails, Domingo could see the Pinta anchored not far up the coast. Chachu ordered Domingo to join the hands boarding the launch to row Columbus ashore, and he was happy to comply. The men pulled diligently against the oars in an effort to deliver their anxious captain-general as quickly as possible. Martín Pinzón met them on the beach.

Domingo watched as the smile that had been on Columbus' face gradually disappeared. He could not make out the words of the two captains clearly, but Domingo could easily see that something wasn't right. Pinzón spoke in an unusually quiet voice and Columbus said little at first. Then Columbus demanded angrily, "Repairs have not even been started? Not even *started!*"

Pinzón tried to hold his own temper. "We just managed to reach land yesterday," he said. "The Santa Maria and the Niña were not even out of our sight when the current started pulling us back out to sea. We've been fighting the sea and that damned rudder this whole time. My men are exhausted. Even so, we were able to begin caulking the ship this morning."

"Caulking," Columbus muttered gruffly, "And the rudder still mangled." The captain-general eyed Martín Pinzon suspiciously, swore under his breath, and walked a few steps toward the boat.

Domingo waited with the others in the launch for orders. Columbus seemed unaware of their presence. He stood with his head down, deep in thought, not many feet from them. As Columbus silently considered what to do, one of the island residents joined them. This man approached

101

Columbus and told him in a voice loud enough for Domingo to hear that Doña Bobadilla had sailed for Gomera four days earlier and was probably there by now. They had apparently passed each other without knowing it as they sailed from one island to the other.

Columbus stared at the man, then seethed in frustration. With his face red and his jaw clenched, he shouted back at Pinzón, "That rudder is to be repaired, *immediately!*" Without another word he turned from them and headed toward the settlement.

In the days that followed their captain-general bore down on all of the men with a vengeance. Every experienced carpenter was brought ashore, as well as hired from the port area, and put to work. Guards were placed around the workers to insure that their tasks were performed without interruption. In addition to working on the Pinta's rudder, the Niña's main and fore sails, which had been triangular in shape, were replaced with square sails to allow her to maintain a speed more consistent with the other ships. Domingo bought supplies, cooked for the workers, helped with the caulking, washed clothes, and went to sleep absolutely exhausted when he was given the chance.

While the men labored, the captains and De La Cosa discussed what should be done to Rascon, whom Martín still believed had intentionally damaged the Pinta's rudder. In spite of Pinzón's suppositions, however, not one of the Pinta's crew came forward to accuse Rascon, or anyone else, of sabotaging the ship. Since the cause of the damage remained unconfirmed, Rascon went unpunished. It was decided that he would accompany them to the Indies. Watching Rascon's reaction to this announcement by Columbus, Domingo guessed that it was the worst form of punishment the man could have received. Although he was coming with them, Pinzón had Rascon watched closely by several of his men.

In six days the rudder, sails, and rigging were finished. A week after the fleet had returned to Grand Canary, without ceremony or congratulations, they again set sail in the direction of Gomera. This time, with all three ships intact.

They stayed in Gomera only long enough to fully provision the ships' stores, which had been sorely depleted by all of the delays. Doña Bobadilla proved to be generous and helpful, making certain that they had everything that was required. The sailors speculated among themselves, with many winks and much laughter, that the captain-general was probably having a few private audiences with Doña Beatriz Bobadilla, who was rumored to be quite beautiful.

Columbus, once again in good spirits, told his men that the voyage westward should take no more than twenty-one days. He had made certain that they had supplies enough to last them at least twenty-eight, just to be safe. He assured them that they had more reserves than they would need, and that all would soon be ready. Francisco kept Domingo and Pedro busy packing and repacking, sorting and resorting, from dawn to dark. Domingo's only breaks from these tasks were given when he was ordered to prepare meals.

Just before leaving Gomera, when everything was proceeding well, the captains received the disturbing news that a Portuguese armada had been sighted in the area. Since Spain had controlled these waters for years, the presence of the armed ships was nothing less than ominous to the men of the fleet. Everyone guessed that they had been sent to intercept their ships before they could head west. It was common knowledge that Columbus had first asked King John of Portugal to support him on this venture, but that Columbus had grown tired of the years of waiting and had taken his cause to Spain. King John may very well have felt betrayed when Columbus turned to Ferdinand and Isabella. And it was quite possible that the Portuguese monarch intended to take his revenge by destroying or disabling Columbus' fleet. The decision was made to depart immediately, before the Portuguese had seen them in the Gomera harbor.

When they left the port, the men watched over their shoulders hoping that the Portuguese caravels would not suddenly appear behind them. Desperately wanting speed to avoid meeting the foreign ships, they received instead a calm sea and little wind to push them from the island. The

Niña and the Pinta might be able to outrun the ships from Portugal on the open sea, but the larger, heavier Santa Maria would be at their mercy. After two anxious days, they could still clearly see the islands in the distance. Somehow, through luck or providence, the Portuguese ships had still not happened upon them as they crawled ahead with painful slowness. Finally, on September 9, the wind picked up. The ships pulled forward with the breeze and, at last, the small fleet moved farther from the Canary Islands. With enough water and food to last until October 6, they pointed due west.

As the land disappeared from view, fears of what lay ahead seemed to reawaken among the men with painful clarity. Several of the sailors stood on deck and wept openly. Others quietly prayed with their eyes closed and their heads bowed low. Some of them had not, until that moment, truly faced the uncertainty of surviving this reckless trip. With their chests tightening, they asked themselves if they would ever see land again. Would their graves be nothing more than the wide waters of the Atlantic Ocean?

Pedro and Domingo stood like most of the others, watching the islands grow smaller and smaller. Pedro looked up at his friend's face. He thought of the journey before them and wondered if they would both come through it. Maybe not. Maybe they would die together, swallowed by the monsters of the sea. Maybe it would be soon. Pedro had heard too many stories of the terrible creatures that lived beneath the waves. Some of the beasts, he was sure, were large enough to swallow their ship whole. These images came to him now, unwanted and terrifying.

Although Pedro had said nothing, Domingo had been watching him, and could read much by his expressions. Crouching down on one knee so that his head was no higher than Pedro's, Domingo searched the boy's large brown eyes. "Pedro," he said, "I've been wondering about the houses of gold. Can you tell me all about them."

Forcing himself to pull his thoughts away from the demons that had captured them, the very young voice said slowly, "Well, they will be huge houses." After thinking a moment, Pedro managed a weak smile and continued. "They will be so big, Domingo, that three mounted war-horses can go in at one time. And the houses will have golden walls and golden roofs that will shine in the sun. They will be so bright, that it will hurt our eyes to look at them. But we will look at them just the same. And we will be invited inside the grandest of the houses to feast with the Great Khan. We will sit on beautiful gold chairs while we eat. And, oh, the food they'll have, Domingo!" Pedro's momentum built with each description. He let his imagination flow freely into his words, and wondrous pictures of the Indies unfolded one after another.

Caught up in Pedro's stories, the two hardly noticed that the vast ocean, slowly and steadily, surrounded the three ships and drew them deeper and deeper into its unfathomable expanse.

Anani

8

Anani sat in the doorway of her home feeling the ocean breeze whisper against her skin. She softly ran her fingers over the magnificent bowl she held in her lap. It was by far the finest thing she had ever made. The color of wet sand and oval in shape, it was engraved with nearly perfect symmetry. The lines and shapes that encircled the pottery depicted the symbols of her family's ancestors. There were handles on each side for a rope to be drawn through, so it could be hung from a post or beam.

Only those of the noble class, those descended directly from ancient heroes, were taught the skills required to produce works of art like Anani's. She was the oldest daughter, and her mother had trained her with a combination of patience and high expectations. This bowl was something she could be proud of when it was presented to the parents of her prospective husband.

These days Anani thought of little else but the festival that was to take place tomorrow in Cubanacan, the large city that lay thirty-five miles inland. These celebrations were held to give thanks to Itiba Cahubaba, the earth mother goddess, and Baibrama, the lord of the harvest, for their blessings of healthy children and good crops. Villagers from all over Cuba would come to the city to participate. Political leaders would officiate over games of skill, using the competitions as a means of binding allegiances and deciding disputes. Their cacique, their chief, was taking a new bride on this special day. Anani had always eagerly awaited the dances and games that accompanied such gatherings. But tomorrow would be different. It would be something much more for Anani. She knew that the event would forever stand out in her memory. At the feast tomorrow, her parents would choose the man who would become her husband.

She glanced over her shoulder to see the pile of gifts that had been sent to her home over the last few months. It was customary for a future husband to bestow his bride with special offerings. But the possessions she had received were of such quality and richness that even her austere grandfather had seemed pleased, and her aunt praised them repeatedly. Rank among her people was inherited through the mother, and Anani was of high noble blood. In addition to her rank, Anani had inherited the rare beauty of her mother. If the gifts had been inferior to her position, the marriage would have been denied. Her parents had not told her who had sent the presents, but she had guessed, had hoped, that they were from the young man who had once touched her face so gently.

Several months ago, Anani's family had been visiting relatives in Cubanacan. It was there that she had first noticed Calichi. She had thought it was only coincidental that she had seen him so often when she walked with her sister and brother, or ran an errand for her mother. But late one afternoon, as she was filling a water jug from the river, Calichi had called her name from the shadows of the trees, startling her. He had walked up to her cautiously, as if he feared she would run from him. But she had stood quite still, returning his gaze. Calichi had slowly lifted his hand to her face. Ever so lightly, he had run the back of his fingers down her cheek and under her chin. Although she had never been touched this way, sensually, longingly, she had not drawn away from him. She had sensed his gentleness. He had smiled at her and had been about to speak when her younger siblings had come bounding noisily in their direction. He had smiled at her and quietly withdrawn back into the forest. They had been alone for only a moment but she had not forgotten the caress.

Her little sister's voice brought Anani back to the present. "What are you doing, Anani?" asked Guanina, just coming around the side of the house. "Mother says we will be leaving soon, and you aren't even ready yet." Guanina was ten years old and had been fittingly named after the hummingbird. Although she was four years younger than Anani, Guanina sometimes thought that her older sister spent too much time dreaming. "Let me help you get your things together."

Anani stood up, patted Guanina on the head, and spoke with gentle affection. "It's all right, little sister. My things are packed, and I will carry my bowl under my arm. You don't need to fuss over me." Both girls turned toward the sound of someone approaching from the direction of the beach.

Rushing breathlessly up to them, their younger brother, Hura, lifted up his small hands and presented the girls with a conch shell larger than his head. Grinning proudly he demanded, "Isn't it the biggest one you ever saw?"

"Hura, you know we must leave in just a little while, and here you are covered with sand," Guanina declared in exasperation, her hands on her hips.

"I'm not very sandy," he said sticking his lip out at her.

Six-year-old Hura looked down at his belly hoping to prove that his statement was true. He only succeeded in starting a small avalanche of sand trickling down from the top of his head to the ground.

"Come with me," Guanina said taking his hand and turning him around. "We have to hurry and wash you off." They headed back to the water with Hura still hanging onto his prized shell. He looked back at Anani and smirked again. Laughing softly to herself, she waved back at him. Catching the scent of pineapples that were carefully cultivated near her home, Anani inhaled deeply, savoring the sweetness. After a few moments, she turned and entered the house, lovingly cradling her bowl.

Inside, her mother was busy packing the last of the things they would need during the long trip to Cubanacan. Nearly twenty-five feet in diameter, the hexagon shaped house was airy, clean, and comfortable. Its walls were constructed by burying the ends of vertical poles in the ground and binding them tightly together. The pointed roof, rising high above Anani's head, was securely thatched with the deep green of palm leaves. She brushed by her hammock as she crossed the room. One of these woven beds was hung from the support posts of the house for each member of Anani's family. At the wall opposite the front door, the girl picked up the pouch of woven cotton that held her personal things, and slung it over her shoulder.

When she turned around she saw that her mother was watching her with a thoughtful expression. "Anani, it would be wise to wrap your bowl so it is protected during the journey."

"I will hold it very carefully, Mother."

Her mother, Tanama, approached Anani and looked into her daughter's eyes before speaking. "If your gift were broken, how would you feel, Anani?"

This question was typical of her insightful, kind-hearted mother. Tanama very seldom insisted that Anani follow her directions. Instead, she gently pointed out possibilities and asked Anani to consider more carefully. In this way, she tenderly guided her daughter, helping her to see the most reasonable choices of actions for herself.

Tanama knew that Anani had put so much of herself, her spirit, into the making of her bowl that it was difficult for the girl to separate herself from it. When the symbols of their ancestors had been marked on its surface, the piece of pottery had become a holy thing. It was something to be honored for what it signified as well as admired for its beautiful workmanship. The woman watched her daughter consider, then take a manatee skin from where it hung on the wall. She lovingly wrapped the cherished vessel, and placed it in a separate cotton sling.

"Are we nearly ready, Mother?"

Tanama brushed a strand of her daughter's long dark hair back over her shoulder and gently patted her cheek. "Almost. When your father returns from the forest we can leave."

Anani knew what her father, Tiburon, was doing in the forest. He was hiding most of the family's hallowed relics, their zemis, in a secluded place where they would safely remain until Tiburon returned from their trip. Images carved from wood, stone, or shell, their zemis were the special benefactors of Tiburon's family. The spaces in their house normally filled with a statue of Earth Mother and the carved masks of ancient relatives were now bare.

Most of the zemis were being hidden, but not all of them. Anani and each of her parents wore zemis in the form of amulets around their necks. A few months earlier, when she had become a woman, Anani had been presented with her own talisman. Hers was very similar to her mother's. It was carved from a white shell and looked something like a miniature totem pole with two figures, each depicting the spirit of an ancestor. Her father wore an especially sacred amulet that had been passed down from three generations before him. Tiburon's great-great-grandfather had been a renowned leader among his people. After the great man's death, a small bone had been removed from his body in a solemn religious ritual. As a distinct tribute to the dead chieftain, this bone had been carefully carved into an image of his likeness, and given to his son. It was worn with the greatest of honor and respect. Since this zemi had come to him, Tiburon had often felt the power that the icon conveyed to protect and to guide him.

The common people of Tiburon's village were fishermen, and life usually was calm and plentiful for them. But Caribs, invaders from the south who stole their young women and ate the flesh of their male victims, occasionally assaulted their coastline. With permission from the powerful cacique in Cubanacan, Tiburon had trained a group of his strongest fishermen in the ways of war, how to use a spear and a bow and arrows with skill, and how to use poison on the points to enhance the chances of a kill. If a raiding party was too large for them to withstand, the people could escape into places that Tiburon had carefully chosen and provisioned deep in the recesses of the forest. Guards were posted regularly in the highest trees along the shoreline to warn the villagers at the first sighting of the Carib canoes. Tiburon felt that the spirit of his amulet had overseen all of these preparations, and had helped them repulse two attacks in the last few years. They had lost only one man in both raids, and their friend had not been captured alive, a fate the men feared far more than a quick death.

Although the chances of an attack while they were away were slight, the zemis were too valuable, too revered to risk them being stolen or destroyed by such people. Tiburon was only acting responsibly in concealing them before his family set out from their home.

Anani hoped that her father would not return for a little while. It was rare that she and her mother found time alone together, without the other women of the village or her younger siblings demanding Tanama's attention.

"Mother, I'd like to talk to you before we leave." Anani sounded so serious that her mother stopped her packing. She sat down, and motioned for her daughter to join her.

"Mother," Anani began, paused, then went on, "There is so much I don't know about being a wife."

With a hint of relief in her voice Tanama said, "I have wondered when you would be ready to talk about such things." Until then, Anani had been reluctant to dwell on the inevitability of her marrying someday. "What is it that you want to know, Anani?"

"For one thing, how do I know that we will get along well together, my husband and me? What if we displease each other? What if he and Father don't become friends? You know how fierce Father can seem to people who don't know him well."

Softly laughing, Tanama said, "You have asked three things rather than one, but I will try to answer all of your questions at once. There is no way of knowing ahead of time what will happen during the long years you will spend with your husband. All you can do is hope that your spouse is chosen wisely, first by us and finally you. Then, as important as finding the right man, you must teach yourself to compromise. Not surrender, but compromise in all things. Be willing to give up half of what you want so that he may have half of what he wants. You are a very giving young woman and this will be easier for you than for some." Tanama continued more gravely, "But, Anani, you must never give more of your spirit than he is willing to give of his. If you do, your life will ultimately fill with bitterness. There must be balance in a marriage."

"But what if he is unwilling to give his spirit to me?"

"If he acts unwilling, you must teach him to, just as you are teaching yourself. Sometimes this can take years but you must not give up. Some young men find it very difficult to learn this, some women too, but perseverance is absolutely necessary in a marriage. Balance and perseverance. Perhaps these are the most important things of all."

"And the man you chose? Do you think he will want to give himself to me?"

"We have tried to choose someone who is as giving as you are, Anani. Someone worthy of you. I think we have found one who will bring you joy and honor. You have asked so little about him that I have wondered if you already know who he is."

"I know who I *hope* he is," Anani said looking down at her hands. "But I don't know anything about him really. That sounds so foolish. I'm not sure why I haven't wanted to know more. Maybe because this has all seemed so far away until just a little while ago. I think I wanted to keep it far away for a while longer. And, I was afraid that you and Father had picked someone other than the one I would prefer."

"Do you want to know who he is now? You know that your father will make the announcement at the ceremony tomorrow. If it is someone you disapprove of, someone you feel you can not be happy with, you must tell us."

Tanama knew the boy her daughter had wanted all along. She had known Calichi since his birth and had watched him as he grew. His family was made up of fine, admirable people of noble rank. Calichi seemed to have characteristics that agreed with Anani's strength, honor, generosity, and sensitivity. If any man could be worthy of her daughter, it was Calichi. Tanama was pleased when he started paying special attention to Anani.

Anani's little sister had seen him touch Anani's face on their last visit to Cubanacan, and had told Tanama all about it. Tanama had watched Anani closely over the next few days and had seen the change in the girl. Without knowing she was revealing her thoughts to her mother, Anani had asked the names of some of the young people in the city, pointing out Calichi among the others. Then Anani had followed the boy with her eyes every time he was nearby, which happened more often than chance would have allowed. On their return trip home, Anani had hummed often, and she had worn a dreamy smile that she would not explain to Guanina no matter how many times the girl had asked. Tanama finally told Anani's father of her suspicions. Not knowing the young man's family as well as his wife, Tiburon had begun his own investigation into whether the boy would be an appropriate match for his daughter. Before he had made his ultimate decision, the gifts had started arriving.

Uncertainty, apprehension, then resolution crossed Anani's face before she finally said, "Yes, Mother. You are right. I need to know who it is."

Tanama took her daughter's hands in her own. "It is Calichi, my daughter, the boy you saw in Cubanacan."

Anani beamed and squeezed her mother's hands tightly. Tanama smiled back at her daughter's joyful face.

"I'm glad to see that he is the one you wanted," she said sincerely. "Your father and I think he will be a good husband to you. Of course, you will have the chance to get to know him much better over the next year. During that time, you must judge him for yourself and decide whether you want to reject every other man you have ever met in favor of him. If so, he is the right man for you to marry."

Anani thought back to her cousin's wedding the previous fall. Looking serene and beautiful, the young bride had been led into her mother's home where she waited alone. A young single man, not her perspective husband, had entered the house and ceremoniously tried to convince the young woman to become his wife. In a voice loud enough for those outside to hear, the girl politely but firmly rejected him and the man left her. This ritual was performed several times as one by one the young men of the village appealed to the bride to choose him over her intended mate. After all of the symbolic suitors had been dismissed, the bride emerged from the house and declared to the community that she had denied all other men. She would have no one but her husband in marriage. Only then had the proud and anxious groom approached Anani's cousin. Their holy man, their behique, had blessed them solemnly. With the ceremony completed, the couple had entered the house together amid the cheers and best wishes of their people. As was custom, the newly joined couple would live with the girl's family.

Now, Anani thought of standing beside Calichi in a little more than a year. She would become his wife. And again she realized how little she knew him.

"I have never even spoken to him," Anani said to her mother.

"You will tomorrow night." Noticing the look of uncertainty that crossed Anani's face, Tanama added, "And believe me, he will be more nervous than you will be."

Anani gave Tanama a doubtful yet hopeful look.

Trying to give her daughter some reassurance, Tanama said, "It will take time to learn each other's ways, but you have lots of time, my daughter. Tomorrow will only be the beginning."

Seeing that her daughter had slipped back into her own thoughts, Tanama released Anani's hands, patted them, and said, "Now, come. Help me finish getting ready before your father returns."

Tiller and Mast

9

In the dim light just before daybreak, Pedro crouched beside Domingo watching him sleep. Pedro held his hands over his mouth in an effort to contain the snickers that threatened to escape every time Domingo mumbled in his sleep. But when Domingo softly muttered, "...so sweet...with me..." Pedro couldn't help sputtering loudly into his hands. This, so close to Domingo's face, was enough to wrest him from his dream. He pried his eyes open just enough to determine the cause of the annoyance, then closed them again and groaned noisily.

"Pedro," he growled.

At this, Pedro laughed out loud. "You were dreaming about Carmen, weren't you?"

"Yes, and I wish I still was," said Domingo grumpily, eyeing Pedro again.

Still grinning, Pedro showed no remorse whatsoever. "It's almost time for our shift so you need to wake up anyway. Most of the men are already eating. Now, get up and tell me about your dream."

"I *should* tell you nothing since you're the one who woke me," Domingo declared in a mock seriousness that he knew Pedro could see through.

"Oh, *please*, Domingo."

Surrendering easily, Domingo sat up, stretched, and let out a huge yawn. "Oh all right, but only because I want to think about it a little longer."

Pedro saw the smile at the corner of Domingo's eyes and sat down happily beside him.

Domingo was actually pleased to go along with anything that delighted the boy so much. Pedro had been much too quiet lately, much too serious, and Domingo had begun to worry about him. Everyone on board was holding their fears in check, but Pedro had seemed to be keeping them somewhere deep inside himself where they gnawed at him and saddened his heart.

"We were in Palos and I was trying..." Domingo began.

"You and Carmen were in Palos?" Pedro chimed in.

"Yes, now let me tell you without interrupting." Receiving an eager nod, Domingo continued. "We were on the beach, standing just at the edge of the water. It was still dark, just like on the morning we left. I could see that three ships were waiting for us to come aboard and I was trying to convince Carmen to come with me, to come to the Indies. I was holding her hand, pulling her toward the launch. At first, she said she couldn't go so far from home, but then she was letting me take her. She was stepping toward me, coming with me. She looked so beautiful, so soft...and she was coming with me."

Pedro watched impatiently as a far-away look overtook Domingo's face. "*Then* what happened?" he demanded.

"*Then*, you woke me up."

"Ah, Domingo, that wasn't the whole dream," Pedro said disappointedly.

"Yes, it was. If you want me to tell you about a longer dream, you had better not disturb my sleep next time." Domingo stood up and rumpled Pedro's hair.

"You're right, everyone is eating," Domingo said. "We'd better join them if we don't want to go hungry."

"I had a good dream last night too," said Pedro as they headed toward the others. "I dreamed that I was eating some of my mother's fresh bread. It was still hot and covered with honey. I could taste it in my dream. Umm, it was like heaven, Domingo. When I get home, I am going to eat a whole loaf by myself, maybe two loafs. I will have plenty of money for my mother to buy all of the flour and honey she wants. We will all eat like lords when I get home." Domingo couldn't guess what had made Pedro turn his thoughts away from whatever had held them captive, but it was good to hear him speaking with some brightness as he described the future.

The two of them headed toward the group of men gathered together at the back of the main deck. The mornings had been cool and refreshing, the days warm but not blistering, ever since they had set sail from the Canary Islands five days earlier, and all of the men were delighted with the change. The pleasant weather and favorable winds had done much to help the men maintain their courage and temperaments.

As Pedro and Domingo ate their sea biscuits and cheese, the pilot of this watch, Sancho Ruiz, approached them. "The captain has told me that you are to man the glass today, Domingo," he said casually, guessing what the lad's reaction would be.

"Yes, sir." Domingo replied almost choking on his mouthfull of food.

He was being given the chance to keep track of the time by turning the half-hour glass throughout his shift. This meant few, if any, trips to the hold. It meant that he would be near the tillerman and the pilot as they steered the ship, as well as discussed and marked their progress. Domingo would be there, under the cover of the stern castle, when the captain checked their bearing and made any adjustments. Of course, he would work on other small jobs too, but Domingo would not be allowed to wander far from the glass for long. Timekeeping was Domingo's favorite duty, mostly because he was close to the officers as they judged the success of the day. The only bad news was that Domingo's absence from the cook pot meant that they would all have to suffer through Francisco's cooking. Domingo had wondered if the men's preference for his own cooking had anything to do with him being assigned the duty of timekeeper so seldom since they had left the Canaries behind them.

A couple of hours later, shortly after turning the glass, Domingo stood looking out at the sea with his back to the pilot, and the tillerman, Alonso Chocero. All three of them had been quietly lost in thought when Domingo heard Alonso ask, "Señor Ruiz, what do you say to me letting

Domingo take the tiller for a moment? She's holding steady and calm, sir."

Domingo turned around and looked between the two men's faces to see if they were only teasing him. Ruiz glanced first at Alonso, as if considering his question thoroughly, then at Domingo whose hopeful look encouraged him to finally answer, "The sea and winds are being kind to us again today, that's true. What do you think, Domingo?"

"Yes, sir. I would love to take the tiller, if only for a moment." Domingo could not help but wonder at his good fortune today, first a chance to be the timekeeper, now the tillerman.

"Stand by him closely, Alonso," cautioned Ruiz.

The tiller was a huge timber that entered the ship from the tiller port in the rear hull, and spanned ten feet into the Santa Maria's main level. The opposite end protruded outside and attached perpendicularly to the giant rudder. The tiller was nearly a foot square where it joined the rudder, thinning to six inches by twelve inches where it reached the tillerman. Ropes were fastened tightly to each side of the tiller's head to provide leverage for steering. In rough weather, it took three or more men handling the lines on each side to stabilize the ship. Today, however, the mild conditions allowed Alonso to manage the tiller by himself.

"Hold her steady to our course," the pilot commanded Domingo. Domingo had been checking the compass and listening to the men all morning, and he knew their course setting as well as Ruiz.

"Yes, sir," he said.

"Get ahead of me and grab your own set of lines," Alonso instructed as he scooted backward.

Domingo approached the huge timber, gingerly straddled it just in front of the seated tillerman, and gathered a line from each side of the tiller in his hands. Excitement rose in his chest, and he rode behind Alonso as if they were astride a massive horse. Domingo's heart pounded harder and faster as he felt Alonso slowly lift himself from the tiller. The tillerman paused until he could see Domingo's legs tighten and his feet press against the deck. Then

Alonso lifted his right leg over the tiller and moved a step away. Standing to the side now, Alonso maintained a hold on his lines, watching closely as Domingo's body felt the ship's innermost connection with the sea for the first time.

Every muscle in Domingo's body tightened as he felt the power that heaved against the rudder. He could feel, more intimately than ever before, the ship moving with the current and submitting to the wind. Gradually, Alonso eased the tension on his lines until he had given Domingo the tiller fully. The tillerman came forward, and he and Ruiz observed Domingo's conduct, looking on as his face displayed the emotions and sensations that held him.

Domingo did not speak and he did not look at his two superiors. At first, he stared straight ahead, too involved with the rhythm of the ocean to think beyond it. He was far back in the ship under the half-deck, with the base of the mizzenmast, the capstan, the main mast, and the forecastle all blocking the view in front of him. From his position, he could not even see the sails or the water in front of the ship. The only way to steer was to use the instrument close at hand. Domingo focused himself, checked the compass encased in a wooden box just in front of him, and held the Santa Maria to her course. "I am steering the Santa Maria," he told himself again and again, to help himself believe that it was true.

He did not see the knowing smile that passed between Alonso and Ruiz, or that Pedro, Rodrigo and Gonzalo were all watching him with pride and pleasure. Time seemed to stand aside and allow Domingo this encounter, and he absorbed these new sensations completely. He reveled in the moment, wanting to hold it in his heart and mind. There was nothing in his world but the compass, the ship, the sea, and the dance that they were executing.

Much too soon Alonso was standing beside him saying, "Well done, Domingo. Perhaps you will be a tillerman yourself one day." And he mounted the tiller, took up the lines, and relieved Domingo of his task.

"Thank you, sir," Domingo managed to say, but the look on his face expressed much more.

Alonso nodded saying, "I still remember my first time at the tiller, son. I have never looked at the sea quite the same since that day. It is an experience that makes a man feel so powerful, yet so small."

Domingo could only agree.

It was a common thing to hear a song spring from the lips of one of the men or a small group of sailors. The Basque's often sang songs of their homeland and their people, and if Domingo was awake during these times, he joined in. Because he worked with the Spanish crewmembers, he had quickly picked up several of their songs, most of them about love or tragedy. But today, after his experience at the tiller, he found himself singing to the sea itself, and pondering its power.

As the day wore on and the watch changed, then changed again, Domingo was given the chore of scrubbing out several newly emptied casks that had held salted cod. He was moving the brush back and forth, trying not to let the smell overwhelm him, when Columbus entered the steerage area to consult with Ruiz. After a brief discussion of weather conditions and the currents, Columbus told Ruiz to hold the course steady.

"We have sailed well the last few days," said Columbus. "And if we can maintain this speed throughout the day we should make forty-eight miles or so."

"Excuse me captain-general, but I believe we will have traveled closer to sixty or sixty-one by nightfall," Ruiz told him politely.

"No, Sancho, it will be closer to forty-eight, I am sure." Columbus said this in a friendly, but firm, tone. The pilot merely bowed slightly to show his respect for the captain-general's superior rank.

This exchange reminded Domingo of a similar scene two days earlier when De La Cosa and Chachu had been talking on the half-deck just before sunset. Columbus had joined the two of them just as they were discussing how far they had sailed that day. When De La Cosa reported his estimate to Columbus, the captain-general had said, "I believe you have overstated your miles by five or six, Señor De La Cosa." De La Cosa had looked at Columbus curiously at first. Then his expression had hardened. Domingo had not thought much of it at the time, but now he wondered whether De La Cosa and Ruiz were both wrong, or if Columbus was estimating their miles faultily. Surely not. He tried to push the idea from his mind and attend to his cleaning of the stinking barrel.

Domingo worked steadily for several minutes and was just making one last rinse of the keg when he heard a man from the Niña shouting something that sounded like, "Look ahead! Something in the water, Captain!"

Domingo left the keg and swiftly climbed to the fore deck. An instant later the lookout in the crow's nest of the Santa Maria called out, "A ship's mast! Fifty yards dead ahead!"

"A ship's mast?" mumbled Columbus who had appeared on the foredeck and stood staring out at the object in front of them. Domingo heard one of the men mutter, "What would the mast of a ship be doing out here, in unknown, untraveled waters? The man must be wrong."

In order to get a better look, Columbus ordered the men to trim the sails and come along side whatever was bobbing in their path. Domingo returned to the main deck where he, Pedro, and several others leaned far over the railing to see what they were quickly approaching.

"Can you see anything, Domingo?" Pedro asked.

"Yes, something."

The shape of the floating timber became unmistakable as they drew nearer. It was indeed the main spar of a ship, a ship nearly as large as the Santa Maria. Before they had quite reached it, Columbus ordered the men to haul the massive pole aboard the ship. Men swiftly grabbed long-handled gaffs and ropes. Leaning over the port side railing, strong arms stabbed into the wood as if it were the hide of a whale. They strained against the monstrous weight until muscles bulged and teeth clenched. The men tried to hold the mast steady enough to rig it to the loading arm yet keep it from ramming against the hull of the ship. And while the hands struggled to hold it, they saw that ropes still clung to the lower half of the mast. The crow's nest had been torn away, as well as the yardarm. The metal base that had secured it to the deck of its ship was still attached, and fragments of wood decking still clung to its underside. Despite their efforts, the eighty-foot timber was so water logged that its weight was totally unmanageable. Columbus had no choice but to order that the mast be released. They all stared as the long shape slid past them, and grew smaller as the wind pushed the Santa Maria forward.

Columbus looked at the faces of the men; most of them still staring back at the mast. Some of them looked confused, some speculating, some pale.

"Men," he said, "That mast must have come from a ship in the Canary Islands. One that was probably caught by a storm while it was moored. The currents simply carried it out this far, just like they are carrying us."

The hands listened to the captain-general, but their expressions told him that they knew of another explanation.

After a moment, Columbus said, "Sometimes there are misfortunes at sea, men. But we must look forward. Resume your duties." The men began to shuffle back to whatever they were doing before the spar had been sighted.

Domingo and Pedro stood near Rodrigo and Gonzalo. Pedro glanced up into the older faces and asked, "Where do you think the spar came from?"

"There was no banner, no way of telling where the ship was from," said Rodrigo. "Do you suppose it was from one of the Portuguese ships?" he asked Gonzalo.

"I don't think it was one of the ships that was following us when we left the Canary Islands. Even if they had managed to pull ahead of us in the night, it looked like the mast had been in the water for at least a couple of weeks. They couldn't have outrun us by more than a day."

Rodrigo thought for a moment. "Then either the captain-general is right about the currents pulling the mast far out from the Canaries, or..."

"Or we are not the first ones to have sailed these waters."

Gonzalo finished. The four of them looked at one another. Domingo pulled his glance away first.

Pedro gazed back once more at the disappearing mast. "And the ones that came before us are now at the bottom of the sea," he said in a voice so quiet it was almost inaudible.

Domingo left them, picked up a barrel that needed cleaning and began swabbing it with his brush. A moment later the brush slowed then was still. He stared unblinking at the bottom of the barrel and could think of nothing but the mast and what it may mean. For just a moment as the spar had rolled, Domingo had caught a glimpse of a mark, a small symbol, that had been carved into the wood eight feet above its base. The mark looked something like a four-tailed spinning ball of fire. This shape, a lauburu, was an ancient symbol of the Basques. This sign had been carved into the main mast of each of his father's ships. His father's ships, and those of his brothers. Domingo closed his eyes, bent his head, and prayed that his brothers were still alive.

Behique

10

"Anani, you must sit still if you want to be ready before the ceremony begins," Tanama said. "I can't comb your hair with all of this moving around." Tanama had never known her daughter to be so agitated. But she knew it was only to be expected on so special an occasion.

"Yes, Mother, I'll try," said Anani stopping herself from shifting her position yet again. "My mind is just so full today. It's hard to keep my body calm."

Anani's family had arrived at her uncle's house in Cubanacan the evening before. They had been met by the excitement of a city preparing for a special festival and the cacique's upcoming marriage. But Anani's nervous movements had little to do with the cacique or anything related to the ceremonies. Her mind was concerned with events much closer to her own destiny. And in spite of her good intentions of just a moment before, she squirmed again.

The comb became still in her mother's hand. "Close your eyes and try to think of something peaceful," she suggested patiently, then resumed her efforts to bring out the shine in Anani's hip-length hair.

Anani took a long breath, shut her eyes, and tried to picture herself swimming lazily in the mouth of the river by her home. Instead of the clear, smooth water, the only image that came to her was one of Calichi watching her. She saw him looking at her intently as her parents formally accepted his proposal.

She knew that today was a lucky day for them to begin their courtship, since it was the wedding day of the cacique. But, still, she was afraid. Not nervous as her mother presumed, but actually fearful of what this day and the future would bring. She had scolded herself for being childish but the panic had continued building. She did not want to disappoint her parents by failing to fulfill their wishes. But what if she found that she simply could not care for Calichi? He seemed amiable but she didn't really know him well enough to judge such things. What if there was a side of him that her parents had not seen, a side that was cruel or would be impatient with her? What if he was kind to her at the beginning but became bad-tempered as the years passed? A part of Anani wanted to turn to her mother and say that she was too young, that she was not ready for this. She started to stir again, then caught herself, and forced her body to remain still.

Tanama pulled the carved wooden comb slowly through her daughter's hair, wishing she could ease the girl's anxiety. She remembered her own worries about Tiburon before her parents had accepted him.

Tanama had always understood Anani. They were much alike, and she could easily sense what her daughter was feeling. She continued combing the exquisite hair in long gentle strokes. While she combed, Tanama began to softly hum a melody that she had sung to Anani from the time she was a baby. Anani listened to her mother's soft voice, the familiar loving tune, and tried to let the repetition of the comb running through her hair ease her tense muscles. After a while Anani's posture began to relax a little.

By now Anani's hair shone and glimmered in front of Tanama and she laid the comb aside. She rose, and walked to the far side of the house. When she returned, Tanama was carrying two covered bowls and a small, brightly colored pouch. She sat down in front of Anani with a thoughtful expression on her face.

"You are a woman now, Anani," she said holding her daughter's eyes with her own. "And on this special day, you will wear the holy markings for the first time."

Anani had foreseen this part of her preparations but was still moved that the time for it had really come. She did not respond, but remained absolutely still out of her deep respect for her faith.

Her mother removed the cloth coverings that had been tied over the mouths of the bowls. Then, with the utmost care and reverence, she removed a stone image from its pouch. She dipped one side of the stone figure into the bowl that contained the juice of the jagua plant. Lifting the carved image up again, Tanama pressed the stone against the center of Anani's right cheek. Pulling the body stamp away, Tanama could see the distinct black pattern of a frog whose belly was adorned with geometric shapes. This mark represented womanhood, the continuation of life, the children that Anani would one day bear. Tanama attentively cleaned the stone figure, then dipped it into the other bowl that held a bright red dye made from the achiote plant. This time Tanama pressed the body stamp against Anani's left cheek, then removed it and observed the results. The two emblems, black and red, stood out boldly against the young woman's golden skin. Tanama gazed at Anani for a moment before she looked down and cleaned the stamp once more. She replaced the figure in its pouch and returned the pouch and the bowls to their special places against the wall.

Coming to sit in front of her daughter once again, Tanama closed her eyes and began to pray. Anani piously closed her eyes at the sound of her mother's first words. In a diffident voice, Tanama thanked the gods and her ancestors for sending Anani to her. Even more humbly, she asked them to watch over her daughter today, and to enhance Anani's wellbeing in the future. When at last Tanama's supplication ended, both of them opened their eyes together. Tanama leaned back on her heels and again studied her daughter. A slow, rich smile spread across her face, and Tanama was nearly overcome with gratitude. "You are truly a gift from the gods, my daughter."

Anani bowed her head. "I hope I will bring you and Father honor today."

Tanama could see that Anani was trying to be brave. She intended to fulfill her duties to her family and her people by entering into a marriage agreement that, at that moment, was no more than something to dread. But Tanama wanted this day to be a happy one for her girl. She

126

had purposely held something back from Anani, something that she hoped would help her daughter now.

"There is a gift from Calichi, Anani, that you have not yet seen."

"A gift, Mother?" Anani asked. She wondered if it might be a chair, a duho, to match the one that he had sent to her parents earlier. Calichi had carved it himself and it was both graceful and intricate. A duho was considered something like a throne, meaning much more than simply an object to sit upon. A duho was a sign of rank and wealth, and was to be used only by the nobility. Calichi's duho had been his most valuable gift to her family.

While Anani reflected, Tanama rose again and went to her family's things stacked against the wall. She brought back a small bundle and handed it to Anani saying, "This gift is not for your father or me. It is for you alone."

The girl accepted the gift and looked inquiringly at her mother.

"Open it, Anani."

Anani loosened the cotton cloth surrounding the gift and folded it back.

"Mother," she breathed in awe as she gazed at the objects in her lap.

Two golden earrings that had been artistically pounded and shaped into identical rainbows lay before her. She picked one of them up and admired its beauty. As if wanting to confirm this unexpected wonder, she asked. "He sent these for me?"

"Yes, my child, for you. For today," Tanama said. "I can see that he chose something that pleases you. He must think very highly of you to offer you such treasures."

"Oh, Mother, look at them. They are finer than anything I ever hoped to have."

"Then put them on."

Anani removed the feather earrings from her earlobes and replaced them with the pair of golden ones. They felt smooth and balanced as she turned her head to show her mother.

"There. You are ready," Tanama said to her smiling

daughter. "Now go see if your little brother and sister have managed to stay clean, while I get ready." Anani hugged her mother tightly before she left the house, her spirits much higher than they had been a few minutes before.

Anani saw admiring looks turned toward her as she headed to the center of the city in search of Guanina and Hura. She mistakenly believed that her earrings were the cause of the attention, and she thought again of Calichi's generosity. She began to notice just how lovely everything around her looked today. There were flowers, parrot's feathers, and intricate carvings decorating the city, especially the area around the central square.

Many women were busy at the fires in front of their houses preparing food for the upcoming feast, and Anani breathed in the wonderful aromas that followed her as she walked. She saw the workers mixing the dry pulp of yucca roots with water, flattening the dough into round, thin patties, then cooking them on heated stones to form cassava. This nourishing bread, though a staple food of her people, was one of her favorites. In addition to the cassava bread, crabs, sweet potatoes, peanuts, shellfish, corn, turtle eggs, squash, berries, manatee, guava, beans, parrots, water fowl, lizards, pineapples, and jutias, a large rat-like animal, were also being prepared with special care for the cacique and his guests. The smells rising from the cooking stones and roasting pits made her stomach start to rumble and tighten, and she hurried her steps.

Anani finally found her brother and sister standing wide-eyed in front of the hut of the behique, which was located next to the large home of the cacique himself. She quietly stood behind Hura, put her hands on his shoulders, and watched with them as the holy man performed his rituals. Many others had also gathered to witness the behique's rites of purification.

The behique, a man greatly admired and just as greatly feared, looked much like a fierce skeleton dancing before them. His emaciated body turned and stepped to music only he could hear. Although not yet an old man, his age would have been impossible for a stranger to guess. The behique was naked except for a belted loincloth, and he looked as if his skin was loosely wrapped around nothing but bones. He had painted himself half black and half white above his waste, half blue and half red below. The holy man's terrible thinness was the result of fasting and purging. These rites were practiced to better enable him to communicate with the gods. Purification was essential for such an ominous role, and was achieved only through his extreme abstinence from sex as well as food. Sexual contact would only serve to reduce his power, to detract from his magic.

He alone spoke directly to the gods. On holy occasions, the behique would pass into their world with the aid of a hallucinogenic potion and return hours or days later to deliver whatever messages they had conveyed. His office was one of great distinction, second only to the cacique.

Anani knew that women had been chosen as behiques in the past, but only after they had reached an age at which their monthly cycles had completely ceased. Then their powers would be less influenced by the distractions of their bodies. Such a life seemed too mysterious and lonely for her to comprehend.

Hura, Guanina, and Anani stood spellbound as the shaman paid homage to the zemi's of the cacique through his strange dance. Anani had seen this rite performed only once before when she was Guanina's age. Her siblings were witnessing it for the first time. As they watched, the behique's dancing became more and more frenzied, and his chanting louder and louder until he was shouting toward the heavens in a unsettling, unearthly voice. Hura pressed his back against Anani's legs and grabbed her hands that still lay on his shoulders. Guanina took a step backward and looked at her older sister for reassurance. Anani tightened her hold on Hura's hands and nodded at Guanina with an expression of courage greater than she felt.

It was not long before the behique's movements and his voice began to diminish again. He slowed his steps until he came to a stop before a wooden stand near the house.

Picking up a tool from the stand, he began chanting words over it, words that were unknown to the others. In his hands was a curved stick that had been carved from the bone of a manatee. It was at least a foot in length, and its handle had been shaped by the skilled shaman to look like a long-billed bird. Anani and her siblings watched as this apparition of a man raised the stick high above his head.

Hura squirmed as the behique held the stick poised in the air. "What is he ...?" Hura started to whisper with apprehension, but Anani quickly hushed him.

The holy man slowly lowered the bone tool down his open mouth and pressed it deep inside his throat. Removing the stick quickly, he vomited the small amount that his stomach had held forcefully onto the ground. He quickly regained his breath. Placing the vomiting stick on the stand once again, he wrapped his bony fingers around the handles of a pair of dark maracas. These gourd rattles he shook rhythmically as he continued chanting and dancing. He treaded in a small circle, beseeching those of the other world in a high, cracking voice to allow him to join them so that he might hear their wishes. If the spirits would only share their dictates with him, his people would obey them, and thereby remain under the gods' protection.

After many pleas, when his legs and his voice seemed too weak to continue, the behique stopped abruptly. He stood silently swaying before his entranced audience. His purification was completed. He was ready. It was time for the shaman to make the magic that would help him see into the other world. This holy rite must be conducted solely in the presence of the cacique and his chosen men. With a face as somber as a grave he turned from them all and entered the house of the cacique.

With the behique's departure, the gathered crowd stirred and began to speak again, but in hushed voices, as if they had just been freed from a hypnotic trance. The fear and fascination that had gripped Anani, Hura, and Guanina, as well as the others, began to lessen immediately.

Hura, still somewhat shaken, turned to Anani and said,

"I thought he was going to kill himself with that white stick."

Anani bent down and held him close, running one of her hands down the hair on the back of his head several times. She comforted him until she could feel his small body relax against hers. Then she stood up and patted Guanina's cheek. Guanina tried to give her older sister a brave smile.

"Come you two," she said, gently taking Hura's hand, "Mother wants to see you before the wedding begins."

As they headed back to her uncle's home, Guanina looked back over her shoulder at the cacique's house and wondered what secret things the men were doing inside. She shuddered, and was grateful that she had never been chosen by the gods to do their powerful work.

The cacique was ready for the holy man when he entered. The leader and his men sat grim-faced in duhos arranged in a semicircle facing the door. A special duho had been placed in the center of the room. Near the empty duho stood a dark wooden table carved to resemble a seated man with a bowl resting on the top of his head. Without a word, the behique approached the table and, still swaying slightly, pulled the contents he would need from a pouch tied to the belt at his waist.

Using great care, he measured out each of the three ingredients. These were the cohoba, tobacco, and finely ground seashells. The holy man knew, as did generations of behiques before him, that the tobacco and shells would enhance the speed and potency of the hallucinogen. He had tested the exact strength and efficiency of the drug hundreds of times during his own lifetime. Today he must not make the magic too strong because he would be needed later during the dance and wedding ceremonies. He was precise with his amounts, knowing just how much of each element would make his magic take effect quickly, yet hold him for only a short time. With his wraith-like finger, the behique stirred the powdered elements round and round the bowl. The cacique and his men watched in as deep a silence as the holy man himself, each well aware of the power of what was to come.

Once the mixture was ready, the behique filled a long bone pipe, and sat down in the duho. He paused for a moment, then, chanting a prayer as he lifted the pipe high over his head, he asked once again for the gods to guide him to their world and speak to him. Lowering his arms he looked directly at the cacique for the first time and bowed to him. He then leaned forward over the pipe and inhaled its contents deeply.

The drug took possession of the food-deprived body almost immediately. Leaning back and closing his eyes, the behique gave himself fully to the magic. He tried to keep his body still as his mind began to shift and lean with strange images, but his body was no longer his to control. He tilted far forward in the duho, bending down so low that his head was almost between his knees. Then the drug began to reveal its secrets.

The behique felt his body being lifted from the duho. He was floating just off the ground, then floating higher, up and away from the cacique's house.

At first, he was afraid because he did not know where he was going. Then, as he was drawn to the cemetery in the center of the village square, he knew that the gods were allowing him to enter their dwelling place. They were accepting him into their presence. His fear grew greater as he hovered, suspended, above the graveyard. With crashing, terrifying clarity he saw the spirits of the dead spring from their graves. They did not look at him or approach him right away but they knew that the shaman was there.

The dead began to circle beneath his floating body, their forms shifting nearer and nearer. Just before they reached him, they disintegrated with sudden flashes of blue, gold, and orange, only to reappear again under him. As they circled, the cemetery dirt began to cave in. The ground crashed and sank until a hole of unimaginable depth gaped open. The spirits suddenly stopped circling. They raised their arms, and pointed from the behique to the hole, directing him to enter its blackness.

Before the behique had a chance to obey, he was plunging down the black tunnel, clawing at the air in a futile effort to slow his plummeting descent. He fell farther and faster, screaming until his breath was gone. Looking downward, he could see that a vast sea was opening up, and he was certain that his body would be crushed when he hit the water. But just as his feet were about to touch the plane of the sea, he stopped, his legs suspended inches above it.

The behique remained very still, then slowly stretched out the leg that was painted blue and touched his big toe to the water. A tiny trickle of the blue ran from his toe, staining the surface of the water. He reached down, touched the water with his white and black hands, and watched as the same thin stream of color ran from each into the water. The black and white dye wandered in small waving lines until they reached the blue and mixed with it, blending all three. The behique watched the new color that had formed from the three separate ones and marveled at it. Then he became aware of the dead souls all around him. They were pointing to him again, instructing him to lower his other leg, the one that was painted red. But the behique was afraid to lower his red leg, dreading what would happen, though he had no choice but to obey the spirits. Slowly, reluctantly, he stretched out until his red toe and the water met. Instantly a blood red color spilled into the water and spread swiftly, the stain growing wider and wider until it covered the entire sea.

The shaman tried to get away from the crimson water. It was horrible, terrifying, but the spirits would not let him move. He was so frightened now that his eyes closed and his body writhed as he screamed. He yelled for help and struggled to avoid the sea beneath him. At last he opened his eyes and the dead were again pointing at something. He looked in the direction they indicated and spotted the small patch of grayish-blue. It was still there, slowly circling in the ocean of blood. But the terror of the red liquid would not release him. He looked up, hoping to reach the tunnel. He pleaded with the spirits to release him, to let him return to his world. Instead, the tunnel began to collapse before his

133

eyes. He cried out pitifully as the walls crumbled and, at last, he began to rise. His body was speeding upward, the walls giving way as he rose. Chunks of dirt and boulders buffeted him, and he waited for one to crush him completely. Twisting and turning to avoid the ultimate collision, he was thrown upward with a mighty thrust. Breaching the earth's surface just as the hole rumbled closed beneath him, he reached the light and air of his own land.

A tragic sadness settled upon him so heavy, so profound, that he could not move. His mind faded until it went dark.

"Behique. Come back to us. Come back, behique." His worried leader leaned over the holy man, calling to him. The cacique and two of his men were holding the behique down on the floor. Their faces were pale as they watched their spiritual chief. None of them could have guessed the strength in the skeletal body of this man. It had taken all three of them to keep him still during his vision. When their holy man had started screaming and thrashing around on the floor with such violence, they had all feared for his life. They had never seen their behique go through such torture while he worked his magic, and they had been touched by the horror he was experiencing.

"Behique," the cacique called again, and the shaman slowly opened his eyes. He looked at the others vacantly for a moment. He tried to focus on their faces but it was difficult with the dream still haunting his mind. He forced himself to relax. He could feel the drug releasing him, but the images he had seen still loomed vividly. Finally he brought the face of his cacique into view and saw the concern written there.

"Can you speak?" asked the cacique. The behique nodded. The men released their protective holds on him and helped him back to his duho. The cacique and all of his men gathered close around the behique so that they would not miss any of his words.

The behique had closed his eyes again and seemed too exhausted to open them, let alone speak. They waited, anxious and pensive, but they waited without a word. With a great effort, the behique at last looked around. He attempted to sit up straighter but fell back. When he was able, he began to tell them of his vision.

"The dead..." he managed, but his voice had been lost with his earlier shouting. One of the men brought him a drink of water and the behique tried again, achieving only a raspy whisper. The men leaned closer still.

Weakly but persistently, the behique told them what he had seen, every detail that he could remember. When he finished he looked around at these brave, strong men and saw a hint of the fear that he himself had felt. That he still felt.

As if he was not sure he wanted to know the answer, the cacique asked, "What does all of this mean, Behique?"

The behique had a concept of what his dream had meant to tell him, to tell his people, but he did not wish to voice it today. Not on the day of the cacique's wedding. Tomorrow would be soon enough to tell them, to warn them, of the vision's message. *How* it would happen was unclear, but the magic had been painfully clear about *what* would happen. Death. Death would come to many of his people, and soon.

"I must think about all I have seen," he whispered. "This vision is unusual and I must meditate in solitude on what the spirits wish me to reveal."

The men looked uneasily at the behique, then at each other, but they accepted his words.

"You must rest now. We will send you some food so that you may recover your strength," said the cacique kindly.

"No food. Not yet. Not yet." The behique did not want to eat until his mind had uncovered the remaining mysteries of his visions. His present state of purity must not be interrupted before then. The cacique accepted this request.

Two of the cacique's men gravely and honorably carried the behique from the great house. Outside, many of the citizens of Cubanacan had gathered, and they looked on with fearful expressions. They too had heard the unnerving screams of the behique. All of them watched the men carry their holy man, who looked more dead than alive, into his own house where they placed him gently in his hammock. As the shaman wished, his two bearers left him alone.

Stepping outside the behique's home, one of the men quietly closed the cane door behind him and turned in the direction of the onlookers. It was Tiburon, Anani's father. He saw Anani standing at the edge of the crowd watching him closely. Her eyes were large and questioning. Tiburon returned her gaze with an unreadable expression, then looked away. He turned from her and headed back to rejoin the cacique and the others.

Sightings

11

Domingo dropped another chunk of fresh dolphin into the cook pot, stirred the soupy mixture, and went back to cutting more of the pink meat. Pedro sauntered up to him, bent over the kettle, and peeked in at its contents. For some reason, this simple action annoyed Domingo. But then, everything seemed to annoy him lately. He had put up with people coming over and peering into his pot several times each day. He was tired of the comments and griping that always seemed to follow their perusal of the ingredients he'd put together for their meal. Domingo frowned down at his bloody hands, chided himself for his nasty mood, and resumed his chopping.

Pedro watched his friend work and said nothing. He had just finished washing the steps that led to the foredeck and was waiting for Francisco to assign him another task. He very much hoped it would not involve helping pump out the foul bilge water. At the moment, Francisco was busy down below checking their food supplies.

The silence grew too heavy for Pedro, and he pointed out, "You look like you've been run through with a sword, Domingo." He aimed a finger at Domingo's waist and said, "Look at all of the blood on your clothes."

Domingo paused only long enough to survey the stain of splattered blood that spread from his waist to his thighs. "Cleaning a dolphin is dirty work," he said.

Pedro turned toward the sea, gazing out at the blue water and automatically checking the western horizon for land. But there was nothing but ocean and the yellow-green plants that danced on top of the waves as far out as he could see.

"I like the look of a clear blue sea much better than this yellowish sea grass. When do you think we will see the last of it, Domingo?" asked Pedro.

"I don't know, but since it hasn't bothered the progress of the ships I'm not going to worry about it," Domingo said testily. Hearing how harsh his words sounded in his own ears, Domingo again felt guilty for his short temper, and he tried again to clamp down on his impatient words.

The grass did not trouble Domingo nearly as much as the men's fear of it did. When the sargasso weed first appeared over a week ago, all of them had been concerned. This was something new, and they were amazed at how great a distance it covered. Some of them initially wondered if the weed would entangle and trap the fleet. This had not happened, but the plant life had not dissipated either. Some of the crew began to ask if it would go on and on until they reached land.

Land was what each one of them longed to see every time he looked up from his duties, each morning when he first awoke, and each night just before falling asleep. As days passed, they searched the horizon more and more frequently. They had left the Canaries on September 6, and Columbus had told them that they should reach the Indies within twenty-one days. Today was September 24, and the men were increasingly more agitated and quarrelsome.

"With so many signs of land, surely we'll reach some soon. Don't you think so, Domingo?" Pedro wondered.

"Soon, yes," Domingo responded only half listening. Pedro had asked him this question so many times lately that he was growing impatient with it. And he was trying to keep his mind on his cooking. The last thing he wanted today were more insults thrown at him like the day before. He was determined to provide the men with a good meal.

Under normal circumstances, his shipmates praised his food, but lately some of them found fault with everything and everyone. Yesterday one of the more ill-tempered among them had made a scene over how foul the food was becoming. The man had loudly implied that Domingo should be replaced by someone who knew what he was doing. The other men quickly hushed the complainer, knowing that Domingo was by far the best cook on the ship. It was true that there was no fresh fruit left, and they had run out of a few of their other stores. But there was still plenty of food, at least enough for another week or two. Domingo tried to make it as varied and appetizing as conditions allowed. The soup he was in the process of making contained potatoes, garlic, and the small dolphin that two of the men had managed to harpoon from the ship. The dolphin meat had a delicious flavor something like salmon that he hoped would please the men. He had even gotten Francisco's permission to issue honey with the sea biscuits today, hoping this would further appease the testiness of the hands.

"Domingo, didn't you hear me?" Pedro demanded after asking another question and receiving no answer at all.

Domingo looked up and saw the mixture of disappointment and frustration on Pedro's small face. "I'm sorry, Pedro. Tell me again. I will listen better this time."

"I asked if you want to hear what some men on the foredeck were saying a little while ago?"

Domingo didn't want to hear about it. He was certain he had heard similar things too many times recently. Complain, grumble, and snarl. Some of the men said very little that was positive lately. But Domingo could see how badly Pedro needed to talk. Trying to sound interested, he asked, "What did they say?"

Pedro leaned closer and spoke just above a whisper. "They said that the captain-general is mad. That he is willing to risk his life to become a great lord, but that we will get next to nothing for risking ours. With the Pinta so far ahead of us, they think we have no chance to win the reward for sighting land first. They said that we are fools to go any further because we will soon be out of food and water. They even said there is probably no land out there for a thousand miles."

Domingo waited for a question, but none came. Pedro just looked at him.

"The men are just afraid, Pedro. They know of no one who has ever sailed as far from land as we have. There is land out there, Pedro, and it is not so far away." Domingo said confidently.

Pedro frowned and looked at Domingo curiously. "How is it that you are so sure, Domingo? You speak as if you have been to the Indies before."

Domingo could not tell Pedro that his family had sailed the Atlantic for ages and knew of the lands, at least some of the coastlines of the lands, they were sailing to. The whalers went ashore to render the oil from the whale blubber before returning home. They did not stay to settle or discover what lay inland. They simply hunted the whales, and had dared to follow the huge animals to the distant western shores. He had been forbidden to tell Pedro any of this, but he would give the child what comfort he could.

"I have seen Columbus' charts, Pedro, and it will not be long before we sight land."

"But how do we know the charts are right? Weren't they just made from stories and guesses of how far the Indies might be?"

"I trust the charts, Pedro. I think they are close to what we will find to be true. And we have enough food even if the captain-general's reckoning is off by several days." Domingo spoke with great assurance. His manner comforted Pedro even more than the reasoning behind his words.

"You are right," said Pedro. "We must trust the charts, Domingo. I only hope that the rest of the men will trust them too."

Domingo could tell that Pedro had more on his mind.

"What's wrong, Pedro?

"I didn't tell you before, but the men on the foredeck also said that the captain-general would deserve whatever happened to him. They said they think the hands from the other ships agree that it would be best if he fell into the sea some night. They claimed that the Pinzóns were beginning to think so too. I didn't like the sound of that," Pedro confided.

Domingo didn't like the sound of it either. Even with his faith in the charts and the ability of the officers, Domingo had let it cross his mind that there wasn't adequate food or water for a return trip. They wouldn't even have subsistence rations if they sailed much further west without reaching land. In spite of himself, he had wondered if land was where the charts indicated it was, and whether the ships were being navigated properly. He understood how the others, with much less assurance than he had, would be near the end of their courage. But he had never thought that they may harm the captain-general out of desperation. Surely, they were just voicing their frustration more than anything else.

"You must try not to listen to such talk, Pedro. Anyway, how could any of the men on the Santa Maria know what the Pinzóns are thinking? They are just talking about things that they shouldn't be. Nothing more."

Pedro thought about this for a moment. "Yes, they are only grumbling. You know, Domingo, at times I wonder if you and I have more courage than some of the older men," the boy said with sincerity.

In spite of his words to Pedro, Domingo found himself remembering how Martín Pinzón had run the Pinta ahead of the rest of the fleet for the last few days. Columbus had repeatedly signaled to him, ordering him to stay with the other ships, but Pinzón had ignored the signals. Yesterday Columbus had sent him a written message using a line cast and strung between the two ships. When Pinzón had sent his reply, the captain-general had not hidden his displeasure.

Domingo and the rest of the crew believed that it was the queen's reward that lured the Pinta's captain into the lead. Queen Isabella had offered a fortune, as well as fame, to the first man to sight land. This reward, 10,000 maravedies a year for the rest of the seaman's life, would be enough to make him quite wealthy. It seemed that Pinzón meant to claim the reward for himself, and cared little about the captain-general's annoyance. After all, the majority of the men in the fleet were from near Palos and loyal to the Pinzón family rather than to Columbus. Domingo asked himself if it was possible that Pinzón had developed plans beyond taking possession of the reward, plans that included harming Columbus.

But that would be crazy. If it were ever found out, Pinzón and those who had supported him would be hung when they returned to Spain. Besides, Martín's younger brother, Vicente, kept the Niña close by the Santa Maria. This would not make sense if the Pinzóns had decided to use their strength against Columbus. It was just as he had told Pedro. The men were simply spending too much time voicing their worst thoughts.

Francisco approached the boys, breathless and dirty, and glanced inside the nearly full kettle. When he noticed the little pile of garlic skins beside Domingo he grunted, "Lots of garlic. Good!" Although he would never voice it, even Francisco appreciated how able Domingo had become at cooking. "Ah, I will miss the garlic when it is gone. But, we'll enjoy it today at least, eh? Domingo, you finish up with that soup. I've already worked up an appetite, and there is much work yet to finish. I will be as hungry as a shark when it's time to eat and I don't want to have to wait for it."

"Yes, sir," Domingo said picking up another chunk of meat. With a jerk of his head, Francisco motioned for Pedro to follow him and the two of them headed for the hatchway. Francisco went down the stairs first. At the top of the steps Pedro glanced around to be sure he wasn't being noticed. Looking back and catching Domingo's eye, Pedro covered his nose with his hand and descended the stairs with a doomed countenance. His exaggerated expression made him look as if he were being led to the gallows rather than into the hold. Just before he disappeared, Pedro grinned mischievously at him. Domingo smiled back at the empty hatchway. It was good to see that Pedro, occasionally at least, was still able to joke like a child.

The following day the winds were so tranquil that some of the stronger swimmers among the crew were allowed into the water. Domingo was grateful to be included in their number. Good swimmer that he was, most of the time Domingo took the precaution of holding onto a rope that was secured to the ship. The water felt wonderful but he did not like the touch of the seaweed against his body. Several shallow dives under the surface served to rinse off some of the grime that had accumulated on his clothes, skin, and hair. Salty but cleaner, and smelling far less pungent, he climbed back aboard the Santa Maria and sat dripping on her deck. Before long, the rest of the swimmers left the water too.

It was close to sunset, nearly time for them to sing the vespers prayers. The western sky was just beginning to redden. Domingo leaned back, closed his eyes, and breathed in deeply. "Yes," he thought, "I definitely smell better."

The Niña was close by their port side. The Pinta was ahead as usual. The air was so calm that Domingo could have held a conversation with one of the crewmen of the Niña and been heard easily. The minutes passed lazily as the men waited for the timekeeper to call out the hour.

The quiet was jarred by the voice of Martín Pinzón shouting from the Pinta. "Land! Land to the south-west!" Every man in the fleet was on his feet and craning to see in that direction. There it was on the horizon, not more than seventy-five miles away.

The cry of "Land! Land!" became a thundering chorus. Men and boys were hugging each other, slapping each other, crying with joy. Columbus and many others fell to their knees and thanked God. The hour of vespers was soon upon them, and the holy songs were sung with the deepest gratitude and reverence. The men aboard the Pinta congratulated Pinzón on the wealth and stature that he would receive for his sighting. He would surely be remembered for ages to come because of today.

After the prayers were concluded, the crews watched the horizon until darkness completely hid their view. Few of them slept that night. Domingo sat up with Rodrigo and

Gonzalo and speculated about the nature of the people of the Indies. What would they be like, and how would they receive the Europeans once they had anchored and gone ashore?

Pedro had tried to stay awake, but had fallen asleep leaning against Gonzalo shortly after nightfall. As the other three talked for hours, Gonzalo held Pedro's head on his lap and thought of his own sons far away on the other side of the world.

Before dawn, they were all lining the rails of the ship waiting for the first close glimpse of land. The ships had sailed well during the night and Columbus had told them that they may be within ten miles of the shore by daybreak. Excited speculations were being made as to how close to the great cities of Japan and China they would land. With the first dull light from the east, the eager expressions grew confused. Then, as the light increased, faces became absolutely grim. There was no land. What they had seen the evening before had been nothing more than squall clouds.

Pedro turned and looked up at Domingo with disbelieving eyes. "It was there," he said pitifully. "Last night it was there."

Domingo could not answer Pedro at first. A deep hollowness had grabbed his gut as he looked at the empty expanse of ocean before him. He was fighting to accept what he saw and to master his own disappointment. Domingo knew that Pedro was hurting, that the boy needed him, but he simply couldn't comfort him yet. He couldn't even move. Pedro held onto the rail and began to cry silently. His shoulders shook but he did not make a sound. As the silent sobs continued he turned his head away from Domingo. Finally, Domingo forced himself to pull his eyes from the horizon and to bend down to the boy.

"Pedro," said Domingo turning the small body toward him and holding his shoulders comfortingly. "The land is there, Pedro. It is a little father away than this, but it is there."

"But I *saw* it. Last night I *saw* it." Pedro's expression still

144

showed an unwillingness to believe the land had disappeared.

"You saw *something*, Pedro. We all saw it, but it couldn't have been land because it's not there any more." Pedro looked back at him with skepticism as the tears continued to flow.

Domingo decided to try a different approach. Putting on a puzzled expression, Domingo continued, "This whole thing confuses me too, Pedro. You are an experienced sailor, much more experienced than I am. Have you ever heard of men seeing things that looked like land, but weren't?"

Pedro slowed his crying to consider Domingo's question. He wiped his eyes and nose on his sleeve and studied Domingo's bewildered look. He thought a minute longer and sniffed twice before saying. "I *have* heard of such things, Domingo." He swiped at his nose with his sleeve once more. Then, as if he were Domingo's older and wiser brother, he began to describe such claims.

"I didn't remember at first," Pedro said, "but it's so. False sightings have probably happened hundreds of times. Domingo, you shouldn't be too concerned. We will surely find real land very soon."

"Thank you, Pedro," Domingo said to him warmly. "I feel better after talking this over." Domingo was surprised to realize that he had spoken the truth. By reassuring Pedro, he had buoyed his own sagging spirits somewhat.

The gratitude and joy that the crew had felt at the belief that land was within reach were replaced by a surly gloom. The personality of each man dictated how he dealt with the weight of his disappointment. For some, it took much longer to regain hope than others. Columbus seemed to be among the first to recover his optimism, and he tried to cheer the hands with reminders of the wealth they would gain when they reached the Indies. Although this did little but increase the grumbling from a few of the worst tempered hands, many of the sailors were heartened by Columbus' words.

Most of the men rallied themselves enough to try catching fish to extend their food supply, but they had little success. On a calm morning, several of the hands stood at the rail with their nets and poles in the water hoping to snag a fish. Domingo had just come up from the hold when he heard Pedro yelling excitedly for him to come see something. He set down his sack and was turning in Pedro's direction when a long, orange object hurled itself across the deck and skidded at his feet. Domingo was so surprised he jumped into the air trying to avoid the flopping thing. He stopped his frantic foot movements as soon as he realized it was a fish, a very strange fish *with wings*. A handful of men laughed heartily at Domingo's antics as they lunged for the fish.

This began a merry chase with men bumping and pushing into each other as they tried to grab the slippery creature. Pedro even appeared in their midst, dodging in and out between the men in an effort to catch the prize. Domingo stood back and watched the ruckus, still amazed at the sight of the odd fish.

A huge groan rose from the main deck when the fish flipped off the ship at the base of the port rail and landed in the sea. Domingo ran to the rail and gasped when he saw more of the same kind of fish leaping out of the water and surging ahead of them at great speed.

"They're flying fish! Watch, Domingo!" shouted Pedro next to him. The two looked on and were joined by most of the men, as the glittering, orange phenomenons put on an aerial display above the water. The sailors hooted and clapped when one particular fish rose thirty feet in the air and glided for nearly two hundred yards.

But the amazing fish were illusive to hooks and nearly impossible to catch with nets. Before long, the flying fish lost much of their novelty and the next few days dragged by with a terrible heaviness. Domingo was quiet, and mindful of the other men, hoping tempers would hold. Often Pedro would join him at the rail, and the two would stand watching the distant horizon without saying a word.

It helped a little to lift the spirits aboard the ships when the winds grew more favorable and birds appeared in greater and greater numbers. But land was not sighted and the date of October 6, the date up to which they had been fully provisioned, loomed ever closer.

Francisco and Domingo murmured in whispers when they discussed how much food was left and how it was to be used. They tried to use their dwindling stores with great care, and reported to Columbus and De La Cosa daily on how things were holding out. The rest of the men were not blind to how the full barrels and bags were decreasing in number, or that Domingo's soup was watered down a little more each day. They could also see the ship taking on more water, and that repairs that could only be made on land would be needed soon.

The majority of the men and boys bore such observations in silence and staunch bravery while they awaited their fates. There were a few, however, that tried to relieve their fears through cruelty to the weaker ones around them. Cabin boys were cuffed and kicked for little or nothing by the likes of these men. Chachu and the other officers tried to keep tempers calm but they could not be everywhere on the ship. The emotions of the most dangerous among them were tightening like a noose.

Addressing one particular complaint of his crew, Columbus attempted to equalize the chance that one of the men of the Santa Maria would be the first to see land. He ordered that the two faster ships were to rendezvous with the flagship every dawn and every sunset for the rest of the voyage since it was during these times of day that it was easier to see greater distances.

October 6th arrived clear and calm, and the crews watched the horizon as if this was destined to be the day that land would appear to them. Columbus warned all of the crews during their morning rendezvous that anyone who falsely claimed to see land would forfeit the reward, even if he later actually did spot it first. So, they watched carefully. Nevertheless, they watched and waited in vain. That evening Martín Pinzón's crew pulled the Pinta close alongside the Santa Maria and their captain hailed Columbus.

"Captain-general, I have been studying one of your charts," Pinzón called out across the short distance. "I believe that if we change our course to the southwest we will soon reach the island of Japan. I think it would be wise to change course this evening."

Columbus did not like Pinzón shouting his intentions across the water like this. He was already displeased with Pinzón for refusing to stay with the flagship. Glancing around, Columbus could see the anxious faces of his men waiting for a reply.

Facing Pinzón again, he cupped his hand and yelled back to the Pinta, "I do not wish to alter course, Captain Pinzón. I believe that due west is still our best route."

"But Captain-general, we have already sailed far beyond your estimated distance to Japan. Surely by altering our direction we will be more likely to meet landfall soon," Pinzón persisted.

"It is possible that we have missed Japan," Columbus responded, "But that is even more reason for not altering our course. If we did bypass Japan, we must head directly west to try to reach the mainland of China as quickly as possible. We will continue west." Columbus was firm in his decision.

Pinzón did not hide his disappointment or frustration. He turned his back on Columbus. A few of the bolder members of his crew threw dark looks in the direction of the leader of the fleet. As the captain-general drew away from the rail he could not help but notice the brooding expressions of some of his own men. When darkness fell, Columbus headed to his cabin without a backward glance.

The next morning, not long after the sunrise rendezvous with the other ships had concluded, Domingo and Francisco were down in the hold deciding what to cook for the hands. Both of them were distracted and wanted to get above deck as soon as possible. With the first light, all of the men had seen something on the horizon, but it was still too far away to be distinct. No one onboard the Santa Maria wanted to risk the reward by making another false claim of seeing the land. Everyone who possibly could do so was watching the shape in the distance, straining their eyes and hoping.

"No more garlic," Francisco complained as Domingo glanced again at the hatchway. "It matters little what we cook if there is no garlic. It will all taste the same. Oh well, we can use the last of the rice. We can stretch it no further. It has no flavor, but without any garlic what..." Francisco began.

Both of them started violently as a booming shot of a cannon rocked the air outside. Domingo jumped toward the hatchway and was six steps ahead of Francisco by the time the older man reached the stairs. He scaled the steps three at a time with Francisco's excited cursing following him up the opening. Domingo nearly tripped on a coil of rope as he raced across the deck. He just managed to catch himself and hurried to join the men and boys crowding the port side of the ship. They were all staring ahead toward the Niña. There was the flag. The banner signaling the sighting of land had been raised high on the Niña's main mast. It was her cannon that had been fired. With her greater speed, the Niña had ranged far in front of them to investigate the manifestation of what they all hoped was a landmass on the skyline. It was her crew that had hailed them to announce the discovery of the land they had sought for so long.

With the brightness of the new day, they all celebrated the sighting with abandon. But as they sailed farther and farther to the west, disappointment once again settled like a crushing weight on the shoulders of each of them. No land showed itself. The sighting had been another false one. Spirits fell like comets, leaving the men feeling even lower than they had when the first wrongful sighting was made. Domingo and Pedro hardly spoke a word that day. The bravest of the crew remained silent with their dark thoughts. Others loudly predicted their destruction until Chachu threatened to chain them below.

In an effort to ease the hopelessness of the crew, Columbus and De La Cosa repeatedly pointed out the many large flocks of birds that had begun to fly over them toward

149

the southwest. The migration of the birds was a powerful indication of where the closest land lay. With this newest sign of land, and the growing discontent of the Pinzóns and their men, an hour before sunset Columbus at last agreed to change course slightly toward the south.

More land birds were seen overhead the next day. The seaweed looked fresher, and Rodrigo even claimed that he could smell the scent of flowers in the air. These signs were enough for the crews to hold on to their last wisps of hope. That night the men could see the birds against the nearly full moon. The flocks were heading in the same direction as the fleet. Each of the captains told their men to put their faith in those birds. They knew where the land was. To this some of the men asked each other, "But how far is the land? How far? And what if we are off course and miss the land altogether?"

On the evening of October 9, the wind shifted to the northwest and the ships were making little headway. An hour before sunset, Domingo heard some raised voices and, glancing in that direction, saw that the launches from the Pinta and the Niña were rowing toward them. Looking more closely, he noticed that the Pinzóns wore solemn expressions.

The crewmembers of the flagship started murmuring among themselves. Domingo heard one man mutter, "Maybe after a meeting between the captains we can turn back to Spain. To keep going is madness."

The Pinzóns boarded the Santa Maria and were motioned by the captain-general to the half-deck. Every hand watched as Columbus, De La Cosa, Martín, and Vicente closed the door to the captain's cabin behind them. Chachu stood guard outside and kept an eye on the men.

"What do you think the Captain-general will decide?" Pedro asked Domingo.

Domingo paused only a moment. "I think he will want to sail on, as will De La Cosa. But the Pinzóns may want to go back, and they have greater influence with most of the men. They may convince our captains to turn around." Domingo

150

watched the door behind Chachu, then gazed out at the western horizon.

"What do *you* want to do, Domingo?"

Domingo looked at Pedro, trying to read the boy's thoughts. "What would you decide, Pedro, if you were the Captain-general?"

"I would ask my good friend, Domingo, what is in his heart before I would decide," Pedro said with a straight face.

With just a hint of a smile Domingo answered, "All right, Pedro. I want to go on. The land is there and I want to see it. I think we have a better chance if we go forward than trying to make it back to Spain."

Pedro considered these words. "I thought that was what you would say. If you, De La Cosa, and Columbus feel that way, I would be foolish to think otherwise. I want to go on too. I just hope those birds really do know where..."

Pedro stopped speaking as the sound of shouting rose from the direction of the captain's cabin. At first, few of their leaders' words were distinct enough to make out. Then Domingo and Pedro clearly heard the voice of Columbus above the others, "Three days longer! I insist on three more days! If we haven't sighted land by then you can have my head!" Complete silence fell. The murmur of softer, calmer voices followed. Domingo and Pedro looked at each other, then gazed at the faces of the rest of the crew. Staring straight ahead, Chachu's face looked like it had been carved in stone. Rodrigo's expression looked resigned, Gonzalo's hopeful. Low threats came from the mouths of the men who were already incensed by what they guessed would be the outcome of the meeting.

Shortly after Columbus shouted down the others, the cabin door opened and the Pinzóns descended from the half-deck, crossed the main deck, climbed down to their boats, and left the Santa Maria without looking back. Columbus and De La Cosa emerged grim-faced and, in a voice loud enough to be heard by all, Columbus ordered Chachu to hold the course steady. Almost imperceptibly, De La Cosa nodded to Chachu.

Many of the men began to raise objections, but Columbus turned from them and reentered his cabin. De La Cosa stood next to Chachu with an expression that did not welcome discussion, and the grumbling men reluctantly resumed their duties.

"We'd better try to get some sleep, Pedro," said Domingo wearily. The two found places for themselves and curled up under the forecastle.

As they settled in, Pedro said, "Well, we got our wish. We're sailing farther. Tonight I think I'll ask God to help guide those birds we're following."

Domingo said goodnight to his young friend, then lay staring at the moon and thinking. He had seen the murderous look on some of the men's faces. He couldn't help wondering how such anger might erupt. It was the kind of dangerous anger that grew from fear.

Domingo closed his eyes and added his own prayers to Pedro's. He prayed that this voyage would not result in mutiny, or the death of their leaders. "But," he told God, "if it comes to that, to mutiny, I will stand with De La Cosa and try to die with honor. I will not return to my people as a mutineer." With this promise, he fell into an uneasy sleep.

Trouble did not wait for the sun to set the next day. No land had been sighted, and the pressure of the crew's fear was expanding with the passing of each hour. The men began gathering in small groups, and their voices were rising. Domingo kept Pedro nearby and was trying to finish up the tasks that needed done before he was relieved.

De La Cosa stood on the quarterdeck and firmly told the men to prepare for the changing of the shift. Voices rose louder. Gonzalo and Rodrigo exchanged a look and moved closer to Domingo and Pedro. Columbus emerged from the cabin, approached De La Cosa, and scanned the faces below them. Columbus turned back to De La Cosa as if to say something, but he was interrupted by a shout from below.

"Is it true, Captain-general, that you have been lying to us all along?" a Basque crewmember yelled up to the officers.

Columbus looked startled, but gathered himself quickly. "Why would I lie to my men?" he demanded with a fierce look in his eyes.

"Have you been lying to us every day about how far we have sailed?" another crewmember questioned.

De La Cosa forced himself to keep his face expressionless. He had strongly suspected that Columbus was keeping a false log ever since they had left the Canaries. Columbus did not so much as flinch.

"Is that what this gathering is all about? Who has been telling you such things?" Columbus roared.

The first man who had spoken called out again, "The pilots of all three ships say that you have lied. You've tried to keep us from knowing just how far we have sailed away from our homes. We've traveled much farther than you promised and *still* there is no land."

Columbus glared at his two pilots but they did not look away from his anger. They were certain that they were right, and they feared that the captain-general's lies might cost them their lives.

The voices grew more menacing and several shouts were thrown toward the quarterdeck. Chachu and the other boatswain slipped billets into their belts as the officers tried to calm the crew. Rodrigo pushed Pedro protectively behind his back, using his larger body as a shield. Gonzalo stepped in front of Domingo, but Domingo gave him a direct look, and nudged him aside. Domingo did not want Gonzalo's protection. He would stand with the rest of the men and face what was to come. Gonzalo understood, and stood at Domingo's side.

Someone yelled out, "With the food running out and this change of wind we'll never make it back to Spain. Your lies and false navigation have doomed us all!" This claim was taken up by many of the other men. A few of them started pushing and shoving those who remained silent. No one had yet bothered Domingo's small group.

It was then that the Pinta and the Niña pulled alongside the Santa Maria for their evening rendezvous. Some of the hands from the other ships saw what was happening and began shouting to the enraged crewmembers of the flagship.

"Silence, you men!" thundered Martín Pinzón to his own crew, and he was reluctantly obeyed. Vicente Pinzón's men remained relatively still aboard the Niña as they watched the scene unfold around them.

"Captain-general!" Martín Pinzón bellowed again, this time across the stretch of water toward the mothership. "May I be of assistance?"

Columbus looked over at Pinzón. "Some of my men seem to think they will never return home," Columbus responded. The approach of the other two ships and the dominating presence of Martín Pinzón had checked the loudest members of the Santa Maria's crew enough for Columbus to be heard.

Directing his authority toward his men once again, Columbus reproached them loudly. "You men, where is your spirit? You are acting like frightened children, not like seamen. The king and queen of Spain have sent us to find the Indies and we will continue until we have indeed found them. Your complaining is useless. We are sailing on until we reach land. Do you hear? Until we reach land!"

The rumbling of dissatisfaction that followed had little time to build before Pinzón's voice boomed across to the Santa Maria.

"Captain-general, I would be happy to come aboard and assist in hanging five or six of the men who are yelling the loudest. That may help quiet the others." Pinzón's men exchanged uncomfortable looks. They did not doubt that he would do what he said.

De La Cosa took a step forward and glared into the eyes of each of the sailors until they backed down one by one. Columbus waited and watched the men as they dropped their gazes before De La Cosa's unyielding expression.

"That will be unnecessary, Captain Pinzón," Columbus said. Then, as if nothing unusual had just happened, he added, "With the wind shifting favorably to the southwest again, we will maintain full sails throughout the night. With the help of the moon and by doubling the watch we should have no trouble spotting land before we get too close to shore."

"Agreed," said Martín Pinzón. Vicente nodded from the Niña. Just then, the hour of 7:00 p.m. struck, and Chachu called out the changing of the shift a little more resolutely than usual. The grumbling men grudgingly resumed their duties.

Before Gonzalo and Rodrigo left their younger crewmates, Gonzalo held out his hand to Domingo. He didn't say a word, but his expression clearly conveyed respect. Domingo took his hand and shook it firmly. As Pedro and Domingo headed for the railing to watch the sun disappear, Pedro leaned close and whispered to Domingo, "I hope I dream about my mother's bread again tonight. That would be much better than dreaming about Captain Pinzón hanging some of our men."

Domingo looked down at him and nodded. "Much better," he said aloud, then repeated it to himself.

The thought of the noose seemed to have been held throughout the night by more than just Pedro. By morning, a gloomy silence prevailed once again aboard the ship. A gale-force wind and a following sea formed rapidly in the early hours and by late morning the ships were surging forward at a great speed. The hands were kept as busy as possible by the officers.

Near midday, Rodrigo was standing on the foredeck when he gave a short yelp and scrambled down the stairs to the main deck. He grabbed a net and threw it out into the water. Grinning broadly, he began pulling the net back toward the ship as quickly as he was able. Domingo, Pedro, Gonzalo, and many others milled about Rodrigo, asking what he was doing, what he had seen, but he told them only, "Wait and see."

When the net was finally aboard, Rodrigo gently unfolded it, searching for something the other men could not see. With the greatest of care, he untangled a small section of the net and slowly pulled from its webbing a small branch. Still clinging to the wood were three red blossoms. As he held it up in the air, the men went wild, cheering and calling to Columbus and De La Cosa. When the captain-general and the master joined them, they all stared at the blooms, and burst out laughing at one another. Their eyes had deceived them before when they had mistakenly thought they saw land where there was none. But their fingers and eyes did not fool them now. The branch had not been in the water long. Land could not be far.

Rodrigo closed his eyes and inhaled the scent of the flower. Everyone laughed again when he said he could smell its delicate fragrance. He just smiled knowingly, gazed lovingly at the pretty red flowers in his hand, and ignored them all.

Less than three hours later someone aboard the Pinta spotted a floating stick and brought it aboard their ship. Upon examination, it was evident that they held in their hands some sort of man-made tool. Its tip could have been sharpened, and its edge carved, only by human hands. They must be close not only to land, but to other people as well. The Pinta fell back to the flagship just long enough to report the crew's find, then raced ahead again. The reward was once again foremost in the minds of the men.

At 10:00 that night, every hand that could keep his eyes open was still on watch. Columbus was on the stern-castle scanning the horizon like the rest of his men. Thinking he saw a tiny light in the distance, Columbus called to Pero Gutiérrez, a representative of the queen, and asked him if he could see the light. Pero said that he thought he could, perhaps, see it also. Because it was so faint and inconsistent, Columbus thought it wise to say nothing of it until he was certain.

He asked all of his men to keep a close watch and added to the reward of the queen by offering one of his own. He promised to personally give the first man to sight land a silk jacket from his own wardrobe.

The quarter moon rose just before midnight and shed

enough light to help the tired watchers. The Pinta was out ahead of the rest of the fleet, the Niña halfway between the other two ships. Pedro had fallen asleep three hours earlier and Domingo was starting to nod in spite of his best efforts. Rodrigo nudged him gently and Domingo jerked himself upright. He mumbled his thanks to his friend and gazed again at the seemingly endless sea. Gonzalo stood quietly on his other side. Each of them silently speculated about what lay just beyond the waves, and when they would reach it.

Domingo found himself wondering where his brothers were. He refused to believe that any harm had come to them. Had his brothers ever sailed to the shore that he would soon walk on? The image of his father rose before Domingo, and with it came a longing to speak to him. Domingo imagined them talking together as they walked along the beach that bordered Lequetio. How he hoped that his father was alright. He had so much to tell him. Domingo then thought of Carmen as he had last seen her. He remembered how she had felt in his arms.

"I'm so far away," he told himself. After a few moments, he managed to control his deep homesickness. At least now, with land so close, it looked like he would be able to return to those he loved. The crews would soon be able to restock their supplies, recaulk the ships, and sail home. The thought of carrying riches back with him was nowhere in his mind at that moment. He wanted only to return to Carmen, to his family, and to his village.

Around 2:00 a.m. a boom from the cannon of the Pinta jarred the night air. Domingo was jolted fully awake by the blast. Was it truly land this time? He scanned the horizon but couldn't see it. Men were shouting, "Where? Where?" Then someone yelled out, "Straight ahead! Land straight ahead!" Straining to see ahead of them, one by one the hands of the Santa Maria took up the shouting.

There it was. Domingo could see it himself now. He ran to Pedro, picked him up, and carried him to the railing. "Pedro look!" he said in the boy's ear as he held him, "We've found land! Look! Look there!"

Pedro looked up startled, turned his eyes in the direction Domingo was pointing, and saw the land. As he stared at the scene in front of him, what remained of his sleepiness fell away.

With a mixture of joy, wonder, and acknowledgement, he declared, "Well, you always said we'd find it." Then he looked back at Domingo and his expression altered. His chin started to quiver and his eyes filled. "Domingo," he started, "We are here. We..." His voice cracked and his arms came up and around Domingo's neck as sobs shook him. Pedro buried his head in Domingo's shoulder, and could say no more.

Domingo patted Pedro's shaking back and said, "Yes, Pedro, we are here," until his own voice was overcome by emotion. All he could do was continue to pat Pedro's small back.

Rodrigo and Gonzalo were dancing with each other like crazy men, weeping, and laughing at the same time. Men who hadn't spoken a civil word to each other in days were hugging like long-lost cousins. Columbus and De La Cosa were embracing. A couple of older boys were belting out irrintzis, piercing Basque battle cries, while swinging from ropes over the heads of the rest of the crew. Chachu didn't even try to calm them. He was happily being pounded on the back by several of his men. Mayhem completely took over the Santa Maria.

By the time the flagship pulled up to the Pinta, its crew was already in a full uproar. The Niña had joined the Pinta a few moments earlier and had added their joyful voices to those of the others.

The man who had, at last, found land was Rodrigo De Triana from the town of Lepe. De Triana had been hoisted up on the shoulders of several of the Pinta's men and was being paraded around the main deck like a king. With the appearance of Columbus, his bearer set him down on the deck and pushed him to the rail nearest the Santa Maria.

"Captain-general!" someone shouted happily, "Rodrigo has something to tell you!"

De Triana beamed and shouted across to Columbus, "I humbly claim the rewards from you and her majesty the queen, sir."

Columbus looked troubled and studied the plain seaman before him. "I am sorry Rodrigo, but I myself saw a light shining from shore not long ago."

De Triana's smile disappeared. Pinzón's brow furrowed slightly and he looked uncertain. Members of the Pinta's crew looked at each other as if they had not heard correctly. Many of Columbus' own men frowned at this claim. Domingo glanced questioningly at Rodrigo. The captain-general had not announced the sighting of land last night. Why would he say such a thing? How could he be claiming the reward that rightfully belonged to De Triana? De Triana tightened his jaw but said nothing.

Columbus read the expressions and heard the rumblings around him. Speaking again to De Triana, he said in an assuring voice, "Do not be concerned, Rodrigo. You and I will discuss this further and all will be well." This comment succeeded in bringing a hopeful look back into the sailor's eyes and relief to the others.

The ecstatic mood of the crews rebounded easily. Land was before them, after all. At the captain-general's order the cannons of the Niña and the Santa Maria were fired, and their booming filled the night sky.

The coastline lay just six miles in front of them. It was so close, in fact, that the overjoyed crews had to be calmed down long enough to haul in most of the sails so that they wouldn't run too close to shore. Once the sails had been adjusted, the men and boys of the fleet stood along the railings, all eyes turned in the same direction. They earnestly thanked God for keeping them alive. Then they thanked their worthy ships.

After seeing him through so much, through what seemed now like years rather than weeks, the Santa Maria had become a permanent part of Domingo's soul. For thirty-three continuous days, Domingo had known the cadence of the Santa Maria's breathing. He had felt her straining against the sea and the wind. He had read her moods as she fought to keep them alive in a boundless expanse of unforgiving water. Her noble efforts had brought them safely to this place. No matter what happened over the course of his life, Domingo would remember this ship with something close to reverence. She had not failed them.

The crews watched the shore with exhausted, excited smiles on their faces. They would go ashore at first light. They were the first to reach the Indies by sea, or so most of them thought. They had not only survived; they would soon share in the wonders and riches that Marco Polo had written about. With these amazing thoughts and hopes, ninety men and boys surveyed the shoreline and waited with painful impatience for the sun to rise.

Hidden behind the bushes and trees that edged the beach, many eyes looked back at the strange men that had appeared in the tall ships. They too were waiting for dawn.

An Omen

12

Eight powerful men supported the litter carrying the cacique as it slowly circled the central square. Anani and her family stood with the rest of the citizens of Cubanacan and watched the litter's progress. Following the leader with her gaze, Anani's expression revealed her admiration. As he passed by with great dignity, her cacique looked wise, strong, and very handsome. He wore a huge headdress of fantastically colored feathers. He was also adorned with an intricately woven cotton mantle that had been beaded with brightly dyed fish bones. On top of the mantle, a gold medallion, the special emblem of his rank, reflected the rays of the afternoon sun.

Noticing the medallion, Anani recalled the story she had heard so many times of how gold had first been given to the Tainos. Ages ago a goddess called Guabonito had bestowed special treasures, including gold, on their first cacique. This was why gold was so highly esteemed. It was more than beautiful; it was holy. She thought of the earrings she wore, the ones that Calichi had given her. Lifting her hand she touched one of them briefly and wondered again at his exceptional generosity. Her mother looked at her and smiled, and Anani turned her attention back to the royal conveyance.

Once the bearers had made a full circle of the area, the litter was carefully lowered to the ground in front of the cacique's house, and he stepped out. Standing erect and composed, he waited for his bride-to-be to join him.

Like those of ancient times, their cacique had been chosen from the noble class, and would serve for the remainder of his lifetime in great honor. He had been given, as was custom, the largest and finest home in the city. His house, which was rectangular in shape and easily distinguished from the smaller, round houses of the other residents, also served as a temple to the gods. His zemis were by far the most powerful among his people. The spirits watched over him with special attentiveness.

Along with his privileges, the cacique was required to bear grave responsibilities. Food storage and distribution, crop planning and harvesting, and hunting and fishing were among the essential functions that he was required to manage. The cacique pronounced judgement on any of his people brought before him for the commission of a crime. The armed defense of his people against the Caribs was up to him to plan and execute. Most importantly, it was the cacique who, through his conduct and leadership, must please the gods so that the Tainos would continue to flourish.

Anani's family looked on as the bride's litter arrived, and was gently brought to the ground before the cacique. An attractive young girl that Anani had never seen before was helped down and led to the entrance of the cacique's house. The ritual of the bride, the show of turning away all suitors but the cacique, began.

While all eyes attended to the bride, Anani became aware of someone moving very gradually toward her right side. Glancing in that direction she saw Calichi inching closer and closer, hardly noticed by the people he was sliding between. Anani snapped her head forward and tried valiantly to keep a calm expression on her face. Tanama and the rest of her family stood to Anani's left. They did not seem to see Calichi shifting unobtrusively among the wedding guests. In reality, Tanama had spotted him even before her daughter had, but she kept her gaze straight ahead and looked as if the marriage was the only thing going on around her.

Without turning in his direction, Anani occasionally saw Calichi's ever growing shape from the corner of her eye. When he appeared again, this time only a few feet away from her, her breathing became unsteady. Only one person, an old woman with an enthralled smile on her face, stood between them. Calichi remained very still, not even looking at her. But his nearness was enough to distract Anani for the duration of the wedding.

Calichi worked as hard as Anani to keep staring at the rite being conducted in front of him. He felt Anani's closeness so acutely that she completely occupied his senses. Instead of the marriage of the couple before him, Calichi thought about their own wedding to come. After their ceremony, lovely, gentle, Anani, would be with him for the rest of his life. He started to imagine how it would be to spend each day and night together. He was drawn to the thought of touching her body for the first time, taking her in his arms, and loving her completely. Abruptly, Calichi forced himself to push these images from his mind. He clenched his fists and made a huge effort to concentrate on what the behique was now saying.

Anani was not thinking as far ahead as their wedding. She thought of today, of being with Calichi. She wanted simply to be able to look at him for longer than a moment at a time. She longed to talk to him and hear his thoughts and feelings, to see his expression when she gave her bowl to his parents.

The behique was almost finished speaking when Anani finally dared to glance at Calichi. He had been waiting, hoping that she would. He looked back at her, held her eyes, and smiled. There was the same gentle smile that he had given her months ago, and it calmed Anani's heart as nothing else could have. A man with such a smile must be a good man. She smiled back at him briefly, shyly, then slowly turned her eyes to the ceremony. Neither of them heard a single word of blessing that the behique intoned in his hoarse, cracking voice.

At last, the cacique and his bride entered his grand house and the crowd cheered their congratulations. Calichi again turned to look at Anani. This time, however, the shape of Tiburon loomed protectively over his daughter. The older man was looking intently at Anani's future husband. Calichi was so surprised that he could say nothing at all. Tiburon continued to stare at him, patiently observing the youth's discomfort and hesitation. Anani shifted her feet beside her tall father and gave what she hoped was a reassuring look to Calichi.

"We are blessed by the gods to have your family with us today, Tiburon," Calichi finally said, humbly and sincerely. Anani stared at the young man, amazed by the extraordinary beauty of his voice. Realizing that this was the first time she had ever heard Calichi speak, she was captivated by the smoothness, depth, and richness of his speech. His voice was as beckoning as warm, rhythmic music.

Tiburon looked pleased with Calichi's courteous words of greeting. "We are looking forward to watching the games and sharing the feast with your family, Calichi. Before we have feasted, we wish to present your parents with a gift that Anani has made."

Calichi looked at Anani with such open pleasure that her cheeks reddened and she looked away. Calichi's parents had already been told of his acceptance as Anani's suitor. The giving of the bowl would be an unexpected and gracious addition to the simple formality of accepting him before both families.

"My parents will be honored to receive any gift from Anani, Tiburon," Calichi declared.

Anani found herself staring at him, wanting him to keep talking so she could hear his incredible voice. How could her father seem unmoved by it? Why hadn't her mother told her that Calichi had been given such a bequest by the gods?

Tanama, Hura, and Guanina joined them, and an uncomfortable silence gathered around the small group. Hura looked with disapproval at Calichi, then at his older sister, then back at Calichi. With a slight pout on his face, Hura stepped directly between Anani and the young man. Tugging on Anani's hand and frowning at Calichi, Hura said, "Come Anani, we must hurry and get to the ball court." The rest of them raised their heads and saw that most of the crowd was already heading along the short stone roadway toward the ball and dance court.

"You are right, Hura," Tiburon said. "We must go to the court and wait for the cacique and his new wife."

When they reached the high grassy walls that encircled the court, the small group climbed its gentle slope and stood gazing down into the arena. Workers were at the far end of the large rectangular-shaped stone floor, busily sweeping it clean. Anani's family took their places not far from the center of the playing field. Duhos had been set up for the cacique and his family at the middle of the western wall, and all but the two grandest of these chairs were already filled by the cacique's other two wives, his children, and his siblings. Next to the cacique's family, the highest-ranking nobility took their places. Those of lesser rank sat gradually farther from the center of the court according to their status.

Calichi left them briefly in search of his own relations. When he returned, Tanama introduced Anani to Calichi's parents and his younger brother, who was about Guanina's age. Though Guanina and Calichi's brother were seated close together, they pretended not to notice each other, and let Hura do all the chattering. Anani and Calichi sat somewhat stiffly under Tiburon's watchful eye. Anani kept hoping that Calichi would speak to her, since she seemed unable to think of anything to say herself. She decided that Calichi must be waiting until Tiburon's attention was diverted by the games. She forced herself to focus on the court beneath them and tried to be patient.

The large crowd murmured with mounting excitement as the sweepers moved down the arena, leaving the stones behind them gleaming. The players were standing outside the arena waiting to be announced.

When at last the cacique and his new bride arrived with all due formality, everything was ready. One of the cacique's officers appeared on the court and raised his arms for silence. He bowed low to the cacique, then in a clear, carrying voice, he announced, "In honor of this holy and celebrated day, three games of batey will be presented. The first match will be a contest between brave women from our own great city." Cheers erupted from the masses and the officer was forced to pause.

When the voices fell again, he continued, "This game will be followed by two more competitions by our local male teams. May the gods and our ancestors bless the participants in today's games. May their performances bring honor to them and to us all!"

Amid wild cheering from the onlookers, twelve young women proudly entered each end of the arena. Each of the team members wore a loincloth and an ornately carved, semicircular wooden belt. This belt was adorned with an elbow-shaped stone in the front, which had been carved to represent the player's protective zemi. The women took up their positions, saluted the cacique, and poised themselves in readiness to receive the ball from the cacique.

The ball was made of bands of rubber, and was not to be touched by the hands or feet of the players. Instead, players used their arms, legs, hips, shoulders, and heads to keep the ball in the air and return it to the other side of the court. The ball was remarkably resilient and sometimes reached deadly speeds. Though well trained and skillful, players had been killed while attempting to deflect the ball with their heads, as well as in collisions against a wall. It was not uncommon for a bone to be broken during a game. The players expected to leave the arena with bruises and cuts, and hoped that their injuries would not be worse. But to be chosen to play was an incomparable honor, and each woman would give her utmost to win the match for her team.

The cacique stood tall and splendid, waited for the behique to bestow a blessing on the players, and threw the ball into the center of the arena. The team on the north end of the court sprang toward the ball, took possession, and propelled it back to the other side of the court. Both teams volleyed masterfully back and forth several times. Then one of the players from the team on the south side of the arena forcefully bounced the ball onto the other half of the court before the other team could successfully return it. A roar of congratulations rose from the audience, and the successful scorer bowed to the cacique. After this first score, the serve was relinquished to the other team, and the action began again.

As Anani had guessed, Calichi had been waiting until their families were interested in the ballgame, then he softly spoke Anani's name. She turned toward him, and watched as Calichi glanced at Tiburon, then slid nearer to her. He was very close now, but she did not turn her gaze from him.

He watched her intently, then looked down at his hands. "I want to say so much to you. It is hard to choose what to say first."

Anani just wanted him to keep talking. She needed to hear the soothing sound of his rich voice. "We have time," she said softly. "You can tell me anything you want."

These were her first words to him. "We have time." He heard them and silently rejoiced that it was so, that they had their whole lives to share, to tell each other everything in the years that were before them. Even more, she had said this as if she were pleased, as if she wanted it no other way.

He had worried, had even feared, that she might have accepted him only to please her family, and that he was not the one she would have chosen for herself. He had hoped that she would want him and that she could, someday, feel true affection for him.

Years before, he had listened to his mother talk about the lovely young daughter of her friend, Tanama. He had followed Anani whenever she would visit, and ask questions of those who knew her. When he was eleven years old and she was seven, he had decided that she was the one he wanted for his wife. Although he had tried not to let her see him, he had observed her many times as she grew. She had become a exceedingly desirable young woman.

Working with every ounce of talent he possessed, Calichi had made his gifts for her and her family, all the while praying that they would be good enough, that *he* would be good enough, to be accepted. And now she was here sitting next to him, and she seemed happy with the thought of joining him for life. Surprised that his own feelings could expand beyond what they already were, his heart was moved by her words. Perhaps he had been naive to think he knew her well. Thankfully, she seemed willing to teach him about herself.

Anani watched Calichi's face mirror his thoughts. When he realized that she was waiting for him to continue, he said, "Yes, Anani, we have time. I want to know everything about you, and I want you to know about me. It will take many talks to learn so much." He held her gaze and said, "I am so happy that we will be together, Anani. It is what I have wanted since I was a small child."

Such openness made Anani respond with candor of her own. "I was afraid to ask my parents who they had chosen for me. I was afraid it was someone other than you."

For the second time that day, Calichi was at a loss for words. He reached toward her hand and touched it gently with his much larger one.

Inconspicuously, Tiburon glanced at his daughter and Calichi, and saw the looks of joy on their young faces. He turned to his wife, who had not missed the expressions of the young couple. The two older people smiled briefly at one another; just long enough to convey their memories of when they were young, and their relief and gratitude that they had chosen wisely for their daughter.

Her parents were not the only ones who had noticed the interaction between Anani and Calichi. Hura's face grew cloudy and he marched over to his sister. Without a word, he plopped down into her lap and stared at the man who had been playing with her hand. Much to Hura's confusion, this action produced a burst of laughter from both of the families. His mother called him back to her side and, after he had reluctantly complied, held him in her own lap. From there, Hura kept peeking over Tanama's shoulder to observe Calichi's movements.

The women's ball game was followed by two more contests played by men's teams, but Anani had little interest in the action on the arena floor. She and Calichi talked quietly together as the afternoon waned. They were still absorbed in each other's words when Calichi's father laid his hand on his son's shoulder. Everyone else was standing, and motioning for them to follow toward the grassy area near the arena. The feast was already being spread out. Tanama and Anani left the others to fetch her bowl, her gift to Calichi's family.

The rest of their group found a wide place on the grass where Anani's uncle and his relations were waiting for them. When Tanama and Anani returned, Tiburon stood formally next to Tanama, and asked Calichi's mother and father to join them. Then, all of them turned their eyes toward Anani.

More calmly than she could have imagined, Anani stepped forward, unwrapped her bowl, and presented it to the people who would soon be her second set of parents. They both accepted Anani's offering with true appreciation. Praising the workmanship and delicate detailing of the bowl, they thanked her graciously. Tiburon made a sign for Calichi to join them, and took a step to the side of his wife. Since custom dictated that all things were inherited through the mother, it was Tanama who now moved forward and spoke to Calichi.

"We choose you, Calichi, to become the husband of our daughter, Anani. We believe that you will care for her with kindness. May the gods and our ancestors watch over both of you." At Tanama's glance, Anani approached Calichi until they stood not more than a foot apart, facing each other.

"Look into each other's eyes," Tanama told them gently. Anani let herself be drawn in by the depths of emotion shining in Calichi's black eyes. Her heart pounded and her skin tingled, and at that moment she knew how right Calichi was for her.

Looking directly at Calichi, Tanama spoke sincerely. "The eyes are the doors to the spirit. Learn to see each other's soul. From this day, nurture compassion and tenderness for one another. Build a strong devotion to each other so that when your wedding day comes, you will be ready to share your lives fully." When Tanama had finished speaking, Tiburon once again stepped forward, and said, "Calichi, today you may sit next to my daughter during the feast, and tonight you may dance at her side."

As the young couple released each other from their gaze and seated themselves, softly spoken wishes of congratulations, smiles, and warm laughter encircled them. Soon afterward, the cacique stood in the center of the large gathering and bid them to enjoy the feast with him and his family. Young and old gave their attention to the delicious food, but Calichi and Anani could not keep from looking at each other. Anani smiled to herself as she remembered her nervous fears of that morning, which seemed so long ago. She marveled at the change in her, how in so short a time she could become calm and reassured. While Calichi looked on, smiling, she silently repeated her mother's words. "The eyes are the doors to the spirit." Calichi's eyes revealed a spirit replete with appreciation, pleasure, and a good share of anticipation. His eyes and his voice were all that were needed to hold her thoroughly charmed, just as her beauty and tranquil grace held him. Neither of them did justice to the bountiful array of food being passed to them.

After everyone had eaten their fill and all were lying or sitting about, lazily enjoying the last light of the evening, the beating of drums filled the air. Deep and resonant, the cadence of the drums beckoned the people of Cubanacan back to the court. The sun was setting, and it was time to begin the dance ritual. With the coming of night, came the awareness that the spirits of the dead would soon awaken and walk the earth. The night was a magical, holy time when few dared to walk alone for fear of meeting the ghost of an ancient one. A spirit might appear in the form of a bat or an owl, or it might speak from within the sweeping branches of a tree. Regardless of the form it took or the nature of its demands, the wishes of a spirit must be carried out. To ignore their dictates was to ask for certain misery. Tonight the behique would be in the midst of his people, guarding them from the power of the dead. He would lead them through the dance as they gave homage to their gods and spirits, those with the capacity to grant benevolence or cause desolation. He would ask, on behalf of them all, for continuing mercy and protection.

Anani felt the magic in the evening air as the drums

grew louder with every step she took toward the court. It was to be the first time that she would be a participant in the dance rather than an observer. Only the adults of the noble class were called to join in and, as the small crowd entered the arena and formed a long line in front of the behique, Calichi proudly took his place beside Anani. She could no longer see their parents but knew that they were not far down the line from them.

Giving herself up to the sensations of the evening, Anani felt the coolness of the stones under her bare feet and the soft easterly breeze against her skin. Although he stood several inches from her, she imagined that she could feel the warmth coming from Calichi's body. Deep within her, Anani perceived that Calichi's heart was beating in unison with the low-pitched booming of the drums. Raising her head, Anani looked at the sky, knowing that the moon would soon rise and replace the fading light of the setting sun. An illusive aura seemed to hang above them all. "Yes," she thought, "there is magic in this night."

In a deep trance, the behique's eyes remained closed as he waited for his people to stand before him. As soon as all of them stood in their positions, the drums stopped suddenly, and silence fell around them like a web. At this signal, the behique slowly opened his eyes, and waited for his mind to rejoin his body. He lifted a flute-like instrument to his lips, and began to play. Not one of the dancers moved as he swayed from side to side playing his eerie music. The holy man and his flute called the souls of the special guardians of his people. These were the first of the spirits to be summoned so that they might protect the dancers from any destructive phantoms who might come among them as the ritual progressed.

Excitement rather than fear ran through the participants, as well as the watchers who sat along the high walls surrounding the court. Never had the behique's presence failed to take them safely through this ceremony. The dance ritual had always ended with reassurance that the gods were pleased with them, that all was well in their world. Their dance was a celebration of the rewards granted to them for following the decrees of the gods. They were a gentle, just people, and the gods had never abandoned them. What did they have to fear with their behique guarding and guiding them?

Tonight, however, it was the great behique himself who was afraid. He was gripped by a fear so overwhelming that it threatened to crush him, and his foreboding was growing ever more dominant. Before the wedding, as he had rested in his hammock trying to interpret his vision, he had gained certainty of its dark meaning. He had managed to perform the marriage ceremony, but his dread had evolved with each passing hour. In his weakened state, the large wooden mask that he usually wore during the dance rite had been too heavy for him to bear. Without explanation, he had asked his assistant to paint the design of the mask directly onto his face and body. Many of the dancers noticed this alteration, but their holy man was not one to be questioned. If their behique had changed an ancient custom, he had probably been directed to do so by the gods. But this was far from the truth. The behique was deeply shaken, and his body felt so feeble that he was using all of his vast mental energy to force himself to concentrate. He was barely able to produce enough wind to finish playing the ancient, mystical melody.

As his tune ended, the behique lifted his head, looked out at his good people, and hoped that he was wrong. Perhaps their gods would come to him now and reveal that his fears were unfounded. This thread of hope was enough to enable him to continue. His assistant accepted the flute from him, handed him a pair of carved maracas, and withdrew.

After taking a moment to gather his strength, the behique called out in as loud a voice as he could produce, "Our gods have been called. Sing and dance with me. Give them thanks for all they have bestowed on us."

The dancers took the hands of those next to them. They watched and listened for the behique to begin. Standing in front of the line of dancers, the behique hoarsely sang out the first words of his prayer as he took several shuffling steps forward. Echoing his exact words and movements, the dancers followed him as if they were one living thing rather than many. The behique continued his steps, sometimes forward, sometimes back, or to the side. He paused in his singing long enough for the dancers to repeat his chant, then he sang the next phrase of the song in a higher or lower pitch.

For the first time in his life the behique tried, and tried desperately, to interfere with what the gods might say to him. In this internal struggle, his mind sought to block the knowledge, the certainty, that he had correctly interpreted their earlier communication. Yet he fought to leave himself open just enough to receive a conflicting message from them. He prayed with every measure of his power and experience, begging for the protection of his people.

Slowly, in spite of his efforts to push it aside, an image began to shape itself in his mind. It was dark and menacing. The behique tried to focus on his song, to strengthen his steps. He refused to let his eyes close in an attempt to keep the perception away. But it would not be refused. His vision blurred as it captured the behique's mind and formed itself fully and clearly before him. It was a single spirit, monstrous in size and draped in a billowing red cloth. The spirit itself shone with a silver light as it came toward him, growing ever larger and larger until it darkened the entire sky. It hung above his trembling body for an endless moment, then looked down at him out of an eyeless skull. Raising its massive, bony arm, the apparition pointed directly at the behique. The horrible arms swung and circuitously waved itself over the entire crowd of dancers and watchers.

The behique recoiled and covered his face with his hands. With the last of his strength he shrieked, "No! Please! Nooo!" and he crumpled to the stones before the stunned dancers.

Tainos

13

Gonzalo, as tired as if he hadn't slept in a week, stood with a few of the other men at the ship's railing and watched the island. A dull light was just beginning to glow in the eastern sky when he jerked his head back to a movement near the trees, blinked, and squinted at the spot. He stared at the place with his breath held. Suddenly he jumped, turned sharply toward mid-ship, and shouted out, "Look ashore! There are men on the beach!"

Clambering over each other to get to the rails, boys and men of all three crews who had slept little themselves the night before, gawked at the shore.

Now and then, a young man showed himself for a moment, then quickly withdrew into the greenery.

"They wear no clothes at all!" someone said in astonishment.

"They have brown skin rather than black!" came another voice.

Pedro was pulling at Domingo's sleeve saying, "They are all naked, Domingo! Where are their clothes?" Domingo had managed to fall asleep just minutes before Gonzalo's yell, and he was still trying to awaken himself fully. He had seen nothing of the men onshore yet. Rubbing at his eyes, he ignored Pedro for the moment. He looked groggily ahead trying to bring the bushes and trees into focus. Minutes passed and Domingo was beginning to wonder if the others had really seen anything. Then, three finely built young men stepped from the forest and pointed back at him. Domingo's eyes flew wide open in surprise.

"Well," he said to Pedro with a look of pleased amazement, "It looks like we certainly *have* found people as well as land."

"But where are their clothes? They are supposed to be dressed in fine silk clothes." Pedro persisted.

"I don't know, Pedro," Domingo answered him at last. "Perhaps this land is still far from the Great Khan's city. Perhaps there are two different races in the Indies. We will have to wait until we've talked to these natives. I just hope Señor De Torres can speak their language."

"They certainly don't look very dangerous," Pedro observed with obvious disappointment. "They lack weapons as well as clothes."

"We will see," said Domingo, "But I hope you are right about the weapons. We came here to trade, not to fight."

Speculation ran through the ships like fire. Columbus, dressed in his most impressive clothing, stood near De La Cosa. Both men wore looks of concerned puzzlement, but they said little to each other. They all watched the islanders and waited until the sun was high enough to provide adequate light to judge the safety of anchoring nearer to shore. Within the hour, the captains had determined that this land was surrounded by a coral reef. They would have to look elsewhere for a safe port. Much to the disappointment of all, they were forced to raise the sails and head north.

As they sailed, Domingo could see that they were circling an island not much more than thirteen miles in length. They traveled five miles, which seemed interminably long to the impatient men, before they found a shallow bay where they could anchor.

Again, the men of the fleet vigilantly eyed the tree-lined shore. At first, the only visible forms of life were clans of screeching monkeys swinging among the higher tree branches. But, just as preparations were being made to bring the launches free of the decks, several islanders moved into the open and gestured toward the ships. Columbus called Luis de Torres to speak to the natives, but with the interpreter's first words the islanders melted back into the trees.

Columbus frowned slightly and said in a quiet voice to De

La Cosa, "These people are nothing like Marco Polo described them to be."

Looking thoughtfully back at him, De La Cosa said in a respectful tone, "We will learn more once we are ashore, Captain-general."

The small launches were lowered from the ships, and heavily armed men climbed into them. Much discussion during the previous night had determined which of the men were to be among the first to land. Columbus and De La Cosa, of course, De Arana, the master at arms, Rodrigo Sánchez, the controller, Rodrigo de Escobedo, the secretary, De Torres, the interpreter, and several men trained in firearms, Rodrigo De Jeres among them, boarded the Santa Maria's launch. Chachu was left in charge of the Santa Maria and he watched the rowboat pull away with the same longing look as his men. Domingo, Pedro, Gonzalo, and the others were only allowed to be silent observers to the landing.

The boats carrying the Pinzón brothers had already cleared their ships and were being rowed steadily toward the island. The men in the boats from the Niña and the Pinta waited just offshore to allow Columbus' launch to overtake them, and for the captain-general to be the first to step into the sandy shallows of the beach.

A step behind Columbus came the others, all of them keeping watch for sudden movements from the islanders. Columbus walked onto the beach, unfurled the banner of the sovereigns of Spain, and jabbed it into the sand. De Arana ordered the men to set up a defensive ring around the leaders as a precaution against attack. All but those who were standing guard knelt down and bowed their heads low. Columbus' voice broke with emotion as he prayed, "We humbly thank you, Lord, for delivering us to this land. We praise you for choosing to protect us from the perils of the sea. We ask that you continue to guide and protect us, oh Heavenly Father. May your name be praised now and forever, amen."

Standing and collecting himself, Columbus ordered the others to bear witness to, and Escobedo to write down, the words that he was about to say. In a voice loud enough for every man of the fleet to hear, he declared, "I take possession of this island in the name of Ferdinand and Isabella, king and queen of Spain. To this island I give the name San Salvador, in honor to our Blessed Lord."

Escobedo stood beside Columbus and officially announced, "By order of Isabella, Queen of Spain, I hereby proclaim the following. Christopher Columbus, by his discovery of this island of the Indies, has hereby earned the title of Admiral of the Ocean Seas. He has also earned the title of governor of this island and all other islands and continents to be discovered by him. What's more, Señor Columbus will, from this day forward, bear the title of Don, as will all of his descendants. On the queen's behalf, I offer my congratulations, Don Columbus."

When Escobedo finished, the other men gathered around their new admiral and offered him their own compliments, as well as their gratitude. Their talk faltered, however, when they noticed native men moving in their direction.

After first spotting the ships, the islanders had sent a runner to the neighboring village to find the cacique and the behique of the island, and they had studied the men from the sea intently. One of the first things that they noticed was that these people from the floating houses had brought their young sons with them, which a warrior would never do. Surely, since these strangers brought their children with them, they came with peaceful intentions.

When the seamen had boarded their small boats and rowed toward the beach, the inhabitants of the island could see that many of the visitors wore colored head-coverings, which had always indicated noble ancestry among their own people. But then, everything on the newcomers' bodies was very strange and their customs could only be guessed. Some of them wore shiny metal coverings on their upper bodies and heads. Strangely, all of the faces of the adults were covered with thick hair. All of them, that is, except the one who wore blue clothing that shone like a sun-lit sea, the one who was now doing all of the shouting. This one, with white hair on his head and no hair on his face, must be the leader of the strange group. The islanders guessed that what the foreigners were performing with their flags and yelling was some kind of religious ritual. These visitors must either be holy men from far away or spirits from the other world. The villagers were simple fishermen, but they knew what must be done to honor the spirits. The strangers had landed and performed their holy rites before their cacique or behique had arrived, but it was only right that they be welcomed without further delay. Several of the young men stepped bravely from the trees and presented themselves to the spirits. The islanders approached cautiously and paused, waiting respectfully to be instructed as to the wishes of their revered guests.

At the sight of the natives drawing near, the sailors standing guard pulled their swords and readied their firearms. De Arana and De La Cosa ordered them to hold their fire. Columbus faced the natives, smiled, and beckoned to them in a coaxing manner. He said to De Torres, "Speak to them Luis. We must find out where we are, and how far it is to the Great Khan." Hearing these words, several members of the crews also motioned for the islanders to come closer. The men with swords, including Columbus, held their weapons unsheathed and ready for any sign of aggression.

Domingo and Pedro watched spellbound from the ship. "Look at them all," breathed Domingo. "There must be forty of them."

"They have painted colors all over them!" said Pedro.

"Yes. Maybe they paint their bodies instead of wearing clothes," Domingo said with wide eyes. "It must mean something special to them, the way they wear the different colors and designs. See how some have just a small part of their bodies painted, like an eye or an arm, while others are almost totally colored?"

"There's red, and black, and white...and look, there is even blue on the face of that shorter man!" Pedro pointed as he exclaimed excitedly, forgetting his discomfort at their nakedness.

"They are a handsome people," admired Gonzalo. "Just look how well they are built, with long straight legs and no bellies. Not a single paunch among them. But then, these are all young men. I don't see anyone over the age of..."

"A girl! Look, there's a girl!" someone down the rail shouted wildly.

All of them did look, and there she was, a very young girl stepping from the shadows and coming to stand next to a man who must be her father. She wore no more clothing than the rest of them, and she approached the strangers within a step of her father. Her face revealed great wonder rather than fear.

As the islanders came cautiously up to the armed men, De Torres walked forward and addressed them cordially and slowly. Trying one after another, he spoke in every language known to the nations surrounding the Mediterranean Sea. He asked them repeatedly yet patiently about their location and about other inhabitants of the area. The Tainos, in their fluent and expressive language, welcomed them formally to their island and asked what the spirits required of them.

The only thing that De Torres was able to determine from this first exchange was that the natives called their island Guanahani. Finally accepting that none of their languages were being even slightly understood, the Europeans allowed the islanders to come close enough to inspect their clothing and their beards.

One of the Tainos was particularly curious about Columbus' sword, which the admiral held up for him to inspect. Admiring the shine of the polished metal, the Taino firmly grasped the blade and moved his hand along its edge. Before Columbus could react, the man quickly pulled his hand away and looked down at a deep cut that had opened up his entire palm. As blood ran freely from his wound, the man looked at the sword then at Columbus with deep reflection. Columbus sheathed his sword, silently cursing the accident and any possible repercussions. De La Cosa, De Torres, and several others came to the aid of the wounded

179

man, but he humbly refused their help. If treatment were deemed necessary by the behique, he would treat the wound when he arrived. But the fact that a spirit would carry such a weapon confused the Tainos greatly.

In an effort to restore a favorable perception of them among the Tainos, Columbus ordered one of his hands to bring out a chest that they had brought ashore. Opening its lid and pulling several articles from within, Columbus placed a red beret on the head of the wounded man and a long string of glass beads in his uninjured hand. Feeling that sanctified gifts had been bestowed on him, the native thanked the spirit abundantly. With this satisfactory reaction, each of the natives was given a modest gift in the form of a hawk's bell that was similar to those used by falconers in Spain, beads, or some other trinket. After receiving the presents of the visitors, the islanders sent some of their people to the village and brought back gifts of their own. With appropriate ceremony, the Europeans were given balls of cotton thread, short wooden spears, live parrots, and a strange dry leaf that the natives called tobacco and for which they seemed to have a high regard.

After several more attempts to communicate, Columbus and De La Cosa, the other captains, and about half of the first landing party returned to the ships. It was time to let some of the other hands walk on dry land for the first time in many long weeks. Seeing the boats heading back toward them, the hands on board the ships cheered and waited without the slightest sign of patience, each hoping to be among the next group to go ashore.

While the last men of the landing party were still climbing up the ship's ladder to come aboard, De La Cosa ordered Chachu to select the next bunch to go ashore. Before Chachu had even had a chance to approach Domingo, Francisco walked up to the youth, laid a hand on his shoulder and asked, "Have you forgotten, Domingo, that the men will still want something to eat today?" Crestfallen, Domingo could only stare back at Francisco. At that moment, he knew he would rather go ashore for an hour than eat for the next week. And he was sure the rest of the men felt the same. But Francisco continued as if he saw nothing unusual in Domingo's expression, "You know we will all be hungry as wolves in a little while. You'd better see what you can gather together while I go ashore and search out what food is available on this island." It took all of Domingo's willpower to hold his tongue.

Pedro had heard every one of Francisco's words. He took a step toward him and said with a serious voice, "Sir, I volunteer me and Domingo to go searching for food. It may be dangerous with all of those painted people ashore. I was wrong about them not being dangerous, sir, because I hadn't seen that they had spears. Did you see their spears, sir? Me and Domingo really ought to go first and make sure it's safe, sir."

How Pedro managed to give this speech with a straight face Domingo couldn't imagine. Unfortunately, Francisco was eyeing Pedro suspiciously. He looked as if he had just about decided to let loose a string of curses to reprimand the boy for being so insubordinate. It was just then that Chachu came upon the three of them and guessed fairly closely what had been going on.

"Francisco," said Chachu. Thinking he was going to be ordered ashore, Francisco puffed out his chest and looked at the cabin boys triumphantly. "Francisco," Chachu repeated, "the men deserve a celebration meal today, and you are the only one with the skill to see that it is done properly. Domingo here doesn't have the experience to prepare a truly special feast." Francisco was sputtering and trying to interrupt but Chachu continued as if he couldn't hear a word the cook was saying. "Yes, I've decided to take these two young men on the next boat. I'll stand guard while they search inland for food we can add to your feast." Domingo and Pedro let out a chorus of excited yips as they scrambled for the launch, without a backward glance at Francisco's red face.

When their boat reached land, Domingo and Pedro jumped out and reveled in the feel of the sand between their toes. *Land*, the word echoed in Domingo's mind, and he reached down and scooped up a handful of sand. Somehow, it was more real now that he could feel it with his own body. On impulse, he picked up Pedro, spun him in the air, and tossed him into the shallow water. Pedro came up sputtering but grinning, and began a rather one-sided splashing war with his larger friend.

The islanders watched the playfulness of the boy and the young man from a short distance up the beach. Before the youths were aware that they were being observed, they were surrounded by many of the Tainos. The island men seemed greatly interested in Pedro. Domingo with his mature build and unshaven beard looked much like the other adult spirits, but Pedro was obviously a child. At first, Pedro withdrew uneasily from the Tainos' outstretched arms. Domingo stayed close beside him, as fascinated with the brown men as they were with Pedro. The Tainos were gentle and inquisitive, and they seemed to think he was something extraordinary. Eventually, Pedro lost much of his apprehension and allowed the natives to touch him. Before much longer, Pedro found himself enjoying all of their kind attentions. Chachu stood defensively nearby, closely watching out for the safety of his younger charges.

When the curiosity and homage of the natives was finally satisfied, Pedro and Domingo were allowed to accompany Chachu and several others as they wandered a short distance inland in search of food and water.

For the remainder of the day, men of the fleet visited the island in small groups. Most were allowed to venture no further inland than the shadow of the trees. Only those seamen searching for edibles under the direct supervision of Chachu had authorization to leave the beach. Still, for today at least, just being able to walk on the beach, to smell the flowers, taste the fresh fruit, and swim in the shallow surf, was enough to satisfy many of the men.

The Taino leaders arrived and met the strangers for themselves. Though little could be understood by the use of words, the mildness of the attempted interactions served to reduce the islanders' uneasiness and enhance their curiosity about the visitors. Some of the island men even grew comfortable enough to venture out to the tall ships. They swam or paddled out in well made canoes, some of which were large enough to carry forty men. Once they reached the ships, they carried on a lively trade of their goods for the sailor's novelties. With the exception of a few very young girls, the women were kept out of the sight of the invaders.

The next day, a cross was erected on the beach, and prayers of thanks were said. Columbus directed that such a ceremony would be conducted before the fleet departed from each of the lands that were found. Later, the bartering continued, as well as attempts to gather information.

When the island's cacique and some of his men came to the Santa Maria in a canoe, Columbus noticed that several of them wore small pieces of gold in their pierced noses. Questioning them, Columbus and De Torres gathered that there was a land to the south where a great king lived who possessed great stores of gold.

"At last," the admiral declared with satisfaction, "The Great Khan. We now have the direction in which to set our course." It was decided that on the following morning they would set sail toward the south.

At daybreak, Domingo was down in the hold sorting through some of the exotic island fruit that the men had dubbed "pineapples" when he heard voices on deck above him. Climbing the steps until his head was just a few inches above the deck, Domingo saw De La Cosa standing with his back to him, his legs spread apart and his hands on his hips. From his posture, Domingo guessed that the ship's master was not pleased.

"*Whose* orders?" De La Cosa asked, questioning Bartolome García, the boatswain from Domingo's shift. García and several hands had just boarded the ship with three Taino men and had placed them under guard against the railing.

The boatswain answered formally, "The admiral's orders, sir."

De La Cosa frowned up at the half-deck where Columbus was just starting to descend the stairs.

Domingo, who had not been noticed by the officers, lowered himself back down the steps and crouched where he could hear every word without being seen.

Columbus approached the two men, ordered the boatswain to see to the comfort of the "Indians", and came closer to De La Cosa. "We discussed this, Juan. You agreed that it would be useful to take a few of these people to Spain and teach them our language. They will be very serviceable as interpreters when we return to the Indies."

"What we discussed, admiral, was some of these people coming with us *willingly*."

Columbus held his voice to an even tone. "It's plain to see that these men think we are gods. They think it a great honor to be coming with us. We've taken only these three, as well as two aboard the Pinta, and one on the Niña. All of them can return to their island, unless the queen wishes it otherwise."

"You tried to get them to come with us yesterday and they all refused, sir," De La Cosa pointed out. "Did these men come of their own free will?"

"We need these men *now*. We don't have time to explain everything to them in a way they'll understand. They can direct us to the great cities of the Indies. They must know where they are. Without that knowledge we could sail around for months and find nothing but poor savages."

De La Cosa perused the faces of the captives. He had to admit that they did not seem alarmed or even terribly afraid. Still, he was not comfortable with taking them. "It won't take long for them to realize we are only men. Right now, they probably believe we are taking them to some kind of heaven, with how little they understand of our language. They may even think we intend to bring them back tomorrow. Besides," he added practically, "if we take these few and something happens so that they never return, how will these islanders react next time our ships approach this harbor?"

"Juan," Columbus said, "you can see for yourself how meek these people are. They would be no threat to one of our ships. The entire population of this island could be overtaken with a handful of our men." Seeing that De La Cosa was still hesitant, Columbus went on.

"Don't forget what these natives will gain if they return with us to Spain. If the queen chooses, and I believe she will, they will be baptized. They will be given a chance to attain eternal salvation. There is no greater reward."

Then, with finality, Columbus concluded, "We are to get underway immediately. Our men must see that the launch is secured behind the ship, then weigh anchor."

Domingo heard the footsteps of both men recede. After waiting a few moments longer, he climbed the steps carrying a heavy canvas bag over his shoulder. He saw the three Tainos and De Torres sitting near the port side of the foredeck. De Torres was using words and hand signals in an effort to explain something. Three armed men stood around the captives. The deck hands were trying to avoid direct contact as they worked the ship's lines around the group of islanders.

When the ship began to move the Tainos looked uneasily at each other and one of them started to stand. The guards stepped closer and motioned firmly to the captives, telling them to stay where they were, but their swords remained sheathed. De Torres smiled at the Tainos reassuringly, nodding at each of them, and repeated soothingly that everything was fine.

The sails were fully unfurled as the ships angled to catch the wind. With the forward surge of the Santa Maria, Domingo could see that the Tainos were even more amazed and disconcerted. As the Indians eyed the guards and listened to the reassurances of De Torres, their expressions evolved from fear to speculation and, at last, to stoic resignation.

Watching them, Domingo could only guess how these island men were analyzing and accepting what was happening to them. He wondered what he would have done if he were in their position, then he turned his glance away from them. Trying to concentrate on his immediate chores, Domingo could feel his admiration for the admiral grow clouded with confusion.

Shortly after getting underway, Francisco, who seemed reluctant to have anything to do with the newcomers, ordered Domingo to take the prisoners something to eat. Domingo thought over his options from the ship's rations and decided that the Tainos would prefer food that was familiar to them. He was cutting up a pineapple when Pedro came up behind him.

"We've taken those natives," he said in a troubled voice.

"Yes," Domingo acknowledged.

"Do you think they wanted to come with us, Domingo?"

Domingo looked at the Tainos then at Pedro. "I don't think so Pedro. We don't have any way of knowing what they believe. They must be trying to understand who we are and where we came from, but mostly what we want with them."

"Will we let them go?"

"I heard the admiral say we will take them to Spain, teach them our language, and bring them back as interpreters," Domingo said. Pedro eyed the Indians for a moment.

"But what of their families, Domingo? These men will be gone from them for months at least."

"I know, but there is nothing we can do." Pedro looked at him disappointedly and was about to say something when Domingo spoke up. "You'd better get back to work, Pedro. Francisco is glaring at you from the fore deck." Pedro glanced in that direction from the corner of his eye, saw the cook glowering in his direction, and headed toward the hatchway.

Not meeting their eyes at first, Domingo placed a wooden platter of the fruit in front of the Tainos and sat nearby, waiting for them to eat. Seeing them so closely, Domingo noticed for the first time that the Tainos' foreheads were unusually broad and slanted back from their brows. He rightly guessed that their impressive lengths of black hair had never been cut, with the exception of the portion that fell down their foreheads. Other than the cropped bangs, their thick hair hung past their waists. The hair on the top of their heads and their eyebrows was the only hair on their

186

entire bodies. Unlike Domingo and the rest of the crew, they were totally comfortable with their nakedness.

The Tainos looked back at Domingo in a studying manner not unlike his own, and Domingo wished that he knew what was in their minds. He wanted very much to speak to them, but realized he would then have to explain their situation. Such an explanation would not be easy. Their facial expressions acknowledged Domingo's offering of food. They showed no trace of malice toward him because of their confinement. But they did not eat the fruit.

Francisco managed to gather together three pairs of worn breeches, handed the clothes to Domingo, and said, "See that they put these on." Domingo wrinkled his nose at the powerful smell that arose from the bundle and looked down at what were little more than filthy remnants. The men had discarded these clothes as irreparable and Francisco had been meaning to rip them up and use them as swabbing rags.

"I'll just rinse them off first," Domingo said. "These are foul smelling, and undoubtedly infested with lice, sir."

Francisco responded to this with a snort, "These heathens don't need to wear anything better than the lot of us. Get them dressed. *Now.*"

Domingo scowled at Francisco's back as the cook turned and left. Crouching down near the group of captives, Domingo, somewhat hesitantly, indicated with hand motions that they were to put on the stinking breeches. When they understood what he was demanding, they looked at each other then at Domingo with barely restrained repugnance. De Torres repeated Domingo's instructions more convincingly to the Indians. With great reluctance and obvious distaste, the men accepted the breeches and pulled them on. Without understanding a word of their language, it was easy enough to see how unnatural the Tainos thought it was to wear the tattered clothes.

Domingo couldn't keep from wondering what it would feel like to live in a place that was always warm and to spend your days wearing nothing at all. He imagined the feel of the sun and the wind on his skin all of the time, rather than just during a quick swim. He wondered if a person would end up with fewer lice than he had been forced to endure during his sailing life. And he felt even worse about forcing the fetid rags onto the Tainos.

As the fleet circled the island, natives on the beach ran along with them, shouting and making signs, beseeching them to come ashore. They gestured that they would give the strangers food and water if they landed. Domingo wondered if they were begging for their young men to be returned to them. Columbus came to the rail, waved at the islanders, and muttered to those near him, "They are giving thanks to their gods for favoring them with our visit." Hearing these words, De La Cosa moved away from the rail and busied himself under the half-deck.

Surprising everyone aboard, an old Taino swam out to the ships and climbed into the launch that was trailing behind the Santa Maria. Before long, they brought the elderly man aboard the flagship too, adding him to their group of captive guides. The other Indians seemed to know him well but it was unclear to Domingo what relationship he might have with any of them.

After trying again to question the Tainos, Columbus ordered Domingo to see that they were fed adequately. He was told pointedly by the admiral that the Indians must be kept healthy. Domingo couldn't keep the guilty look from his face whenever he neared the quiet group of men and saw the questions in their eyes. But he was exceedingly curious about them, and he visited them more often than was necessary.

De Torres noticed Domingo's fascination with the natives and often asked him to sit with the Indians whenever the interpreter needed time to himself. Even after the incident with the breeches, it wasn't long before the Tainos began to accept Domingo's care. They seemed to sense his genuine interest in them, and his willingness to see to their needs. But what also influenced them to accept Domingo was his singing.

The day after they had left San Salvador, Domingo was absorbed in the job of scrubbing out his cook pot, hardly aware that he was singing to himself, when he glanced up and saw that all of the Tainos were watching him and listening to him closely. They motioned for him to come to them and, when he was near at hand, indicated that they wanted him to sing again. Gonzalo was standing not far away at the time, and he grinned broadly at Domingo. "Go on, go on, sing to them," he said. A little embarrassed, Domingo squatted down, thought for a moment, and began to sing a song about a ship sailing the ocean in search of whales. He started softly but, seeing the encouragement on the faces of the Tainos, gradually raised his voice to its fullest level. He sang the rich melody with heart and depth. When he had finished, the Indians gestured with enthusiasm, asking what the sound coming from Domingo's mouth was called in his language. After Domingo told them, they repeated the word "song" several times so that they would remember it.

And remember it they did, many times a day. Columbus, noticing that the music seemed to please the Tainos, encouraged Domingo to keep singing to them. So, Domingo's duties expanded to include serenading the Indians onboard the Santa Maria. He took the teasing from the other seamen in stride, and admitted only to Pedro that he actually enjoyed singing to the islanders.

All through the hours of their second day of captivity, Domingo could see that the Tainos were learning as much about the men of the fleet as the other way around. The Indians spoke softly to themselves when they did not want to be overheard. And, although much of what the Europeans did and said was incomprehensible to them, they soon seemed to lose their belief that there was anything supernatural about the seamen. Domingo noticed that the awe had left their eyes as they watched the men move about the ship.

During the middle of that night, the clamor of yelling and cursing, and the sound of running feet wakened Domingo. "An Indian is escaping! He's rowing away!" someone bellowed. Stumbling to his feet, Domingo joined in the general confusion. He managed to gather that a dugout had pulled along the side of the Santa Maria and one of the captives had leaped into it. By the time the alarm had been sounded, the rowers in the canoe were pulling swiftly away. The sailors were clumsily trying to lower the launch in the dark but Domingo could see that by the time it was in the water the Taino craft would be out of reach. Columbus furiously ordered that the guard on the remaining captives be doubled.

Shortly afterward, the admiral paced the quarterdeck and spoke with agitation to his officers. "That Indian will undoubtedly tell the other natives about being captured, and everything else about us. As you know, we need the help of these islanders if we're going to find China and the Khan. And help will be harder to find if the islanders know too much about us. Another escape *must not* be tolerated." He pondered for a moment, then went on. "The use of chains would eliminate the risk of losing another captive. But if we use them the Indians may either refuse to guide us, or guide us to some disaster." To De La Cosa and De Torres he said, "See that the guards are more watchful, at *all* hours. And give the captives more gifts. See that they understand we mean them no harm."

Somewhat suspicious of the captives now, Columbus still chose to follow the directions of the remaining Tainos. According to the Indians, there was an island close by where people wore arm and ankle bands made of gold. The following day the fleet landed on this supposedly rich island, but it took only two hours to realize that there was no sign of gold here. There was, therefore, no reason to remain any longer.

As the ships' anchors were being raised, a canoe smoothly approached the Niña. Before anyone could stop him, the Taino captive that had been aboard jumped into the dugout and grabbed a paddle. The man dug powerfully into the water, straining with the other Taino paddlers in a desperate effort to escape the large ships.

Columbus roared at the Niña's crew, "Catch him, men! Bring him back here!" The sailors of the Niña leaped toward the launch and had it in the water within minutes. The rowers boarded, braced their feet, and hauled away in fast pursuit of the dugout. They chased and hunted the canoe the rest of the day, but with no success. Spotting it again the next morning, they tried to overtake it, but failed once more. Eventually, they found the empty dugout abandoned on the beach.

While the remaining crewmen awaited the outcome of the search for the escapee, Domingo and several others noticed an islander paddling close to the Niña. The Taino slowed his dugout, held up a huge ball of cotton, and indicated that he wanted to make a trade. Columbus saw this man too, and ordered that the native be delivered to him once. When the Taino refused to come willingly, several of the Niña's sailors leaped into the water and grabbed him.

De La Cosa, seeing what was happening, neared Columbus and said, "Admiral, we are risking a great deal if we alienate these people. Why capture one of them in so rough a manner? He will not cooperate with us."

"Don't worry, Juan. I do not mean to harm him. Watch and you will learn my intentions," Columbus answered evenly.

The frightened man was brought aboard the flagship and presented to Columbus. Much to everyone's surprise, the admiral received the Taino in grand fashion and welcomed him warmly. The bewildered guest was presented with a red beret, a string beads, and hawks bells. Columbus graciously refused to take the ball of cotton offered in exchange for the gifts he had just bestowed. The seamen gently returned the man to his canoe with many kind words and watched attentively as he paddled back to shore.

No sooner had he reached the sand than his fellow islanders surrounded him and began asking questions. From the islander's excited expressions and gestures, as well as the reactions of his listeners, it was clear that the Europeans were being described quite favorably.

Columbus turned to De La Cosa with a look of satisfaction and said merely, "You see how simple these people are? Any damage that might have been done by the ones who have escaped has, hopefully, been repaired." De La Cosa bowed but did not respond.

Columbus and De Torres questioned the captives from San Salvador more carefully as they began, little by little, to understand each other better. They were made to understand that vast amounts of gold could be found on an island further west. Believing that where he found gold, he would find a direct trail to the Khan, Columbus chose to follow this path. The fleet spent the next week exploring two islands, which Columbus named Fernandina and Isabella, but gold was as scarce on these islands as it had been on San Salvador. It was on Fernandina, however, that Domingo made a discovery of a different kind. Here he saw a Taino woman for the first time.

The natives of Fernandina had come to the ships to trade shortly after their arrival and had encouraged the Europeans to come ashore. Domingo and Rodrigo had been included among a landing party led by Columbus. The group of explorers was directed to a village by a number of Taino men. While the sailors stood in the center of the village, women and children began to show themselves. They cautiously encircled the strange visitors.

Domingo could not help staring at the women. The young girls wore nothing at all, and the women wore only a cotton loincloth. He had never seen a woman's body before. Their breasts, which immediately caught Domingo's attention, were well shaped, and small, except for those of the women who were nursing infants. Their dark tan legs were long and smooth. Domingo felt his face redden as he caught Rodrigo smiling at him, and forced himself to end his breast and leg scrutiny. This only made Rodrigo laugh out loud.

"They don't seem to mind our looking, Domingo. We may as well enjoy it while we have the chance."

Domingo followed this advice and took full advantage of this unusual opportunity to study the female form. He tried to be a little more subtle while observing them than he had before. He noticed a young mother carrying a baby with its head bound to two flat pieces of wood. Puzzled by this, he looked around and saw another baby wrapped in a similar fashion. Domingo wondered if this custom explained why these people all had slanted and broadened foreheads. Perhaps they viewed this trait as desirable. Other than their foreheads, which Domingo found too foreign a feature, the faces of the Tainos were very attractive. Their teeth were white and straight and their eyes were large and appealing. And their bodies were beautiful.

Before Domingo had spent nearly enough time with the natives surrounding him, Columbus was ordering them to move further into the island's interior to search for more villages, and any signs of gold. As the sailors left the village, Domingo was suddenly struck by the image of Carmen watching him. He tried to push this uncomfortable notion aside, and he fell in line with the others. They trudged along heading deeper into the forest. Domingo kept his eyes focused straight ahead.

As De Torres worked each day to understand the Tainos aboard the flagship better, he often called Domingo to join him. The Indians acted more at ease with Domingo and Pedro than anyone else on the ship, and Domingo's presence seemed to reassure them. It wasn't long before De Torres noticed that Domingo was picking up their language faster than he was himself, which surprised him. The interpreter had always learned the speech of others with speed and relative ease. Pulling Domingo aside one afternoon, De Torres asked him about this. Domingo thought it over, then explained as well as he could.

"Well, sir, it's curious, but their language is...built more like Basque than like Spanish. Rather than adding more words to change a thought or describe a thing, the words themselves must be added to more often."

De Torres furrowed his brows, trying to understand, so Domingo made another attempt.

"It was difficult for me to learn Spanish, sir, because there were so many words to learn. In Basque, it is much simpler because there are fewer words. We change the Basque words slightly, adding sounds to the beginning or the end of the word to change its meaning. It is similar in the Taino tongue, this subtle changing of a few words."

De Torres thought he was beginning to comprehend. After considering this further, he realized that by using Domingo's explanation he was able to grasp the meanings to some of the Taino words that had eluded him. De Torres had never learned to speak Basque, so knew nothing of the workings of the language. But it struck him as extraordinary that the Basque tongue would have anything in common with the speech of this distant people. With the passing of the days, De Torres encouraged Domingo to join them each time they sat down to their language lessons.

Everywhere the ships were anchored along the coastlines the generous inhabitants were questioned. The Tainos never failed to give them assistance, even carrying great casks of water and food out to the ships for them. Eventually, the islanders of Isabella told the strangers what they had already heard from other Indians. There was a much larger island to the south, called Cuba, where there were great treasuries of gold owned by a powerful king. Not only this, but along Cuba's coastline great ships had been seen that were sailed by skilled navigators.

Hearing of the great ships, Domingo wondered, as he had many times, where his brothers were and whether they were safe. The image of the broken mast he had seen in the sea had not left him. Could these great ships be any of his father's ships?

Columbus interpreted the news of the ships to mean only one thing. He told his men that this Cuba was the island of Japan, and the ships undoubtedly belonged to the Great Khan himself. He told them that, at long last, they were getting close to their goal, and he ordered the ships pointed toward Cuba.

The admiral's excitement spread quickly to his crew, and Domingo was not immune to its effects. He slept little as they sailed ever closer to the island, and he had a feeling that its shores would truly hold treasures beyond his imagination.

Hura and his young friend, Aji, were standing in the knee-deep water of a small pool just off the beach. The two boys held miniature spears at the ready as they stared into the water and waited. They had been happily occupied by their less than successful attempts at fishing for over an hour when something far out to sea caught Hura's attention and he turned his gaze in that direction. Startled at what he saw, Hura motioned to his friend to turn and look. The children lowered their spears and stood gazing as three distinct white spots out on the ocean grew larger and larger as they neared the shore. Eventually, Hura and Aji could just make out the hulls of the ships and the red crosses on the billowing sails.

Fearful now, Hura said, "Come. We must tell our parents."

"But what are they? Great canoes of some kind?" Aji asked in bewilderment.

"Come!" repeated Hura, backing away. When his friend joined him, both boys broke into a run and disappeared into the trees. Neither of them looked back or slowed his pace. As they breathlessly neared the village, Aji ran toward the south, shouting in the direction of his house for his mother and father. Hura didn't slow his pace until he had reached his own home in the center of the community.

"Mother! Father!" he yelled as loudly as he could. "Mother!"

Hura burst through his doorway and almost collided with Anani, who was hurrying out to see what Hura was shouting about.

"Mother and Father are at the pool, Hura," she said placing her hands on his shoulders and trying to calm him. "What is it?"

"There are some magical canoes coming to our beach! They're coming closer and closer. I saw them!"

"Magical canoes? Hura, what exactly did you see?"

"I saw three of them. They are as big as our house only taller, and they had clouds hanging above them. Anani, we must go get Father! The canoes will be here very soon!"

"Were they Carib canoes, Hura?" Anani asked, trying to keep the fear from her voice.

"No. No. They are much larger and have clouds over them. Oh, Anani, you don't understand. You didn't see them!"

"Can you show me where you saw these ships, Hura?" Anani asked.

"No, Anani! We must bring Father home!"

Anani could see how shaken Hura was, and she gathered her little brother into her arms for a moment. Hura, small as he was, was usually so fearless, always trying to imitate their father's character. It was not like him to react like this. He pulled away from her with questioning eyes.

"Yes, Hura, we will go get Father," she said.

Anani took his hand and they stepped outside. She spotted Guanina ambling slowly toward them with a basket of corn braced against her hip. Anani called out to her sister and motioned for her to quicken her pace. One look at her siblings' faces told Guanina that something was wrong.

Before she had a chance to speak Anani said, "Guanina, take Hura and go find Mother and Father at the pool. Tell them that they are needed at home." When Guanina started to ask why, Anani stopped her again, "Hura will tell you about it on your way. You must hurry." The tone of her older sister's words made Guanina nod once, and move with Hura rapidly down the path in the direction of the pool. Anani stood deep in anxious thought, trying to control her apprehension as she watched them leave. Once they were out of sight she turned and, progressively quickening her pace, headed down a side path toward the beach.

Lowering her body and moving quietly through the underbrush as the trees thinned, Anani could now see the ocean ahead of her. She couldn't see any magical canoes but she still moved very carefully behind the cover of branches and leaves. Slowing her movements as she eased forward, Anani suddenly froze in mid step and stared at the picture before her. Three huge, inconceivable crafts lay just off shore. For a moment, she could only gape at what she saw. Her mind raced in search of an explanation but found none.

Ever so slowly she lowered herself to the ground and crawled deep within a thicket of tall shrubs.

Anani lay hidden in the bushes, watching with her mouth open and her eyes wide as the man-like creatures moved around inside the amazing vessels. Who were they? What did they want here? Apprehension gripped her anew when she saw them lower small canoes from the larger ones and begin rowing toward the beach. They were heading directly toward her. They would reach the shore not far from where she hid. Her eyes never left the little boat in the lead. When the first of the launches landed, Anani could clearly see that a Taino was with the mysterious men. This puzzled her greatly. Why would one of her own people be with such men?

At least she guessed that the others were men, rather than some other kind of creature. They were terribly fierce looking with that thick hair hanging from their faces, and bulky clothing covering their entire bodies. Some of them even had a silver covering like a turtle's shell over their chests. Many had light or dark brown hair rather than black.

Barely breathing, she watched the hairy men walk up and down the beach in front of her, then come together as a group around the only one of them with a clean face. This one had white hair hanging to his shoulders and a grave expression on his face. Anani supposed that this man must be the leader since he shouted something in a strange language and all of them began moving into the trees. They were going in the direction of her village! With her heart beating violently, she moved swiftly but with great stealth from her hiding place, and she sprang up the side path. She must warn her people.

She had almost reached the village clearing when she noticed that many people were already running into the deeper forest on the far side of their community. She must not have been the only one from her village who had been watching the strangers. Hurrying toward her own house, she saw her father waiting in front of it and scanning the area with a worried expression.

"Anani," he said with great relief at her arrival. "Quickly, daughter. They will soon be here." He turned in the direction of the trees and motioned her in front of him. Anani paused only to ask about the rest of their family but Tiburon nudged her forward. "Your mother, sister, and brother, as well as our zemis, are already safely hidden," he told her as they hurried toward the cover of the dense forest. Just behind the last of their fleeing neighbors, Anani and Tiburon reached the first of the trees, and faded into the shadows and the deep green foliage.

Encounters

14

Shouts from the seamen as they scrambled to lower the sails and anchors disturbed the quiet of the wide, blue river. Domingo tied down his line, turned, and took in the beauty of the island that the Indians called Cuba. The scene was enough to impress him so deeply that he often recalled its images long afterward. From the ship, he could see a vast variety of tall waving trees. Birds sang out strange melodies from the heights of the branches, their brilliantly colored feathers reflecting the rays of the sun when they moved. The bushes bloomed with flowers of unimagined colors, sizes, and shapes. The weather was ideal for exploring the fantastic land before him.

Domingo had resigned himself to the inevitability of having to wait until later in the day before he would be allowed to go ashore when he overheard De Torres asking Columbus to allow him to be among the men in the first boat to land. Columbus listened to De Torres' explanation of how Domingo had learned much of the language and ways of the Tainos over the past two weeks. The admiral briskly nodded his approval and went on to more pressing matters. Domingo, almost dancing with excitement, helped lower the launch as quickly as possible.

By the time Domingo and the others reached the village, it was totally abandoned. Columbus gave strict orders that nothing belonging to these people was to be disturbed.

"It is imperative that I be taken to the king of Japan," the admiral reminded them ominously. "We must be looked upon as friendly visitors, not as any kind of threat."

With this clearly understood, Columbus allowed them to search the houses for signs of gold, pearls or any other goods that might have been obtained in trade from the city of the Khan.

Domingo, De Torres, and a Taino, who had been given the name of Palo by the sailors, entered one of the larger houses and stood admiring its interior.

"They are a clean people," De Torres said appreciatively. He walked to one of the walls and, after sifting through and uncovering various articles, picked up a small statue of a woman carved from stone. He called for Palo and showed him the statue.

"Earth Mother. Holy god woman. Zemi," Palo tried to explain in the language De Torres spent hours each day teaching him.

Domingo inspected one of the hammocks, marveling at its design. "Is this some kind of bed, Palo?" he asked, also in Spanish.

Palo shook his head at the new word, "Bed?"

"A place to sleep," explained Domingo closing his eyes and tilting his head in a pantomime of slumber. "A bed."

Now Palo said, "Bed, yes, called hammock. Hammock high up so no crabs reach."

Domingo carefully lowered himself onto the hammock and stretched out unsteadily into the netting. "This is wonderful, Señor De Torres! You must come lie in one." De Torres smiled at him indulgently, but shook his head and began analyzing the carved images on the back of a low-legged chair.

Climbing free of the net bed and slowly circling the walls, Domingo pointed up at a huge wooden mask. The carving of the mask had been masterfully done, its features superbly defined. What appeared to be ivory had been set into the wood to form the eyes and teeth. "What is this, Palo?" Domingo asked with admiration.

"Zemi of...grandfather." Palo pointed to the mask's eyes and teeth. "Bones from grandfather. Great holy in mask zemi." Domingo looked incredulously at De Torres. De Torres stared at the mask then at Palo. De Torres asked carefully, "The bones in this mask are from an ancestor, a grandfather of one of the natives?"

"Ancestor, yes. Much holy," Palo said with finality.

Domingo stared at the mask for a moment longer, then moved uneasily away and joined De Torres as he continued to study the chair.

When they concluded their search, Domingo's group joined the others. Although many fascinating items had been discovered, none of the landing party had found anything in the way of pearls, gold, or any other treasure. The officers were quiet as they returned to the ships. It was painfully clear that they had not reached Japan.

Knowing that information from the Cuban Tainos was essential, and realizing that the natives would continue to flee from the Europeans, De La Cosa suggested sending Palo back to shore by himself to speak to the villagers. Columbus agreed to this plan and allowed Palo to be rowed near to the beach. Once they were close in, Palo dove from the launch and swam toward shore. The rowers returned to the Santa Maria at once. Palo reached the beach easily, and waited alone on the sand until two native men approached him cautiously. A few brief words were exchanged, and Palo was led inland, away from the vigilant eyes of the seamen.

When Pedro could no longer see Palo, he asked Domingo, "Do you think we'll see Palo again? Do you think he will want to stay with these Indians or come back to us?"

Domingo wondered why Palo would want to come back to join the ships, but he did not voice his thoughts. Instead, he said, "All we can do is wait and see what he'll do, Pedro."

Palo was taken to the house of Anani's uncle, and questioned thoroughly by Tiburon and the other leaders of the village. Over an hour later, Palo returned to the beach and shouted to the sailors that all was well, that the islanders were coming out to meet the fleet.

After Palo had left the village, the rulers had decided that they must learn more about the strangers before the meaning of their arrival could be determined. These visitors did not appear to intend them harm. Rather than attacking the Tainos, the men from the sea had sent a spokesman to say that they came with peaceful intentions, that they wished to give them gifts. Still, caution was needed. After choosing a group of men to keep guard over the women and children still hidden in the forest, Tiburon joined those bound for the canoes.

As the watchers aboard the ships waited hopefully, sixteen canoes were pushed away from the shore and paddled out to them. Palo was in the first canoe to reach the Santa Maria, and he came aboard as a successful ambassador. Tiburon and the others were welcomed, and gifts were generously bestowed upon them.

The workings of the flagship interested Tiburon greatly, especially the sails and the tiller. Palo, knowing Tiburon to be an important man, accompanied him on a tour of the different decks. When the two Tainos climbed to the half-deck, they approached Domingo and Pedro, who had been watching the Indians intently. Palo pointed to Pedro and spoke seriously in his own language, "This boy works very hard, harder than some men." Indicating Domingo, Palo said to Tiburon, "This one sings like a night bird. He sings of a land far away. I believe he may be a young behique, although he knows little magic yet."

Domingo understood most of these words but wondered what a behique was, and what magic he was supposed to know. Pedro whispered, "What did he say?" several times before Domingo had a chance to explain. Tiburon studied the two thoughtfully, then directed his attention back to the Santa Maria.

Tiburon was allowed little more time to investigate the ship before he and three other Tainos were brought to Columbus. They were asked many questions, primarily about the location of gold and a man called the Great Khan. One of the Tainos sitting with Tiburon guessed that the Great Khan the strangers sought must be the cacique of Cubanacan. The man began to explain about the cacique to Columbus, but Tiburon silenced him with an intense glare. This speechless exchange did not escape Columbus, however, and the admiral dismissed the group soon afterward. Different groups of natives were then questioned, and Columbus learned that the location of the cacique was only a day's journey from their present location. This, and the

fact that the cacique had gold and many men, was soon volunteered.

That evening, after consulting with his officers,
Columbus decided that a small delegation should be sent to
meet this cacique of Cubanacan, and to invite him to the
ships. There was no telling how the Great Khan would react
to their presence, but a well-instructed handful of men
might be well received.

Those finally chosen to go were Palo, De Torres, one of
the local villagers, and Domingo's friend, Rodrigo De Jeres.
Rodrigo was selected because, years earlier, he had successfully visited and returned from the village of an African
king. It was believed that this experience dealing with foreign dignitaries might prove useful. Columbus carefully
instructed De Torres and Rodirigo on how to address the
Khan and what information to share with him. This small
band of men then gathered food for their trek, gifts for the
cacique, and their own courage. With the well wishes of all,
they left at the first signs of light the next day.

Domingo and most of the men were put to work beaching
the Niña so that badly needed repairs could be made. They
understood that no more than one ship was ever to be out of
service at a time. Although things appeared calm enough,
the remaining two ships must be available in the event of an
attack. After the Niña was made seaworthy, the Pinta, then
the Santa Maria would be hauled ashore.

The officers kept the men working hard for the next few
days while they waited for the envoy to return from their
meeting with the Khan. The men were told that under no
circumstances were the villagers to be harmed since they
were valued vassals of the great leader himself. No male
Indian was to be cheated in a trade, and no woman was to
be touched against her will. To enhance the potential success of these orders, the men were restricted to the ships or
the camp unless they were on strictly supervised missions.

As days passed and the Europeans continued to exhibit
blameless behavior, the villagers grew more comfortable

with their presence, and they intermingled with them more freely. Those in hiding returned to their homes, but not until guards were posted who could announce the approach of any of the seamen. Because of Tiburon's wariness, Anani's family was among the last to leave the security of the forest. Even then, Tiburon asked that they not leave the village. Anani obeyed her father, but she found a place at the edge of their community from where she could watch the movements and actions of the strangers from afar.

Four days after the small group left with the goal of contacting the cacique, whom the foreigners called the Khan, Anani was startled by a runner bursting from the forest and asking for the village leaders. By the time she reached the runner, Tiburon, Tanama, and the others had already gathered around and were listening to the messenger.

"The cacique is coming," he said, steadily regaining his breath.

"The cacique! The cacique is coming!" echoed around the gathering.

"He is coming with his son, a man called Calichi, and his guards to meet with the white haired cacique," the messenger continued.

Anani jerked her head in the direction of her mother and could tell by Tanama's expression that she too had heard Calichi's name.

"We must prepare to welcome him," an elder announced but the messenger immediately stopped him.

"No, you must wait. The cacique has asked me to tell you of the message sent from the behique."

Everyone became still. Messages from the behique usually imparted good news, but on the cacique's wedding day, the behique had fallen into a mysterious illness. Most took this and the news of his collapse during the feast dance as signs of evil things to come.

"Tell us the behique's news," Tiburon encouraged.

"He asks that you remember the ancient warning of the great behique many ages ago, the warning of men dressed in clothing who would one day come to our island and destroy our people."

Some of the younger listeners looked doubtful and began to question their parents about this unknown prophecy. Many of the elders remembered the age-old tale and recognized the possibility of it applying to them now. An uncertain murmur circled the gathering.

"But surely that warning referred to the Caribs. They wear more clothing than we do. They have tormented our people for generations," someone reasoned.

The messenger raised his arms to quiet the rising voices. "The behique has instructed me to tell you this, and to ask that you avoid the strangers if you can. They may be more harmful than we suspect."

The runner did not mention that the behique had tried to convince the cacique to stay away from the visitors as well. After meeting with De Torres and the others, the cacique hoped that the newcomers brought good rather than evil among them. He had decided to talk with their strange cacique and judge for himself.

"I have spoken the words sent from the behique. The cacique will speak to you himself when he reaches the village. This is my message." He turned away from the crowd to find water, food and rest after his long run.

Domingo was just about to call the men to eat when he heard shouts coming from up the forest path. "They're back! De Torres and De Jeres are back!" Men threw down their tools and rags, and whatever else occupied their hands, and ran to meet their shipmates to hear the news. They crowded around the new arrivals and gawked at the magnificently dressed cacique and his men. Chachu ordered the sailors to step back so that the leaders could speak to one another.

De Torres formally introduced the cacique to Columbus and the captains. Since the cacique was obviously a man of importance, and because the Santa Maria was beached at the moment, the entire delegation was rowed out to the Pinta to provide a more impressive meeting place. Domingo stood on the sand with Pedro and Gonzalo watching the two boats row away from shore.

"We will be the last to hear what they found out," said Gonzalo with resignation.

Pedro was still staring at the cacique. "Just look at him. That Indian is so...so noble looking. Do you suppose he's a messenger from the Great Khan?"

Gonzalo shook his head and said again, "We will be the last to hear, but Rodrigo will tell us when he can. At least our men are alive. The fact that the Khan didn't have them killed is a good sign."

"Maybe we'll be allowed to visit his city tomorrow," Pedro speculated hopefully.

Domingo grinned at him, knowing the boy was still picturing the golden houses. "Maybe, but I don't think we'll be allowed to go anywhere until the work on the ships is finished." Fighting his own impatience, Domingo turned his attention to his responsibilities. "Right now," he said, "I'd better call the men to eat."

As the discussions progressed aboard the Pinta, Columbus began to understand that this cacique before him was the one he had presumed would be the Great Khan. Realizing his mistaken hope, the admiral was barely able to maintain polite conversation as he tried to hide his disappointment.

After gifts were presented to the cacique, Martín Pinzón offered to show him around the Pinta. As Martín, Palo, and the cacique left the others, Columbus watched them go with a gloomy expression. He was only half listening as De Torres and Rodrigo began to tell him about their visit to Cubanacan.

"When we first arrived, Admiral, the people of Cubanacan believed we were gods," said De Torres. Somewhat embarrassed, he continued, "They...mostly the women, sir, kissed our hands and feet to determine if we were actually made of flesh and bones. They showed us every courtesy we could have imagined."

Rodrigo agreed with the interpreter, and went on to describe the layout of the city, the houses, the crops, and many of the customs.

De Torres broke in to explain, "They have a curious practice of burning the leaves of the plant they call tobacco and inhaling its smoke. They showed us how these leaves are harvested and dried. Then they demonstrated how to push the tobacco into a piece of hollow wood, set it afire, and breathe in the smoke as it burns." Columbus and De La Cosa exchanged a skeptical look at such a story. Seeing their glances, De Torres added, "These people seem to find the effects of the smoke pleasant and relaxing."

Columbus slowly shook his head, but motioned to De Torres to continue.

Reluctantly, De Torres said, "There is very little gold, or other treasure, to be found near Cubanacan, sir. However, we were informed that the gold is not far from Cuba. According to these people, there are unfathomable amounts of gold on an island to the southeast, an island called Bohio."

Columbus listened to this news closely. "I have heard of Bohio from the coastal villagers, but they also call that island Babeque." He considered as he eyed De Torres. "Babeque may prove rewarding to us. Perhaps, Señor De Torres, you have brought some good news back with you after all."

After further discussion and civilities were exchanged, the admiral tried to persuade the cacique and his two companions to stay aboard the Pinta overnight. The cacique acknowledged the honor that the white-haired cacique was offering him, then politely but firmly declined. Columbus hesitated a moment before accepting the cacique's refusal to stay. He badly wanted to take this fine example of the Indian people back with him and present him to the queen. However, repairs were still needed to his flagship, and holding the cacique against his will could lead to trouble.

Ultimately, the admiral agreed to accompany the Taino leader back to the island, with the understanding that the cacique would meet with him the following morning. The cacique told Columbus that he agreed to this condition. Then the group returned to shore and the cacique politely made his farewells.

He did not return to the ship the next day.

After the cacique left their company and headed toward Tiburon's village, Domingo and the rest of the men gathered around the officers to hear the news. Columbus briefly explained their situation, and announced that a new course would be set toward Babeque. The fleet would leave Cuba just as soon as the repair work on the ships was completed.

Instead of the good fortune the men had hoped to hear about, they heard orders to double their efforts on the cleaning and caulking. The grumbling rose like a chorus as the group began to breakup.

Pedro lifted sad eyes to Gonzalo. Trying to raise his own drooping spirits as well as Pedro's, Gonzalo said, "No one ever told us the life of an explorer was a predictable thing. Good things will come, Pedro. We must all be patient."

The three of them headed to where the Santa Maria, lay braced on the sand.

Domingo picked up a scrub brush and said, "The gold seems to be running just ahead of our ships. But I'm glad we got to see Cuba, even without the gold."

Gonzalo and Pedro looked at their friend for a moment. Then each of them busied himself with his own chores.

Even with the additional hours the hands spent laboring to mend the ships, it took four more days to make them all seaworthy. After a final inspection of each ship, Columbus ordered preparations to be made to set sail the next day.

Francisco pointed out that Domingo had little time to gather what was still needed to feed the men, and sent him to the village to make his last trades.

During his visit aboard the strange vessel, the cacique had gathered much from Columbus as they talked. The admiral's face and voice had revealed a great deal. It had surprised the cacique to read the stranger's desire to hold him captive. Distrustful now of these white-skinned men, the cacique remembered the warnings of the behique. He spent the next three days under cover of the forest observing the strangers and meeting with the village leaders. Then, he and his son prepared to return to Cubanacan. But they would not stay in the city long. The cacique would return to the coast with his entire force of fighting guards. It would take only a day or two to prepare his men and start back to Tiburon's village. For now, bringing his warriors was just a precaution, but they would be ready if they were needed.

Calichi, uneasy that the strangers were camped so close to Anani, remained behind when the cacique left the village. Tanama welcomed him into their home.

Calichi had intended to keep a watchful eye on the strangers when he had declined to return with the cacique. He had also hoped to spend much of his time with Anani. Tiburon, however, apparently had other ideas. Anani's father found endless tasks for Calichi, including standing watch over the village until late into the night. Still, though Calichi spent far less time with Anani than he would have liked, he found great pleasure with her when they did manage to be together. His happiness was dampened only by the proximity of the invaders.

It was early afternoon and Calichi was standing watch, thinking about the manatee hunt that Tiburon, two other hunters, and he would be going on at the end of the day. He was imagining how pleased Anani would be if they were successful. The meat of the huge animal would feed many families, and its bones made countless useful tools. His thoughts were interrupted when he noticed one of the strangers coming up the path that led to the village.

After watching closely for days, Calichi had come to recognize many of the foreigners. The man approaching was the one who cooked for the seamen and was often with the smallest of their boys. Calichi had wondered about this stranger. This one seemed friendly with the Tainos who traveled with them, and apparently knew much of their language and signs. He did not seem to be a leader like the older one who knew their speech, but rather some sort of caregiver. This combination of curiosities had often held Calichi's interest, and he had observed Domingo in particular as he studied the workers on the beach. Calichi had seen Domingo visit the village twice before, but never alone. Careful not to reveal his position, Calichi moved in the direction of the path that Domingo was walking along. Domingo was only a few paces away from Calichi when he stepped onto the path and gave him a sign of welcome.

Domingo returned the sign, and gave his full attention to the strongly built Taino before him. Calichi waited politely for the visitor to say something, but when Domingo waited also, Calichi began.

"Do you speak our language?"

"Some, yes," Domingo replied.

Calichi was pleased and fascinated. This stranger did not seem threatening at all, merely as curious as he was himself.

"I see that you are coming toward the village."

"Yes," said Domingo, trying to choose the right words. "I trade." He swung the canvas bag from his shoulder and showed the contents to Calichi. There were hawk's bells, strips of ribbon, berets, and other small items inside.

"What do you want in exchange for these?"

"Food," explained Domingo. "Food for men."

Domingo wanted to explain that they were leaving in the morning, but he did not have the authority to reveal such things to the Indians. Columbus had only told the natives that they would leave "soon", which the Tainos interpreted to mean "later." But since they were leaving, Domingo found that he wanted to tell the man before him how beautiful he found this land, how fascinating its people.

Domingo also wanted to express these thoughts because he never intended to return to Cuba. He longed for his family and his homeland with such intensity that, at times, it was painful. He had seen so much, and learned so much on this voyage. And if the stories of Babeque's riches were true, he may even return home with a modest share of the gold. But he did not want to take such a voyage again. Unknowingly at the time, Domingo had been right when he had told his father that one trip sailing the ocean would be enough. Then, he had only wanted to convince Aitor to let him leave Lequetio, and he was willing to give up all future trips to be granted just one. Domingo had gradually come to realize that, once he was safely home, he would have little interest in voyages beyond his own bay.

He was convinced that other Spaniards would come to Cuba. Perhaps many would come here. What that would mean to the Tainos, Domingo could not guess. Even if he could express all of this with his limited knowledge of the Taino tongue, Domingo knew he was not free to do so. Instead, he watched the Indian youth and waited for him to speak.

Calichi wanted to know more about these men. Pointing to Domingo's chest, he asked, "What do they call you?"

Domingo smiled at this. "Domingo," he said.

Calichi repeated Domingo's name quite clearly. Domingo's smile broadened. He pointed to Calichi and raised his eyebrows questioningly.

"Calichi," he said. "My people tell me that you live far away in another world. What is it like there?"

Domingo asked him to repeat his words to be sure he understood, then paused for a moment in thought. At first, he pictured the large buildings and rich art displayed within the cities. He mentally compared that world to Cuba, and was about to point out some of the major differences in the two societies. Then he thought of the similarities between their cultures, and he realized that there were many. Finally, he responded, "My people fish, raise crops, hunt."

This answer surprised Calichi more than a little. He had been told of great wonders that existed in the other world. He had heard stories of strange land animals as large as a manatee, and of booming sticks that could kill an enemy from far away. Perhaps these had been nothing more than wild tales. Calichi wondered what these strange people were really like.

"Do your people dance and sing?" Calichi asked.

"Yes. My people...much dance and sing."

"Is it forbidden to show me one of your dances?" asked Calichi gravely.

Domingo didn't bother to answer. Instead he put down his sack and moved Calichi back a few steps. He raised the Tainos arms and bent them at the elbow so that they formed

211

right angles away from his body. Calichi held this position with great solemnity and patience. Domingo started to dance slowly to a tune he sang, and nodded encouragingly at Calichi.

At first, Calichi found it disconcerting to watch Domingo's grinning face while he performed a rite that had always been deeply religious to the Tainos. Perhaps dancing wasn't religious to these strangers. Perhaps they danced for pure enjoyment in his land. Holding this thought, Calichi tentatively began to follow Domingo's steps with deep concentration. It wasn't long before Calichi progressively gained confidence in his movements.

Domingo was quite impressed with how proficient a student Calichi was showing himself to be, and he picked up the pace ever so slightly. As they danced faster, and Domingo sang louder, some of the villagers quietly gathered around them. Their audience watched in amazement as Calichi, now smiling almost as broadly as Domingo, stepped, leaped, and twirled with the stranger.

When at last Domingo's breath and song ran out, the two dancers stood panting and looking very pleased with each other.

"Calichi good dancer," Domingo proclaimed with sincerity. Gazing around at the small crowd that had gathered, Domingo remembered that he had an errand to complete. To his dancing partner he asked, "Calichi come village? Help Domingo trade?"

Calichi thought this was an excellent idea. What better way to keep watch on a stranger than to stay at his side? Besides, he was beginning to find this one fascinating, even likeable. Calichi signaled his agreement and headed up the path in front of Domingo.

Anani and Guanina were sitting in front of their house, each working on a piece of pottery, when Anani saw Calichi and a stranger heading toward the village center. Tanama had been standing by the door watching unnoticed as her daughters worked. She had seen the stranger even before Anani had.

"Come inside, girls. Quickly," she said. Anani glanced

over her shoulder as she entered the doorway, and caught Calichi's eye just before she disappeared inside.

Domingo noticed this brief exchange, but was quickly distracted as several villagers approached him with goods they wanted to exchange for what he carried in his bag. With Calichi's help, Domingo was able to barter for more than he had hoped. In addition to the food, he was able to acquire several of the net beds, hammocks, which he had admired ever since he reached the islands. He was already speculating on how they could be hung around the ship. They would certainly be more comfortable than the wooden decks.

More than satisfied with his new supplies, Domingo faced Calichi and said, "You good help, Calichi." Domingo had purposely held back two of the hawk's bells when the trading was being conducted. He held these up to Calichi and indicated that they were for him to keep.

Calichi looked at the bells but did not take them. "I have nothing to give you in return for these gifts," he explained as if that was the end of the matter.

Domingo searched for the words. "You give help. You help Domingo. Help is good gift." He reached for Calichi's hand and put the bells into his palm.

Calichi considered this stranger thoughtfully. There were a hundred questions he wanted to ask, about Domingo's world, his life. But he could see that Domingo was ready to leave. He was already slinging his overfilled sack onto his back.

Domingo faced Calichi, looked at him for a long moment, and said in Basque, "I will remember you, Calichi."

He turned and left the village with several Tainos who had agreed to help him carry the provisions back to the ship. Calichi watched him go, remembering their dance.

Anani stood near her doorway, and also watched the young stranger leave.

That evening, as all three ships lay peacefully in the water, a canoe approached the Santa Maria. Columbus invited the six young men it carried, who were interested in trading, to come aboard. Once the Tainos had climbed the rope ladder and were standing on the main deck, Columbus ordered his men to seize them, take them below, and keep them quiet.

When it was nearly dark, Columbus watched a small group of men who were carrying hunting spears as they headed up the coast. As soon as they had disappeared from view, the admiral sent the three launches ashore. The timing was well planned. Columbus knew that the Tainos believed that spirits awoke when full darkness fell. By the time his mission was completed, none of those who were still in the village would dare to interfere.

The men in the boats landed silently, circled the village, and listened from the darkness of the trees. They waited patiently to determine the best of their many alternatives. At houses where they heard only the voices of women and children, they entered, covered the mouths of the terrified occupants, and carried them from their homes. The captives were herded back to the beach. With the three boats now full, the seamen rowed back to the ships. The captives, seven women and three children, were forced up the ropes. Tanama, Anani, Guanina, and Hura were the last to be jostled onto the decks of the flagship.

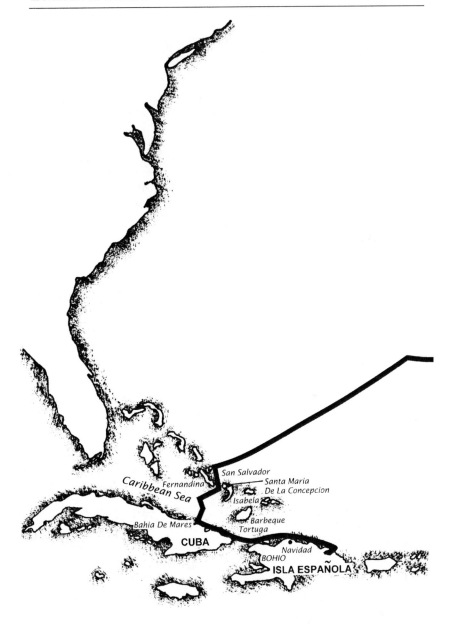

San Salvador to Isla Espanola

Separations

15

In the deepening darkness, Domingo could barely make out the faces of the captives as they stumbled across the main deck and were led down into the hold. It was light enough, however, to see that there were no men in this group. Domingo didn't understand. Why would the admiral crowd the ship with captured Taino women and children? He could think of no reason for ordering such an action.

Domingo noticed that he wasn't the only one aboard who was uncomfortable with what was happening. For once Pedro was too astounded to say anything at all. De La Cosa's features were stormy, and he appeared to want nothing to do with this night's raid. It was De La Cosa's shift, but the ship's master stood back in silent protest, and Chachu followed his example. One of the pilots and the other boatswain carried out Columbus' orders to secure the prisoners below.

Domingo's shift had ended not long before. Even so, De Torres motioned for Domingo to join him as he followed the last of the women down the steps. Domingo didn't move. "Get going, lad! Señor De Torres wants you below!" Francisco barked at him. Domingo glanced at De La Cosa, and was surprised when the ship's master gave an almost imperceptible nod toward the hatchway, signaling for him to obey the order. With great reluctance, Domingo walked to the opening and down the stairs.

The six young men who had been captured earlier in the day were trying to reassure the frightened women and children. Their words were soft and their expressions displayed brave acceptance.

"The strangers have told us that we will be returned to

our village as soon as we are taught their language," one of the youths said to Tanama. "We must learn their words so we can speak with them when they visit us again. It won't take long. All will be well."

In a gentle voice, De Torres told the women where to sit among the barrels and crates in the crowded hold. The interpreter glanced over his shoulder and said, "Domingo, come give me a hand."

Domingo stood like a statue at the bottom of the stairs. De Torres approached him and was about to speak when he was cut short by Domingo's demand. "Why?"

Amazed by the uncharacteristic hardness in the youth's voice, De Torres said firmly, "I will explain later, Domingo. Right now, I need your help."

Domingo did not move.

De Torres' tone softened, but he stared at Domingo intently, "Domingo, they need your help, our help." When he saw that Domingo was still waiting for an explanation, De Torres added, "We *can not* change that they are captives, Domingo, but we *can* try to see to their needs." The two exchanged a long look. Finally, Domingo turned toward the Tainos.

By the light of candle lanterns, Domingo stepped past the armed guards toward the huddled group of captives. He looked over the confusion of stores and bodies, and forced himself to think beyond his shame at being a part of this. He could at least attempt to make the captives as comfortable as possible.

Domingo had just started rearranging a huge pile of ropes when he heard Columbus' voice drifting down from above. He could not make out the words clearly. When De Torres sent him to fetch clothing for the new captives, Domingo gave up trying to listen to the admiral, and concentrated on his work. After much searching, Domingo located what he hoped would be enough to cover them. At least the clothes, although threadbare, were clean. He had spent hours on the beach tending a huge kettle in order to boil the lice and filth out of the clothing. The fact that the clothes did not stink made it easier for him to hand them to the women and children. One by one the women kept their eyes lowered, and tugged on the garments without protest.

Anani and her family were closest to the hull of the ship in an area where little light reached them. Tanama was trying to comfort Hura, whose brave shell had finally given way to weeping. Guanina and Anani sat close together in silence as their wide eyes watched every movement of the strangers. When Anani saw the young bearded man coming toward them, she remembered seeing him in the village. Calichi had told her that his name was Domingo. Calichi had said that they had danced together, and that this stranger seemed to be a good person. She wondered what Calichi would think of him when he learned that she and her family had been taken.

Her mind raced with questions. Where were Calichi and her father? Had they returned from his hunting trip yet? Would these foreign men keep their word and return her and her family to their village? How long would they keep them in this damp, stinking darkness?

Domingo had only a few more shirts to distribute. Holding out one of them, he found himself staring into two beautiful eyes filled with equal shares of fear and anger. He recognized this girl. He had seen her today in the village. She was the one who had looked at Calichi in an intimate way. Remembering this, Domingo was struck by an unwanted suspicion. Could this be Calichi's wife? Domingo looked more closely at the older woman, the younger girl, and small boy who sat nearby. Were these people the girl's mother and siblings? Or were they Calichi's mother and siblings? Had they stolen Calichi's wife and entire family?

Guilt and regret overwhelmed him, and Domingo turned away from Anani's gaze. He handed out the last of the shirts without meeting any of the other women's eyes. He heard two of the women weeping mournfully for their husbands, but the others remained still. Palo went to the crying women and told them that word could be sent to their husbands explaining that they would be brought back home one day soon, and even those who wept grew quiet.

Domingo returned to the task of rearranging the ship's

provisions to allow more room for the Tainos. He reminded himself several times of De Torres' words, "We can not change that they are captives, but we can try to see to their needs." He would do what he could to help these people.

Domingo realized that Columbus must have finished speaking to the men when he saw Pedro coming to join him. Pedro said nothing at first. With wide eyes, he gazed at each of the captives' faces.

Noticing Hura, who was tall for his age, Pedro guessed that the boy was his own age. Hura looked up and met Pedro's eyes. The two studied each other for a few moments.

Pedro, still watching Hura, asked Domingo, "Do you know the name of that boy?"

"No, Pedro," Domingo did not want to look at any members of Calichi's family.

"Will you ask him?"

"You can ask him, Pedro. You have learned enough Taino to ask him his name," said Domingo as he heaved a small barrel to the top of a crate.

"I don't remember their words like you do. Please ask him, Domingo."

Seeing that Pedro's tenacity had taken hold, Domingo sighed heavily and nodded.

Carefully shifting his way through the bodies, Domingo stepped toward Anani and her family. Pedro was following him so closely that when Domingo stopped in front of the small group, Pedro bumped squarely into him. Domingo lurched forward from the unintentional shove, but managed to stay on his feet. Anani and Guanina glared up at him. Tanama's expression was unreadable. Domingo quickly averted his gaze from the women and concentrated on Hura. He drew Pedro from behind his back, and saw that Hura was as fascinated by Pedro as the other way around. Hura's fear and sadness, for the moment, had been replaced by a child's curiosity.

Pedro crouched down and smiled at the Taino child. Without hesitation, Hura reached out and touched Pedro's hand as if he wanted to determine if this strange boy's skin felt the same as his own. When he discovered that it felt just the same, Hura returned Pedro's grin. Anani and Guanina had stopped frowning the moment they saw Pedro. They looked on with softer expressions as the two boys examined each other with their eyes.

Seeing the change in the girls' attitudes, Domingo wished he'd thought of bringing Pedro among them sooner. They responded to the boy naturally, as a loving woman would to any child.

"This boy called Pedro," Domingo explained in Taino, patting Pedro on the top of his head. Then he looked at Tanama, pointed to Hura, and asked, "What this boy called?"

"I am called Hura," Hura answered before the women around him had a chance to speak. Once these few words were out of his small mouth, Hura did not hesitate to voice question after question that he had been holding inside. Directing his questions to Pedro, he wanted to know all about him, the ship, and why they were brought here.

Pedro avoided any attempt to answer the question of why the Indians had been taken. He did not know the answer himself. He turned to Domingo and asked him to translate. Domingo agreed, then found it difficult to keep up with the rapid flow of thoughts between the two young minds.

In the middle of the boy's talk, the attention of everyone in the hold was abruptly diverted by the noisy rise in activity above their heads. Muffled though they were by the decking, excited voices could be heard shouting back and forth.

Tanama suddenly stiffened, and strained to hear more clearly. Her daughters looked at her with concern, but she raised her hand to silence their questions. With her body rigid and her eyes wide, Tanama held her breath. The talk above them stopped. A few moments later, large bare feet began to climb down the steps and into the hold.

Revealing his entire frame as he descended the last of the stairs, Tiburon turned toward them. Before he reached the final step, his entire family, Tanama in the lead, had leapt up and rushed to surround him. Tiburon took Tanama by her shoulders and looked into her face to see that she had not been harmed, then he glanced at each of his children. In spite of her best efforts to hold her emotions, Tanama began to cry quiet, grateful tears. Tiburon was with them. Whatever was to happen, they would be together.

When they saw Tiburon, Domingo and De Torres exchanged uncertain glances. Why would Columbus order this Taino to be taken when he was obviously a leader among his people? As soon as he was seated with his wife and children, Tiburon answered this question himself. He said that he had come to the ship alone. He had asked the leader of the seamen to allow him to stay with his family and, after some discussion, he had been granted his request.

Overhearing this, Domingo was greatly impressed by the courage and loyalty it took for such an act. Thinking again of Calichi, Domingo wondered why Anani's husband had not come with Tiburon. Domingo glimpsed at Anani as she sat listening to her father. No doubt Calichi would have wanted to be with his beautiful young wife. But, perhaps Calichi was not her husband after all. Anani felt him watching her, and stared at him until he looked away.

Every one of the captives knew of Tiburon's rank, as well as his strength and wisdom. The mood of the Tainos changed noticeably with his coming. They held onto their hope and pushed much of their fear aside.

It was not until later, when most of the others were asleep and the strangers were out of hearing, that Tiburon told Tanama and Anani of his plan.

Speaking very softly, he said, "Anani, Calichi intends to come for us in the morning."

Anani had said nothing of her feelings about Calichi's absence. When her father had appeared without him, she had been torn between relief that Calichi would be safe and disappointment that he had not come to her. She had told herself that Tiburon had refused to let Calichi come. This was the right thing for her father to have done. Anani had begun to feel grateful that Calichi would be spared their unknown future. She had been trying to tell herself that it was better this way, even if it meant that she would never see him again. At least he would live. But the pain of this acceptance had been terrible, and Anani now clung to Tiburon's words.

"We have sent our swiftest runners to the cacique to tell him what has happened. It is my hope that he and his men are already on their way back to our village. When they arrive, they will send many canoes to these ships and pretend that they wish to trade. They will even bring gold, which the strangers hunger for. While the strangers are distracted, Calichi will bring his canoe to the other side of this ship and we will escape."

"But, Father, I believe these strangers plan to leave very soon. What if the cacique is not already coming? What if he doesn't come in time?" Anani asked searching Tiburon's face.

Tiburon paused only slightly. "I have told Calichi that he *must wait for the cacique.*"

After giving the two women time to understand the full meaning of this, Tiburon continued. "We must not risk any more of our people. The village leaders wanted to act at first light, but we have too few men to fight against these invaders. Calichi and the others must wait for the cacique and his fighting men."

Knowing Calichi, Tanama could not help but ask, "In spite of your order, Tiburon, do you think Calichi will wait if the cacique is late in coming?"

Tiburon looked again at Anani. "He wanted to come with me, daughter. I was shouting before I finally convinced him that he would be of more help if he stayed. Even so, I was afraid that I would have to ask the others to restrain him when I left. Perhaps he knew that I would have had him held if he had not accepted my wishes. He agreed at last, but only because I gave him no choice." Tiburon sat remembering the dreadful anguish on Calichi's face when he had left him behind.

He ran his hand across his face, exhaled deeply, and answered Tanama's question. "If the cacique is late, Calichi undoubtedly plans to ignore my orders. But he will not be allowed to. I have left instructions with my men. If it is certain that the cacique will not come before these ships leave, Calichi will be given a drink that will make him sleep for many hours. It is a cruel thing, but it must be so."

Tanama sat very still. She looked at her children and was filled with a terrible foreboding. She leaned her head against Tiburon's shoulder and tried to borrow some of his strength.

With a pain in her chest, Anani accepted the wisdom of her father's actions. He had wanted Calichi to stay safely behind, if he could not rescue them. She pictured him at their home waiting for news from the runners. She saw his handsome face clearly. Would she see him again? Oh, what would happen tomorrow? Would Calichi and the cacique come for them in the morning?

Tiburon interrupted their thoughts. "We must pray to the spirits that the cacique arrives before the strangers leave Cuba."

The three of them fervently pleaded for help from their gods, their ancestors, and their zemis. Anani prayed for hours. She prayed until her mind grew weary, and sleep surrounded her like a mist, and she surrendered her tortured mind to its numbing comfort.

Anani awoke to the foul smell of the hold and the movement of the ship. She jerked awake with a cry, and stared up into the faces of her parents. Their expressions told her everything. The cacique had not arrived in time. Calichi would not be coming for them. Her father's men had drugged him. Calichi would wake long hours from now and she would be gone. Anani sat mutely, her eyes glazed, as her mind registered these facts one by one. She and her family were being taken from their home. She was being taken away from Calichi, perhaps forever.

Her face became completely blank and she grew so still that she looked as if she were frozen in place. She was barely breathing when she at last recognized her mother's fearful voice calling to her. But Anani still could not move until she felt Tanama's arms embrace her. Then, even as she gave into her grief and her shoulders shook with her sobbing, Anani could sense that the ship was gaining speed. She heard the flap and groan of the canvas as the sails billowed and captured the breeze. The ship pushed forward, heading east, away from her home, away from Calichi.

Domingo waited impatiently on the main deck for De Torres to emerge from the captain's cabin where the interpreter had been talking privately with Columbus. De La Cosa was on the poop deck overseeing the final adjustments to the sails. He was giving Chachu instructions before the changing of shifts would end their watch. When De Torres finally appeared and climbed down to the main deck, Domingo quickly approached him.

"What is it, Domingo?" De Torres asked distractedly, but not unkindly.

"It's the Indians, sir. Will they be brought up to the main deck while they eat?"

De Torres answered him frankly. "The admiral has just ordered me to keep the Indians in the hold until we are far from their villages. He is concerned, and is right to be, that they will try to escape."

"But, sir," Domingo asked, "How long will it be before they can come up?"

"I don't know, Domingo. Perhaps a long time."

Picturing Anani, Hura, and the others being left down in the foulness, Domingo frowned deeply. Anything would be better than that kind of existence.

"Sir, what if we tied them when we brought them up? If I were in their position, I would prefer wearing ropes to being left down with the stench and the rats."

De Torres rubbed his forehead wearily. "The ropes would prevent them from escaping, Domingo, but they would not solve all of the potential problems."

"But, sir..." Domingo began again, but De Torres stopped him.

"Listen to me, Domingo. I know what it means to keep them down there, but there is one good reason for the

Indians, at least the females, to be kept in the hold. One that you may not have considered." Domingo's face began to register his understanding.

"How long do you think we could keep the men from the women if they were allowed to roam around the ship?" De Torres went on. "Tying them would do little to discourage the attentions of some of our men. And Columbus *intends* to keep our men away from the females. While you and I were below last night, he warned all of the men to stay away from them. Nevertheless, it's unlikely that all of them will heed his warning." Under his breath, De Torres exclaimed. "We will be lucky if we don't have a mutiny over those women!" Catching himself, and realizing he had said more than he should have, De Torres glanced around.

He continued in a lower voice. "Domingo, we must carefully consider how we deal with the Indians. For now, they must be kept below. But perhaps, when we are farther from their own land, we can bring them up in groups that are small enough to be well guarded. There are *some* men of honor aboard, you know, like those who are protecting the Indians."

De Torres placed his hand on Domingo's shoulder. "Come, we must eat. Your shift will start soon, and you will be kept busy seeing that the Indians are fed."

"Sir, " Domingo had to ask him one last question, "If the women weren't brought aboard to please our men, *why* were they taken?"

De Torres searched for the right words.

"The admiral said last night that the women were taken to provide mates for the male Indians we have already captured. He told the crew that, years ago, he sailed with the Portuguese who captured Africans and sold them in Europe. He recalled that the large black males gave them a great deal of trouble. He believes that the male Indians will behave better on this voyage, as well as when we return to Spain, if they have mates."

"But why weren't they allowed to bring their own mates?" Domingo asked.

De Torres chose to ignore this question, and he continued. "You know as well as any of us, Domingo, that we have managed to find almost nothing of the riches we thought we would in the Indies. These Indians may be all that the admiral has to take to the queen when he returns. These natives may prove to be very valuable to him. He evidently wants them whole and sound when he presents them to Her Majesty." Domingo looked away from him, and De Torres concluded, "If there were reasons for taking the women beyond these, I don't know them, Domingo. I must follow orders just as you must. Now, come along. Let's see what we can find to eat before the day gets any older."

By the time Domingo was halfway down the steps to the hold, he could hear tormented moaning coming from where the Tainos were being held. As he neared them, he saw that many were suffering from seasickness. An unmistakable odor rose up to meet him and he fought to steady his own stomach's reaction. Pedro came up behind him, followed by De Torres. Pedro covered his nose with his hand. They all grimaced at the scene before them, but immediately went to work. Rags were dispensed to those who could help clean up the mess left by the sickest members of the group. They handed out buckets and the Indians were instructed to use them when they relieved their nauseated stomachs, as well as their bowels and bladders.

De Torres organized a chain of reluctant bodies, and before long men were handing full pails from one person to the next, across the hold. The slopping pails were passed up the stairs, across the deck, and to the rail, where the contents of the buckets were finally tossed overboard. The hold, foul smelling before, became so fetid that the stink was enough to disrupt the stomachs of the hands who were used to the rising and turning of the ship.

Tiburon could not keep from succumbing to the sickness. To his shame, he vomited violently and repeatedly into a bucket. He couldn't stop until his body was empty and weak. Completely exhausted, he could do no more than lay back on a pile of ropes and try to steady his breathing.

Anani was ill, but she managed not to vomited. She was holding Hura when he suddenly lurched forward and retched, missing a nearby bucket by a foot. Pedro appeared beside her and silently helped swab up after Hura. Tanama tended to Guanina the best she could as she fought her own nausea.

After what seemed like hours, when the odious chore of cleaning up was at last completed, Domingo and Pedro climbed the steps to catch a desperately needed breath of clean air. They leaned out over the railing and inhaled deeply until they began to feel light-headed. Once their own stomachs had settled somewhat, they exchanged a rueful glance, and with heavy feet descended the stairs once more.

It was now their job to give food to any of the Tainos who were willing to try to keep it down. But they did not accept what was offered to them. Most turned away with a groan at the mention of food. At least everyone seemed too tired, miserable, and empty to vomit any more. Many of them were mercifully able to fall asleep. After Domingo and Pedro had repacked the edibles, they heard Francisco bellowing above for Pedro, and the boy gladly left his duties in the hold for awhile.

Domingo, with the help of two of the guards, began again to move some of the huge containers of food and other stores away from the Tainos in an effort to give them a little more space. Sweat was soon dripping down their backs, but they did not slow their efforts until the many heavy crates and casks had been rearranged. When they finished, the guards gladly changed duties with two hands above. Domingo sat down heavily and wiped away the sweat that trickled down the side of his forehead.

Anani sat with her back against a keg, cradling Hura's head in her lap as she watched Domingo. Exhausted, he was sitting on a crate against the far side of the hold with his head hanging down so low that she could not see his face. His dark beard spread out like a palm leaf on his chest. She had been watching him and the small boy, as they worked. The two of them, and the older man, who could speak their language a little, had been kind to her people. Perhaps

Calichi had judged this man's, Domingo's, character correctly. The guards standing over them had not been cruel, but they looked at the Tainos as if they were not people at all, as if they were something less.

She gazed down and studied the sleeping face of her little brother. His smooth, young features showed none of the strain of their situation, just peaceful dreaminess. Anani's countenance softened greatly as she observed him, and she lifted her hand to stroke his dark hair ever so gently. With a sad, quiet sigh she slowly raised her head again, and found herself staring directly into Domingo's eyes.

He had been looking on as she examined the young boy's face with such tenderness. Instead of turning away from him, Anani forced herself to hold his searching gaze. She stared back at him, trying to read his thoughts, and was surprised to see that the young stranger was troubled. Her expression asked what she could not voice. "Why are you troubled when you have mastered us so completely?" He did not look away. So, still speaking only with her eyes, Anani continued. "What kind of person are you? Does your heart hold some kindness? Or do you care for my people only because you have been ordered to do so?"

Domingo guessed that she was asking him what would happen to her. He wanted to give her an answer. Even more, he wanted to give *himself* an answer. He looked at her uncertainly for a long moment. Then, even as he recognized the great limitations on his own authority aboard the Santa Maria, he forced his own doubts aside. He smiled at the island girl. It was a gentle yet confident smile that showed itself in his eyes more than on his mouth. It was a smile to generate trust and reassurance. She watched him in wonder. She understood that his smile was an unspoken promise, a promise to try to help her. But Anani did not know that it was also a commitment Domingo was making to himself, a promise that he would not forget what he had been raised to believe. Riches and power did not dictate the value of a human being. Each person has their own worth, and the right to live among their people in peace. These Tainos had been stolen from their homes. Domingo would do what he could to see that they came to no harm, and that they were returned to their homeland someday.

It was a strong promise to make to a strange girl, without a single word being spoken. Domingo knew the seriousness of this promise and the dangers of its possible consequences. And yet, his soul felt calmer now. Wondering at this, he gazed down at his hands. Anani looked down at Hura again. After a few moments Domingo stood and headed for the stairs that led to the main deck. He could feel Anani watching him as he climbed each step.

The fleet set sail on Monday, November 12, in the direction of an island that the Indians called Babeque, which they claimed held much gold. All day the ships moved eastward, following the Cuban coastline. That night, when the ship was as quiet as a church, the admiral proved that he meant to enforce his threat to punish any of the crewmen who tried to use a Taino woman.

While both of the guards dozed, two men crept stealthily down from the main deck. They paused on the lower steps and surveyed the guards, then the sleeping women. Very slowly, they inched toward the nearest women. She was not much older than Anani. One of the men clasped his hand roughly over her mouth while the other grabbed her around the waist. They lifted her and carried her toward the front of the hold, but they had underestimated the girl's strength. The terrified girl twisted and fought in their arms so violently that their grips loosened and they dropped her.

Her screams woke not only the guards, but the entire ship. Before the men could retreat up the stairs they were surrounded by several shipmates. Within minutes, Columbus, De Arana, and De La Cosa had learned what had happened, and had agreed on what must be done.

De Arana, as master-at-arms, stood on the main deck with the two guilty men before him. With a stern face and a commanding tone he declared, "You men are hereby sentence to be roped to the main mast for twenty-four hours." De Arana raised his head so that his voice was sure to carry,

"The rest of you men be warned. The sentence for the *next* man who tries to take one of the females aboard this ship will be *four days* tied to the mast, *without food*." The men looked uneasily at one another. A man pinned to the mast that long, exposed to the elements and given nothing to eat, had a good chance of dying. Even if he managed to survive, he'd never live down the shame of such a punishment. The men knew De Arana meant what he said. Those among them who had been weighing their chances of getting their hands on one of the women began to rethink their plans.

The next day, Columbus ordered the ships directly toward Babeque, estimating it would take only two to three days to reach the island. But strong winds forced them back to the coast, then westward again in an attempt to reach a safe harbor. Here they remained, impatiently waiting for the wind to change.

Columbus named the harbor Port of Prince, and wasted no time before going ashore to do some exploring. When he returned, he told De Torres that the Tainos could safely leave the hold. De Torres hurried to Domingo and, with a broad smile on his face, asked him if he would like to give the captives the news. Domingo let out a loud yip, pumped De Torres' hand several times in thanks, and anxiously hurried below the decks.

The Indians had gradually become more accustomed to their awful environment, and had managed to keep down a little food. But they were utterly miserable in the dank hold. Domingo went to the guards and told them that the Indians were to be taken upstairs. He turned and scanned the Taino faces until he found Anani's.

In Taino he said, "You come up with me. You all come up." He motioned for them to follow him up the stairs.

Anani's expression lightened as his meaning became clear, and a murmur of surprise and relief rose up around her. She stood up on slightly wobbly legs, and helped Hura and Guanina to their feet. The Tainos moved toward Domingo quickly, as if they feared he would change his mind. Anani had to keep Hura from bumping into people in his impatience to get to the main deck. When she passed

230

Domingo at the top of the stairs, she said, "Thank you," very softly, and walked with Hura to where her parents and Guanina stood at the rail.

It wasn't long before the Tainos were standing in the sunshine, rejoicing in the open sky and fresh breeze. Several of the armed sailors stood close by, watching them carefully. Domingo watched too, and was happy to see them breathing in the clean air and stretching their stiff limbs.

After awhile, he came over to Anani's family and asked if they would like to see the rest of the ship. Tiburon eyed him for a moment, then accepted the invitation for all of them. Domingo found himself walking next to Anani as he explained, in his still clumsy Taino, the details of the Santa Maria. Several times when Anani met his eyes directly, he faltered slightly with his descriptions. De Torres joined the tour, but let Domingo do most of the talking. When the group at last returned to the main deck, Francisco ordered Domingo to see to their meal, and he reluctantly left the Indians.

After Domingo had gone, De Torres gathered the Tainos in a semi-circle around him and began to instruct them in the Spanish language. Anani was determined to learn the strange words quickly so that she could return to her home, and she concentrated deeply on all that was said. The Spanish lesson did not hold Hura's attention for long, however, and he soon wandered over to investigate what the man was putting into the huge black pot.

Domingo smiled at the child, and waited to see if he would sit beside him. When he did, Domingo started to explain what he was about to cook for them all when a thin shadow fell between them. Domingo gazed up at Anani. She reached for Hura's hand, intending to take him back to the lesson.

"I want Hura stay," he told her in her own language. She hesitated and glanced back over her shoulder at the rest of her people.

"You stay also?" Domingo invited. Anani looked at him curiously.

Domingo stammered slightly as he went on. "You stay

231

and tell me...about you." This brought a thoughtful expression to Anani's face, and she lowered herself until she sat next to Hura.

"What do you want to know, Domingo?"

It surprised him greatly to hear her use his name, and it pleased him very much.

"About your family," he said. He had been about to ask her if she was Calichi's wife, but had thought better of it at the last moment.

"Hura is my brother, Guanina, my sister, and Tanama and Tiburon are my parents," Anani answered him with dignity.

Domingo watched her, and waited a moment before asking, "Your *whole* family?"

Anani's brows drew together and her expression darkened. At first, she did not respond. Then she said, "Any other family I have is not with me."

In spite of himself, Domingo blurted out, "Have you a husband?"

Domingo saw the pain come to her face, saw her head lower, and he deeply regretted his impetuous words. He didn't know what to say now, but he searched his mind for something that might sooth her.

Hura had been watching and listening to the two of them. Softly, trying to help his sister, he said "She was to marry Calichi, but he could not come and save us."

Hura had barely spoken these words before Anani got to her feet, pulled Hura up beside her, and hurried back toward De Torres with her little brother in tow.

Domingo grimaced and called himself every kind of a fool. When he finally paused in his self-recrimination, he asked himself why he had been so impatient to find out if Anani was Calichi's wife. Why didn't he just keep his mouth shut? Had he been trying to relieve his own guilt? Guilt that his people had taken the wife of someone he had thought well of? He told himself that this must have been so. But now he felt terrible for making Anani sad with his pointless question.

He dared to glance over at her, but she was turned away

from him. He looked at her long hair, the curve of her back as she leaned slightly forward. He dearly wished he had not asked her the question. And yet, he reluctantly admitted, he felt relieved by Hura's answer. No less guilty, but less troubled somehow. Perhaps, he was relieved for some reason that had less to do with Calichi and more to do with Anani. He tried to push this thought aside, but he was so distracted as he mulled it over that he let the knife he was using miss its intended target. With a long slice, he cut deeply into the base of his left thumb instead of the fish he was holding. He dropped the heavy blade with a clatter onto the deck, and grabbed for the cleanest rag within reach.

His hand, though not so deeply cut that it would be permanently damaged, was already bleeding a great deal. Pedro was the first to notice Domingo's ineffective attempts to bind the wound himself, and came to help him. In spite of Domingo's embarrassed objections, Pedro called the ship's doctor over to look at the cut. As Domingo tried to sit still under the doctor's prodding, insisting all the while that the cut was nothing, he silently repeated his list of the types of fools he considered himself to be.

Later in the day, Columbus went out in the launch again to study the bay with some of the crew. De La Cosa had watched the behavior of the Indians for hours, and felt it was safe to allow small groups of Indians to swim near the ships. This announcement was met with immediate acceptance. Tiburon, Domingo, and several of the young Taino men were the first to jump overboard. Domingo immediately felt a searing pain in his bandaged hand as the salty water reached his cut. Clenching his teeth, he waited until the worst of the pain had subsided then tried to ignore it altogether. He treaded water and watched the graceful movements of the Indians in the ocean.

They swam like dolphins, stretching and gliding through the water with little apparent effort. Soon they began diving deep into the sea, staying under for unbelievable lengths of time. Domingo watched Tiburon dive down and waited for him to surface. After what seemed like a very long time,

Tiburon startled Domingo when he sprouted from the water right in front of him, holding a huge shell in one hand.

"Conch!" Tiburon announced.

Too surprised to say anything else, Domingo returned "Conch!" Having no idea what it meant.

"Conch," Tiburon repeated shaking the shell in front of Domingo's face. "It is very good to eat."

Domingo nodded to signal his understanding. He turned and yelled for one of the men to throw him a net. When the net was lowered to him, he put Tiburon's conch into it and grinned at the chief.

In no time, Tiburon, Domingo, and the other swimmer added not only more conchs, but also many oysters to the net. It grew so heavy that it took most of the hands to haul it back up onto the deck. When De La Cosa ordered every-one back aboard, there was a look of satisfaction on the faces of many of the swimmers. Domingo landed on the deck close to Tiburon and held up two of the conchs.

"I cook tonight. Much good," he said in Taino.

Anani watched her father smile at Domingo's words. She turned away from them both.

Guanina had observed Anani and Domingo earlier, and she had noticed how quiet Anani had been all afternoon. She kept her eyes on Domingo now. He was a stranger, but he had helped take care of them when they were sick, and she perceived him as a different sort than the rest of her captors.

As she watched him start his fire and set the pile of conchs near the pot, she could see by his puzzled expression that he didn't know the first thing about cooking them. Guanina turn to her mother and spoke quietly with her for a moment. Tanama glanced over at Domingo, then back at Guanina, paused uncertainly for a moment, then nodded. Guanina walked over to Domingo and shyly asked him, "Would you like me to show you how to cook these?"

"Oh, yes. Yes, show me," he said.

Domingo looked so relieved and grateful that Guanina couldn't hide her smile. She sat down next him and began her patient instruction. When all was prepared, the men were called to a blessedly welcome meal.

The sailors, glad as they were to partake of the feast that the sea and the Tainos had provided, were somewhat disappointed when not even one of the oysters contained a pearl. Still, they praised Domingo and Guanina noisily. Uncomfortable with the compliments from anyone other than Domingo and Pedro, Guanina lowered her eyes and sat very close to her mother.

With the presence of the captives, Columbus decided that changing the timing of the work shifts would allow for better and easier management of everyone aboard. Domingo found his hours of sleep shifted, but he still worked with the same men. Pedro, Rodrigo, Gonzalo, and Francisco were still his closest coworkers. The admiral also had the six Cuban youths moved to the Niña to provide more elbowroom and better security. This decision was thoroughly questioned the next morning when two of the young Indians escaped. They simply swam ashore and disappeared into the thick greenery of the island.

The watches were once again tightened around the remaining captives.

Martín Pinzón chafed with impatience as the days at Port of Prince passed one by one. The admiral, however, appeared to be in no great hurry to leave the lushness of the harbor. In fact, he seemed delighted with the new sights and sounds of the area. Pinzón's frustration built until he felt he could hold his silence no longer. One evening he asked the admiral to meet him on the beach and Columbus did not keep him waiting. Their greetings were cordial enough, but before long their voices rose loud enough for Domingo and every other man in the fleet to hear them from the ships.

"As I've said before, we are taking too many chances with the ships. We sail to close to these strange shores for safety, then we sit and sit when we finally find a decent harbor. We need to keep moving if we ever want to find the rich cities."

"*We* are taking too many chances?" Columbus demanded. "Don't you mean *I* am taking them?"

Pinzón did not hesitate. With his jaw set and his brow

low he said, "Yes, Admiral, I do think you have made some decisions that have been less than advisable. And I think we should have left port days ago."

"*I* will decide when we sail, *Captain*!" Columbus shouted. "Do you forget who is in command of this fleet, this voyage?"

Pinzón yelled even louder than the admiral. "I wish I *could* forget who is in command of this voyage! It would have a better chance of succeeding!"

Before Columbus could respond, Pinzón spun around, stormed to his launch and had his men row him back to his ship.

When at last the wind that Columbus had been waiting for blew across the bay, they set their sails again in the direction of Babeque. By midmorning of the next day, they had drawn near enough to the island to see its outline. They were within just thirty-five miles of it when the wind shifted once more, blowing directly at them.

The Taino whom the sailors called Palo and two of the other Indians from San Salvador stood against the port railing of the flagship looking north rather than in the direction of Babeque. They could see the island that the strangers called Isabella clearly from here. There own island was not far to the north of Isabella. For several moments, they dared to hope that the changing of the wind would cause the fleet to head north. If so, perhaps they would find an opportunity to elude their captors and make their way back to their village. As they stood watching and longing, they heard the orders called out to turn the ship once again to the south, back toward Cuba.

Palo looked grimly at the man next to him. "I thought that if I learned their words and helped them learn ours that these strangers might let us go. Now I see that we must find gold for them. Only then will we be taken back to our homes." His companions silently agreed.

Even returning to Cuba did not prove to be an easy task. Now the wind and currents seemed to be working in unison against the fleet. The ships crawled along the rest of that day and the next, making little progress. Hours passed with the fleet barely moving.

Sunset was nearly upon them again when Rodrigo suddenly turned to Gonzalo and asked, "What is the Pinta doing? Look at her. She's turning to the east."

And so she was. Rodrigo spun around to notify De La Cosa of this strange happening, but the master was already staring after the caravel. A low rumble rose from the crew as each of the men stopped what he was doing and gawked in disbelief at the Pinta. De La Cosa had sent Chachu to inform Columbus, and in moments, the admiral was at his side.

At first, Columbus was incredulous. "What the devil is that man doing?" he fumed. The admiral glared at the Pinta, then glanced quickly in the direction of the Niña.

"The captain of the Niña shows no sign of attempting to follow his brother, sir" De La Cosa informed him. Columbus saw for himself that Vicente held his smaller ship quite near to the Santa Maria.

"Signal the Pinta!" Columbus bellowed, and seamen jumped to build the signal fire. But their signal, clearly visible to anyone within five miles, was completely ignored. The crewmembers had been trying to reassure themselves that the Pinta would come about when Pinzón saw that the rest of the fleet was holding its course. But the Pinta did not turn. A strange hush descended over the men as the realization of what was happening settled upon them. The admiral's face grew menacing in its anger.

"His insubordination has reached total betrayal," Columbus said in a voice so low it was barely audible. "He means to beat us to the gold."

De La Cosa said nothing. Pinzón's defection was inexcusable, of course. The voyage would be in greater jeopardy the longer he stayed separated from them. Still, De La Cosa had seen how dark Pinzón's mood had been lately. What was more, he understood Pinzón's frustrations. De La Cosa had questioned some of Columbus' decisions himself, like taking the captives, following the coastlines too closely, and lingering in places that did not match the descriptions of the

Indies. At times, the admiral's lack of experience commanding men showed itself too clearly.

But Columbus had been the creator of this voyage. Without him, it would never have been possible. They had reached what appeared to be an unexplored section of the Indies. This was no small thing. If they wanted to reach home again, their chances were much better if they worked together. And, most importantly, Columbus was the admiral. At sea, that was enough. An admiral, or any captain in command for that matter, was to be obeyed.

De La Cosa looked again in the direction of the Niña. Vicente Pinzón stood on the fore deck looking ahead, to the south, as his brother continued to sail eastward away from the fleet. De La Cosa's admiration for the young captain expanded greatly as he watched him. Duty to the fleet, to the voyage, had caused Vicente to stay with them. He had held honor above his willingness to support his own brother. And De La Cosa had seen that these two brothers were close to one another in spirit. Staying with the admiral and his men required a strong will and a good soul. Even so, De La Cosa was sure that Vicente's heart was heavy as he sailed close beside the mothership.

Columbus continued to stare after the Pinta. He did not order the Santa Maria to follow her. His last words before turning toward his cabin were, "Hold your course, master of the ship." The cabin door closed softly behind the admiral, and De La Cosa obeyed the order he had given him.

Shifting Tides

16

Domingo watched Anani's family while they ate, and wondered what was wrong. He had noticed that the Tainos aboard were growing more restless as the Santa Maria and the Niña headed further southeast, down the Cuban coast. While the Tainos looked uneasily to the east, the crewmembers looked northward with their own worried expressions. The Pinta had not been seen since she separated from them two days earlier.

At first Domingo had thought that the Indians were apprehensive because they were being taken farther and farther from their homelands. But when the ships neared the eastern end of Cuba, and they could see a new stretch of land across a wide water passage to the east, the Indians pointed toward it with dread. They became even more quiet and preoccupied. Concerned that they were truly afraid of something on the island ahead, Domingo decided it was time to ask Anani.

His skill with the Taino language had been improving daily, and the Indians were learning Spanish little by little. But even with a greater confidence in his words, he waited for the right moment to raise his questions. He had not spoken more than a few sentences to Anani since the day he had asked her about Calichi. Many times Domingo had conversed with other members of her family. Since Hura had become a constant companion for Pedro, both of them were around Domingo much of the time. Domingo had watched Anani closely, protectively, but he had refrained from interacting with her directly. Today, he hoped she would be willing to talk with him.

In the late afternoon, when Anani and Guanina were sitting apart from their parents near the hatchway, Domingo took a breath, walked up to the two girls, and squatted down near them.

"Anani, Guanina" he hailed them both, but he looked directly at Anani.

Guanina, who had helped him to prepare meals more than once recently, smiled at him. Anani looked at him guardedly, but with no sign of anger. "Domingo," she said in return.

Determined not to upset her this time, Domingo said, "Anani, I would like to ask you something."

Anani waited for him to continue.

"Are your people...uneasy?"

The two girls looked at each other, and Guanina was about to answer him when Anani said, "Yes, Domingo. We are afraid."

Pointing to the east, Domingo asked gently, "Is it something about that land?"

Guanina fidgeted nervously at the simple reference to the island.

Domingo glanced at Guanina then back at Anani.

"The island is called Bohio," Anani said in a very low voice. Guanina fought to control another shudder. She moved closer to her older sister as if she were suddenly cold and needed warmth.

Anani put her arm around Guanina and continued, "On Bohio there are people called Caribs. They are also called Cannibals by some. These people have been enemies of our people for ages and ages. They are terrible."

"Why are they terrible, Anani?"

"For many reasons," she said. "Their warriors have arrows and they poison the tips. Their victims suffer an agonizing death. But to die by poison is not the worst way to die. Our people pray that they will be killed in battle rather than be taken back to the Carib villages."

Domingo could see the fear in her eyes but he encouraged her to continue. Anani spoke so quietly that he had to lean very close to hear her.

"When they capture our men, they butcher them slowly.

240

They drink their blood and roast their body parts so they can eat them one by one." She hesitated only a moment before going on. "It is even worse for the women. The women are not allowed to die. The female captives, some of them mere children, are kept in an open pen day and night. Any man or boy in the village may use them whenever he pleases. Then, if a woman bears a child..." Anani looked directly into Domingo's wide eyes and whispered with a pained expression, "The babies are eaten at special feasts. The Caribs consider them... delicacies."

Domingo went pale. He wanted to doubt Anani, but he could clearly see the open fear on her face and on Guanina's face as well. But surely, they were mistaken. The two girls obviously believed these things. They must have been told such ungodly things for some reason. But, what he had just been told was no more than a story, surely. His mind fought to reject the fact that such people could be real, that such things could really happen.

Anani could see that Domingo did not want to believe her.

"What I have said is true, Domingo. I knew two young women who were taken by the Caribs. I saw a man who escaped from one of their villages and heard his words. He had a large indented wound on his shoulder. He said that they had cut that piece of his flesh away and eaten it raw while they waited for him to bleed to death. He pretended to die, and the Caribs left him because they were busy with other captives. When night fell, he slipped away from them. Somehow, he lived and found his way home. And, Domingo, he is not the only captive who has managed to escape from the Caribs. I have heard other such accounts."

Domingo could only stare at her. For an awful moment his mind pictured Anani being taken by the Caribs and subjected to the horrors she had just described. So strong was the image that he was about to reach out to her, to comfort her, but he caught himself and lowered his hand. Anani did not miss his movement. She gazed at him in surprise. Domingo turned away from her, toward the island to the east.

After a moment, he asked, "Anani, are you sure the Caribs come from Bohio?" His mind still wanted to protest what he had heard.

Anani considered his question before answering. "We have always heard that they come from the direction of Bohio."

"But perhaps they come from a land further east," he insisted.

"I don't believe so, Domingo, but it is possible. None of the people from our village have traveled as far as Bohio. I do not know what lands lay beyond it."

Tiburon noticed his two daughters talking so seriously with Domingo. When Domingo realized that Tiburon was observing them, he motioned for him to join the small group. Tiburon sat with them, and soon confirmed everything that Anani had said.

Feeling almost sick at the possibility of such horrors, Domingo left the group and reported the information to De Torres. Within minutes, Tiburon was repeating his stories to Columbus and De La Cosa.

"Bohio? But I thought Babeque and Bohio were two names for the same island," was the admiral's first reaction to Tiburon's explanation about the Caribs. Tiburon pointed out that Babeque lay further to the north than Bohio did.

Impatiently directing his remarks to De Torres, Columbus said, "So they are two different islands, and there are man-eating Indians on one of them?"

Domingo could easily see that Columbus did not believe Tiburon. Judging from De La Cosa's expression, he intended to learn more before he decided what to believe. De Torres was inclined to give credence to Tiburon's descriptions.

Walking away from the Tainos, Columbus said to De La Cosa, "They must be exaggerating. Captives being eaten. Still, it sounds like these Caribs are warriors. They may well be some of the Great Khan's people. We may have to visit Bohio if we don't find what we hope for on Babeque." Then, a new thought occurred to him and Columbus added,

"No wonder the Indians run from us. They probably think *we* intend to eat them too!"

Late that night Anani's mind dwelt on how Domingo had looked when he had reached for her. She had seen concern, and perhaps something more, in his brown eyes. There was gentleness and warmth inside him, she was sure. Domingo was not like the other strangers. As the ship rocked lightly with the current, she fell asleep, remembering Domingo's eyes.

For nearly two weeks, what was left of the fleet sailed down the Cuban coast. They were forced to contend with heavy rain, contrary winds, and strong currents. When the conditions were very bad, the officers found a bay to wait it out, and some of the crew were sent ashore. If the shore party found a village, the inhabitants usually fled before them, and the explorers were often left to wonder at the strange things the islanders had left behind. A sailor discovered a human skull kept in a small basket that hung from a post inside a house. In a village further east, the landing party saw some houses that were divided into rooms by suspended mats and strings of shells. Here too, they saw a number of islanders who had dyed their entire bodies red. Although these finds were fascinating, the gold they sought remained elusive, and they pushed farther ahead.

During the days, Domingo, De Torres, and the Tainos worked to improve their ability to understand each other. When Domingo was not on duty, and sometimes when he was, he found more and more opportunities to be with Anani. Often the two would talk about what the men had found on the island. Anani would patiently explain what the articles were used for, how they were made, and their importance. Domingo loved learning all about Anani's culture, but even more, he loved hearing her tell him about it. Her voice was delicate and sweet, and he no longer heard the hint of anger in her words. Her sorrow even seemed to be lessening. Whatever she felt at being held captive, she was careful never to speak of it. She seemed to have decided that the blame for the taking of her family did not belong to Domingo. She even smiled at him occasionally, usually when he misspoke or drew the wrong conclusion from her words. It was a gentle smile, like her voice, and it softened and illuminated her lovely face. A time or two Domingo said the wrong Taino word intentionally, just to see her smile.

Pedro, who noticed most things aboard his ship, did not miss what was happening between Domingo and Anani. He admitted to himself that Anani was lovely, but he was uneasy for his friend. He hoped Domingo would do nothing foolish. Although greatly tempted, Pedro decided not to say anything to Domingo, not unless he felt he must to protect him. Still, as a precaution, Pedro began to listen for any suspicious rumblings about Domingo among the men. He would keep his eyes and ears open, and warn Domingo if necessary.

When the fleet reached the eastern tip of Cuba and no gold had been found, Columbus planned one more attempt to reach Babeque. In addition to gold, he hoped to locate the missing Pinta, which was never far from his thoughts. Who knew what could have happened to the ship while it was on its own?

The wind, however, seemed determined to keep the Santa Maria and the Niña away from Babeque. On the morning they were to have set out, mighty gusts blew into their faces. There was little choice as to the direction they could take if they wanted to advance at all. The prows of the ships were reluctantly pointed to the southeast, toward Bohio. None of the Tainos slept much that night.

As the shores of Bohio drew nearer, Anani's family and the rest of the Indians willingly remained in the hold. Domingo prayed that his optimistic supposition had been correct, that the Caribs came from a land beyond Bohio. He stood watching the shoreline and thinking, "If the Caribs are here, there will be a battle. But how many of them live here? Perhaps many times the number of men on our two ships." He recalled with dread the poison arrows they used against their enemies.

The night before, as the ships neared Bohio's western coast, Domingo and many others on the decks had seen the smoke of signal fires rising from the forest just off the beaches. Whatever people lived on this island, they had seen the ships, and were preparing for them. Domingo intended to stay close by Anani in the days to come to see that no harm came to her.

Standing at the rail, wondering what dangers the next few days would bring, Domingo's imagination carried him far from the Santa Maria, back across the long miles he had come, back to his home. Perhaps because it was his eighteenth birthday, the first time that the anniversary of his birth had been spent away from them, the thoughts of his loved ones were deeper and more clear than usual. The faces of his family members appeared before him one by one. They were smiling. He imagined that he could hear their warm laughter. Missing them terribly, Domingo wondered if they were thinking of him today.

Then, he pictured Carmen standing alone with her hand raised to block the sun from her eyes as she looked out to sea, to the west. She was waiting for him. He closed his eyes tightly and lowered his head.

Domingo had tried to hold the images of his village and his people at a distance for many days. The memories of his family, but mostly of Carmen, had become troubling and guilt-ridden. Now, with the uncertainties posed by the unknown land before him, he allowed himself to face what he felt for the island girl. He had not intended, had not wanted to grow fond of her. At first he had told himself that he was simply acting with honor, as his parents had taught him to do. But as his protectiveness evolved into desire, he realized that his drawing closer to Anani meant turning away from Carmen.

This haunted him painfully now. He asked himself how it was possible to feel so strongly for Anani, yet feel no less strongly for Carmen. His conscience churned and bucked, but he forced himself to look at his disloyalty to his betrothed. His heart tightened and his head hung even lower. Yet, even as he reproached himself for being something less than he had always believed himself to be, Domingo knew that he could not turn away from Anani. She needed him too badly, and he cared for her too much. He would do whatever he could to protect her. Feeling unworthy yet greatly in need, Domingo asked God to help him, to help them all.

He raised his head very slowly and stared again at the island. A strong breeze whipped his face, whirling his hair and beard. This was his life, this day, this moment, standing here on this deck and facing this strange shore. There was no certainty that he would ever reach his home again. He must survive today before he could face tomorrow. He must keep Anani from any injury beyond what she was already suffering. No Carib, or other threat, was going to come near her. Not if he could prevent it. Anani was down in the hold right now, and she was badly frightened. Domingo pushed himself away from the railing. He turned and walked to the steps, then descended into the hold.

As the ships eased along the northern shore of Bohio, Columbus called the men together and told them that he intended to name the island Española, after the queen's homeland. He also laid out his plan for approaching the new area.

"We'll follow Española's shoreline and learn what we can about these natives," he said. "No one will be sent ashore until we determine how dangerous the people are. Keep a close watch on the beaches, men. It's possible they will try to attack the ships. I want to hear about every native spotted."

With the passing days, the weather turned gradually cooler and rain fell more often. The change in weather added to the apprehensions of the sailors. The men spent hours each day scanning the tree-lined beaches, looking for Carib warriors. The inhabitants of Bohio seemed in no hurry to show themselves to the newcomers, however. The crewmembers could see many canoes along the beach, and occasionally glimpsed a fleeing islander, but that was all.

After several uneventful days, even Tiburon began to relax a little, and wonder if Domingo had been right about the Caribs coming from another land. These islanders were not behaving like Caribs.

Columbus wanted desperately to go ashore, to find out what gold the island held, but he was uneasy about the safety of a landing party after all of the stories that had been told. One afternoon he called Tiburon and the three Indians from San Salvador together to question them one more time. Domingo and De Torres were called upon to act as interpreters for the admiral.

Columbus addressed himself to the four Tainos before him and said, "We have seen no sign of the Carib warriors on this island you call Bohio."

Palo, quite calmly, said in Taino, "The Caribs do not live on Bohio. They come from a land to the south called Caniba."

De Torres was almost too surprised to translate. Everyone gaped at Palo, Tiburon most of all. Columbus could not hide his consternation.

"Palo," he demanded, "You've known for days that we have been waiting to go ashore because we thought the Caribs might attack. Why did you say nothing about Caniba before now?"

Palo answered, "I did not understand that you wanted to know about such things."

Everyone stared at him again. Columbus turned his attention to the other two men from San Salvador.

"Is what Palo says about Caniba true?"

They both nodded.

"And is it safe to go ashore here in Bohio?"

Again, they nodded.

Relieved at the news but disgusted that they had needlessly wasted so much time, Columbus waved the Indians away from him. He immediately began planning the landing for as soon as possible.

With the wind howling at them from the northeast, it was not long before the sailors located a harbor, and dropped their anchors. The landing party was dispatched, but returned to the ship late that day with little to report. Near noon on the second day, however, they rowed back with a comely young woman. Domingo stood on the main deck with the other hands, watching the launch draw nearer.

The girl's obvious terror only increased when she saw herself being taken closer and closer to the strange craft. As the men dragged her aboard, she screamed and twisted in an attempt to escape. De Torres whispered into Columbus' ear and left them. He returned a moment later with Tanama, Anani, and another Taino woman. When the girl from Española saw Tanama, she ran to her and threw her arms around her legs. Tanama's relief that the native girl was not a Carib was nearly as great as the child's at seeing one of her own kind. Tanama quickly bent down and comforted the girl, speaking soothing words and caressing her long hair.

Under the watchful eyes of the ship's officers, Tanama said gently, "These men do not mean to hurt you. This man," she pointed to De Torres, "told me that he only wants to talk to you. Do you understand?"

The girl searched Tanama's face for assurance, then asked, "They have not harmed you?"

"They are not like the Caribs," Tanama said, "They have taken us from our home, but they say we may return when we have learned their language. They teach us their words every day. If you talk with them, they say they will let you go home."

"Are they gods?" the girl asked with wide-eyes.

"They are strangers," Tanama answered.

Reassured somewhat, the girl slowly turned toward De Torres and Columbus, but she kept a tight hold on Tanama's hand.

"Get her something to wear, Domingo," Columbus ordered. In a moment Domingo returned with a used tunic and carefully handed it to the girl.

While she submitted to being dressed by Tanama, the girl watched the men warily. Not until Columbus greeted her formally through the interpreters did she speak to them. She answered several general questions about her people and the island. Then the girl said quietly, "I am the daughter of the cacique. If you release me, and do not take any more of our people, you will be treated well by my father."

With this surprising and reassuring news, Columbus himself brought her gifts of bells, rings, and glass beads. He had De Torres tell her that these things were being offered to her as signs of friendship.

The girl accepted the gifts willingly, but her gratitude was nearly painful to watch when she was told that the men would take her back to the beach right away. She bowed before Columbus and said to Tanama, "They must be gods, with such kindness and so many wonders." She turned away before she could see the look on Tanama's face.

With much care, and great hope that she would speak well of them to her people, she was rowed to the shore and accompanied part of the way back to her village.

They waited several days, but no word came from the cacique or any of his people. Finally, a handful of men including De Torres were sent cautiously ashore. They had not gone far inland when they were surrounded by many islanders, and greeted warmly.

The cacique's daughter turned out to be a valuable emissary. The girl had finally concluded that the visitors could only be zemis who had come to them from heaven, with compassion in their hearts, and bearing mysterious gifts. She had told her news to her entire village, and the strangeness of the visitors seemed to confirm her words.

The landing party, though happily astounded at the reception they received, found neither gold nor any other kind of treasure they were looking for. When the men returned to the ships, the decision was made to continue eastward, through the passage between Española and an island the Indians call Tortuga.

News spread among the coastal villages of their eminent arrival, and of their reputed goodness. Rather than bracing for war against the Caribs, the men of the fleet found themselves overwhelmed with an outpouring of attention and generosity that was hard to comprehend. Thousands of islanders came out to the ships, some swimming three miles just to see the holy strangers, and to give them simple gifts. Unlike the Cuban women who wore long loincloths, the women of Bohio wore no clothing at all. Many of the people dyed their skin, and the predominant color chosen was red.

Domingo, Anani, and Guanina were standing on the Santa Maria's foredeck watching the approach of a number of canoes, when Guanina suddenly pointed at a man in the nearest dugout. "Look, Domingo," she said. The Taino she was directing Domingo's attention to was within ten feet of the ship's ropes, and was standing up. Domingo heard Anani catch her breath as she saw what Guanina had. At first Domingo did not know what he was supposed to be looking at. "Look at his shoulder, Domingo," Guanina said softly, no longer pointing in the islander's direction. It wasn't until the man stood on the main deck not far below them that Domingo clearly saw what Guanina had been pointing at. An ugly scar, roughly the size of a hen's egg, showed itself plainly on the man's left shoulder. Domingo turned and looked at Anani, intending to ask her about the man. Before he had a chance to speak, Chachu hailed him from the half deck, beckoning him to come and act as interpreter for De La Cosa. Not wanting to leave Anani, and wondering where the devil De Torres was, Domingo had no choice but to obey.

It turned out that De La Cosa and Columbus were both speaking with another Indian who bore a scar similar to the one worn by the Taino Domingo had just noticed. The islander was showing Columbus a handful of arrows and attempting to explain their nature.

With evident relief at Domingo's arrival, Columbus asked, "What is he telling us about these arrows?"

"He says they came from Caniba, sir."

"Caniba! Ask him how he got them."

When this question had been relayed to the Indian, and answered, Domingo said to Columbus, "There was a battle, sir. The Caribs attacked them a year ago. This man retrieved the arrows after the fight."

250

Domingo asked the officers if he could question the man about his scar. They gave him permission to do so, and Domingo asked the islander, "Were you wounded in the battle?"

Instead of answering right away, the Taino called to the other scarred man, who was standing on the main deck. Once they stood together in front of the officers, the one Domingo had questioned before said, "Near the end of the battle, we and several others were surrounded by many Carib warriors. They had ropes and intended to tie us so they could take us back to their island. We struggled to free ourselves, and managed to escape. But Caribs bite the flesh from their enemies' bodies as they fight, and they marked us with their teeth. Many of our men did not escape them as we did."

Domingo relayed these grizzly words the best he could.

Unsettled, the officers found that they had no more questions to ask. The Taino men were dismissed to explore the ship, and trade what they had brought. After the Indians turned away from them, Columbus leaned toward De La Cosa and said under his breath, "Holy Mother of God." De La Cosa and Domingo both nodded as they stared after the departing Indians.

Hoping he would no longer be needed, Domingo looked back toward Anani and saw that she had been watching him. Domingo remembered that the men standing next to him, and even he himself, had doubted Anani when she had first spoken of the Caribs. Now they had been shown proof that what she had told them was the truth. Even so, there was no hint of victory in her expression. She looked back at him with attentiveness, nothing more. His attention was diverted from Anani when he noticed that a young Taino man was approaching her with a look of great interest on his face. Domingo asked to be excused from the officers and returned to her side without delay.

A few evenings later, Columbus entertained the son of a village cacique in his cabin. He was pleased when the young man told him that he would invite his noble father to come to the ships very soon. Two days later this cacique appeared

on the beach riding in a litter and accompanied by at least
two hundred men. He came to the ship, greeted Columbus
formally, and gave Columbus a beautifully crafted belt. He
also gave the admiral a few small pieces of gold. Thrilled at
the sight of the glittering nuggets, the admiral informed the
cacique that he would like to trade his gifts for more gold.
The cacique seemed happy to comply with this request, and
additional small amounts of gold were obtained through
bartering over the next few days.

Raising the hopes of all aboard, an old man told
Columbus where there was as much gold as they could ever
want not far to the east. His information was not ignored.

As they moved slowly eastward, the island people continued to come to the ships. The natives welcomed the
strangers by bringing them food and whatever other possessions they had to give. Anything the sailors gave in
exchange was gratefully accepted as a thing of high value.

Among the visitors to the ships was a large group of dignitaries that had been sent by the great cacique of Bohio,
Guacanagari. Domingo was included in the group chosen to
welcome Guacanagari's men. He learned that this mighty
chief had sent his officials to invite Columbus to his city.
The ambassadors presented Columbus with an ornately
decorated belt. Hanging from the magnificent belt was a
carved mask, detailed in gold. In spite of their generous
invitation to accompany them overland, the admiral chose
not to leave his ship. Instead, he sent a party of six men
including Rodrigo De Escobedo, the secretary of the fleet,
with the cacique's officials. De Escobedo had an extremely
limited knowledge of the Taino language. Even so, he was
instructed to tell Guacanagari that Columbus would come
to see him as soon as they had reached the harbor near his
city. After the briefest of lessons from De Torres and
Domingo, De Escobedo departed with the Taino ambassadors.

In the meantime, Palo and Tiburon were sent to a nearby village to question the inhabitants. They returned with
the chief of the village, who was pleased to inform the
leader of the strangers that the gold he sought was on this

252

very island. It was reportedly located not many miles to the east. This seemed believable since the Europeans had begun trading their beads and other trinkets for larger and larger nuggets of the precious metal.

Two days later, De Escobedo and the other men returned to the fleet with stories of their grand welcome in Guacanagari's city.

"The Indians carried us from place to place on their shoulders, Admiral," De Escobedo said. "They treated us as if we were kings. We were paraded around the city right behind Guacanagari, and everyone cheered our coming. His city is much grander than anything we have yet seen in the Indies, sir. It has a great plaza and wide, smooth roads of stone."

Columbus asked, "What did you learn about Guacanagari himself?"

"I'm afraid I understood only a little of what Guacanagari said to me, sir, or of what he asked me to convey to you. But I can tell you that he is a very impressive man, Admiral, and that he is looking forward to your arrival."

"Were you able to find out if he controls the mining of gold on this island?"

"No, Admiral. But he did give us some pieces of gold, as well as many other gifts." De Escobedo brought out the articles Guacanagari had sent him back with, and Columbus admired each one in turn. When he finished, he turned to De Escobedo and smiled. "Congratulations," he said. "You have done well."

That evening brought even more good tidings to boost the spirits of the men and the admiral. Several Indians from the nearby village told the seamen that Bohio itself had much gold, but that the land of Cibao had even more.

After considering this, Columbus speculated aloud to De La Cosa, "Cibao is very likely Japan. We *must* be close."

"I hope so, Admiral," De La Cosa said cautiously.

"Guacanagari may be able to confirm our hopes. And do you know what day it is today, Juan? It's December 23. Wouldn't it be auspicious if we were to arrive at

Guacanagari's city in two days time, on Christmas day? It would be a blessing indeed to have the chief welcome us and justify our expectations on the birthday of our Lord."

"It would indeed, sir," De La Cosa smiled.

The admiral's excitement was felt so strongly by the crew that it was difficult for many of them to sleep that night.

On Christmas Eve morning, with renewed hopes and high intentions, the hands sailed their faithful ships toward the east under a light wind. The day was lovely, and everyone aboard admired the beauty of the island as they glided slowly along. In their off-duty hours, Domingo and Pedro stood with Anani, Guanina and Hura repeating the Taino names for the birds, turtles, fish, trees, mountains and every other thing their Cuban companions pointed out. De Torres came up to them and encouraged Anani and her siblings to use the Spanish words for the objects they saw, and the interpreter stood over the young group, supervising them like a wise tutor.

The early evening watch was about to change when Columbus ordered the Tainos to the hold. Domingo wondered the reason for this since the Indians had recently been allowed to remain above decks until dark. He gave Anani what he hoped was a reassuring smile as she headed toward the hatchway. It wasn't long, however, before Domingo realized that the admiral's command had been given as a precaution.

As soon as the Indians were secured below, Columbus faced the crew and said, "In honor of this holy night, an extra ration of wine will be given to the men who are just coming off duty."

Wild cheers erupted from the crew. Columbus smiled and held up his hands to quiet them.

"Just be sure that you hands who are about to start your shift keep your minds on your work until you are relieved. Merry Christmas, men."

The Niña was sailing along slightly ahead and further out to sea than the flagship. But it was near enough for her crew to hear the loud, merry voices and hearty toasts that rose from the decks of the mothership. Vicente Pinzón followed the admiral's example, and holiday wine rations were soon being poured aboard the smaller ship too.

Pedro looked up at Domingo and frowned ruefully. "It looks like we will have to wait four long hours before we get to have our Christmas toast," he said.

Domingo laughed at Pedro's tragic expression. "You sound like an old sailor who can't survive four more hours without a drink." Then, knowing full well that Pedro would be given his share of wine just like every other hand aboard, he added mischievously, "Besides, they'll probably give your drink to me since you're too young for straight wine."

Pedro had read Domingo's teasing face before he even finished speaking, and he punched him playfully in the shoulder. "We'll see who handles their wine better, you or me."

When 11:00 came at last and Domingo, Pedro, and the others received their Christmas wine, Columbus and De La Cosa raised their own cups to accept the toasts of the men. Afterward, Columbus stood on the half-deck surveying his contented crew. He turned to the master of the Santa Maria and smiled broadly.

"Well, Juan," he said, "It has been a long two days and I slept little last night. I am going to the cabin and rest for awhile."

"Of course, Admiral," De La Cosa said.

"With such a calm night and a quiet sea, you should have little to deal with."

"Yes, Admiral," De La Cosa agreed.

With the gentle night and the wine warming their insides, Pedro and Domingo became drowsy within minutes of emptying their cups. They settled down in two small places on the open deck, grinned at each other sleepily, and began to whisper about the Christmas celebrations of their past. The memories brought a longing for their families, and a prayer that they be granted the chance to see them again. The magic of the blessed night encircled the two young sailors with deep feelings of hope and well being. Then, imperceptibly but unresistingly, a mellow dream-filled sleep descended on the pair.

Dead tired himself, De La Cosa called to the helmsman and told him that he was going to lie down for a little while. The helmsman was ordered to call him if there was any change in the wind or the weather. Then De La Cosa left him to find his own bunk in the cabin.

Domingo was jolted violently awake when someone kicked him hard in the back and tripped over him. He heard De La Cosa and Chachu yelling, calling urgently for the men to wake up. Something was terribly wrong. His first thought was of Anani. Had something happened to her? The moment he jumped to his feet, he could feel that the ship was not floating free in the water. A general alarm exploded around him. Something was wrong with the Santa Maria. Pedro leaped up next to Domingo and glanced fearfully at his friend. It was just after midnight and the scant moon shed little light on the confusion aboard the ship. They heard Francisco hollering their names, and Pedro left Domingo's side to fight his way through rushing bodies, heading in Francisco's direction. Domingo ran through the noise and chaos to the stairs that led down to the hold, and almost collided with De Torres.

"Stay where you are most needed, Domingo! I'll see to the Tainos," the older man ordered. "I'll call for you if you are needed below," said De Torres, and he pushed Domingo aside as he rushed down the steps.

Columbus and De La Cosa ran back and forth along the rails surveying the situation, both of them shouting questions and orders to the men nearest them. What had first felt like the gentle landing of the Santa Maria on a beach changed suddenly to a jerking and shifting of the ship. A wave brought her up, then firmly down, onto the sharp prongs of a coral reef. An ominous and terrifying grinding sound came from beneath the ship. Men jumped out of his way as De La Cosa rushed passed them and climbed below. A few moments later he thundered back up the stairs.

Domingo sucked in his breath when he saw the expression on De La Cosa's face. The ship's master looked as if someone had just shot a member of his family. The terrible anguish of losing his ship battled with a dreadful rage that the Santa Maria had been exposed to such a risk.

It was then that Columbus found De La Cosa and barked out, "Take the anchor in the launch and drop it behind the ship! We'll use the capstan to pull her free!"

De La Cosa said with a firm voice but the same disturbing expression, "It's too late. She's breached, and water is already coming into the hold. We must get everyone to the Niña. We need to send the boat for help if we hope to get everyone off in time."

"We *must* save this ship!" Columbus shouted at him again.

De La Cosa exploded, "She's *my* ship! *My* ship! And she's breached and going down! We *can't* save her! She's already impaled on this shoal! And I don't intend to let those aboard drown in a hopeless attempt to drag her backward!"

Columbus did not seem to hear him, and he bellowed even louder into De La Cosa's face, "Get to the boat! Get that anchor to the stern of the ship!"

De La Cosa spun away from the admiral and shouted to several of his strongest hands to follow him. Domingo bounded once again toward the hatchway to help Anani, but Chachu grabbed his arm before he reached the stairs.

"Help those two men bring up the boat!" he yelled over the noise, and shoved Domingo to the rail. The launch was trailing the ship on a line, and Domingo hauled on the rope with the other men until it was along side. No sooner was the launch within reach than De La Cosa, Chachu, and their men leaped in and grabbed for the oars. De La Cosa took an oar himself. Domingo heard the ship's master mutter, "My ship," just before the boat pushed off. They rowed with all their strength, straight toward the Niña.

Columbus watched the boat in disbelief, then began yelling curses after them. De La Cosa ignored him completely. The ship he had worked most of his life to earn, and that he loved like only a captain who had sailed her for

257

years could, was going down. There was no hope of saving her. He had no doubt of that, not after seeing the damage that had already been done to her hull. But he was not going to lose his men, nor any one else on board if he could help it. So he disregarded the order of the man who had paid no heed to his repeated warnings of the possibility of just such a grounding.

When the panting rowers were within shouting distance of the Niña's crew, De La Cosa called out and told them what had happened. Vicente Pinzón and his men moved to respond to the hail with the greatest possible speed.

On the Santa Maria, Columbus ordered men to carry the ballast up from below and throw it overboard. When that action gained nothing, he gave the command to cut down the main mast. But these attempts to lighten the Santa Maria were not enough to fight the undertow of the water that pulled her down without mercy.

With the launch from the Niña just ahead of him, De La Cosa raced back toward the Santa Maria as fast as he and his weary oarsman could row. Just before they reached her, the great ship rose up once more, then crashed down against the teeth of the reef. The leaking crack in her belly broke wide open and water came roaring into her hold.

Domingo felt the ship stiffen and heard the bone-chilling sound of her hull rupturing. Screams rose from the hold. He lunged forward, shoving men aside as he bulled his way to the stairs. But even before he had reached the hatch, he saw Hura bounding up the top steps. The boy was followed immediately by Guanina, and the rest of the Tainos. Domingo grabbed Hura, then Guanina, then Anani and pulled them out of the way of the rushing men. Tiburon followed him, sheltering Tanama in his arms.

Horrified men and cabin boys were running everywhere, cursing and snapping at anyone in their way. Domingo scanned the faces. Where was Pedro? He couldn't see Pedro. He shouted to Tiburon that he had to find the boy, and took three steps into the turmoil when the boy appeared from nowhere and ran right into him. Domingo scooped him up, and brought him to huddle close with the rest of his small group. Rodrigo was not far behind Pedro. De Torres, Rodrigo, and Domingo ushered their charges under the forecastle, and tried to keep them safely together.

As the currents turned the ship clock-wise in the water, she tilted to the starboard side. Men fell to the deck, and women screamed and grabbed for a support. Water continued to rush into the gut of the flagship. Some of the terror-stricken men regained their feet and turned to the admiral, awaiting his orders. But many others turned instead toward De La Cosa who was just climbing up the ship's ropes.

When the ship's master came aboard, Columbus and De La Cosa glared at each other murderously. But there was no time to exchange words. Some of the crewmembers were already piling into the boats by the time Columbus gave the order to abandon the Santa Maria. Columbus sent his secretary after his logbook and charts, then followed after him to be sure everything was safely removed from his cabin.

Groups of sailors, then Tainos, were taken over to the Niña as speedily as the rowers could ferry them. Those aboard the small boats cursed, or cried, or prayed, or remained in shocked silence.

Domingo stayed with Anani, and he and her family were among the last to reach the already over-weighted Niña. The Indians were crowded into the hold, while the crewmembers jostled for what scanty space was available above deck. The miserable humans onboard had little more than room enough to stand.

As the long night wore on, rumors of what had happened to cause the wreck began to circulate around the Niña. The helmsmen of the Santa Maria, it was said, had left the tiller in the hands of one of the cabin boys so that he could take a nap. Then, as the boy had leaned against the swaying tiller, even he had fallen asleep.

When Domingo and Pedro heard this news, they stared at each other for a long time, then gazed back at the dark outline of the upper third of the Santa Maria still showing above the water. Their ship, their loyal Santa Maria, had been left under the control of a tired, unsupervised cabin boy.

Finally, Pedro asked the question that he had been holding inside for two hours. For those two interminable hours he had been too afraid of the answer to ask. "Domingo," he whispered, "How will we get home now?"

Domingo avoided the boy's eyes. He could give Pedro no answer.

Navidad

17

The first rays of the morning sun sparkled across the sea as the launches pulled away from the heavily burdened Niña and headed toward the beach. Faces were grim and tongues were silent as the passengers unloaded. As soon as the last person stepped into the shallow water, the launches pulled away and returned to the ship.

Domingo stood in the sand beside Pedro, gazing back at the next group to be brought ashore, and trying not to look at the wreck of the Santa Maria. Her upper deck still hung above the water line.

Domingo remembered wearily that it was Christmas day. How strange that such a tragedy would happen in the early hours of Christmas morning. What reason could God have had for allowing them to lose their flagship? No answer came to him.

It was not long before everyone was on land, and they turned to face the admiral. Columbus looked as downhearted as the rest of them. De La Cosa looked worse. The two stood only as close to each other as was necessary.

"The food and other supplies must be unloaded from the Santa Maria," said the admiral. "I'm sending Señors De Arana and Gutiérrez to Guacanagari's village for help. It shouldn't be more than five miles from here. They should be back within a few hours with men and canoes, but we can't wait for them. We'll start the unloading immediately."

"What's to happen to all of us, Admiral?" one of the older hands asked from the middle of the throng.

Columbus looked at the worried faces in front of him. "Perhaps I'll be able to discuss my plans with you tomorrow. For now, we have work to do."

Columbus walked away from them, sat on a fallen tree in the shade, and put his face in his hands. De La Cosa and Chachu began organizing the men into groups assigned to specific duties. Once assignments were given, the hands quietly went about their tasks, burdened by fear and weariness.

When there were no Europeans close at hand, Tanama touched Tiburon's elbow and asked softly, "What must *we* do, husband?"

"For now, stay with these men. We don't know what kind of people these islanders are. Until we do, it may be safer with the strangers."

"Do you think they will let us go soon? We've learned many of their words, and they've found some of the gold they've been demanding," Tanama said.

"Perhaps. But for now we're still being guarded." Tiburon inclined his head in the direction of three armed sailors talking together not far away. "We must continue to help these strange men, and see what the gods decide for us," Tiburon said.

Pedro dropped the potato he had been peeling in the sand and stood up with his mouth hanging open.

"Hey! Pedro what are...?" Domingo started, then he saw what Pedro was staring at. Just coming into view around the curve of the eastern shoreline, a magnificent fleet of canoes was moving swiftly toward them. De Arana and Gutiérrez were in separate canoes just behind the front of the group. De Arana stood up and shouted a greeting to those on the beach.

"Look, Domingo. The Indian in the lead canoe. That's got to be Guacingari," Pedro breathed.

"*Guacanagari*," Domingo corrected as he gazed at the impressive sight. "And it looks like he's come to help us."

Some of the sailors shouted and waved back at the canoes. Others yelled for the admiral to come see as they ran to the edge of the water and watched the canoes pull closer.

Even after the canoes landed and the Indians were approaching the camp, Pedro seemed rooted to the sand. He kept his eyes focused on the chief. "What kind of bird can grow feathers that long?" he asked in reference to Guacanagari's headdress. The bright feathers stuck out four feet from his head, starting at one ear, running over the top of his head, and ending at the other ear, forming a huge colorful fan. Pedro also saw that the man wore a mantel with symbols of every color. And gold hung from his ears and nose.

Domingo had taken a few steps out in front of Pedro and was staring at the Indians along with the rest of the men. When Guacanagari reached Columbus, Domingo listened carefully.

With De Torres translating, the cacique said to the admiral, "Honorable visitor, the men you sent to me have told me of your misfortune. You must not worry unduly over the loss of your ship. My people and I will help you forget your loss." Guacanagari stepped closer to Columbus, wrapped his powerful, brown arms around him, and embraced him like a brother.

Pedro demanded, "What did he say?" But Domingo shushed him impatiently and said, "Just a minute, Pedro."

Columbus recovered from his surprise enough to return the hug. He pulled away and thanked the cacique warmly. Then the admiral explained that what he most needed was to have the goods removed from the damaged ship, and safely stored.

Guacanagari told his people what was to be done, and returned to his canoe. Taking a paddle, the great cacique himself helped row to the Santa Maria and unload her.

"Will you look at that, Domingo," Pedro said.

"I'm looking, Pedro. I'm looking," Domingo reassured him.

"He's picking up barrels and hauling them just like our own hands," Pedro said. "And he's the leader of all of these Indians."

"Yes, he is. But he certainly doesn't seem to be afraid of work," said Domingo.

He turned back to Pedro then looked at the sand at the boy's feet. "Now how about picking up that sandy potato and cleaning it off. These men are going to be hungry soon."

The Indian captives helped sort and stack the provisions as they were carried onto dry sand. But when the people from Guacanagari's city began heaving the stores onto their shoulders and toting them inland, the captive Tainos were told to stay on the beach. Columbus remained behind while Guacanagari left to manage the moving of the goods to his village.

Two hours later, the cacique sent his own brother back to the admiral with news. Two huge houses had been filled with their goods, and Guacanagari's personal guards were now installed around them. Two more houses had been set aside and were available for the strangers' use.

Anani was so glad to be on land again, and to be beyond the terror of the night before. This morning, working beside her family and Domingo, was almost enjoyable. But she had seen that Domingo was struggling to hide his anguish over the sinking of the Santa Maria. His brow was often furrowed with deep concern and he spoke very little.

Late in the day, Anani watched over Hura while Domingo and Pedro organized some of the food containers still on the beach. Her parents were further up the beach trying to talk with some of the local Tainos, but they were having trouble understanding each other. Domingo focused on his job, seldom looking over at her, and Anani wondered if he was dreading what she herself was hoping. She hoped that the sinking of the ship meant that her family and Domingo would stay here on the island. If so, they could borrow canoes and make their way back to Cuba.

She continued to concentrate on Domingo as he worked. They had been together almost constantly these many weeks, and he had protected her and attentively cared for her through everything. Last night, that terrible night, he had not left her, not until she had been taken to the hold of the Niña. Even then, he had tried to join her but there had been no room, and he had been ordered to remain above. During the most horrifying moments of the ship's sinking, Domingo had seen to her family's safety before his own. He had not left any of them. He was a kind man, a man of courage and honor.

During the night, she had realized that she wanted Domingo to return with her to her village. She *wanted* to be with him. This realization had startled her at first. But she did not deny it. The more she considered it, the more her spirit told her it was right. Still, there were so many questions that she had no answers to. What would her parents say? Even if they approved, would her village accept him after his people had kidnapped them? She didn't even know if Domingo would be willing to come. His life was so different. *He* was so different.

And if he did come with her, she would be choosing Domingo rather than Calichi as her husband. This thought brought her up short. What about Calichi? She pictured his sweet smile and splendid voice. Did he still think of her after so long? He probably thinks I am dead, she concluded sadly. By now, he had probably chosen another girl to be his wife.

As evening approached, Domingo came over and sat in the sand next to Anani and Guanina. He nodded to them and managed a weak grimace that Anani guessed was supposed to look like a smile, but he said nothing. He looked so tired.

Anani smiled gently at him and said, "We should go for a swim. It would refresh us all."

He looked at her and, slowly, returned her smile. A real one this time. It was the first one she had seen all day.

"Yes," he said. "I'd like that very much."

Startling both of the girls with his sudden change of mood, Domingo jumped up, and threw off his shirt. Calling out to the two guards to announce his intentions, he ran toward the sea. The two girls followed close behind him. They dove into the water and came up grinning at the pure pleasure of the water washing around their bodies. The three hardly had time to do more than get wet before Hura and Pedro came splashing into the ocean like noisy puppies.

Domingo pushed onto his back and closed his eyes, luxuriating in the feel of the water, letting it cleanse his troubled spirit as well as his body. He hollered for Pedro and Hura to stay close to shore, then started swimming farther out. When he felt his arms and legs growing heavy, he floated on his back again. He stared at the sky for a long time, and tried not to think at all. At last he turned back and swam lazily toward shore with long, slow strokes. When he was within twenty yards of Anani, he treaded water and watched her. She did not see him. She swam with absolute ease, staying parallel to the beach. All he could think was, "She swims like a goddess." He drank in the sight of her, the way her body glided through the water.

She took a deep breath and dove. When she surfaced closer to shore, her feet found the sea floor. She took a few steps until the waves could brush no higher than her waist. She turned around, saw his expression, and smiled.

Domingo stared at her and his breath caught. The wet shirt clung to her body, revealing every detail. He swam closer then stopped again, fifteen feet in front of her. He knew that Guanina, Hura, and Pedro were just up the beach. He also knew the guards and Anani's family were watching them. So he did not come close enough to reach for her.

"You look too beautiful to be real," he said.

She looked down, very pleased, and ran her hands gently through the water.

She heard someone swimming toward them and turned to see Guanina.

To Domingo, she said, "Come. Let's swim while we can."

Before long, however, Francisco found them, and the swimmers were called from the water. Anani and Guanina left them to join their family. Domingo and Pedro were ordered to wash clothes until the officers had decided where each of the men was to sleep. Even though Domingo hated to leave the water, the swim and Anani had done much to rejuvenate his spirits.

While Pedro and Domingo stayed by the huge kettle and took turns stirring the clothes around in the boiling liquid, they talked about what it would be like to stay in one of the two houses Guacanagari had made available.

"Do you suppose we can sleep in one of those hammock beds, Domingo?"

"I've been hoping the same thing," said Domingo. "I wonder how many hammocks can hang in one of their houses. Anyway, I imagine we'll be the last to get one of the hammocks."

"Domingo, isn't it something, the way these people are treating us, I mean?"

"Yes, it's amazing," said Domingo. "We are total strangers to them. They greatly outnumber us, could kill us all if they wanted to, and they show us such...kindness. It is something, Pedro."

"Do you suppose it's because it's Christmas?"

"Well, Pedro, they don't know about Christmas?"

"Oh. That's right," said Pedro, and he grew quiet and thoughtful.

Pedro's words made Domingo reflect on the spirit of the special day for awhile. His thoughts bounced from Christmas to the way Anani had looked in the water just a short time ago, and suddenly he was seized by the desire to give Anani a gift. The notion took a firm hold of him. He knew that she was not Christian, that Christmas meant nothing special to her, but he wanted to give her something anyway. But what could he give? He had nothing.

He spent the next half-hour working, and trying to think of a present for Anani. When an idea finally came to him, he couldn't help smiling. He would shave his beard. If he could persuade De La Cosa or one of the other officers to lend him a razor, he would shave. The rest of the men would think this was a wild thing to do. No sailor ever shaved his beard before he reached home. The length of a seaman's beard was a thing to take great pride in and to show off whenever possible. It told the story of how long a sailor had been away at sea, and, if Domingo ever *got* back, he would have been at sea for a very long time. On the other hand, who knew if they would ever make it home? Why not shave his beard? He imagined Anani's reaction to seeing his clean-shaven face for the first time. Perhaps he wouldn't seem so foreign to her without his beard. Perhaps she would even find him attractive. He dwelt on this possibility a great deal as he waited for the opportunity to approach one of the officers.

In the end, it was Pedro who obtained the borrowed razor. Domingo had no more than mentioned his intention to him before Pedro had disappeared. Within minutes he was back, proudly holding the blade up to Domingo. Domingo had not missed the fact that Pedro had not even questioned the reason behind his odd request. Looking at Pedro's still grinning face, he realized that Pedro had probably known how he felt about Anani for quite awhile. The boy had never spoken a word about it, neither of judgement, nor of criticism.

"You are a good friend, Pedro," he said with feeling.

"You'd better hurry, before that razor is missed," Pedro said

"Missed?" Domingo asked in surprise, "You didn't ask to borrow this?"

When Pedro's smile only broadened, Domingo laughed out loud.

"Pedro," he chuckled shaking his head.

Domingo laughed again and, following Pedro's advice, quickly headed toward the river to shave.

Sunlight was fading when Domingo returned to the beach. He could see Anani's family already being rowed back out to the Niña. Anani sat in the launch with her back to him. Good. He didn't want her to see him until he could see her reaction to his clean-shaven face.

The sailors around him were picking up supplies from the beach to take with them to Guacanagari's village. One of them straightened up and noticed Domingo's face.

"Good heaven above! Domingo looks like a damned native!"

Loud laughter and good-natured curses erupted as the other men joined in.

"Where's your beard, Domingo? Did one of the island girls cut it off?"

"You didn't have to shave just because it's Christmas!"

"That young man will never make the rank of captain!"

"This island air must have got to him!"

Domingo knew that their teasing was inevitable, and took it as well as possible. But he refused to offer any explanations. De Torres approached him, succeeded in suppressing his own comments, and put his hand on his shoulder.

"Never mind these pirates, Domingo," he said. "The admiral wants me to stay ashore in case Guacanagari or any of his people need to get a message to him. He and Captain Pinzón will stay aboard the Niña tonight, and the admiral wants you on the ship, too. He wants you nearby in case he needs to speak with any of the Taino women." As he finished speaking, a look dawned across De Torres' face, as if a new thought had just occurred to him. He studied Domingo speculatively for a moment. The interpreter's look was too shrewd, and it made Domingo a little nervous.

But De Torres said only, "It's been a very...eventful Christmas. Let's hope it can at least end quietly, shall we?" He left Domingo with the same thoughtful look on his face, and joined the procession of men heading into the forest.

Pedro was already on board when Domingo climbed the ropes of the Niña. The boy wore the expression of a true co-conspirator. The Tainos were already in the hold, and the sun was setting fast. With his heart pounding, Domingo walked to the hatchway and descended the steps.

Domingo saw Anani before she saw him, and he quickly went over and sat down in front of her. The light from a single candle lamp was dim, but when she looked up at him she gasped in surprise.

"Domingo!" she exclaimed, her hand flying to her throat. She stared at him as if to reassure herself that it was indeed Domingo sitting before her. He wore a wide grin, but no beard. She continued to gaze at him, carefully studying this new face of his. The skin beneath where the beard had been was lighter than the skin around his eyes, but his mouth and chin were strong and handsome. She decided that she liked this face very much. It had been hidden under that dreadful beard much too long. When she reached this conclusion, her eyes showed her thoughts.

Tiburon, Guanina, and Tanama were watching them. Guanina giggled into her hand, but her parents closely observed Anani's face without saying a word. They exchanged a wise, knowing look.

Anani said, "I'm glad that you took off your beard, Domingo."

"It is a gift to you, Anani. Today is Christmas, a very holy day. I wanted to please you."

Anani was more than pleased. Her heart was touched by his gift. She didn't know if it was painful to remove a beard, and she hoped it had not hurt him, but she was grateful for his generous action.

Anani started to speak again, but the voice of the Niña's boatswain roared down on them from above.

"All hands above decks! Admiral's orders!"

Domingo looked up at him then back at Anani. He saw disappointment on her face, but she quickly hid it with a smile.

"I thank you for your gift," she said.

"Rest well," he said. Then he turned and climbed to the main deck. Before he reached the top step, he heard Guanina's exclamation of delight and surprise at "Domingo's clean face!"

Domingo and Pedro were waiting to receive their morning orders the following day when one of the men on watch called out, "Three canoes approaching, Admiral!"

"It's Señor De Torres and Guacanagari, sir," the crewman shouted.

Columbus and Vicente cordially welcomed Guacanagari and several of his family members to the Niña. After greetings had been exchanged, Guacanagari pointed to De Torres and said, "This ambassador tells me that I may address you as Admiral."

After De Torres had translated, Columbus said, "I would be honored if you would do so, Guacanagari. I also ask you to accept my thanks for all you did for us yesterday. We are greatly in your debt."

"We are happy to help you, Admiral. I have brought you a gift that I hope will lighten your heart after your misfortune."

Guacanagari held out a woven pouch and poured the contents onto the deck in front of him. The sizable pile of gold glittered in the sunlight.

"Your gift does indeed lighten my heart, Guacanagari," said Columbus delightedly. He ordered gifts to be brought to the cacique, and Guacanagari was most pleased with the hawk's bells. He admired their lovely shape and color, but held them almost reverently as he rang them. He listened to the sweet, clear tone and asked Columbus, "Is the magic of your zemis inside your gifts?"

After hearing this question translated, Columbus hardly paused, "There is a kind of magic in the bells, yes."

Guacanagari nodded with satisfaction. "I see that you find joy in the beauty and magic of gold. I will bring you more gold tomorrow, if you wish. Some of my people may want to trade gold for some of your gifts. Would that please you?"

"I would like that very much, Guacanagari. Is there much gold on your island?"

"There is much gold, yes."

"Admiral," said De Torres quietly in Spanish, "Our men are already trading their personal things for gold with the villagers. What Guacanagari says is true."

Guacanagari said, "Admiral, though there is gold here on Bohio, there is much more on the island of Cibao, to the east."

Domingo leaned close to Pedro's ear and told him what Guacanagari had said. Pedro was so excited that he yelped out loud, and Domingo had to walk him away from the group of leaders before he started dancing for joy.

Columbus smiled broadly at Guacanagari and asked if he would care to eat with him. But the cacique said that a feast was already being prepared in the admiral's honor on shore. His invitation was readily accepted.

Columbus' outlook continued to improve as he spent the day feasting and receiving more gifts from Guacanagari. Among other things, the two discussed the threat of the Caribs to the cacique's people. Columbus assured Guacanagari that the king of Spain would see that the Caribs were destroyed.

"If any Carib survives one of the battles, he will be brought before you, Guacanagari, with his hands tied behind his back," Columbus said. "It will be up to you to decide the punishment of all prisoners."

To prove the power of Spain to the cacique, Columbus had his men fire a musket, then a small cannon into the trees. The frightening demonstration brought Guacanagari's people to their knees, but the cacique himself stood firmly by the admiral. Through De Torres, Columbus assured the cacique that he and his men were grateful friends, and that their weapons would be used only against Guacanagari's enemies.

Before nightfall, the admiral assembled all of his men together on the beach.

"I'm sure you have all heard about the gold here on Española," he said. "Most of you have even traded for some. You've seen the generosity and gentleness of these people. After seeing these things for myself, I have come to realize that the loss of the Santa Maria was actually a blessing from God. If the accident had not happened, we may not have found out about the gold. And would not be forced to start a settlement here."

A murmur rose from the men, and Columbus' officers ordered the men to be quiet.

"I am sure that God wanted us to start a settlement for Spain on this island, and that is what we will do. You know that all of us can't return to Spain on the Niña, and that some of our party must stay behind. It will be the duty of those who remain on Española to search for more gold, and hopefully find the mine. But even before they start to search, they must build a fort to house them, and as a precaution against attack. I don't believe there is danger from Guacanagari's people, but there may be an attack by the Caribs, so a fortress is necessary. A year's worth of provisions will be left at the fort. That will give me more than enough time to reach Spain and return for the men here. And, men, I have decided to name the settlement Navidad, since the Santa Maria went down on Christmas day. May the Lord's blessings fall on the men who are chosen to build and strengthen Navidad."

The admiral's declarations were met by assorted reactions. Many of the men had already considered the hard fact that most of them would be left on Española. The Niña would never make it back to Spain if she was overcrowded. Some of the sailors had thought of little else but how nice it might be to stay. They intended to take full advantage of the generosity of the island girls and the gold until other ships returned from Spain. Other men greeted the announcement with dread that they may be among the ones chosen to stay. They wanted nothing more than to go home.

Domingo was one of those who had contemplated being ordered to stay. He wondered if Anani and her people would be allowed to remain here also. He was torn between his feelings and wishes, between home and Anani. He finally told himself his future would not depend on what he chose anyway. Their fates were in the hands of his superiors. The hands would be told what was to come only after Columbus had consulted with the other officers and a decision had been reached. Domingo had no choice but to wait until then.

Construction of Navidad started with the rising of the sun. The fort was to include a large moat, a storage cellar, and a watchtower. Since much of the material they needed could come only from the Santa Maria, some of the men were set to work dismantling their flagship. Most of the others, including Domingo and Pedro, began digging out a foundation. They labored under the sun, sweating, and wondering who would stay and who would sail home.

De La Cosa and Columbus, faced with the obvious challenges ahead, formed a stormy truce. These two and Vicente Pinzón sat together and discussed which of the men were to stay, who was to be put in command, and what provisions would be left.

It was finally decided, with a few exceptions, that the crew from the Santa Maria would remain on Española. The Niña's crew would stay intact, as much as possible. They knew the captain, the ship, and each other, which should mean easier sailing. From the Santa Maria, the Spanish boatswain, one of the physicians, one of the pilots and a few others would sail with them. A small number of the Niña's crew would join those who were building Navidad.

"That's settled, then," said Columbus.

"There are two more that must come back with us, Admiral," said De La Cosa. "The young man, Domingo, and the boy, Pedro."

"Why are these two so important to our return?"

"I made a promise to Domingo's father that I would bring him home, unhurt, as soon as I could. And Pedro is too young to remain here."

Columbus and Vicente considered this request. The Niña would already be over-manned. With so many Indians aboard, they would be stepping over each other the entire trip back.

"I have heard that Domingo is a good cook," Vicente said with a raised eyebrow.

De La Cosa added, "And they are both hard workers."

Columbus looked from one to the other and shook his head.

"All right. Domingo and Pedro sail with us. I don't enjoy the thought of eating bad food during our long voyage home either."

Late in the day, while Columbus and Guacanagari were sharing a meal, a messenger arrived with news important enough to be delivered to his cacique immediately. The man was brought before the two leaders. After greeting them formally, he said, "Guacanagari, our men have seen another ship, much like the one in our harbor. It is just down the coast."

When De Torres translated this news, Columbus came to his feet. He had heard no word of the Pinta in over a month. With Guacanagari's permission, the admiral questioned the messenger as to the location of the ship. He turned to the cacique and said, "Forgive me Guacanagari, but I must make every effort to reach our other ship as soon as possible. I must leave you now and meet with my men."

With a new sense of urgency, the men working on Navidad were pushed even harder. The admiral did not intend to let the Pinta out of his reach again.

For once, Domingo was grateful to Francisco when he growled at him to leave his digging and prepare the mid-day meal. Domingo willingly headed for the river, pulling off his wet, filthy shirt as he walked to the riverbank, and knelt down. He splashed the cool water over his face, then his whole head. The water felt so good that he flipped great handfuls over his back and chest. Standing up, he shook his head back and forth sending a spray of water flying. He took a deep breath and admired the beauty of the forest around him. Then he turned and strode back up the path in the direction of what would soon be the fort.

He thought of Anani and wondered what she was doing. Hoping he might have a word with her before he started cooking, Domingo veered off the path and headed toward the beach. As he drew nearer, he could hear female voices at the edge of the trees, and he ducked into the thick vegetation. Maybe he could sneak up on Anani and watch her without her knowing. He moved slowly forward until he could see Anani sitting in the sand with her back to him. She was looking up the coastline away from the other of women. There was only one guard, and he was talking to a young woman at the opposite end of the group. Tiburon, who had always been the most watchful of the women's guards, was standing close to the shoreline gazing at two men being rowed out to the Niña.

Domingo circled wider so he could approach Anani on the side farthest away from the others. He scouted the foliage carefully until he found a thick bush that would shield him nicely, and stealthily crawled closer and around the outside of the shrub. He lay still for a moment to catch his breath. Raising his head, he peeked out in Anani's direction.

There she was, not twenty-five feet to his right. Hura was sound asleep, with his head in Guanina's lap and his feet almost touching Anani's leg. Tanama sat cross-legged in the shade to Guanina's right, chatting with another woman.

His heart was pounding as he checked once more to be sure Tiburon's attention was still occupied elsewhere. Then he picked up a small shell and tossed it at Anani. It missed her back by a foot. He found a small stick and threw it more carefully. It landed just to her left, but she saw it fall and looked quickly in his direction. He raised up just enough for her to see him, putting his finger up to his mouth so she would not call out.

She wondered why he didn't come out of the jungle and join her. Then she saw him beckoning for her, signaling for her to be quiet, and she understood. She turned her head back toward Tiburon, then her mother, and then the guard. None of them was looking her way. Anani glanced ever so casually back in Domingo's direction, as if she were doing no more than eyeing the landscape. Domingo motioned again for her to come to him.

After one more scan of the people around her, Anani stood up and stretched lazily. She wandered very slowly along the trees in Domingo's direction. When she was almost in front of him she bent down and picked up a shell. As she studied it, she sat down in front of the bush that hid Domingo, letting little more than her legs stick out. Tanama glanced at her daughter, saw that Anani was simply looking at a shell, and resumed her talk with her friend. Guanina's head began to droop onto her chest, as Hura's slumber became contagious. Tiburon was still watching the activity near the Niña.

Domingo reached up and ran his hand gently down the length of her hair. He had wanted to do this for so long.

Anani froze for an instant, then forced herself to relax, and continued examining her shell.

"Your hair is so pretty, Anani," Domingo said softly.

Anani smiled at her shell.

Domingo slid his hand under her hair and moved his hand slowly across her back. Anani did not pull away. Instead, she turned her body toward her family so that she could see Domingo if she looked to her right. He slid his fingers from her shoulder to her elbow. Anani shifted the shell to her left hand. When he took her right hand she turned and looked at him. He smiled.

She loved the way his face looked without the beard. She could already see a dark shadow where the beard was starting to grow back, but she could still see all of his handsome face. Yes, it was a very handsome face.

Domingo leaned over her hand and kissed it ever so gently. He looked up at her, and her expression encouraged him. He kissed her hand again, pressing his lips warmly against her skin. Without releasing their hands, he raised himself up until he was kneeling. He pulled on her hand, drawing her towards him. Anani's eyes jerked back to the people on the beach. Luckily they were occupied, because Domingo's next tug caught Anani off guard and pulled her all the way over. She tumbled into him, and he grabbed her to keep her from falling all the way over. "Oh, I'm sorry, Anani!" he whispered. Before she responded she hurried to peek back out at her parents. With a deep sigh, she leaned back into the cover of the greenery, and moved very near Domingo.

They stared at each other. Unable to stop herself, Anani started to giggle silently at the clumsiness of their clandestine meeting. Domingo took her hand again, and drew her in as he leaned toward her. Anani stopped laughing. When Domingo's lips touched hers, she stared at him. As his kiss deepened she closed her eyes and, after a moment, pressed closer to him, lengthening the kiss. Domingo cupped her face with his hands and kissed her again, more thoroughly, reveling in the warmth of her response, the sweetness of her mouth.

Anani drew away from him just long enough to look into

his eyes, as if to reassure herself. Then, with some resolution reached, she closed her eyes once more and tilted toward him. He complied to her unspoken wish with the passion he had felt for her for so long, for what seemed like ages. He kissed her fully, his arms wrapping around her waist and tightening his embrace until she was pressed against him. He moaned at the feel of her exquisite body, the soft warmth of her mouth. Nothing mattered except what he felt for her. He wanted only to hold her like this, to touch and kiss her.

Anani pulled her lips away. She stiffened suddenly, then began pushing against his chest, pushing him away.

"Domingo," she whispered frantically. "Domingo!"

It wasn't until he released her that he heard Tiburon's booming voice, worriedly calling his daughter's name. And he was heading in their direction.

Anani shoved Domingo back further behind the bush, hurriedly straightened the shirt that had twisted around her, and moved as casually as she was able back into the open. Domingo groaned again, this time with frustration. With his heart still racing, he crept out just far enough to see Anani. Her cheeks were flushed, and she did not look directly at her father when he met her and asked where she had been. Her voice was a little shaky when she said she had been exploring. The two voices receded as Tiburon accompanied her back up the beach.

Domingo turned over and lay on his back, waiting for his body to grow calmer. He could still feel Anani against him, still taste her. He tried to force himself to think of something else, to breathe more slowly.

He focused his mind on the fort. With a start, he realized that Francisco was probably looking for him by now. The men would hang him for sure if he kept them waiting for their food too long. He got up, dusted the sand from his clothes, and made his way back in the direction of the site for the fort.

The men exchanged curious glances as Domingo serenaded them the entire time he was preparing their meal.

Just when had the young man learned to love cooking so much?

That night there was another meeting, this time in the hole that would eventually be the cellar of the fort. The men stood anxiously waiting to hear the names of those who were to remain at Navidad. Domingo and Pedro waited with the others for fate to announce itself.

Thirty-nine names, beginning with the officers, were read off the list. After each name was read, a duty or title was assigned. Diego De Arana was to take command of the fort, accompanied by Pero Gutiérrez and Rodrigo De Escobedo. Pedro and Domingo stood tensely side by side as the names were called. They heard Chachu's and Gonzalo's name shouted out, then Francisco's. Not until the last name was read, and instructions were being given to the soon-to-be settlers, did Domingo and Pedro understand that they were to return to Spain together.

Pedro turned to Domingo. "We stay together," he said, nearly overcome with relief.

"Yes, Pedro. I thank God for that," said Domingo sincerely.

But Pedro could see the uncertainty mixed with the relief on Domingo's face. He guessed that Domingo was concerned about Anani.

Within minutes, the issue regarding Anani and her family was also resolved. Columbus announced that he intended to take the Indians from San Salvador and Cuba with him. Guacanagari's brother and cousin had asked to accompany them back to Spain, and they would be made welcome.

Domingo wondered what Anani would think of the admiral's decisions.

After the meeting with the sailors, Columbus and De Torres talked with the Taino captives. The Indians were told that they would see incredulous wonders in Spain, that they would meet the great king of their land, and that they would be given more gifts than they could imagine. Then they were told that they would stay in Spain only a short while before being taken back to their islands, their own villages. The eloquence and sincerity with which these promises were conveyed were enough to convince many of the listeners that to stay with these men would be best.

Anani turned away from Columbus and the interpreter. She saw her father and mother at the edge of the gathering. They were looking into each other's eyes. They had stopped listening too.

The construction of Navidad continued to progress well over the next few days, and the islanders did much to help the seamen. One afternoon an Indian came running into camp looking for the admiral. When the messenger was brought to Columbus, he reported seeing the Pinta again, just two days journey to the east. Hearing this, Columbus decided that they must set sail as soon as final preparations could be made.

In anticipation of the departure of Columbus and his men, Guacanagari's people prepared the finest of feasts, and welcomed all of the visitors. During the celebration, the cacique ceremoniously presented Columbus with a beautiful mask crafted of gold. Then Guacanagari removed his own crown and placed it on Columbus' head.

In return, the admiral presented Guacanagari with a fine scarlet cloak, a silver ring, and a pair of boots. With great solemnity, the admiral placed the cloak on the cacique's shoulders. Columbus then took off his jeweled necklace and secured the clasp around Guacanagari's neck.

"Please accept these gifts as signs of our gratitude, and of our friendship, Guacanagari," Columbus said. "I will think of you often when I am away, and will look forward to our meeting again."

The chief received these things and words with joyous appreciation. Each of the powerful men, through De Torres, promised to hold the other in the highest esteem, and to help each other whenever he was needed.

After the ship was loaded and the partially completed fort stocked, there was still time for some final instructions.

The admiral spoke firmly to the men remaining behind about the need for maintaining a good relationship with Guacanagari and his people. The settlers must remember to use restraint always, even while searching for the gold mine. Above all, they must harm none of the Indians. They were, most specifically, not to use force against any of the women. De Arana was given full authority to punish any man who failed to comply with these restrictions.

Columbus had hoped to leave on January 2, but the winds did not agree with his plan. The next day the wind continued to show its contrary nature. The gusts blew so hard during the evening that it was impossible for the launch to pick up the Indians that were to sail to Spain. Columbus had no choice but to let them spend the night on the island. The precaution was taken, however, to post extra guards around them.

Domingo and Pedro remained on the island along with the Tainos. They were sent to one of the houses that was set apart from where Anani and her family would sleep. It was the farthest Domingo had been separated from her for a long time, and he was uncomfortable about it. When Pedro found out that they had to sleep on the floor instead of in a hammock, he voiced his disappointment quietly, but repeatedly. Domingo finally told Pedro to go to sleep. He lay awake worrying about Anani's safety until he could no longer keep his eyes open, and he fell into a fitful slumber.

At dawn, the men who were setting sail were given a few minutes to say good-bye to the new residents of Navidad. Pedro and Domingo found Rodrigo near the middle of the milling men, giving Gonzalo a bear hug. Once Gonzalo could breath again, he looked at them and smiled.

"The next time I see these two they will be famous explorers, eh, Rodrigo?" Gonzalo declared.

"And the next time we see you, sir," said Pedro, "You will be a rich lord with mountains of gold."

"I hope so," Gonzalo chuckled. "I do hope so, Pedro."

Francisco managed to find them in the crowd, and barked at Domingo and Pedro as soon as he drew near. "And who is going to look after the two of you now?"

Francisco glanced at Rodrigo.

"I guess that duty will fall to you, Rodrigo. Heaven help you!" In spite of his rough sounding words, Francisco was smiling. He gave Pedro and Domingo each a awkward hug and slapped Domingo on the back.

"I have already heard complaining from the men about having to eat my cooking again. You have spoiled them, you know. Take care of yourself, Domingo." Then he added to Pedro, "You too, small one. You keep working like you have been, and you'll own your own ship one day."

Domingo and Pedro wandered through the group shaking hands and hugging the men and boys who had become like a second family to them. All they had been through had formed a strong bond between them. A few of the men let their tears fall freely, unashamed of their sadness at parting from dear friends for many months.

Standing slightly apart, Chachu was firmly shaking hands with De La Cosa. Chachu sniffed hard, and his eyes were slightly red, but no tears were visible.

"I'll try to keep this wild bunch to their tasks, sir," Chachu said.

"I know," said De La Cosa. "I will come back for you as soon as I can, Chachu."

"Yes, sir. I know you will."

When Domingo and Pedro drew nearer, Chachu cleared his throat and looked at them. His glance settled on Domingo and he suddenly remembered how he had played the alboka for the lad in the Canary Islands, and the fight that had followed.

Thinking of that time, he said to Domingo, "If things get too quiet around here, I can always play my alboka." He walked to a pile of stores at the base of a nearby tree and pulled the instrument from a leather pouch.

"How did you ever save it, sir?" Domingo asked in amazement.

With an incredulous expression, Chachu asked, "Did you think, after all the years I've kept this alboka with me, that I would leave it behind?"

They all laughed. Then the two younger seamen said good-bye to Chachu and left the men, allowing them to have a last moment alone before they separated.

Domingo and Pedro were walking down the path toward the beach when De Arana hailed Domingo, and beckoned to him with a wave of his arm. Once the three were together, the master-at-arms told Pedro to go on ahead so that he could speak to Domingo alone. Pedro trotted off and De Arana turned to Domingo. "Well, young man, the winds of fate have chosen to separate us," he said.

"Yes, sir. They have."

"You must give my regards to your family, Domingo. I hope you find your father well when you reach Lequetio. But, of course you will. Aitor was always as strong as an ox."

Domingo nodded at the truth of his last statement.

De Arana reflected, "It seems like a long time since we left Lequetio, doesn't it, Domingo?"

"Yes, sir, a very long time." Domingo recalled listening in the dark outside the window of the Berria house as De Arana and his father argued about Columbus and his plans. It was the first time Domingo had heard of the journey. It seemed like that night happened ages ago.

"Aitor probably won't even let you take off your hat before he'll be asking all about the voyage," De Arana continued. "I'm not sure he'll care too much about whether we found the Great Khan, established a trading fort with the Chinese, or came home with our holds filled with gold. But he'll want to know where we landed, and the likelihood of getting the fishing rights." He sighed heavily and said, "I just hope the queen will consider granting us those rights once she hears how few of her goals we have managed to accomplish. Still, Columbus will present everything that has happened, even losing the Santa Maria, in its best light. I am still optimistic that she will be pleased with us. You can tell Aitor that." Domingo nodded that he would.

"Well," said De Arana as he shook Domingo's hand in both of his own, "Take care of yourself, Domingo."

"Yes, sir. I will. I wish you God's blessings, and great success here in Navidad."

"I will need His blessings if I hope to keep this crew in line," De Arana said with a laugh. More seriously, he said, "I hope we see each other before too long, Domingo." Then turned and headed back up the path toward the fort.

While the men of Navidad were parting with those who were sailing, Columbus was giving his final farewell and thanks to Guacanagari. When at last the good wishes and farewells were made to the men left behind, the sailors and Indians were taken aboard the ship.

Crowded but ready, the Niña opened her sails to the cooperative wind, cleared the reef-ridden bay, and headed east in search of the Pinta.

Swords and Arrows

18

Life aboard the Niña took some getting used to for the former crewmembers of the Santa Maria. Captain Vicente was admired and obeyed by his men, and the ship's operations ran smoothly enough. But, it took time for everyone to adjust to the personalities in the new mix of men, and the Niña's crew had to get used to having so many Tainos aboard.

Domingo felt well accepted, especially since the old cook had been granted his request to remain at Navidad. With the smaller size of the ship and the Indians helping with chores, Pedro found his duties much lighter than they had been aboard the flagship. They were cramped for space because of so many bodies, but their spirits rose with the hope of finding the Pinta soon.

Since Vicente and his hands worked well without help from Columbus or De La Cosa, the two commanders of the Santa Maria often became restless. This impatience grew, along with their worry when the Niña started leaking. Pumping out the hold became a continuous duty for the men. The Tainos were allowed to avoid the wet, foulness of the hold as much as possible.

Late on their second day away from Navidad, Domingo brought his rag and brush, and joined Pedro as he scrubbed the fore deck. The boy had just paused in his cleaning and was staring out ahead of the ship. He didn't look in Domingo's direction, but he knew by the sound of the footsteps who had approached him from behind.

"It's strange without Francisco here to yell at us," Pedro said. "There's no one to make me jump when I'm working. I almost miss him."

"Me too," grinned Domingo, "*Almost.*"

"I wonder what Francisco is doing right now. Do you think the men at Navidad will be alright, Domingo?" Pedro asked, wiping the hair from his face with the back of his hand.

"If they can keep from fighting with each other," Domingo said, "and if they remember what the admiral said about how to treat the Indians, they should be fine. That is, at least until the new fleet comes back for them."

Pedro shook his head and laughed suddenly. "I guess *we* should be worrying about getting home. There'll be no one to come for the men at Navidad if we don't make it back to Spain and tell the queen about them."

"That's true," said Domingo, still smiling. "We need to get home for them as well as for us. Let's hope the admiral knows the way."

They maneuvered along the coast in the direction of the bay where the Pinta had been sighted by the cacique's scout. From the Indian's description, it would take another day or two to reach the spot.

Vicente didn't like the look of the shallow water near the shoreline, and had sent a man up the main mast to scout for hidden reefs. When the seaman had climbed high up and settled into position, Vicente shouted up to him, "How does it look ahead?" Rather than answer the question, the sailor pointed up the coast and yelled out, "The Pinta! The Pinta straight ahead!"

The Pinta was sailing straight toward them. The two ships approached each other, and several of the men shouted greetings, but there was nowhere for them to anchor. The Niña was forced to double back to find a decent harbor. This time, the Pinta followed. All hands waited tensely for the meeting between Columbus and Pinzón.

When the ships were secured, Martín Pinzón boarded the Niña and met the grim face of Columbus. The Niña was a small ship and there was no captain's cabin. What was said could be overheard by most of the hands. Domingo and

Pedro pretended to be busy around the cook pot as they listened.

Before Columbus could speak, Martín said, "Admiral, I ask you to accept my apology for our long separation. On the day we were parted from one another, the sea currents and the wind prevented me from immediately reuniting with the rest of the fleet, as I wanted to. I proceeded with the wind to Babeque but found no gold there. The Indians aboard my ship spoke with some of the natives of Babeque. They told me about the gold here on Bohio. I came here fully expecting to meet our other two ships."

The admiral had maintained a stony silence throughout Pinzóns speech. Now he asked evenly, "And you, Captain Pinzón, have been within forty-five miles of us for over ten days. Were you not told by the Indians that we were nearby?"

Martín hesitated only briefly. "I heard that you were near. But I was certain that you would head east to meet us, just as you did. I didn't come to join you because I have been ill for many days. According to the ship's physician, I have contracted some sort of parasite. During my illness, my men had some success trading for gold."

"How much gold?" Columbus asked.

"A respectable amount, Admiral. I told my men that they could keep half of all they acquired in trade. They proved to be quite resourceful. Also, Admiral, I learned that the mine itself is less than sixty miles up the river we anchored in."

Columbus took a step toward him. "The mine. Are you sure?"

"As sure as I can be without seeing it for myself," said Martín.

"The mine," repeated Columbus under his breath.

Feeling that he was close was not the same as hearing where the mine actually lay. This was what he had been searching for, praying for.

Pinzón interrupted his thoughts. "There's more, Admiral. I found out there is an island to the south of Cuba called Tamaye where they mine *gold nuggets* the size of beans."

"The size of a bean," Columbus echoed thoughtfully.

The day after rejoining the Pinta, the Niña was thoroughly pumped out and caulked in an effort to stop the leaking. While waiting for the Niña to seal, Columbus decided to relieve a little of the crowding on the Niña by transferring a few of the Indians to the Pinta. It was when the Tainos were being shifted, and Columbus boarded the larger ship to speak with Martín, that the admiral saw six unfamiliar Indians. All of them, four males and two females, were naked. When Martín was questioned about them, he explained calmly, "I took them from the village near the river where we traded for gold."

The admiral burst out angrily. "You took them! You just took them! You will take them *back* to their village! Do you understand?"

Martín's expression darkened.

"What purpose would returning them serve?"

"You, Captain, have evidently given little thought to the rest of the men who started out with on this voyage with us. We have a settlement to think of now. These Indians may very well be under Guacanagari's reign. You've taken them by force and that action may..."

"By force?" Martín was livid. "And what have you done, more than once? How did you come by the Indians boarding my ship right now if not *by force?*"

"The circumstances were different then," Columbus snarled. "I didn't take them when doing so could endanger our own men, men who have to *live* among these Indians."

"When I took these Indians," Martín said very slowly between clenched teeth, "I didn't *know* that our men were going to be abandoned on this island. I didn't *know* that their ship would be sunk from beneath them."

Both men glared at each other, their faces dark and their breathing heavy.

Columbus leaned forward and said with barely retrained fury, "They *will* be taken back."

He turned and men scattered to clear a path as he left Martín's ship.

The pressure only mounted between these two powerful

men. To a lesser degree, Vicente also became tangled in their struggle.

The Pinzóns were brothers, and captains of ships they had managed to keep from running aground. Their crews were fiercely loyal to them. Columbus had only a handful of his original crew around him, and De La Cosa. It was De La Cosa who stood by the admiral now, after all that had happened between them. These two sided together, but they were greatly outnumbered. Columbus had the rank of admiral and the backing of the queen, but he had allowed the ship he had commanded to be destroyed. And he was a long, long way from home.

The tension and mistrust that had existed before they had first reached the Indies surfaced again, but this time it ran deeper. The admiral had absolutely no faith in Martín's loyalty, and he did not feel secure with Pinzón's men when Martín was around. He even began to doubt Vicente and his crew as well.

Martín had no intention of losing his ship or his influence to this would-be admiral who could not even keep his own ship afloat. He would do what he must to return the Pinta and the gold to Spain. He had little doubt that the queen would be pleased with the bounty and glory he had gained for their country on this trip. In his mind, his success far outweighed that of Columbus.

Vicente was under Columbus' direct command while the admiral was aboard the Niña, but he acutely felt the strain of both Columbus and Martín demanding his loyalty. He tried to maintain a tenuous balance between them. Still, Martín was his own brother. And Columbus had already lost one ship.

Domingo and most of the crewmembers watched their leaders' ominous interactions with dread. They had two ships left, and they wanted both of them to return safely to Spain. Domingo watched the admiral pacing the decks of the Niña while he clumsily sewed a patch onto his pant leg. Pedro watched the admiral too, and kept very quiet. He leaned over to Domingo and whispered, "Heaven save us from such headstrong commanders. I hope they keep away from each other long enough for us get home."

It took two days to reach the river where Martín Pinzón had spent sixteen days, trading for gold and recuperating from his mysterious illness. Immediately after they dropped the ships' anchors, Columbus ordered the Indians Martín had captured to be dressed and taken back to their village. Pinzón didn't interfere, but he refused to accompany the landing party ashore.

Wanting to leave the area right away, Columbus directed the fleet to head east just as soon as the wind was with them. As long as they were heading east, and along an island where the Indians were willing to trade generously for gold, they would follow the coast. Though moods were tense, equilibrium was maintained through the next couple of days, and the crewmen hoped that their captains' tempers were permanently cooling.

On January 13, a Sunday, the breezes they had been enjoying died away completely, and the fleet was forced to anchor in a beautiful bay surrounded by high, jagged rocks.

Anani and most of the Tainos stood with Domingo and De Torres on the main deck, scanning the impressive landscape with the crew. It was a lovely beach, quiet and beckoning. Domingo had informed his superiors the day before that it would be wise to add to their food supply before returning to Spain. With this in mind, the Niña's launch was sent ashore to gather sweet potatoes and any other fresh food that might be found. Domingo and Rodrigo were among those ordered to go ashore. The pilot, Sancho Ruiz, was to command the seven member landing party while it was away from the ship.

Though they had little fear of trouble from the islanders, four of the men, including Ruiz and Rodrigo, wore swords while they went exploring. The group found a narrow path leading from the beach and moved into the forest.

The birds overhead filled the air with their musical calls. Domingo inhaled the exotic scents that hung in the air.

They had not gone far when Ruiz, who was in the lead, stopped suddenly. He glanced back quickly at Domingo, motioned emphatically for him to come up the line, then snapped his head forward again. It was not until Domingo was almost beside Ruiz that he saw the armed Indians blocking the path ahead of them.

A group of five natives, armed with bows and arrows, spread out in a semi-circle twenty feet ahead of them. The two groups eyed each other warily. The native men standing in front of Domingo had much rougher features than the Tainos. Their faces were colored as black as charcoal and their hair was pulled back and secured so that it hung down their backs. A web of brilliant parrot feathers fanned out from the back of their heads in a magnificent display of color. Domingo noted their weapons, their lack of fear, and how their features differed from those of the Indians he had seen throughout the islands. And he remembered Anani's description of the Caribs.

"Can you speak to them?" Ruiz asked in a hushed tone, never taking his eyes away from the Indians.

"I'll try to, sir."

Domingo stepped forward slowly, holding his hands up to show his peaceful intentions. Trying not to look uneasy, he kept careful watch for any sudden movement of their hands that held bows. He remembered Anani telling him that the Caribs used poison on their arrows, and he tried to push this thought aside.

Addressing himself to the man wearing the largest array of feathers in his hair and standing in the center of the band, Domingo said him in Taino, "We mean you no harm. We are from a land very far away."

The Indians seemed greatly surprised by his greeting, and they looked at each other uncertainly. A member of their group said something back to Domingo using dramatic gestures. Domingo couldn't even guess what he was trying to say, but he tried again in Taino, "We wish to trade for food."

Again the Indian said something to him.

"What the devil is he saying?" demanded Ruiz.

"I can't make out his words, sir."

But the attempts of the two spokesmen had succeeded in

bringing the two groups a few feet closer to one another. Finally, Domingo began using hand signs.

Through the universal language of bartering, the Indians expressed their admiration for Domingo's beret. They were willing to trade two bows and a good supply of arrows for it.

"Well, give him your beret then, Domingo," said Ruiz.

Domingo pulled off his beret. It had been a gift from his father.

"Go on, Domingo. It's the only thing they seem to want," said Ruiz. "I'll see that you get another one."

Domingo reluctantly held out the hat and was given the bow and arrows by the satisfied Indians.

Further attempts at interaction failed, and Domingo shook his head in frustration.

"I can't understand them, sir. They don't seem to speak much Taino, and they aren't willing to part with any more of their bows and arrows."

Ruiz considered this, then said, "Let's see if we can get some of them to the ship. Maybe one of our Indians will have some luck with them."

Domingo returned to the Indian group and motioned for them to come with him. Hesitantly, they followed him the short distance back to the beach. When the islanders saw the ships, they pointed and shouted in amazement. Domingo and Ruiz focused their efforts of persuasion on the Indian that they guessed to be the leader, the one now wearing Domingo's beret. At last, he agreed to come back to the ship with them.

As the launch neared the Niña, and Anani saw the Indian in the boat, she turned to Tiburon and asked apprehensively, "Is he a Carib, Father?"

But it was the brother of Guacanagari who answered her. "He is no Carib. He is a Ciguayo. The Ciguayos have learned many of the Carib's ways, but they usually fight against the Caribs rather than with them."

De Torres and the Tainos aboard had little better luck translating the Ciguayo dialect than Domingo had had. They gave their visitor small gifts, and asked whether there was gold nearby by pointing to the pieces that he wore and gesturing toward the island. The Ciguayo spread his arms wide to indicate that there was much gold in this area.

De Torres questioned him about the islands nearby, whether there was also gold on them. Through signs and words, the Indian described an island to the east of Caniba called Matinino. When the Ciguayo paused, De Torres and Domingo exchanged an amazed look. The interpreter said to Columbus, "He says, Admiral, that there is an island farther to the east that is inhabited solely by women."

"Solely by women?" Columbus eyed the Indian speculatively. "This isn't the first time I've heard of such a place. See what else you can learn about this island."

But De Torres was able to gain little else that was useful.

Columbus was shown the bows and arrows that had been traded for, and he studied them with admiration.

"Ruiz, you and your landing party return this Indian to shore. Take some of our trade goods with you and see how many more bows and arrows you can gather. And, Ruiz, these natives are armed. See that each of your men is too."

After their visitor had been taken to the boat where he waited to be rowed back to land, Ruiz had each member of the landing party arm himself with a sword. Two crossbows and two muskets were wrapped in a section of canvas and stowed in the boat, just in case they were needed.

Domingo slid a scabbard onto his belt then lifted the blade from its sheathing, feeling its weight in his hand. He hoped he would not have to use it. His father had seen that he was given instructions in arms, but Domingo had never used a sword in battle before. He looked up from the sword and saw Anani's troubled face. She had been watching his every move and her face showed her apprehension. She was troubled about these Ciguayos. They used bows and arrows, possibly poisoned arrows, and now Domingo was going back amongst them.

Putting on a confident expression, Domingo gave her an inconspicuous wave of his hand as he passed her. He climbed with the others into the launch and took one of the oars.

Half of the men were already standing on the beach and Domingo was helping pull the boat onto the sand when he heard Rodrigo shout in warning. Domingo turned swiftly around, and froze in place.

"Don't move, men. Stay very still," Ruiz ordered.

Over fifty Ciguayos were emerging from the forest. Each one carried a bow and arrows. Each one had a war club suspended from his belt.

Rodrigo took a step backward, thinking to get the crossbow from the launch.

"I said don't move!" hissed Ruiz. Rodrigo obeyed.

The same Ciguayo who had accompanied them back from the Niña ran out ahead of the Europeans. He shouted at his people, telling them to put their weapons down. At first, no one complied. Then, uncertainly, they lowered their arms to the sand.

They approached the newcomers with little sign of fear, and surrounded the landing party. The Ciguayos examined them with great interest, now exhibiting more curiosity than intimidation. Ruiz and his men moved further onto the beach, not far from the trees, and showed the Ciguayos their trade articles. Domingo was called on again to make out the Ciguayos' words and hand signs, but he had little success.

Using hand signs, Ruiz managed to consummate a deal for a couple of bows and several clubs. But when he attempted to buy more of the weapons, one of the Ciguayos moved away from Ruiz defensively. He said something in a threatening voice that Domingo could not understand, but his meaning was clearly defiant. He surveyed the people around him, then shouted something to his men. Suddenly the Ciguayos spun around and ran back to their weapons. They grabbed not only their arms, but also short ropes from where they had lain in the sand, then turned and raced back toward the strangers.

The members of the landing party stared with dread as the Ciguayos rearmed themselves. They were caught outnumbered and outdistanced. They could never reach the boat before the arrows could reach them. Domingo and each of the other men drew his sword. Rodrigo had crept back to the boat when the Ciguayo had shouted, and he now panted up to them with two crossbows in his arms. He thrust one of these at a man standing next to Ruiz. They had already been fitted with arrows.

Domingo felt the firm weight of the blade in his hand, and watched the Ciguayos approach. He saw that they were carrying ropes. They wanted to take them alive. Domingo knew what happened to men who were taken alive.

Ruiz's men followed the pilot's lead when he began walking cautiously backward toward the boat, facing their enemies. With a loud cry, several of the Ciguayos charged at them, their war clubs raised high. Rodrigo fired his crossbow at the man in the lead. The arrow pierced his chest, throwing him backward, and burying itself so deeply in his body that only the fletching showed. Seeing their comrade fall, many of the Ciguayos turned from their assault. Others crashed into the band of Europeans. Swords swept broadly in an effort to defend against the many clubs.

Two warriors, one somewhat taller than the other, faced Domingo boldly. The taller man was the first to raise his club. He swung the deadly piece of wood, missed, and jumped away from Domingo's responding sword thrust. The other man tried next with no more success than the first. The two alternately attempted to get in close enough to land a stunning blow without being stung by the blade of their adversary. Domingo's agility allowed him to step and duck before the sweep of their clubs could stun him. But the Indians had swiftness as well, and Domingo did not touch them with his steel. Quickly realizing that they were gaining little, one of the two Ciguayos moved to Domingo's opposite side.

Now Domingo began to swing more wildly, desperately trying to watch both of his opponents at the same time. His sword grew heavier with each stroke and thrust, and sweat began to roll down his back and arms. He heard a hard "thud" and a sailor fell to the sand several feet to his left. From the corner of his eye, he saw the tall Indian signaling something to the other Ciguayo. In an instant the shorter man swung at Domingo's knees just as the taller man brought his heavy club in a gliding arch directly toward Domingo's head. But Domingo had anticipated such a simultaneous attack. With precise timing, Domingo dove under the swing of the taller man, clearing the invisible circle that the three had formed, and out of reach of the shorter Ciguayo's swing. He came up like a cat and spun around to face his foes again.

At that instant a terrible cry of pain rose from several yards behind Domingo. He glanced in that direction while keeping his opponents in view. The stroke of a sailor's sword had sliced deeply into the buttock muscles of the Ciguayo he had been fighting, toppling the Indian to the sand. The wounded man had fallen forward and was writhing on his belly in agony.

The painful wail of the fallen man paralyzed the other Ciguayos for a moment. Domingo stood crouched and ready as his two adversaries stared at the grisly gash inflicted on their fellow warrior. One of Ruiz's men near the outside of the ring of fighters raised his sword to kill his temporarily motionless enemy, but Ruiz quickly shouted an order to stay his hand. The sailor standing closest to Ruiz lifted his newly loaded crossbow, but Ruiz slapped it down just before he fired, and the arrow struck nothing but the sand.

The Ciguayos inched toward the injured man, picked him up, and backed away from the strangers. They continued to withdraw until they were only a few feet from the line of the forest, where they stopped and did not move further.

The landing party stayed very still for a moment, then they too began backing up. They held their swords ready in their hands. Their eyes darted from one Indian to the next watching for any sudden movement. The seaman who had been knocked down in the fight was having trouble standing. Rodrigo lifted him and helped him limp along toward the boat. Never taking their eyes off of the Ciguayos, they reached the launch and got inside. After the others were aboard, Domingo and Rodrigo pushed the boat away from the beach and jumped in. Someone thrust a musket into

Domingo's hands. No one spoke. Domingo tried to breathe evenly and steady his stomach. The men in the launch continued to stare back at the shore until the Indians had retrieved their fallen warriors, and disappeared into the trees.

Anani and Tiburon had been watching the beach, and were the first to see that the landing party was in danger. They had shouted to De Torres, who looked ashore and saw the battle for himself. He let out an alarmed yell for the admiral. The Niña was over a mile from shore. The Pinta was even farther out, and it had the only remaining launch. Before the Niña's crew had even been able to get an answering signal from the Pinta, the skirmish was over and the landing party was retreating to the ship.

While the fight had lasted, Anani had watched in terror as Domingo swung his sword against the two Ciguayos. She had held the rail so tightly that her hands had cramped. Then she had held her amulet and prayed to her zemis, begging them to spare Domingo's life. Tiburon had sadly observed his daughter's misery as she helplessly watched the struggle on the beach, and heard her twice mutter Domingo's name.

When the men came aboard the Niña and retold the details of the fight to Columbus, the admiral considered the ramifications of the conflict aloud.

"There is always the possibility that these people will seek revenge. They pose no real danger to us, but the men at Navidad may be vulnerable." After considering a moment, he continued. "Since Guacanagari's people were not involved in the fight, there is no reason for his Tainos to retaliate against our men. It is likely that these Ciguayos will learn of the settlement but today's battle should give them a healthy fear of our weapons. They'll most likely stay far from Navidad."

Columbus, seeming quite satisfied now, announced, " I intend to take some of these Ciguayo warriors back to Spain. The queen will want to see how they differ from the other Indians."

Domingo, Rodrigo, Ruiz, and the others who had gone

ashore shifted uneasily and exchanged glances. Anani and Tiburon wondered if this strange white-haired cacique could possibly mean what he had just said.

That evening Ruiz made good his promise to replace Domingo's beret. Though it was not the one his father had given him, Domingo accepted it gratefully. He turned it around and around in his hands thinking that he would never forget today, the day he lost his old one.

To the surprise of the sailors, the cacique of the Ciguayos came to the ship the following morning. In spite of the conflict of the day before, he showed no sign of aggression. He was warily brought aboard, fed, and given gifts. Pleased by his reception, the chief promised to send Columbus a crown of gold the very next day, and he carried out his promise. Along with the crown, the many Ciguayos who canoed out to the ship brought sweet potatoes, cotton, and other provisions to trade.

Upon questioning four young Ciguayo men, who seemed to have a good understanding of the islands lying to the east, the admiral was very much impressed with their knowledge. He was so impressed, in fact, that he had them detained in the hold overnight. In the morning, the Niña sailed out of the harbor with the four youths still aboard.

Although Columbus intended to sail to the island of Matinino to capture some of its female inhabitants, he was forced by the winds to abandon this scheme. On January 16, the breezes blew strong and steady, directing them toward Spain. The two caravels were leaking again, and the crews were more restless than ever to reach home safely. Much to the satisfaction of the seamen, and the despair or sad resignation of the captives, the fleet left the islands of wonder and disappointment behind them. As the ships pointed toward Europe, every person aboard prayed that they would be allowed to see their homeland again.

The working shifts that would be maintained for the duration of the journey were assigned, and Pedro and Domingo were given back the hours that they had adhered to on the way to the Indies. While exploring the islands and starting to build Navidad, the shifts of duty had been vari-

298

able depending on what needed to be done. But aboard ship, a routine was mandatory. In no time, the crew was performing smoothly.

Just after finishing their mid-day meal, Domingo and Pedro climbed to the back rail of the poop deck and watched Española growing smaller in the distance. By the time they had sailed another mile or two, the beautiful island would be out of sight completely.

For awhile, they just watched in silence. Then Pedro said with a reflective voice, "I've been thinking about all the things we've seen since we left Spain, Domingo."

Domingo waited patiently until Pedro began again.

"I never dreamed of places like we've seen."

There was another pause, then, "And just think of the *thousands* of naked people. I saw so many naked people, I nearly forgot how unnatural it is to go around naked all the time."

Domingo smiled to himself.

"And you had your first real fight with a sword!" Pedro was still hugely impressed at how Domingo had handled himself against the Ciguayos.

"Yes," said Domingo, "and I thank God those Indians didn't use their poisoned arrows. They could have killed us all with those arrows."

"Domingo, I'm not sure people will believe us when we get back home and tell them about everything."

Domingo thought about this. It was true that they had seen a great many strange and wondrous things. A *great* many. But he knew his family would believe him. The men in his family had been bringing home wild stories for generations.

Pedro's young voice had a sad, far away quality when he interrupted his friend's reflections. "You know, Domingo, we never did see the golden houses."

Domingo leaned down, crossed his arms along the edge of the railing, and rested his chin on his arms. His head was only inches from Pedro's.

"No, we never saw the golden houses." He looked at the boy. "But we got pretty close, Pedro. The admiral thinks they are somewhere east of here, in a place called Japan. Anani says the island's name is really Cibao. She says she's never heard of any golden houses, but then, she's never known anyone who came from there. Maybe the houses are there after all. And like you said, we did see things that were pretty amazing, like the Taino cities. Weren't they something to tell our families about? And remember that canoe that was trimmed with gold and big enough to carry a hundred and fifty people?"

Pedro brightened little by little as he and Domingo recounted what they had witnessed over the last few months. When Española vanished altogether from their sight, the two friends turned around and looked to the northeast, toward home. Hura soon found them. The youngster listened with large eyes as Pedro turned his talk to the subject of his mother's delicious bread.

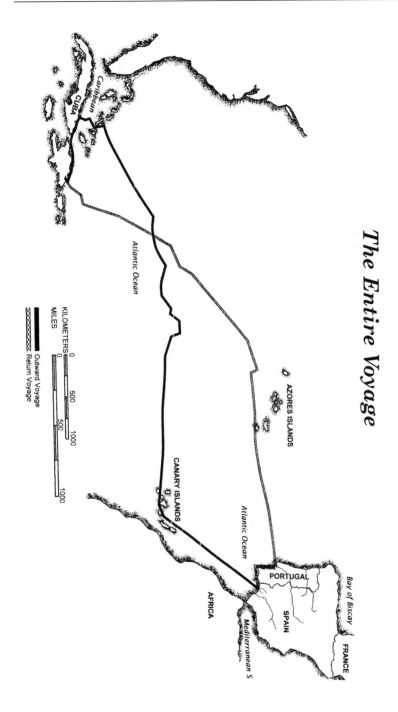

The Entire Voyage

The Wind

19

Days, then weeks passed with fair weather and good breezes. The sailors began to talk more and more of loved ones waiting for them back in their own villages. Domingo avoided such conversations whenever possible. He tried not to think of home and the outcome of the choices he had made, and was yet to make. His mind was full enough with worries about Anani's future without dwelling on his own, or that of the girl who was waiting for him in Lequetio. Every time Domingo asked De Torres what would happen to the Tainos the interpreter told him that they would be returned to their own islands, if that was what the queen chose. But Domingo didn't trust that Isabella would choose to release the Indians. If she didn't, Anani's fate could be something to dread. During quiet moments, he was tortured by the knowledge that he may not be able to protect her once they reached Spain.

Domingo and Anani took pleasure in each other whenever an opportunity was allotted to them aboard the small, cramped ship. Domingo spoke to her more often in Spanish now, knowing it would be better for her if she became more fluent in that language. She was quick to learn and Domingo, when none of the crew was too near, started to teach her to read and write. Anani was fascinated by these lessons, and Domingo took great pride in her steady progress.

As they traveled further to the north, the air grew cold, much colder than the Tainos had ever experienced. January disappeared and February grew to middle age, and all the while the cold intensified. Europeans and Indians alike bundled into coats, canvas, and anything else available to them.

At times, even the terrible smell and filth of the leaky hold was easier to tolerate than the biting chill above deck. The seawater turned frigid and people scurried to avoid it as it splashed across the main deck or swirled through the hold.

One morning before it was fully light, the early sun was surrounded by gray clouds and the sky darkened again. Domingo had just checked on Anani and her people and was now sorting through the dwindling supply of firewood. He felt the Niña surge and listened to the wind strengthening. He piled the wood onto a square of canvas, slung the load on his back, and plodded up the slightly swaying stairs.

He had just stepped onto the main deck when the Niña's prow rose high and pitched forward, knocking Domingo forcefully to his knees. Wood scattered in every direction. He stood slowly, spreading his legs wide apart to steady himself on the rolling ship and just managing to keep his feet under him. The wind whipped him suddenly, flinging his new beret high in the air and overboard. Men were scurrying awkwardly to their positions on the ropes and straining to adjust the billowed sails. Columbus, De La Cosa, and Vicente were shouting orders but the wind mocked their efforts by swallowing their words. The admiral climbed to the stern castle holding tightly to the rail, and studied the storm's assault.

With the first blasting gusts, the sea began to stir as if it were a newly awakened beast. Within minutes, the wind howled with a gale's force. The waves rose, tossed, and angrily collided into each other. As men scrambled to lower the sails, waves broke over the rails, knocking some of them to the deck, and spilling over them. A sailor fell a few feet in front of Domingo. The man lost his hold on the rope and was being washed toward the starboard railing. Domingo and another seaman leaped to grab him but the next wave crashed down on Domingo while he was off balance and he went down too. The sailor he had been trying to help hit the rail first, then Domingo smashed against him. Somehow, Domingo managed to regain his feet and help his breathless shipmate to the center of the deck before the next wave caught them.

Rain began to fall in torrents and the wind hurled the drops against faces and legs, stinging cruelly. Men strained and grappled with the wet ropes, fighting to bring the sails down before they were shredded.

Once the sails were secured, most of the crew were ordered below. They could be of no further use until they were called for, and the officers did not want to risk letting any of their men get tossed overboard.

Before Domingo could make it down to the hold, De La Cosa appeared inches from Domingo's face and shouted for him and another man to help with the tiller lines. Domingo grabbed Rodrigo as he hurried to the back of the ship.

The helmsman and Ruiz were standing on opposite sides of the tiller, fighting to keep it stable, but they were being tossed around like dolls. Domingo and Rodrigo each grabbed a rope behind one of the struggling men, but even their added strength did little to steady the wild whipsawing of the tiller. The Niña pitched and rolled violently with the repeated pounding of the waves. Two more sailors joined them, and all of the men labored and pulled until their hands were raw and their legs aching, and still the Niña bucked and turned beneath them. A huge wave rose behind the caravel and flung itself against the stern of the ship. Icy water exploded through the rudder port, and drenched the men battling to control the tiller. The man behind Rodrigo lost his foothold and went down. He came up again with the rope still in his hand and blood running from his lower lip.

Vicente appeared, wet and breathless in front of the tiller, then De La Cosa and Columbus also became visible.

"We must head straight into the waves!" Columbus yelled to Ruiz. "We will direct you! Watch the compass!"

Columbus stationed himself above them at the front of the stern castle where he could try to gage the onslaught of the waves. The wailing of the wind was so loud that Columbus had to shout his directions to De La Cosa, who shouted them to Vicente, who shouted them to the team at the tiller.

At first, Domingo's physical efforts were so great that his

body heat offset some of the cold. But soon the repeated drenchings and the whipping wind chilled him and his shipmates to their bones. Their hands grew numb and their grips, in spite of their best efforts, began to slip. Another following wave exploded through the rudder port, flinging its icy weight at them, and Domingo fell to one knee. It took all of his strength to rise again.

Before the men lost all feeling in their hands, and their legs would no longer support them, they were relieved by another team, and ordered to the hold.

Domingo and the others reached the hatchway with difficulty, stumbled down the steps, and sat panting to the bottom of the stairs, too exhausted to move. Each of the men had at least one bleeding hand. The Niña's physician brought his salves and bandages, and tended to their wounds as the men regained their breath and a little of their strength. Domingo hardly raised his eyes to the doctor when it was his turn to be tended. He didn't even try to lift his hands.

When Domingo finally lifted his head to look around, he saw one of the Tainos toward the stern of the ship vomiting into a bucket. He noticed the rising smell of seasickness. His eyes searched for Anani until he saw her not far to his left. She sat with her head leaning back against the ship's side and her arms crossed over her stomach. She was unusually pale.

She had been terrified when Domingo had not come to the hold despite Pedro's assurances that Domingo was all right. When she saw Domingo descending the steps at last, she had started to approach him but had been overcome by another wave of nausea. She had been forced to sit down before she could reach him. She sat there watching the doctor bandage him, waiting for him to look in her direction. When Domingo's eyes finally met hers, she managed to give him a shaky smile of reassurance.

Domingo could see that she was sick, and fighting to hide her fear. He got unsteadily to his feet and moved to her side. Each of them pretended, for the sake of the other, that they

305

were not afraid. They sat close together as the tempest raged, forcing the Niña to pitch and lunge relentlessly.

The storm persisted throughout the day, that night, and into the next day. Deep into the second night, the winds eased slightly, and the hopeful crew raised the sails a little. But within a few short hours, the wind began to blow even stronger than before, and the sails were hurriedly brought down once again. As the battered, exhausted people aboard the Niña used every measure of their strength to keep from capsizing, they wondered how long their craft could withstand the power that assaulted them.

No one was immune from the seasickness that enveloped the ship, but the Tainos suffered far more than the experienced hands. Few even tried to eat the cold food that was offered, and even fewer kept it down if they tried. With little or no food and the demands of the storm, the men, women, and children grew weaker.

During the second night of the storm, the Niña's crew had continuously signaled the Pinta in an effort to keep the ships together. The Pinta returned the signals, and Martín and his men battled to stay near the smaller caravel. Then, though it did not seem possible, the wind increased in force. Lightning flashed over the ships and the roaring cracks of thunder ripped the air again and again. Rain fell so thick and heavy that nothing beyond a few feet was visible.

Domingo was among a new group of men struggling to hold the tiller when the ship was caught between two opposing waves. The waves hit both sides of the Niña at the same time, and she swung halfway around, leaning horribly to the port side. The tiller swept in an unstoppable arch and flung all of the men to the ground. One man crashed against the side of the ship with such momentum that he was knocked unconscious and fell like a stone to the deck. The others scrambled to untangle themselves from loose lines and each other while trying to avoid being crushed by the wildly swinging tiller. Domingo felt someone grab him from behind and yank him to the side of the ship. He turned around and faced Gonzalo who was still holding onto Domingo's belt.

"Grab hold of the ship you fool!" Gonzalo yelled.

Domingo gratefully did so and he nodded his thanks to Gonzalo. He squinted across the ship and saw De La Cosa holding the unconscious sailor against his chest with one arm while he held himself to the hull of the ship with the other. Vicente made his way to them and ordered them to abandon the tiller. It was useless to try to control the ship any longer. They had no choice but to leave the Niña in the hands of God.

The men helped De La Cosa with the unconscious sailor as they limped and struggled down into the hold. The last man closed the hatch behind them, then was tossed to the floor by the heaving of the ship. The hurricane roared above their heads as waves broke one after another onto the decks.

Domingo was trying to breathe evenly when a terrible image arose in his mind. He imagined the Pinta colliding with them, its larger prow splintering the Niña's hull like kindling and throwing them all into the sea. The sea was so cold. He forced himself to push away the horror of this picture, and to control his panic. He heard Pedro call his name, and Domingo somehow found his way through the huddled bodies and shifting stores to the terrified boy. He brought Pedro with him until he found Anani and her family. Hauling Pedro's shaking form onto his lap, Domingo held him in his arms, and sat close to Anani. He took a deep breath and closed his eyes. Now the Niña had to fight the horrible storm all alone.

The torment of that night did not ease with the coming of a gloomy dawn. As if to taunt the absolute misery of those on board, the wind blew with even greater intensity. Thunder continued to be heard over the roaring of the wind, and the pummeling of the waves against the deck overhead. And the men and women wondered anew how the small ship could survive the onslaught against her.

Columbus braced himself against the side of the stairs and stood up. He scanned the faces before him until he had their attention. Shouting to be heard, he said, "There is only one power mightier than this storm, and it is in heaven alone. The time has come for every one of us to beg for mercy and deliverance."

Many heads bowed at these words, but the admiral had not finished.

"To show our devotion, I propose that one of us make a pilgrimage in honor of the Holy Mother of God when we next set foot on land. When that day comes, the chosen man will visit the nearest shrine dedicated to Mary and offer prayers on behalf of us all. Do you all agree?"

Heads nodded and men mumbled "yes" and "we agree."

Columbus reached under the stairs, felt around for a moment, then pulled out a canvas bag. He reached into the bag and lifted a single garbanzo bean.

"We will each draw a bean from my hat," he yelled. He took out his knife, and worked it twice across the garbanzo. "The man who draws the bean that bears the cross I have just carved, will fulfill the pilgrimage. Understand?"

Everyone nodded again. One by one, they came up to draw a garbanzo. Before half the crew had drawn, the admiral drew the bean with the cross. He stared at it a moment, then solemnly promised to carry out the pilgrimage.

When the storm continued to blow with no less intensity, two more lotteries were held, and promises to fulfill pilgrimages were made. But the tempest only defied their efforts, and roared on. Finally, every man vowed to go ashore wearing nothing but his shirt to offer up prayers of thanksgiving, if only they would reach a shore. And still the storm did not abate.

In one last weak effort to stabilize the lightweight Niña, Vicente ordered several men to tie themselves to the ship and fill empty water and wine kegs with seawater. When this strenuous task at last had been carried out, the heavy barrels were lowered back into the hold. But such efforts accomplished precious little against the might of the hurricane.

The day wore on and the wretched humans in the hold were continually battered by the savagery of the waves that tossed their ship.

Near sunset, the admiral withdrew to a corner of the

hold, taking his parchment and his pen with him. He told the men that he intended to write down some prayers as an act of devotion, but some supposed that this was not his true intention. De La Cosa, who had a terrible bruise on the left side of his jaw from being thrown against the rail by a wave, watched his commander start writing. Then De La Cosa nodded once, and lowered his head.

Domingo observed the admiral as he sat atop a barrel and moved his pen quickly along the page. "He's documenting our voyage," Domingo rightly guessed. Almost abstractly, as if the scene he was observing had little to do with himself, Domingo continued to speculate about the inner workings of the admiral's mind. He followed the motion of Columbus' pen with his tired eyes.

"He will surely keep his logbook with the ship, in case we survive," Domingo thought. "But, in case the ship goes down, he is writing a separate record. He will probably set the second accounting adrift. Then there will still be a chance that it will reach someone on land. Is he describing, right now, the islands we found, or the people, or the gold?" Because of his weariness, Domingo almost smiled to himself. "Most likely, he's asking the queen to remember him kindly."

He saw Columbus pause, and a look of longing and regret crossed the admiral's face. Then he resumed his writing. "No," Domingo decided, a little ashamed for his earlier thoughts, "He's asking for someone to look after his sons. He's thinking of them now."

For the last hour, Domingo had been thinking of his own family. He had pictured his mother, then his father. He had last seen his father lying sick in bed. He didn't even know if Aitor was still alive. He wondered if his amuma still lived. Even his brothers, who had been at sea just as he had, might not have survived the last eight months. His chest tightened at the thought of them. How he wished he could see them again, well and whole. He wanted desperately to see them all, as he had thousands of times before, sitting by the fire in their kitchen.

When Columbus finished writing, he told the men that

he meant to throw his prayers into the sea as a holy offering. He carefully wrapped his pages of parchment in a waxed cloth, tied it securely, and placed it inside a small keg. Once the cask was tightly sealed, he had two men toss it into the turbulent waves. When this had been done, the admiral sat back down with the rest of the men.

De La Cosa caught the admiral's eye, and he nodded again. They had prayed and the admiral had sent their history into the jaws of a raging ocean. All the men of the Niña could do now was wait for death or the end of the storm.

Darkness overtook them, and they sat swaying, wet and weak, in the dim light of two candle lanterns. Not long after night had come, Domingo noticed De La Cosa suddenly sit bolt upright, and hold stock still, listening. Almost afraid to hope that God had finally answered their prayers, Domingo listened too. De La Cosa's ears had not deceived him. The wind seemed to be easing up. Then, unquestionably, the wailing of the wind quieted, and the Niña began to roll almost gently.

Except for the few who were too sick to notice, those in the hold gradually became aware of the change. Voices rose one after the other, and people tried to find room to stand. De La Cosa was the first one up the stairs, then Vicente. Columbus followed as quickly as his older, aching legs would let him. The hatch was thrown open, and the three men climbed the last steps and stood on the main deck. They searched the sea and sky with their eyes. The rain had stopped and the clouds were parting. Though the ocean still rose in great swells, the wind was continuing to subside.

Columbus quickly gave permission for everyone to come up out of the hold.

Vicente scanned the horizon again, then once more, his eyes probing the ocean's surface for what he desperately hoped to find. But the Pinta, carrying his brother and many of his friends, was nowhere to be seen.

Domingo and De Torres helped Pedro, Anani, and some of the weaker Tainos up the steps. They were among the

last to reach the fresh air and to get a glimpse of the moon-
lit sky.

Great fatigue, as well as the dark clouds that hung
threatening in the east, dampened the relief many felt. Still,
more than a few offered prayers heavenward for this time of
relative peace. More than one of the men knelt down and
kissed the wet decks of the loyal Niña for keeping them all
alive through the nightmare of the last few days.
Cautiously, they raised some of the sails, and moved steadily northeast through the night.

With the light of dawn, land was sighted not far ahead.
Domingo and Pedro huddled together on the foredeck and
took in the vision before them. It was an island surrounded
on all sides by high rocky cliffs.

"Well, it may not look too friendly, but it *is* land," Pedro
said.

Columbus came up next to Pedro. "It must be one of the
Azores," the admiral said.

"The Azores, sir?" asked Pedro.

"They're about eight hundred miles from Palos. And they
are ruled by Portugal," Columbus said, still staring at the
cliffs.

Domingo's anticipation immediately mixed with deep
apprehension. If the inhabitants of the island were
Portuguese, a country that didn't look kindly on sailors from
Spain, their reception was not likely to be favorable. If the
locals thought that the Niña had come from profiteering
along the coast of Africa, which was Portugal's by treaty,
things could go badly when they anchored. And how would
the Portuguese deal with them if they discovered that
Christopher Columbus captained their ship? The admiral,
after all, had left King John of Portugal without his permission, and now sailed under the flag of the Spanish monarchs. King John may even have offered a reward for
Columbus' capture.

They approached the island cautiously, circling it until
they found a rocky harbor in which to drop anchor. As they
were securing the ship, several curious island residents
appeared near the shoreline. Though Columbus spoke

Portuguese well, he brought De Torres to the railing and had him ask the islanders exactly where they were.

The men on the beach, astounded at the sailors' appearance as well as De Torres' question, looked at each other then back at the ship. One man finally yelled back, in Portuguese also, "The Azore Island of Santa Maria."

Columbus sucked in his breath, then turned to his men. "Did you hear? We have landed on an island named for the Blessed Virgin. She heard our prayers after all."

With further questioning, De Torres also learned from the islander that there was a chapel nearby named for Saint Mary.

Portuguese land or not, they had made a vow to visit the first church dedicated to the Holy Mother that they could walk to, and the men were gratefully willing to fulfill that pledge. Columbus allowed half the men to strip down to nothing but their shirts, and go ashore to pray at the chapel.

Much to Domingo and Pedro's disappointment, they were not among the first group to head for shore. While the older men were set to work on badly needed repairs to lines and sails, the younger hands ordered to clean out the hold. With the Niña at rest, several of the Tainos began to feel well enough to help the sailors with their duties.

Domingo didn't begin to feel uneasy about the landing party until he came up from the hold and saw De La Cosa pacing the stern deck and glancing toward shore. When Domingo realized how late the day had grown, he looked toward land too, and wondered what was taking their men so long.

Another hour passed, and tension was rising throughout the entire the ship when De La Cosa spotted their launch rowing back toward them. But instead of their own sailors, the launch was manned by what appeared to be a Portuguese official and some of his soldiers. Columbus ordered four men to load their muskets and keep them visible.

Portuguese law," Columbus barked.

"I think we will decide otherwise once we have seen what

The launch rowed near, but not too near the Niña. The Portuguese men were well armed. The leader stood up in the launch and declared in Portuguese, "I am Captain Juan De Castaneda, governor of this island. I wish to speak with your captain."

Columbus, who already stood at the rail, answered the man in his own language. "I am captain of this ship. What authority do you bear that you to come to my ship in my own launch? Where are my men?"

"Your name, captain?" demanded De Castaneda.

Columbus' eyes were already darkening. In a tightly controlled voice, he said, "You, Captain, are addressing Don Christopher Columbus, Admiral of the Ocean Sea and Governor of the Indies. My titles have been bestowed upon me by the sovereigns of Spain."

De Castaneda and his men burst out laughing. It struck them as highly amusing that such a boast could come from a man dressed in filthy clothes and standing aboard a tiny, battered ship.

"An admiral? Does Spain always provide her admirals with such grand ships? And Governor of the Indies, is it? You ask me to believe that you've sailed to the Indies and back in that tiny wreck of a caravel?"

Again De Castaneda and his men laughed at the ridiculous claims.

Columbus threw away all pretense of politeness. In a terrible temper he shouted, "If you are holding my men, Captain, you will release them at once!"

De Castaneda stopped laughing. "That I will not do," he stated flatly. "But you, Admiral, will surrender to me *at once.*"

"Didn't you hear that I have gained my authority by direct order of the king and queen of Spain?" asked the admiral ominously.

Now De Castaneda was also losing his patience. "Spain has no authority here! *I* am the authority on this island. Your men are in my prison and you will join them until you are all judged for your crimes."

"Crimes! We have committed no crimes, even under-
313

you carry in your hold," said De Castaneda. "Pirates on their way home from Africa have stopped here before."

"Once more, Captain, I order you to release my men," said Columbus precisely.

"And for the last time, I tell you that your orders mean nothing on the Island of Santa Maria."

"If you do not set my men free, Captain," said Columbus threateningly, "I will sail on to Spain with what hands I have. And when I *return*, I will bring back enough ships and men to take you and every other Portuguese on this accursed island back to Spain in chains! I suggest you reconsider your position!"

"And I suggest, Admiral," De Castaneda said mockingly, "That you reconsider yours. I act on behalf of King John of Portugal. I have your men, and I doubt you can sail that rowboat you are standing in without them. I will give you an hour to think over what I've said."

With that, De Castaneda gave a signal to his men and was rowed back to shore. Columbus watched them go with an unreadable expression.

Domingo stood with the rest of their skeleton crew and waited for the admiral's decision. They had only a handful of experienced sailors left on board. How could they hope to sail the Niña with so few? And what if they encountered another storm?

Instead of answering the worries of his men, the admiral waved for De La Cosa and Vicente to follow him to a quiet place on the stern deck. After their meeting, the hands were ordered to repair the ship as best they could, and to fill more barrels with seawater.

Domingo shook his head when he heard the command. It meant they were heading back to sea without the rest of their crew. What would happen to those left behind in the Portuguese jail would not be pleasant.

Hardly had the latest orders been carried out when the wind began to pick up again. Their harbor was far less than ideal, and as the Niña rocked in the strengthening wind, an anchor line was cut loose by the rocks of the bay. This occurrence left little choice but to turn the Niña out to sea.

Through most of the night, a new storm buffeted the ship, and the sparse crew was sorely tried in their efforts to hold a position. Domingo was so exhausted by the middle of the night that he stumbled down the stairs into the hold, crawled across the floor to Anani and her family, and slept like a dead man. He was wakened well before sunrise, to take his turn above deck again. At dawn, he could see Santa Maria Island not far off.

Domingo heard Columbus call out an order to turn the Niña back toward the island. It was brutally obvious now that they could not survive the open sea with so few hands. For all their sakes, they must try again to recover their imprisoned men. If they failed, at least they would share the same fate.

Not long after the Niña anchored, two priests, a notary, and five of their own Spanish sailors, rowed out to the ship. When their lost men set foot aboard they were welcomed heartily with hugs and endless questions. While everyone talked at once, Domingo hurried off to get the hungry seamen something to eat.

Columbus, Vicente, and De La Cosa greeted the Portuguese arrivals with formal respect. The notary politely asked if he could inspect Columbus' letters of authority from the king and queen of Spain, and was allowed to do so.

While the man was reviewing this document, Columbus asked, "Has your governor reconsidered my words then? Is he now willing to release all of my men?"

The notary raised his eyes and spoke with great diplomacy. "Last night Captain De Castaneda...questioned your men, sir. Based on what they told him, he has indeed reevaluated your words. He has sent me to confirm your claims, as well as theirs. I was told to review the paper that supports your titles, and inspect your cargo to insure that you are not carrying goods from Africa. I am then to report back to him on all that I see. What he will ultimately decide regarding the rest of your men, I do not know."

When the notary had thoroughly reviewed the letter of authority and the cargo of the ship, he turned in amazement to face the admiral. "It appears that everything you and your men told Captain De Castaneda is true, Admiral Columbus. These people," he said pointing to the islanders, "Look nothing like Africans. As a matter of fact, nothing aboard this ship is similar to what I have seen taken from the African coast. As remarkable as it seems," he couldn't help smiling, "You must have sailed to the Indies, just as you claim. I will relay these observations to Captain De Castaneda, sir."

The hour had grown late by the time the notary concluded his inspection, so the three Portuguese visitors remained aboard the Niña that night. Early in the morning, they were allowed to row back to the island, leaving the Spanish sailors behind.

Two hours after the notary and priests returned to shore, the remaining prisoners were released. Filthy, half-dressed, and hungry, they rowed themselves as fast as their arms could propel them out to the ship.

The Niña stayed near Santa Maria Island only long enough for the crew to take on a little fresh water and firewood, and to give their ship the minimum of repairs. The sooner they left Portuguese land, the safer they would all feel. When the wind blew from the west that night, they sailed before it toward Spain.

If the weather remained fair, it was conceivable that the Niña could reach Palos in little more than a week. The hopes of the bedraggled crew rose with each passing mile. The first day came and went with calm winds. Food was not plentiful, but with careful rationing, it would last until they reached home.

Domingo started telling Anani all about Palos. Her amazement, and sometimes her outright doubt as to the truthfulness of his stories amused him. When he tried to describe an ox and cart to her, she just smiled and slowly shook her head at him. The thought of a huge beast being willing to carry people in a wooden box that rolled along behind its body was just too much to accept. Domingo had to bring De Torres over to convince Anani that such a thing really existed. She was especially curious about the queen, and would sit patiently listening for as long as Domingo would talk about the great lady.

Anani never asked when she would be returned to her homeland, or whether Domingo would come back with her. She knew that the answers to these questions were not in Domingo's power to control, at least not totally.

Late on the second morning away from the Azores, one of the sailors who had been imprisoned overnight on the island started sneezing and complaining of a severe headache. By that evening, several other sailors were showing various signs of mild sickness. The ship's physician, Dr. Alonso, told Columbus that the symptoms appeared to indicate the onset of influenza. The sick seamen were allowed as much rest as possible and the remainder of the crew and the Indians were left to carry out the necessary duties of the ship.

The following day Domingo and Anani were sitting in front of the cold cooking box concentrating on her lessons. Domingo was spelling out a Spanish word for Anani using a stick and the sand of the fogon in lieu of a pen and paper. Pedro came up to them and sat down nearby. Domingo glanced up at the boy and noticed the concern on Pedro's face.

"Is something wrong, Pedro?" he asked.

"Hura is so quiet today. I think he's feeling poorly," Pedro replied in a troubled voice.

Anani looked from Pedro to Domingo, and then stood up and scanned the ship. She saw Tanama beneath the fore deck, holding Hura in her lap. In Taino she said, "I am going to see Hura."

When Anani reached her mother and little brother, she saw that Hura was covered with a section of canvas. She raised questioning eyes to her mother.

"He keeps saying he's cold, and that he just wants to sleep," Tanama said forcing herself to speak calmly.

"Would it be better to take him down in the hold?" Anani asked hesitantly. She knew how awful it was down there, but it would be a little warmer.

317

"No. There is death in that place. I feel it," said Tanama in a haunted voice. Then, seeing the fear on Anani's face, Tanama regretted speaking her thoughts aloud and tried to reassure her daughter. "I will keep him in the clean air for now, Anani. But I will hold him close so he will stay warm."

While the two women were talking, Domingo came up behind Tanama. It was plain to see that Hura's cheeks were flushed. Domingo spoke softly to Tanama, and Hura tried to look up at him. But he immediately closed his eyes again, moaned softly, and turned away from the light. Domingo said a few words of comfort to Tanama and Anani, then left them in search of Dr. Alonso.

Domingo found the doctor tending to a Taino woman who was already warm with a fever. "One of the Ciguayos is also sick," the physician told him. "I don't recognize this disease. It may be something I've never seen before." He saw the concern on Domingo's face and patted his shoulder. "I'll come see Hura as soon as I can."

"Do you think it's a deadly illness?" Domingo asked, needing to know the truth.

"Our men don't seem to be affected by it as severely as the Indians," the doctor said with a furrowed brow. "But, it is too early to say what the disease will do, how the symptoms will develop."

Within hours, the virus had spread through much of the ship. Most of the sailors showed no more serious symptoms than a headache, a runny nose, and weariness. But the Indians became weak with fatigue, and experienced terrible head and muscle pain, chills, congestion, and then fever.

Over the next two days, despite Tanama's and the physician's efforts, Hura's fever rose with the severity of his symptoms. Tanama's own face grew red, and her breathing congested. Anani, insisting falsely that she felt fine, gently tried to take Hura from her mother so that Tanama could rest, but she would not let anyone else hold her son. Domingo futilely tried to keep Pedro away from Hura in the hope that he would not succumb to the same illness, but Pedro stubbornly insisted on staying with the young Taino boy.

Darkness fell and brought another storm with its coming. Although this storm began more gently than the one they had experienced earlier, the wind and rain increased steadily until everyone not absolutely necessary to keeping the Niña on course was ordered into the hold. The misery of the sick Indians increased greatly in the foulness below the decks. The storm continued to rock the ship unmercifully throughout the entire night and into the morning.

Domingo and Rodrigo, both wet and exhausted, climbed down into the hold after their latest shift battling to control the tiller. Domingo wiped his runny nose with his sleeve and looked about for a place to sit down. He was just getting up when a long mournful cry rose from nearby, stilling him completely. He searched for Anani and Pedro in the dim light, and saw that they were both staring at something to his left. Following their gaze, Domingo saw a Taino woman leaning over someone and sobbing. He and several others gathered around the woman. She was now weeping and praying in Taino at the same time. Rodrigo reached her first, looked down at the woman lying on the floor, and called grimly for Dr. Alonso.

The woman who had been crying looked up at Tiburon, who was among those near her, and said in Taino, "She is dead, Tiburon. My sister is dead." Her voice cracked and her tears continued to fall. One by one the others joined the woman in her grief, and cried aloud at the loss of her sister and their friend.

The doctor came, and Domingo waited for him to speak. After examining the prostrate body, Dr. Alonso looked up and said to one of the nearby sailors, "Tell the admiral that one of the Indians has died." Domingo turned away and went to comfort Anani.

Very soon, the messenger returned from Columbus with orders to remove the body of the dead woman. When this intention became clear, the cries from the Tainos intensified, and they begged the sailors not to take the body of their loved one so soon. But the seamen had their orders. For the health of the others, this action was necessary. Domingo was commanded to help them. He hesitated, asking that a prayer be said for the woman first. In response, he was told that it would be a sacrilege to do so, since she had not been baptized.

Sacrilege or not, as he helped the other men pick up the young woman's body, Domingo silently prayed for her soul. She had been a good, gentle woman whom he had come to know and care about. After all she had been through, he would not let her die, and send her body to the bottom of the sea, without a prayer.

He, Rodrigo, and a handful of others carried the lifeless form up the steps, fought to maintain their footing on the wet, bucking deck, and tossed the body up and over the railing, and into the heaving waves.

Hours passed, and the storm raged around the ship as the disease burned through the bodies of those aboard her. Domingo was passing out some of the last of the sea biscuits when he looked up and saw Anani swaying forward then backward, her head bent down as if in terrible pain. He handed the rest of the biscuits to Pedro and hurried to her.

It was not until he got close that he noticed the look on Tanama's face. She was staring straight ahead of her, seeing nothing, while Tiburon called her name again and again. Domingo could see that Tanama was still breathing, but she did not respond to her husband's voice. Then Domingo saw Guanina. The young girl had her face buried in Anani's shoulder, and her body shook with her sobs. Domingo's gaze followed Guanina's arm until he saw her hand tightly clamped around the end of Hura's shirt. Domingo kept his eyes on Guanina's clenched fist and the small piece of Hura's shirt, unwilling to look beyond it. He understood what he would see, even before he raised his eyes to the boy's small face. Even so, Domingo's breath caught in his throat as the full realization of Hura's death fell upon him.

Pedro came up beside Domingo, and looked at Hura and his family. He turned to his friend and asked in a shaken whisper, "Is Hura dead, Domingo?" Domingo did not have to say anything. Pedro had known the answer before he had asked. Domingo gathered Pedro in one arm and Anani in another, and held them both.

Rodrigo had been watching in sad silence just a few feet away. When someone moved to approach Tiburon's family in order to confirm the death of the little boy, Rodrigo held up his arm and stopped him.

"Not yet," he said. "Give them their grief. Give them that much."

At last, Dr. Alonso came to look at Hura. Tanama seemed to hear him no more than she had heard Tiburon, and she would not let the doctor take Hura him from her. She would not even let Tiburon take him. Several sailors came up to the group intending to take the child's body by force if necessary, but Domingo stood in front of them and told them firmly to wait.

Tiburon tried again. He bent down in front of Tanama's face and said, "Tanama, will you let me hold Hura? I want to hold our son."

Tiburon held her eyes with his own, letting her see that he shared her immeasurable pain. Very slowly Tanama loosened her hold on her little boy, and allowed her husband to pick him up.

Tiburon cradled the small body tenderly for a moment in silence. Then Tiburon lifted his face solemnly toward the ceiling. He kept his eyes closed, and started singing. It was a low and mournful song, a prayer to his zemis. He asked them to accompany Hura to their world in safety, and to watch over him. He reminded them what a fine boy Hura was, how brave and good, especially for one so small. Tiburon sang until his sorrow overcame him, and his song died away. He looked through his tears at the face of his son one more time. Then, ever so slowly, he held Hura's body up to the doctor.

During the night, Tanama's fever rose higher, and she no longer had the will to fight it. An hour before dawn, Dr. Alonso was called again. Her family, Domingo, Pedro, De Torres, and the doctor were close beside her. Tanama looked at Tiburon sadly, longingly, and closed her eyes for the last time.

Domingo's fear for Anani rose with each death. Time and again, the body of a Taino or a Ciguayo was carried up the steps, and the sea's tossing waves became their graves. And all through the days and nights that followed Tanama's death, the wind shifted and hurled itself against the Niña.

On the fifth day of the storm, Domingo watched hopefully as Guanina and Tiburon began to improve. Their fevers had fallen, their pain had eased, and their color was better. Throughout the day, he watched for signs that Anani was getting well. Pedro stayed with Anani constantly, and Domingo left her only when he was needed at the tiller.

The crewmen were near absolute exhaustion, but the haggard officers tried to encourage them with news that they were within a day or two of land. The men were so weary they could barely gather the energy to hope this news was true.

Domingo sat next to Anani and put his hand to her forehead, then her cheek. He forced himself to smile as he looked at her, and said, "I think your fever has come down a little, Anani."

Anani could see how hard he was trying to help her, and she managed to smile back at him.

"Domingo, I must talk to you," she said in Taino, her voice not much stronger than a whisper.

He leaned closer to her face so that he could hear her.

"Yes, Anani. What do you want to tell me."

"I feel my mother close by, Domingo, and Hura too. Soon I will go to the other world so that I can be with them."

"No, Anani," Domingo said gently yet insistently. "We are very near my land. You will get well there. I will take you into a house where you will be warm and dry."

"I do not believe that I was meant to see your land, Domingo."

"You're wrong, Anani. Look at Guanina and your father. They are getting better, and you will too."

"Those two were always the strong ones, like palm trees that sway with the wind. My mother and I were like reeds, and Hura too."

"No, Anani." Domingo could no longer keep the fear from his voice. "You must not say these things. You must think of getting well."

Anani looked at him lovingly and realized that she could not make him understand what she knew with certainty. She was dying. She was not afraid of her own death. She would be with her mother and Hura. But she was terribly sad for her father and her sister. She looked over at these two now. Guanina slept with her head on Tiburon's shoulder. Tiburon was watching her through eyes that looked years older than they had been a week before.

"My father is very brave, and Guanina is much like him. But I hope, someday, they are allowed to return to their home. They should be with our people."

Domingo started to say something, but Anani interrupted him.

"Domingo, I want..." she said and closed her eyes as if to gather some of her dwindling strength. When she opened them again, she reached up around her neck and tried to unfasten the chord that was tied around it. But she could not manage to loosen it.

"Help me, Domingo," she said.

So he lifted her to his chest and untied the knot as she leaned against him. Then he lowered her gently down again. He handed her the amulet that she had worn, but she shook her head at him.

"I give it to you, Domingo."

Domingo lowered his head, overcome by his emotions, knowing what such a gift meant.

He looked up and saw what she felt for him on her face. He wanted to tell her she was wrong, that she would not die, but he would only weaken her further if he tried. It was plain to see that Anani had no doubt of her eminent death, but Domingo refused to accept it. He turned his gaze to Tiburon. Anani's father laid Guanina down and came over to them. He looked at Anani then at Domingo who held his daughter's talisman in his open hand.

Acceptance settled upon Tiburon, and the proud man reached up and touched Anani's face.

"My little flower. So much like your mother," he said.

Anani smiled at him. Then she closed her eyes and slept. The two men stayed by her and prayed silently, each to his own supreme beings. Domingo held Anani's hand and prayed that she would live. Tiburon understood her better. He knew that his daughter, his Anani, would not live. So he prayed that her suffering would end, and that her spirit would soon be united with her mother and little brother.

Without warning, the seemingly endless storm gathered its strength and crashed suddenly down upon the Niña, shredding her lowered sails and pitching the ship violently. The waves rose so high, colliding and whirling around them, that all attempts to steer the ship were abandoned. Every man aboard was ordered into the hold.

When they were all below, De La Cosa noticed Domingo and called Dr. Alonso to him. After a few words with the physician, De La Cosa came toward Domingo. He asked quietly about Anani, then sat not far away from them. Before long, Rodrigo, then De Torres came over and sat next to De La Cosa. None of them said a word.

As the ship was rocked viciously by the hurricane, Domingo held Anani and did his best to protect her from being tossed and bumped. Tiburon tried to help hold her too, but the Niña was under the power of a heartless tempest, and those aboard were thrown from side to side without pity. Anani occasionally moaned, as if she was fighting the storm in her sleep, but she did not open her eyes.

Before morning, Domingo fell into an exhausted sleep. He held Anani against his side with his arm over her shoulder, her head resting on his chest. He felt her move and jerked awake. But Anani had not moved on her own. Tiburon was lifting her away from him.

With the utmost gentleness, Tiburon laid his daughter on the floor, and began to sing his prayer of death.

Domingo stared at him, then at Anani's face. She looked

like a sleeping angel. For a moment, his mind refused to acknowledge what his senses revealed to him. He heard Pedro beside him saying, "Oh, Domingo. Domingo." He put his arm around Pedro to comfort him, and still he would not accept what was before him. Something in Domingo held him apart, barely breathing, as he looked upon the scene as if he were a stranger to it all.

Tiburon's song trailed away. Pedro looked up at Domingo and was frightened by the look on his face. He tugged on Domingo's arm and called his name again, but Domingo did not respond. It was not until two men stepped forward and leaned down toward Anani that Domingo finally reacted. He took a long step forward and shoved the men near Anani so hard that they both tumbled backward. The two fallen men came to their feet with determined expressions. They would have jumped Domingo if De La Cosa had not stopped them.

Ignoring everyone around him, Domingo knelt down and bent over Anani. He studied her peaceful beauty. Beautiful Anani. He reached over and gently smoothed the hair back from her forehead. In the breath of a whisper he said to her, "You should never have been taken from your home."

The two men moved toward Anani again. Domingo stood up quickly and glowered at them. A look of complete hatred darkened his face, and his hand moved slowly to the hilt of the knife at his waist. Before he could lift the blade, De La Cosa leaped to him and grabbed his arm. He was amazed at the strength in Domingo's arms, and he held it motionless with a great effort. The muscles on the hands and arms of both men swelled as each fought to gain dominance. De La Cosa's chest pushed against Domingo's and the two stared at each other, breathing hard between clenched teeth, their faces inches apart. If Domingo drew his knife, his punishment was death. De La Cosa rightly guessed that, at that moment, Domingo didn't care. The two men held the gaze of the other, muscles straining, neither of them allowing the other to move.

With a bang of the hatchway door, Columbus descended the stairs and saw Domingo and De La Cosa locked together. Domingo and De La Cosa did not change their positions or loosen their grips. Three other seamen who crouched nearby, intending to assist De La Cosa if they were needed, took a step forward when they saw the admiral. But Columbus ordered, "Stay there, men!"

De La Cosa felt his depleted reserve of strength weakening and knew he could not stay Domingo's hand much longer. Still pushing his weight against Domingo's arm, he uttered, "Her father and sister still live, Domingo. They need you now. Drop your hand."

As if he hadn't heard, Domingo continued to stare at De La Cosa, his hand still tightly gripping the hilt of his knife. Then, slowly, he turned his head to look at Tiburon and Guanina. Pedro sat beside Anani's sister. Guanina and Pedro stared back at him in mute fear. Tiburon's eyes were numb with grief. Pedro cried out to him, "Domingo. Domingo, no." Gradually, Domingo released his hold on his knife and lowered his arm. De La Cosa carefully took the knife from Domingo's belt, and took a step back from him.

Pedro came to Domingo, and pressed his small forehead against his friend's hand. After a moment, Pedro raised his head and held up Anani's amulet.

"You dropped it in your sleep," Pedro said in a weak voice.

Domingo took the talisman and looked at it through tear-filled eyes. After a moment, he closed his hand around it tightly and shut his eyes.

Columbus shifted passed De La Cosa and came up to Domingo. The admiral looked down at the face of the lovely Indian girl, then at Domingo, whose expression was tortured even with his eyes closed. Columbus waited for Domingo to look up, but he didn't. After another moment, the admiral slowly turned away without a word. Domingo showed no sign that he knew the admiral had approached him. He simply stood unmoving, his eyes shut and his fist clenched around the amulet.

Before the seamen could approach Anani's body again, Rodrigo put his arm around Domingo's shoulders, and turned him away. When Domingo looked up into Rodrigo's solemn face, he could see understanding and compassion written there. Domingo allowed Pedro to lead him to Guanina and Tiburon. He sat down heavily beside them and tried to suppress his own suffocating pain. He turned to what was left of Anani's family and tried to give what little comfort he could.

In the dark hours before the dawn of March 4, one of the hands spotted land looming through the clouds dead ahead of them. The men scurried to the tiller to keep from being smashed against the rocky cliffs of the shoreline. When the sun finally rose, after enduring the wrath of the hurricane for seven days and nights, her sails in tatters and her sides badly beaten, the Niña entered the calm waters of a wide river.

Several of the men recognized the place. It was the Tagus River, the river that flowed by Lisbon. At the end of their strength and hope, they had reached land. But they had reached the land of Portugal.

The House

20

In the village of Cascais on the banks of the Tagus River, people were picking up the wreckage of their hamlet with tenacious resolve. Though the wind still blew with force, the worst of the storm had blessedly passed. At its full strength, the tempest had been ruthless, and few of their houses were unscarred. Some of the villagers tried to repair their roofs in spite of the wind. Some looked for lost animals, and still others, started cleaning up the mud and mess. When one of them shouted and pointed toward the river, men and women stopped what they were doing to stare in disbelief at the small caravel scudding swiftly past them in the water. Her hands were fighting to keep her in the middle of the river as the wind pushed them forward.

It looked more like a ghost ship with its shredded sails and gaunt crew than anything real. The villagers looked at one another, crossed themselves, and wondered in amazement how any ship could have come through the storm that had beaten down on them from the sea for the last week. Over twenty-five ships had been sunk by the violent storms of the past four months, and the last squall had been the worst of them all.

A man from the village ran along the riverbank and shouted at the Niña, asking, "Where have you come from?"

"The Indies!" was the unbelievable answer he received. Dumbstruck at the mere possibility that it was true, the man stopped abruptly and gaped at them as their small ship continued on its way. He said a prayer that the sailors would keep their weakened caravel afloat long enough to reach a safe harbor.

Further up the river, the wind died down greatly, and

several of the Tainos were allowed to come up from the hold. Guanina stood next to Domingo, her eyes wide at the sight of the buildings, the people, and the unimaginable animals that they passed. Tiburon was on the other side of his daughter, and he grunted in amazement at the sight of a horse, and again when he first saw a cow. In a strange, unemotional voice Domingo explained to them what each of these new creatures was called, and its usefulness.

Anani would have known the names of the animals from their lessons together, Domingo thought. Then he closed his mind to such reflections and blanketed himself in the mantle of detachment that had been with him since Anani's death. Since then, Domingo had seldom spoken unless it was in answer to a question from Guanina or Tiburon.

When the Niña reached the most out-lying port in Lisbon and she was securely anchored, the men armed themselves. A few of the exhausted officers went ashore in search of food, and to face what the Portuguese would do to them. With them, Columbus sent a letter to King John, telling him of his arrival. Since the king would know soon enough anyway, Columbus decided to send word to John himself, hoping his letter would give rise to a more tolerant reception.

The Niña had anchored near a powerful Portuguese man-of-war. And some of the men groaned and cursed when they saw a launch pull away from the huge ship and head toward them. They had no hope of winning a fight against the Portuguese, but they were prepared to fight anyway if need be. They rested their hands on swords, and loaded guns while they watched the boat draw closer.

Domingo helped the Indians down into the hold and returned to take a position at the rail. When the boat was within hailing distance, all of the hands of the Niña could see that the Portuguese sailors were heavily armed. A man who looked like a nobleman stood up in the launch, and asked to speak to the captain of the ship.

"I am in command of this ship," said Columbus. "Who are you, sir?"

"My name is Bartolomé Diaz, Captain. I am the master of the ship that lies beside yours. I have been ordered by

Captain Alvaro Dama to request that you meet with him aboard our vessel."

"Forgive me Señor Diaz, but I must refuse your invitation," said Columbus evenly.

Diaz did not fail to notice that this Spanish captain had not yet given his name.

"Then, perhaps, you will allow the master of your ship to accompany me to meet with my captain," Diaz said.

Columbus did not even look in De La Cosa's direction. He placed his hands firmly on the rail and said, "I will die fighting before I allow even one of my men to be taken from this ship."

So daring a statement, coming from a man totally at their mercy, amazed the Portuguese seamen. Diaz lowered his brows but kept his voice steady. "You have not told me who you are, sir."

Columbus looked at his men, knowing he could be sealing their fates as well as his own. They returned his gaze unflinchingly.

The admiral looked back at Diaz. "I am Don Christopher Columbus. I have been named Admiral of the Oceans Seas by Queen Isabella and King Ferdinand of Spain."

"Well, Admiral, you are in a Portuguese port and are being asked to report on where you have been, and what you were doing there. You can plainly see that you have no power to withstand us. You have little choice, sir."

"As I said, I am under the orders of Spain and I will not be threatened into giving an accounting to you or the captain of your ship. But, Señor Diaz, I will tell you this much. I have just returned from the Indies."

If they were amazed before, the Portuguese were now astounded. For a moment, Diaz did nothing but scan the bruised ship and the disheveled men aboard her.

Diaz held his reaction in check. "The Indies, you say, Admiral?"

"Yes, the Indies."

"And do you have some proof of this claim? Something that I may take back to my captain?"

Columbus ordered some of the Tainos to be brought up,

and in a few moments, Tiburon and a woman were led to the rail.

"These are people of the Indies," said Columbus watching Diaz and his men closely. "But they will remain aboard my ship, just as my men, until I receive word as to how my people and I will be treated here."

The Portuguese ship's master gazed at the Tainos with complete fascination. At last, he said, "I will tell my captain all that I have heard and seen, Admiral." He gave a signal to his men, and was rowed back to his ship.

While the Niña's crew waited uneasily for a response to their bold stand, they kept their eyes on the cannon ports of the large ship. If the man-of-war fired on them, it would all be over in seconds.

But no cannon was fired. Instead, several launches pushed away from the Portuguese ship and moved toward the Niña.

Domingo could see Diaz, and who could only be Captain Dama, with the other men in the lead boat. To Domingo's astonishment, the sound of pipes blowing and drums banging erupted from the launches. Several of the rowers raised banners, banners of *greeting*, and waived them back and forth with wild enthusiasm. Domingo stood next to Tiburon and stared at the cheering, smiling Portuguese.

Unbelievably, the men of the Niña were not only being tolerated, they were being *welcomed!* And more than that, they were being shown great honor. With music and pageantry, the officials of the Portuguese navy greeted the bone-weary sailors from Spain.

These fellow seamen were the first of many to come to the harbor to meet Columbus and his crew, see the Indians, and marvel at the strange things he had brought back from the newly-claimed lands. The news of where they had come from traveled from mouth to mouth until crowds gathered, and milled continually around the Niña.

Domingo, still armed, stood guard over the Taino survivors with a face so grim that not even the most curious of the townsfolk dared to come too near them.

The citizens of Lisbon were kind and generous even

before a letter arrived from King John ordering them to give Columbus anything that he asked for. The king's letter also commanded Columbus to come visit him.

Though he was fearful of the outcome of his meeting with the sovereign, Columbus knew that he had no option but to comply. The admiral chose his pilot, Sancho Ruiz, the Taino, Palo, and another Indian in relatively good health to accompany him on his visit with the monarch.

Before Columbus left them, word came to the sailors of the Niña that an epidemic of the plague was sweeping through Lisbon. Knowing this, the men willingly stayed close to their ship to avoid being contaminated with the deadly disease.

During the four days that the admiral was away, the Niña's crew gradually regained some of its strength. The work to provide their unfailing ship with new sails, and other general repairs, was aided greatly by the Portuguese shipbuilders who were eager to accomplish the king's wishes. In addition to helping with the caravel, the folks of Lisbon provided plenty of food and even articles of clothing. The Indians were given adequate clothes for the first time since they entered the colder climate above the tropics.

Vicente Yañez Pinzón lost no time in asking many of the locals if there was news of the Pinta, but no one had heard of the ship. Although discouraged somewhat, Vicente still held out hope that his brother had made it back to Spain without needing to land in Portugal. He had boundless faith in his older brother's abilities captaining a ship. If there was anyone who could have brought the Pinta through the storms, it was Martín. When they reached Palos, he would know.

By the time Columbus returned from a surprisingly agreeable visit with King John, the Niña was in good enough condition to sail to Spain. Not wanting to tempt fate, or the good intentions of the Portuguese king, the decision was made to leave at once. Sincere thanks were given to the many good townspeople who had given them desperately needed aid.

As they sailed down the Tagus River, the men joyfully

told each other that they would reach their own country in two days. They began to plan their homecomings with great excitement.

Domingo found it hard to look forward at all. He was too suspended in the past. His heart and mind seemed always to be remembering Anani's smile, her words, and her touch. At times, as he listened to the anxious anticipation of his fellow crewmembers, it seemed as if he was a stranger in their midst.

The short distance to the coastline of Spain was sailed smoothly, and on March 15, a Friday, the Niña sailed into the Rio Saltés and up the Rio Tinto toward the city of Palos.

When Palos came into view, the crew stood on the deck of their caravel, and hooted and howled wildly. They fired a cannon salute toward the town to announce their return. Men yelled until they lost their voices, and pummeled each other on the back in their elation at seeing the familiar silhouette of the city.

Domingo looked on with little more than a stoic detachment. He wondered what would happen to the Tainos. And, as he had throughout his entire voyage, he questioned whether his father had survived the illness that had gripped him when Domingo had left for the Indies. His anxiety had grown in intensity as they neared Palos. He hoped he was strong enough to hear the answer when he asked about his father at the inn where they had stayed.

Domingo kept Guanina and Tiburon near him as the Niña drew closer to shore.

Men aboard the ship who were seeing their home town again after so long called out to those nearest to them on the beach. They shouted requests that word be sent to their families that they had come home from the Indies. By the time the Niña came to rest, a good share of Palos was astir with the news.

When the Niña's anchor fell with a splash into the Rio Tinto, the sound held Domingo's attention distinctly, and he recognized that it marked, with finality, the end of his voyage. He had made it back to Spain. Yes, he had come back, but he had not returned as quite the same person. His body and soul had changed. He felt scarred, perhaps beyond recovery.

Columbus and then the others knelt on the deck, and the admiral led the men in a fervent prayer of thanksgiving for their deliverance home. When he finished, he stood again and faced the men.

"You have served me well, men. And we have made it home, with God's help. We have much to be proud of."

The admiral went about the ship, shaking hands one by one, and congratulating each man warmly.

Rodrigo turned to see where Domingo was. With their arrival in Palos came the sharp realization that he would never see many of the crewmembers again. And he was concerned about Domingo, whom he had come to regard as the grandson he hoped to have one day. Rodrigo was afraid Domingo did not realize that Columbus would soon leave to meet with the monarchs and claim his rewards. The admiral would take very few of his men with him when he left. The majority of them would be dismissed to find their own ways back home. Rodrigo knew Domingo would find it difficult to leave the Indians. But he must leave them. There would only be more sadness if he didn't. Domingo must go home if he was to heal from all that had happened. He must remember who he had been before they sailed from Spain.

Rodrigo spotted Domingo near the forecastle talking with Tiburon, Guanina, and two other Indians. He also saw Columbus heading down the row of men toward Domingo. Rodrigo moved quickly, reached Domingo before the admiral did, and stood watchfully close by.

When Columbus reached Domingo and held out his hand, Domingo's arm remained stiffly at his side. The admiral reached down, took Domingo's hand in his, and shook it. Domingo stared ahead and said nothing.

"I understand, Domingo," Columbus said under his breath. Then he turned toward Rodrigo.

"But you don't, admiral," said Domingo distinctly, keeping his eyes straight ahead.

Columbus paused in mid-stride. He stood absolutely still. He opened his mouth as if about to speak, then closed it again, and kept moving as if he had not heard Domingo's words.

After each of the sailors had received an acknowledgment from the admiral, a boatload of men was sent ashore to locate an inn where the people, parrots, carvings, gold and other treasures from the Indies could be housed. They soon returned and began loading the launch with goods. The Indians remained aboard while the non-human articles were rowed ashore and stored under heavy guard. Only after the hold was empty would the Indians and the rest of the hands be allowed to go ashore.

While waiting for their turns in the launch, the men embraced one another heartily and voiced their parting good wishes with much feeling. Many made plans to get together at a future date. Some even boasted that, someday soon, they would return to the Indies.

Domingo too said his farewells to the men who had become like a family. When it was time to say good-bye to Rodrigo, Domingo's speech faltered. The older man looked at him and smiled in his gentle way, his poet's eyes holding Domingo warmly. With one hand on Domingo's shoulder and the other shaking his hand firmly, Rodrigo said, "If God is willing, Domingo, we will meet again."

"I hope he grants me that, Rodrigo. Thank you for...thank you for standing by me, always. I am grateful."

Rodrigo smiled again. "I would like to meet the family who raised so fine a son. Go home to them as soon as you can, Domingo." When Domingo did not respond to this, Rodrigo went on, "You must go back to your people, Domingo. They may need you as much as anyone here." Rodrigo could see the understanding in Domingo's eyes.

"Who knows?" Rodrigo said, "You live on the coast and I am a sailor. Perhaps one day I will sail to Lequetio and see you all. Just be sure you are there when I come, eh?"

Domingo nodded, but could say no words. He did not know when or how he would go home. Guanina and Tiburon still needed him, and he did not know if he could face those he loved in Lequetio.

Rodrigo released Domingo, said one last farewell to

Pedro, and climbed down the ship's ropes and into the launch. When the boat reached the beach, he turned back and waved at them one last time before turning and heading toward the town.

Domingo and Pedro remained onboard with the Indians while most of the other men and officers left the ship. As they waited, Domingo sat among the Tainos and answered their many questions as well as he could. But he did not know the complete answer to their most pressing one. What would happen to them now?

Domingo was helping Guanina into the launch when he heard a loud cheer rise up from the crowd on the beach.

"The Pinta! The Pinta!" He turned his head quickly and there she was, sailing toward the Niña with her banners waving. The Pinta had come through the storm after all.

Vicente had been ashore twice already and had returned to the Niña to see that she was made secure before the last of the crew left her. He was bent over the railing of the fore castle checking her anchor line when he heard the shouting. He jerked his head up and saw his brother's ship. Lifting his hat from his head, he waved it in the air, and yelled more wildly than any of the others. When he saw his brother, Martín, standing on the Pinta's foredeck, he cheered even louder, repeatedly shouting his name.

It was not until later that Domingo learned what had happened to the Pinta during the long days since they had last seen her. After the two ships had been separated, the hurricane had forced the Pinta to sail far to the north from their desired course. She had ultimately landed in Galicia, just north of the Portuguese border, and four hundred fifty miles from Palos. Martín Pinzón had sent a message overland to the queen and king of Spain announcing his return, and asking for an audience. He had received a blunt reply early in March. Martín was told by the monarchs that it was the admiral's duty to report to them, rather than his. They would wait for Columbus' return to learn the news of his journey. Deeply disappointed, Martín left Galicia and made his way back to Palos by sea. He still knew nothing of the whereabouts, or even the survival, of the Niña.

The Pinta's anchor had barely been lowered, before Martín Pinzón had his men row him to a quiet spot on the beach, and accompany him to his home. He was very ill. Within days, the captain of the Pinta died, and his physicians were helpless to explain the nature of the sickness he had contracted during his voyage.

De Torres and a handful of guards accompanied Domingo, Pedro, and the Indians to the inn. Nearly shouting to be heard over the noisy crowd that followed behind and lined the streets, the interpreter said to Domingo, "I've heard that the queen and king are presently in Barcelona. Columbus intends to leave as soon as possible to meet them there. Any of the Indians who are well enough to make the journey will be taken with him."

Domingo listened to this news, but kept his questions for another time.

A wide-eyed, stammering innkeeper met Domingo and the others at the door to a large inn and led them to a private dining room. The man gaped at the Indians and asked if they were dangerous. De Torres assured him that they were not, and saw that the man was well paid before he ordered him off to see to some food.

They had no more than sat down to a hot meal when three Indians from the Pinta and their guards joined them. The newly arrived Tainos were instructed to sit and wait for more food to be brought. They obeyed silently, eyeing their strange surroundings with great uneasiness.

Domingo looked over at their amazed and frightened faces. Including these three, ten Indians had survived the return voyage. Twenty-eight captives had been aboard the two ships when they had left the Indies, and only ten had lived to reach Spain. Anani, Tanama, and Hura were among the eighteen who had died along the way. He had lost Anani within hours of reaching land. Domingo quietly pushed his bowl away and turned to face the fire.

That evening, Domingo found his way to the old inn where he and Aitor had stayed so many months before. After pausing outside for several minutes, he forced himself to enter, and asked for the girl who had helped his father during his illness. While he waited for Margarita to come, he felt his stomach begin to tighten, and tried to brace himself for what she would tell him. It was not long before he saw her coming down the hall toward him. When she looked up at Domingo, he could tell by her expression that she remembered who he was. She drew near enough for him to speak to her. He opened his mouth, then closed it again. Finally, he managed to ask, "Did my father live, Margarita?"

She smiled warmly, understanding his hesitancy to speak sooner. He didn't know yet. "Oh, yes, sir. Your father was strong enough to take a ship that was heading back to your village. He left within a month of your sailing."

Domingo's relief was so overwhelming that he felt his legs weaken, and sat down heavily on a nearby bench. He put his hands over his face and said a fervent prayer of thanks. After taking a few deep breaths to regain his composure, he looked at Margarita again.

"Thank you for your kindness to him," he said with such intensity that Margarita looked down at her hands.

Domingo placed a small pouch of coins on the table behind him. The money was an advancement from De La Cosa on the wages he had earned but had not yet been paid. Domingo smiled at her, thanked her once more, and left the inn.

De Torres came to the inn that housed the Indians and found Domingo talking with Tiburon in the dining room. Guanina was with Pedro at the end of the room warming herself by the hearth.

De Torres sat down next to Domingo, and told him quietly that he and the Indians would be leaving the inn within the hour. Domingo thought he had heard the interpreter wrong.

"What did you say?" he asked.

"I know we have been back only a couple of days, but I

told you before that the admiral was anxious to go on to Seville, then to Barcelona. He has asked me to prepare the Indians to leave today."

"Today. Well, if we must be ready within the hour, I had better get..."

"No Domingo, I said that the Indians and I will be leaving, not you."

Domingo stared at him. "But, surely, I am to go with you."

"No, Domingo," De Torres repeated. "You are free to return to your own people." De Torres' voice was kind. He had guessed beforehand what Domingo's reaction would be to his news.

"But, sir, I will be needed on the way to Barcelona," he started. "The Tainos need me to stay with them."

"I will be with them, Domingo. I will watch over them well," De Torres said. "It is time for you to go home."

Domingo started to protest again, to try to make De Torres understand, but Tiburon laid his hand on the younger man's shoulder.

Although his knowledge of the Spanish words was still not strong, Tiburon had followed the meaning of the conversation between Domingo and De Torres.

In Taino he asked, "Are we to be taken to your great cacique, Domingo?"

"Yes, Tiburon," Domingo said, unable to keep the sadness from his voice.

"And you are not to come with us?"

De Torres answered before Domingo could. "He has been ordered to return to his own people, Tiburon."

Tiburon looked at Domingo for a long moment. "It is right that you go back to your family, Domingo. They will be watching for you. It is what you must do."

De Torres understood the conflict that Domingo was battling and said, "Domingo, you will not be *allowed* to accompany us. You have been given no choice in this."

Domingo turned toward Pedro and Guanina. Pedro was trying to explain something to her.

De Torres said, "Domingo, I have spoken with De La Cosa

and he said he will accompany you most of the way back to your village. He will take you overland and it should take no more than eight or nine days."

When Domingo did not even face him, De Torres added, "He will take Pedro home too. You can help De La Cosa look after the boy during the trip."

Instead of acknowledging what De Torres had said, Domingo walked over and sat down on the bench beside Guanina. She turned to face him and could see immediately that Domingo had something grave to tell her. She watched his eyes and waited for him to speak.

"Guanina," he started in Taino, "We have spoken of the queen and king many times."

Guanina nodded.

"It is time for you and your father to go to see them," he said.

Guanina studied him carefully. "And you are not coming. You will stay here?" she asked.

Domingo took her small hand and looked down at it instead of at her face.

"No, Guanina. I will not stay here, but I will not be coming with you. Pedro and I will go to our own homes, to be with our families. They live in villages far from here."

Guanina said nothing until he raised his eyes to her again. She sounded a great deal like Tiburon, brave and wise far beyond her years, when she said, "That is as it should be, Domingo. I want you to go to your village. People are not happy if they are not with their own families." Then she lowered her head until her cheek lay upon his hands, and she began to cry softly.

Domingo was thinking of Guanina's tears ten days later as he stood alone on the lower slopes of a mountain that rose above Lequetio. He tried to tell himself that Guanina would return to her own home some day, just as he had returned to his. Lowering his gaze, he saw the familiar outlines of the church, the beach, and a hundred other things that he had wondered if he would ever see again.

340

He and De La Cosa had parted from Pedro after spending a night with the boy's grateful family. They had been overjoyed at their son's return. The money De La Cosa had given them for Pedro's services was a small fortune to them, and they had blessed his name many times during their stay. De La Cosa had promised to come back for Pedro as soon as he had acquired another ship, which he intended to petition the queen for very soon.

When the time came for him to leave, Domingo had knelt down and hugged Pedro for a long time before letting him go.

Pedro had turned his large brown eyes on his friend. "You will take care of yourself, won't you Domingo?"

"I will, Pedro. You were a fine teacher to me aboard the Santa Maria. I will not forget what a help you were. Perhaps someday, you will join my brothers on a whaling ship. Would you like that, Pedro?"

"I must sail with Señor De La Cosa, Domingo. I gave him my word long ago. But thank you," Pedro had said.

"You must keep your word, of course," Domingo had agreed. "But, I am sure I will see you again before much time has passed. We Basques have a sense for such things, you know."

"Yes, Domingo," Pedro had said in the same serious tone.

Then Domingo had joined De La Cosa and walked away from Pedro's house with a heavy heart. When Domingo had turned back, he had seen Pedro still standing in the road watching them, a tiny figure in the distance. Domingo had taken off his beret, the beret De La Cosa had given him, and waved it at Pedro. Then he had turned toward home.

Yesterday, before De La Cosa had parted from Domingo, he had wanted to talk about the future.

"I intend to sail my new ship back to Lequetio after I bring Chachu and my other men home from the Indies. I have been thinking about doing some business with your family, Domingo. I know of a good market for their whale oil, and I'd like to speak to you and Aitor about it when I return. Besides, I would like to see that family of yours. Perhaps your amuma will dance with me again."

De La Cosa had grown quiet for a moment then had said, "You were a valuable hand to have at sea, Domingo. This voyage was a true test of a man. A true test. I know you said that you don't intend to sail again, but if you change your mind I would be proud to have you among my men."

"Thank you, sir," Domingo had managed to say.

De La Cosa had taken his hand and shaken it like Domingo was his equal. Then he had headed up the path that led to a town further along the coast. Domingo had stood and watched him go, admiring him greatly, and recalling some of the many times that he had led them well. "What would have happened without him?" he asked himself.

Now Domingo stood alone above his town. A breeze blew softly from the sea and he looked out at the water. The sun was nearing the western horizon. He closed his eyes, breathed in the sea air, and thought of Anani. He thought of her and all that had happened since he had last stood near this place. Would his family even recognize him as the same person who had left here almost a year ago? He hardly recognized himself. He felt so weary, as if he had aged a lifetime in the past year.

As acutely as he wanted to see his father and mother again, Domingo dreaded the hurt and the disappointment he would bring with his return. Breaking off his betrothal to Carmen would bring them shame. Such things were not done. And what about Carmen? What about *her* shame, *her* pain? With anguish, he tried to close his mind to Carmen. He had no choice. He couldn't marry her now, so he must terminate the betrothal.

He wanted desperately to be with his family. He wanted to hear them call him by his nickname, Txomin, as they had since he was born. He wanted to know that the whole world had not changed while he had been changing, and that the people he loved were still here, still the same. He wanted to see that they were alright. They must be alright. The desire to confirm the wellbeing of his family grew in him until it became a pressing need.

His feet moved forward and continued to carry him down the hill. When he reached the road that led into town, he quickened his pace.

It was near twilight and most of the people were in their homes eating their evening meal. If anyone saw him, with his beard and ragged clothes, he doubted that they would recognized him anyway. For this he was glad. He didn't want to talk to anyone else before he had seen his family.

Domingo hastened his pace and was almost loping by the time he neared his house. It was less than a half mile in front of him now. He could see it. As he drew nearer, the lines of the house became clear. He had almost reached the farmyard when he saw two figures emerge from the entrance. He knew the two men. They were the village doctor and priest. The possible explanation as to why these men, of all men, would be at his house sent a chill of fear through his body. A doctor and a priest.

"No," Domingo whispered. "Please, God..." He started running, his legs carrying him rapidly to the front of his home.

He came rushing toward the two men, then past their stunned faces before they could stop him. Bursting through the door and into the kitchen, Domingo saw his amuma carrying a platter piled with strips of white cloth and ran to her.

The old woman was so startled by the sudden intrusion that she tossed the tray in the air and gave a holler for help. Then, to her further amazement and fright, this strange man, whom she hadn't been able get a good look at, picked her up off the ground and hugged her so tightly that she could hardly breathe. Not until she heard the familiar, dear voice saying, "Amuma, Amuma," did she know who this wild man was that held her so close.

The priest and the doctor came running to her aid, and grabbed Domingo in an effort to save the old woman from the madman. Domingo let himself be pried away from his grandmother. An instant later, to add to the confusion of the two men still gripping Domingo roughly, Amuma threw her arms around the stranger and began crying with joy. With comical expressions of disbelief, the old woman's rescuers let go of Domingo and looked at each other, then back at the two people hugging one another in front of them.

Enara rushed into the kitchen wringing her hands on her apron, and was brought to an abrupt halt by the scene in front of her. A scruffy looking pauper was embracing her mother-in-law in the middle of their kitchen. But an instant later Enara's hand flew to her mouth and she ran to Domingo trying to call his name in a voice that would not make a sound. Amuma released her grandson and turned him to his mother just as Enara reached him. Domingo swept Enara into his arms and held her as she wept, held her as her body shook with her sobbing and, finally, let his own tears fall unheeded onto her hair.

"Txomin," she said again and again as she cried, "Txomin."

Before long, a loud, impatient bellow came to them from one of the bedrooms, "What is going *on* in there?"

It was Aitor's voice. Domingo put his mother down, wiped at his damp eyes, smiled at her, and hurried to see his father.

Throwing open the door to the bedroom, Domingo looked in, and there was his father. Aitor was sitting on his bed with his left leg, splinted and newly bandaged, stretched out on top of the bed covers. The initial look of surprise on Aitor's face at seeing this bearded foreigner appear at his door was so vivid that Domingo laughed and said, "Don't you know me, Father?"

But he had known his son before Domingo had said a word. Aitor's startled expression immediately melted into recognition, then profound emotion. He could not speak. It was Txomin. His Txomin had come home. Not even trying to hide his feelings, Aitor opened his arms and, when his son was within reach, wrapped them tightly around him. Under his breath he said, "Thank you, Lord, for answering my prayers."

Aitor had almost given up hope of seeing Domingo again,

but he had never stopped praying for it. And now Txomin was here beside him. He held his son for a long time before releasing him. Aitor straightened his arms and held Domingo by his shoulders so that he could look at him.

Aitor immediately perceived a profound difference in his Txomin. It was more than the beard and the long hair that had changed his son's appearance. No sign of Domingo's boyhood remained. His body was terribly lean except for his powerful arms. But, it was in Domingo's eyes that Aitor saw the deepest change. His son's eyes held suffering and an awareness that Aitor seldom saw in one so young. Domingo had seen much since he had last been in his house. Aitor, understanding a great deal without knowing any details, pulled his son close once more, and held him tightly until the women came into the room.

After the doctor and priest realized that it was Domingo who had charged so wildly, they too welcomed him home with enthusiasm. Not wanting to interrupt Domingo's homecoming with his family, the two men did not stay long. But before they left they warned him that, by the next morning, the entire town would learn of his return. This evening and tonight, however, his family had Domingo to themselves.

After the commotion caused by his arrival had quieted a bit, the four Lacas sat down by the fire in the kitchen. Aitor had his broken leg propped up on a stool, but looked healthier than he had for a year. Domingo looked at them in turn and smiled from deep inside. "At least a million times, I imagined you all in this very spot," he said.

"Now, tell me all about my brothers. You could not all be so happy if any news from them was bad."

"If you had gotten home three days sooner," Aitor said, "You would have seen them for yourself. They left to deliver a shipment of whale oil down the coast. They should be back in a few days."

"Domingo," Enara said with a grin, "You became an uncle while you were away. Kepa has a new baby girl, and she's as pretty as her mother. And Eneko has finally set a date for his wedding. It's to be May 20th."

With the thought of the wedding, Enara realized that Domingo had not yet asked about Carmen, and she said kindly, "Carmen is well, Txomin. Her father was...angry when he learned you had sailed, but Carmen refused to listen to him when he said she had to marry someone else." Enara was about to declare how happy Carmen was going to be to see him when she noticed the look on Domingo's face. He was staring down at his hands, and would not meet her eyes. After a moment, Enara changed the subject as smoothly as possible and eventually brought her son back into the conversation. Before long, their talk was flowing easily again.

When Domingo asked about Aitor's leg, his father admitted, somewhat embarrassed, "I got a little too close to that young bull of ours a couple of days ago."

"Yes," said Enara, "And I'm glad you didn't hear the string of words that came out of his mouth when the doctor set his leg."

They all laughed warmly at this.

"That's why the doctor and the priest were here for supper tonight," Aitor quipped. "I invited the doctor to thank him for setting my leg so well, and I had to invite the priest to ask for forgiveness for the language I had used while the leg was being set."

Laughter filled the room again, then a steady stream of conversation continued to flow. Domingo could not get enough of the comforting voices around him. He wanted to listen far more than he wanted to speak.

His parents and grandmother sensed Domingo's reluctance to talk in detail of his voyage, and they told him that he could tell them all about it after he had rested.

Amuma was particularly concerned about his lean appearance. She ladled out a bowl of hearty lamb stew for him and, much to the contentment of his grandmother, he occasionally moaned with pleasure as he ate. Before Domingo ate anything else, however, he insisted on taking a bath. Tomorrow was soon enough to shave his beard.

When he appeared again in the kitchen wearing clean clothes and smelling noticeably better, Enara and Amuma proceeded to feed him until he couldn't take in one more bite of their delicious food.

Hours disappeared as they continued to tell Domingo all about the latest happenings, sometimes talking all at once in their excitement. Domingo reveled in their company. He was truly with his family, in his family's house. For now, for tonight, he did not want to think beyond this.

Their talk at last faded with the deepening of the night, and the Laca family sat in contented silence watching the flames of the fire. Domingo's head began to nod. The adults surrounding him smiled at each other knowingly. Enara and his grandmother roused him gently, accompanied him to the room that he had shared with his brother since he was a baby, and bid him good night. Amuma closed the door and looked at her daughter-in-law.

"Txomin is home at last," she said. She smiled broadly and patted Enara's arm.

They let Domingo sleep late the following morning, and had a breakfast big enough for five sailors waiting for him when he awoke. The two women bustled about the kitchen spoiling him so outrageously that Domingo couldn't help grinning at them. He asked them to sit down with him while he ate, and they complied. Aitor hobbled in from outside on a crutch and joined them.

Knowing that they were extremely curious about his voyage, between bites of food Domingo mentioned, "By the way, I remembered how to make some of your dishes when I was cooking aboard our ship, Amuma."

Delighted to hear any of the particulars of his journey his elders prodded him to tell them more. One eager question led to another until Domingo found himself recounting the trip, more or less, in chronological order. He did not mention Anani, or even her family, and he only briefly told them of the storms. These things were still held deep within him. The wounds they had left were only beginning to heal.

After Domingo had eaten, Aitor said to him, "How about

taking me to town in the oxcart so I can share my newly returned son with Carmen and the rest of our friends?"

Domingo glanced away from him and said, "Father, I'd like to stay close to our house and just rest."

Aitor was mildly puzzled but easily accepted this. Domingo probably was not ready to retell all of his stories over and over again. "Well then," Aitor said, "How would it be if I let just Carmen know that you're home?"

"Not today, Father, please," Domingo replied.

Aitor, Enara, and Amuma studied him closely. Before any of them could ask Domingo his reasons for not wanting to see Carmen, he stood up and said that he wanted to walk around the yard awhile. Then he left the room, and left the three concerned people in the kitchen to wonder what was wrong.

Aitor wisely left his son to himself until early evening. As darkness approached, he found Domingo sitting in one of the stalls, petting their week old foal. The mare had been moved to the pasture where she could get a little exercise. Aitor heard her just outside the door, pawing softly at the ground. He eased himself down, next to his son, and scratched the little filly behind one of her ears.

"Txomin," he said, "I want you to tell me about your trip. Not what you've already told me. I mean tell me what happened to you while you were away."

Domingo understood what Aitor wanted to know, and he looked away from his father. Aitor merely waited, then waited some more.

The first few words were terribly hard for Domingo. Soon however, his story, every piece of it, began to emerge and fall together. He held back nothing from Aitor now. He told him all about Anani, that he had loved her, that he still loved her. He said that he could no longer consider marrying Carmen, not after all that had happened. It wasn't until he had nearly finished that he looked at his father, expecting to see shame and disappointment on his face. What he saw instead was deep concern, and love.

"This voyage of yours hurt you more deeply than I ever imagined," Aitor said. "If I had known all that you would have to deal with, I would never have let you go." There was no judgement, not a sign of reproach in his voice. Aitor understood his son well, and could clearly see how Domingo's sense of responsibility and loyalty had first drawn him to Anani.

"Father, not all that happened to me was bad," Domingo reflected.

"No, not all bad. You became a man while you were away, Son," he said. "I guess manhood is seldom achieved without pain." After a little while he asked, "Txomin, have you stopped loving Carmen?"

Domingo thought this was the strangest of questions considering what he had just told his father, and his expression revealed his thoughts.

"Think about it before you answer me, Txomin. Did you stop loving Carmen, even when you felt love for this other girl?"

Domingo considered more fully what Aitor was asking. He remembered vividly how he had felt while he was on the ship, how much he had missed Carmen. He remembered his confusion as to how he could love Carmen and, at the same time, be so strongly drawn to Anani. Later, when his interest in Anani became more passionate, he had felt so terribly guilty. He had told himself that it was impossible to love them both.

But *had* he stopped loving Carmen? Had his feelings for her really changed? Thinking it through, Domingo slowly decided that it wasn't as simple a matter as whether he still loved Carmen. His caring so deeply for Anani, and his actions toward Anani, had changed what Carmen could be to him. It had also changed what he could be to her. Carmen would never want him now, not when Anani was so much a part of him. Anani was not just a chapter of his past; she was alive in his memories.

He looked at Aitor and said, "No, Father, I did not stop loving Carmen, even then. But that does not change what happened."

"You are right, Son," said Aitor, "It does not change what

happened. But it makes all the difference in what may happen in the future."

"I don't see how it changes anything, Father," said Domingo.

Instead of explaining his meaning further, Aitor said, "Carmen will have heard that you are home by now. If we don't send word asking her not to come, she will undoubtedly be here to see you before long, in spite of what her father may have to say."

"I can't see her, Father. Not yet," Domingo stated flatly.

Aitor considered for a moment, then patted his son's shoulder with resignation. "I will send her a message that you are not well from your trip yet, and that you need time to rest before you see her." Aitor pictured Carmen wanting to come and help care for him. "Perhaps I should also tell her that we would like to tend to you ourselves in order to keep her from any harm."

Domingo understood the truth behind this deception.

"Thank you, Father," he said.

He helped Aitor to stand, let the mare back into the stall, and the two of them headed back toward the kitchen.

Aitor was thinking carefully about all that his son had told him. He would have to discuss everything with Enara and his mother. They would have to know why Domingo wanted to call off his betrothal. Between the three of them, perhaps they could help his son.

The Relic

21

Enara finished cutting Domingo's hair and stood back from the stool he sat on.

"So, it is really you after all," she said smiling.

Aitor had helped Domingo shave his beard before Enara had started working on his hair. Now Domingo looked more like her son than a hardened seaman. Still, she could not help worrying as she stood in front of him surveying his aggrieved face. His sadness was obvious, though he did his best to hide it. And because he did, she did her best to hide her worry.

Aitor had told her and Amuma what had happened between Domingo and the island girl, and how it was still affecting him. Now that he was home, Enara was determined to find a way to help him regain some of the peace he had lost. She had decided that cleaning him up and seeing that he had a lot of good food and rest would not be a bad way to start. What would happen between Domingo and Carmen she did not know. She could only try to strengthen his mind and body after his ordeal at sea. She and Amuma would talk more about it tonight when they were alone. They would decide what could be done, if anything, to heal his heart.

Domingo stayed close to the house during the next few days, seldom going outside unless the sun had already set. He spent much of his time in the kitchen, which pleased the women of his house greatly.

Feeling restless one day, Domingo announced that he would show his mother and grandmother some of the dishes he had cooked while he was aboard the ships. Reluctant to taste his creations at first, the two women and Aitor were surprised and impressed by the tastiness of the meals he prepared.

Within a week of Domingo's return home, his brothers came back from their trading trip, and the Lacas came together for a homecoming celebration. They had just finished a wonderful dinner with good wine and satisfying food, when Kepa's young wife, Catalin, came up to Domingo with her new baby in her arms.

"You've hardly had a chance to meet your new niece," she said. "It's time you got to know her better." She carefully placed her baby in Domingo's arms, showed him how to hold her head, and stood beside him smiling at the two of them.

Domingo held his niece gingerly, and gazed into her large brown eyes. The baby looked back at him as if she found him fascinating too. Domingo grinned and glanced at his brother, then his sister-in-law. "She's going to be as pretty as you some day, Catalin," he said. The young mother blushed with pleasure.

Kepa came over and rested his arm on Domingo's shoulders. "One day you and Carmen will probably have seven daughters, Domingo," he said. Kepa did not see the look that spread across Domingo's face, or the faces of the older members of the family. Domingo grew quieter as the evening wore on.

When it was time for Kepa to pack up his little family and head back to their own house, Domingo walked out into the yard with them.

"You are a lucky man, Kepa," Domingo said with his eyes on Catalin and the baby.

"Yes, Txomin, I am," Kepa agreed. "I have my family, and now I have you home." He slapped his younger brother on the back, and headed down the road with Catalin.

Domingo and Eneko talked late into the night from their cots across the room from each other. For once, Domingo was telling Eneko all about his sea adventures rather than the other way around. It felt good to talk to his older brother after so long. Domingo could sense a difference in the way his brother treated him now. Eneko was more patient and less judgmental of what Domingo said and felt. It seemed as if Eneko considered Domingo more of an equal because of all he had experienced.

When everything else had been said, Domingo told Eneko all about Anani. Eneko said nothing for awhile, and then only, "Sometimes, when a man is at sea, it is like he is in a different world altogether."

During the first few days of Domingo's return, he avoided staying outdoors for long periods of time to avoid meeting Carmen. Some of Domingo's friends came to see him, but whenever the conversation turned to Carmen and his plans with her, Domingo immediately changed the subject. He asked them about what had happened to them while he had been gone, and answered their many questions about his voyage. But Carmen was a topic that his friends learned to avoid.

As more time passed and still Carmen did not come to his house, Domingo began to wonder why she was staying away. She had been told only that he was ill from his voyage and needed rest. It surprised him a little that Carmen would let an illness keep her from visiting for more than a day or two. As far as Domingo knew, she had not even sent word asking about him.

Domingo started doing some of the work around the farm to help out while Aitor's leg was healing. Then, more and more often, he and Enara found themselves working side by side in the field or pasture. Enara noticed when her son would pause in his work and look up the road that led from town. At first, he watched the road uneasily, as if he dreaded what he might see. But as spring unfolded its beauty and the days grew longer and warmer, Domingo looked up the road with a thoughtful expression on his face. Enara never asked him what, or rather whom, he was looking for.

Aitor made a routine of complaining that work was piling up at his warehouse and on his ships in the hope that Domingo would offer to accompany him to the harbor. When at last Domingo agreed to go with him, Aitor considered this a big step toward his son's willingness to accept whatever was to come.

Domingo drove the oxcart slowly down the dirt road as Aitor made plans to do a hundred different things once his splint was taken off the following week. Domingo watched carefully for a glimpse of Carmen, especially when they rolled passed the road where she lived. But neither on the way to the harbor or on their way home again did he see her.

No one in his family even referred to Carmen now, not around Domingo at least. Not a word. Even so, Aitor's question about whether Domingo had stopped loving her continued to run through his mind. Each time he considered this, the answer came back to him more clearly. He had not stopped loving her. What he felt toward Anani seemed almost to be a separate thing, in a separate lifetime. No less strong, just independent of his life now. It was as if he had been a different person entirely when he had known her. But even if it was true that he loved Carmen, it was also true that he had betrayed her. It would be heartless to carry out his betrothal as if nothing had changed, as if he had never met Anani. Domingo knew Carmen well enough to have no doubt that she wouldn't accept him after he had told her everything. But, with each new morning, he was more certain that he must tell her.

Domingo had been home several weeks and he still had not seen Carmen. He began to tell himself that it would be best to go see her soon. He knew he couldn't wait forever to tell her how he had changed, what he had done. She needed to know so that she could plan her life without him. Carmen would marry someone else. He would lose her. No, that wasn't quite right. He had lost her the moment he had let himself love Anani. This judgement weighed on him during the day and tormented his dreams. It became so heavy a burden that he finally mentioned his intention to talk with Carmen to his family one evening. Their reaction was much calmer than he had anticipated.

"Do what you feel is best, Txomin," Aitor had said solemnly.

Enara had looked from her son to her husband then said, "Yes, Son."

Eneko and Amuma had nodded but remained quiet.

Domingo had almost hoped they would try to talk him into waiting a bit, to think through what he would say to Carmen more carefully. But he knew that would only postpone what must be done. The sooner he told her, the better it would be. His "sickness" had lasted a suspiciously long time. She had to realize, after all this time, that he was avoiding her. This must have caused her anguish and confusion. Her feelings of rejection had most likely kept her from trying to see him before now. She had every right to be deeply hurt, when so much time had passed and he had not come to her.

Domingo looked around at the sympathetic faces of his family members. And for the first time, a thought occurred to Domingo that he had not so much as considered before. Perhaps, Carmen didn't even care that he had stayed away. He felt a terrible chill grip his chest. He had been gone for most of a year. All that time, undoubtedly, her father had wanted her to reject him and choose someone else as her husband. What if she had finally agreed, and had chosen someone else? If she had turned her affections to another man, she would have been relieved rather than hurt that he had not come searching for her.

He stared at the fire. This terrible thought explained a great deal. He had been a fool not to realize it, not even consider it, as a possibility. He had been so sure of her faithfulness to him that he had ignored what now seemed obvious. Domingo turned back and scanned the faces of his parents, then his grandmother, and finally his brother. "They all know," he told himself. "They have probably known for a long time."

Domingo stood up, silently left the kitchen, and walked outside. He wandered around the house several times, breathing in the fresh air and trying to steady himself, to think clearly.

Would she even be willing to talk to him now? If she did agree to see him, how could he explain why he had waited so long to visit her? If she were still wavering between a new man and him, his confession about Anani would end her confusion with finality. But he had no choice. He must go to her and talk to her about all that had happened, if she would let him. After she had heard his story, he would have to live with what she would say to him in reply. Her response would be decisive. Nevertheless, it was useless to wait any longer. He would go tomorrow.

He slept little that night, imagining the many ways that Carmen might react when she saw him. Every image was a torment. By morning, his body and his soul felt wretched. When he appeared in the kitchen the next morning his family spoke very little. They let him know by gestures and looks that they would be there for him after he had seen Carmen.

When they had finished eating, Aitor told Domingo he wanted to talk to him, and Domingo followed his father into to his bedroom. Once there, Aitor asked Domingo to help him take down a wooden box from a high, recessed wall-shelf. They both sat on the bed, and Domingo waited for Aitor to open it. Instead, Aitor held the closed box on his lap and looked back at his son.

"I have something to show you, Txomin, something to give you," he said. "But first I want to tell you what it is and why I want you to have it."

Domingo nodded and listened attentively to his father's words.

"A year or two before my father died he gave me this same gift. He told me that his father had given it to him, and his grandfather had given it to his father. He said that it had been passed down from father to son for at least seven generations. But the thing itself was made many, many years before our ancestor found it. I believe it may be thousands of years old."

Fascinated, Domingo forced himself to withhold his questions as he listened to Aitor.

"I have been waiting for the right time to give it to you, Son. Today, I think, is a good day. I am giving it to you rather than either of your brothers for many reasons.

Eneko will receive this house as his inheritance. Kepa already owns his own ship and has a fine family started. They will probably both be wealthy men, and perhaps you will too one day. But I've known I would give this to you since you were small. You have always understood things that have a value beyond wealth, Txomin. You feel things so deeply. I always believed that this gift would mean the most to you."

Domingo watched with great anticipation as Aitor opened the box and lifted out something not much bigger than an open hand. It was three-pointed, and Domingo could see that it had been made of bone.

"It is a horn, Txomin," he said. Aitor lifted the bone instrument to his lips and blew on the largest of the three points. He gently played a short melody from the three musical notes that the horn produced. The music sounded deep and ancient.

"I know of your love for music, Son. All of our people love music, it's true, but when you sing, I can see that you feel it in your soul. Although this horn is too old to be played except on very rare occasions, I want you to have it. I want you to remember your love for music. I have not heard you sing since you came home, Txomin. I want this horn to help you remember how to sing."

Aitor placed the horn, the relic of his ancestors, in his son's hands. Domingo looked at it carefully then raised his eyes to his father.

"I'm grateful, Father," Domingo said with warmth. "I will take care of this, always." He studied the horn with care, and a look of wonder came over his face. Then he surprised Aitor greatly. "I think I may know where our ancestor first found this horn, Father," Domingo said quietly.

"How could you know that, my son?" Aitor asked in amazement.

Domingo told his father about the cave in the mountains that he had found years before. He described many of the other items in the cave that he had dug up over time, and how one or two of them were quite similar in design to the horn. Finally, he told Aitor about the carved boat he had unearthed just before he had left for Palos, and how he had interpreted finding it as a sign that he would be allowed to sail.

When Aitor heard about the small boat he shook his head slowly and smiled.

"I never heard that the horn had come from a cave, only that it had come from a secret place. I was told that our ancestor had taken this horn, and had later returned to bury something that he had made with his own hands in the same spot. He did this to replace the item he had taken. He didn't want to offend any gods that may have been keeping watch over the holy site. Do you suppose the boat you came across is what he left there?"

"It may have been," said Domingo. "The boat didn't seem to be as old as the other things, and it was made of wood rather than bone or stone."

Both of them looked at the horn again.

After a moment, Domingo asked Aitor a question to which he already suspected the answer. "Why did you give me this special gift today, Father?"

Aitor sighed and placed his hand on his son's shoulder. "Because I wanted you to remember how many ages your people have survived, and to remember all they have lived through."

"All they have lived through," thought Domingo, and he reflected on all that he had lived through during the past year.

Aitor continued, "A man can survive much in a lifetime, Txomin, and sometimes he is required to. I don't know what Carmen will tell you, Son. But no matter what she says, what she decides, you must accept it. You must look ahead and continue with your life. I hope that by having this ancient horn, by remembering what it represents of our past, you might be able to deal with the days to come a little better. Whatever happens during your talk with Carmen, I want you to look to the future."

After a pause, Domingo carefully put the horn back into the box and carried it to his room.

As he left the house and headed toward town, toward

Carmen, and tried to hold his father's words in his mind. The walk to the village seemed longer than it ever had before. In spite of himself, his steps slowed as he neared Carmen's house. Three houses down from hers, he stopped altogether. He hoped she would just happen to come out of her father's shop, which took up the bottom floor of her house, but she didn't. He forced himself forward until he was standing at the front door to their shop.

Raising his hand Domingo pushed the door open. Carmen's father looked up, immediately recognizing him. A sly smile of triumph appeared on Imanol's face as he crossed his arms over his chest and waited for Domingo to speak.

"I've come to see Carmen," Domingo said.

Rather than replying, Imanol turned his back on Domingo and disappeared into the back of the house.

Very soon, Carmen appeared in the hallway. She glanced fleetingly in his direction then walked very slowly toward him, avoiding his gaze.

She was lovelier than he had remembered. Domingo was caught so off guard by his sudden, unepected, yearning for her that he almost forgot all that had happened in his life since he had seen her last. Here was his Carmen. He wanted only to put his arms around her for a very long time. He wanted to bring her nothing but joy, not the terrible sorrow he had come to deliver.

She stopped just a few feet in front of him. A long silence held them both. Finally, Carmen lifted her head and looked at him. Domingo could see that she was trying to hide what she felt, what she knew. Perhaps she felt as deep a dread of the words she intended to deliver as he did himself.

"Carmen..." he began, then stopped. He wanted to tell her how he had missed her, how much he needed her to love him. But, she was looking at him with such an empty expression. And those things were not what he had come to say.

Gathering his courage he went on, "Carmen, I have a great deal to tell you."

"Let's go outside then," she said in an unreadable tone.

The two of them walked west of town, over the stone

bridge and to a grassy place overlooking a sandy beach. The painful silence held them captive the entire way. When they reached the edge of the embankment, Carmen sat down facing the ocean and Domingo sat close beside her.

She continued to stare at the water as he began, haltingly, to tell her about his trip. She did not turn to look at him as his words flowed, and every detail of his experience was drawn out and laid before her. He kept nothing back. Even when he told her about Anani, he let her see who she had been and what she had meant to him. And still Carmen did not look at him. She closed her eyes only once, for a moment, then she let the sea hold her gaze again.

After he had finished, Domingo watched her anxiously, but she said nothing. He started to tell her he was sorry for hurting her, but she held up her hand.

"I know you did not want to cause me pain, Txomin," she said with difficulty.

He waited for her to speak again, but she seemed to need time for her words to come. The two of them sat mutely for a few minutes as the breeze whispered through their hair and the waves rolled to the sand below them. With great effort Domingo forced himself to remain still, and prayed that Carmen would not say what he feared was coming.

When she spoke at last, Domingo tried to prepare himself to accept what she said calmly.

"Your amuma came to me the day after you returned. She told me everything she knew about your voyage. She explained nearly all that you have just told me yourself. Then she said you were struggling to understand what to do now. It was right of her to tell me all of this, Txomin."

At last Carmen turned and looked at him. "All this time, I have been thinking about what she said."

Domingo did not want to hear her next words. He knew he must not only hear them, he must also accept them. But, instead of listening to her, he started talking again.

"Carmen, I have no right to hope this, but I want so badly, more than anything else, for you to be my wife someday. I ask for the chance to prove that I still love you, that I will never hurt you like this again. I will wait as long as you ask, Carmen. I want you to be with me, always." At these words, she looked away from him again.

Domingo knew he was being foolish, that he needed to let her talk. But for some reason he could not have easily explained, he started telling Carmen about the cave. He told her how and when he had found it. When she did not interrupt him, he went on. He described each of the things he had found there, the ancient tools, the paintings on the ceiling and walls, and finally, the carved boat. He tried to explain how he had felt when he found the vessel, and how it had encouraged him to pursue his quest to sail.

At last, he moved in front of her and knelt between her and the sea. Holding her eyes with his own, Domingo told Carmen about the gift he had received from Aitor that morning, and all that his father had shared with him.

Then he said, "I would like to show you the cave, Carmen. Will you come with me to see it some day?"

She did not answer him. Instead, she stood up, walked away from him, and faced the sea again. Domingo tried to give her time to think but could not bear the thought of her leaving him. He wanted her so badly. In no more than a few moments he got up and approached her.

When he reached her side, she began to speak. "So much has happened, Txomin, to you and to me. I've come to realize that we can't always control what happens to us, but we must survive it. Your father is so right about that."

After a pause she continued, "While you were gone, I had a terrible dream. I dreamed that your ship went down and that all the men were drowning. I saw you in the water, going deeper and deeper. You were reaching for help, for me, Txomin, and I couldn't get to you. I couldn't help you at all. I woke up crying, and I knew something was terribly wrong. This dream came to me many times, haunting me for months. It wasn't until your amuma came to me, and told me what had happened, that I understood what was wrong."

Carmen still did not face him, but she went on, "It was hard for me while you were away. My father was furious when you left. He found two suitors and told me to choose one of them to replace you. I refused, and he was angry with me the whole time you were gone."

"Then...then your amuma came. After she had told me everything, I thought that part of my heart was dying."

Domingo moved closer and reached for her, wanting desperately to comfort her, but she stepped away from him, and somehow he found the strength to remain still.

"I have considered each of the two suitors carefully, Txomin. Both of them are good men. They would each be a husband that a woman could be proud of. One of them is younger, so he is closer to my own age. In the last few weeks, I have given a great deal of thought to a life with him. It would please my father greatly if I married him. But I knew I could not tell him my final choice until you came to me, and we talked. I had to see you and hear your voice again, Txomin."

Domingo could barely breathe. He held his body motionless, his words unsaid.

She looked at him now, and slowly reached out her hand. It was small but strong, and he held it in both of his as if it were the most precious thing in his world. He took a step nearer and she did not move away.

She faced him, and he saw that her eyes were wet with unshed tears. Yet her face was less troubled, her mind resolved. "I know who I must choose. I want to tell you my choice before I tell my father." She took a breath and searched his eyes with her own.

Very softly, but clearly she said, "No, Txomin, I will not go with you to see the cave. That is something you must do with our son. I am sure, somehow, that we will have a son one day. As he grows, you will teach him the things that your father has taught you. And when we are very old, you will give him your father's gift."

Glossary of Names

Domingo Laca (Txomin) . . . . .Protagonist

Carmen Barrutia . . . . .Domingo's betrothed

Aitor Laca . . . . .Domingo's father

Enara Laca . . . . .Domingo's mother

Eneko and Kepa Laca . . . . .Domingo's brothers

Amuma . . . . .Domingo's grandmother

Christopher Columbus . . . . . .Captain-general of the fleet

Juan De La Cosa . . . . .Owner / Captain of the
Santa Maria

Diego De Arana . . . . .Master-at-arms of the
Santa Maria

Martín Alonso Pinzón . . . . . .Captain of the Pinta

Vicente Yañez Pinzón . . . . . .Captain of the Nina

Dr. Juan Sanchez . . . . .Physician of the Santa
Maria

Chachu . . . . .Boatswain of the Santa
Maria

Luis De Torres . . . . .Fleet's interpreter

Pedro . . . . .Cabin boy of the Santa
Maria

Francisco De Henao . . . . .Cook of the Santa Maria

Gonzalo Fernandez . . . . .Sailor aboard the Santa
Maria

Rodrigo De Jeres . . . . .Sailor aboard the Santa
Maria

Anani . . . . .Young Taino woman from
Cuba

Tiburon . . . . .Anani's father

Tanama . . . . .Anani's mother

Guanina . . . . .Anani's sister

Hura . . . . .Anani's brother

Calichi . . . . .Anani's intended husband

Guacanagari . . . . .Taino chief

Author's Sources

-James Shreeve, *The Neandertal Enigma*, 1996

-Mark Kurlansky, *The Basque History of the World*, 1999

-Jon Bilbao Azkarreta, *America y los Vascos*, 1991

-Rodney Gallop, *The Book of the Basques*, 1998

-Luis De Borandiaran Irizar and Jose Miguel de Borandiaran, *A View from the Witch's Cave*, 1991

-George Sanderlin, *Across the Ocean Sea*, 1966

-Robert H. Fuson, *The Log of Christopher Columbus*, 1992

-Samuel Eliot Morison, *Admiral of the Ocean Sea*, 1942

-Samuel Eliot Morison and Mauricio Obregon, *The Caribbean As Columbus Saw It*, 1964

-David Henige, *In Search of Christopher Columbus*, 1991

-Guadalupe Chocano, Ignacio Fernandez Vial and Consuelo Varela, *The Nina, the Pinta and the Santa Maria*, 1991

-Zvi Dor-Ner, *Columbus and the Age of Discovery*, 1991

-Ferdinand Columbus, *The Life of the Admiral Christopher Columbus, 1534-1539* (1959)

-Gianni Granzotto, *Christopher Columbus*, 1987

-Alice Bache Gould, *Nueva Lista Documentada de los Tripulantes de Colon en 1492* (1984)

-Fray Bartolome de Las Casas, *History of the Indies, 1552* (1971)

-Antonio M. Stevens-Arroyo, *Cave of the Jagua*, 1988

-Irving Rouse, *The Tainos, Rise & Decline of the People Who Greeted Columbus*, 1993

-David E. Stannard, *American Holocaust*, 1992

-William Keegan, *The People Who Discovered Columbus*, 1992

-Fatima Bercht, Estrellita Brodsky, John Alan Farmer, and Dicey Taylor, Taino, *Pre-Columbian Art and Culture from the Caribbean*, 1998

photo by Debra Geraghty

The author, Christine Echeverria Bender, is shown aboard the Nina out of Corpus Christie, Texas. Christine resides with her family in Boise, Idaho. For more information about Christine and future projects please visit her at;

www.christinebender.com